THE WONDERS WITHIN THE STARLIT INN

FOUR MAGICAL CHRISTMAS encounters ... one special inn

ERIN R. HOWARD
BRETT ARMSTRONG
DAWN FORD
J. L. BURROWS

EXPANSE Books

INHERITING PEACE

ERIN R. HOWARD

For anyone needing a little more peace in this Christmas season.

chapter one

IT'S NOT every day a girl gets invited to the Thanksgiving dinner of a relative she's never met *and* inherits an inn.

And it's not every day that the girl decides to uproot her entire life for the opportunity to run said inn.

That only happens in the movies. It's not real life. Except here she was—Maggie Benson, the new owner of the Starlit Inn—trying not to fall through the rickety front porch steps.

An icy breeze lifted the ends of her dark burgundy hair and tossed it in her eyes. Shivering, she risked pulling her hands from her coat pocket to grip the railing. It wobbled under her weight as she took the next few steps. Luckily, she missed the sagging parts of the stairs and made it across the porch to the front door.

So far, so good.

Taking a deep breath, she dug the key from her pocket and slid it into the lock. After a few moments of finagling the key, the lock clicked, and she pushed open the large, wooden door. Damp, musty air tickled her nose. She cleared her throat.

Was it possible for a house to be even colder inside than it was outside? Maggie shivered and heaved the door closed before shoving her hands back into her pockets.

Heat. She needed heat and fast. But where was the thermostat? A quick survey of the large lobby revealed nothing but a chilly, worn room with outdated furniture and an enormous stone fireplace. The hearth had seen better days—but the same could be said for Maggie. The only highlight that lifted her spirits was the high wooden beams running along the ceiling. It gave her hope that this room *could* be beautiful.

She pulled her jacket tighter and went to the counter. Dust coated the countertop, except for the space in the middle where a manila envelope sat with her name scribbled on top.

The estate lawyer must have left it for her. Hopefully, it was a detailed report from the previous owner. Perhaps they also included a how-to manual about operating this place. Maggie eagerly opened the envelope, but the only contents were two sheets of paper.

So much for help getting started.

The first page was a brief letter from the lawyer congratulating Maggie on the new ownership and wishing her luck on her turnkey new adventure. At the bottom of the page, handwritten in a messy script, was a note. "Your first guests arrive on December twentieth. I will email you a copy of the reservations on file."

Guests already? Maggie took another look at the room and frowned. She was led to believe the Inn was in great shape, but this place was far from ready for guests—especially at Christmas. Lodgers would want something warm and inviting. Something homey and magical.

Maggie frowned at the word *magical*. Actually, that was the last thing Rose told her before she left the very weird and awkward Thanksgiving dinner. *"Maggie, dear, the Starlit Inn is a magical place where anything can happen."*

Unfortunately for the Starlit Inn, it looked as though magic was far from reality. Not that the place couldn't become beautiful. Maggie could imagine an oversized Christmas tree in the lobby, decked out with homemade ornaments, and lit up with white twinkling lights. Candles flickering in the windows and garland hanging on the mantle.

"I think it's going to take a lot more than magic to make this place presentable."

"Excuse me, Miss?"

Maggie dropped the papers on the counter and spun to find an older man holding a clipboard.

He gave her a sheepish look. "I'm sorry. I didn't mean to startle you, but your door was open."

She lowered her arm, willing her heartbeat to return to normal. "But I closed it."

The man chuckled. "Sometimes old doors don't stay latched very well. I can fix that."

"I'm sorry—who are you?" Maggie should be concerned, but the man had kind eyes and a grandfatherly tone to his voice. What she wouldn't give to have had a grandparent growing up.

"I'm Walter. I was hired to fix your archway at the end of the driveway."

"Oh, that's right. I didn't realize you were coming today." Maggie straightened the papers from the lawyer and turned to the second page, which had today's date and time for the repairs. Heat warmed her face as she walked around the counter and held out her hand. "I'm Maggie Benson."

He shook her hand. "Pleased to meet you, Miss Benson."

"Likewise." She cleared her throat again, wishing she had her water bottle handy. "So, you're going to fix the broken bricks of the archway?"

Walter glanced at his clipboard. "I have a couple of men coming to help with the archway and wooden sign, and we'll look at the boiler." He paused. "It's old, but I'm sure we can get this place warmed up. In the meantime, I can start a fire for you."

A wave of relief washed over her. "Thank you so much. That would be wonderful."

"Don't want you to catch a chill, so I'll get started in here."

"Sounds good." Maggie watched for a few minutes as the man set down his toolbox and arranged the wood inside the fireplace. He then meandered back to the front desk. Antique mailboxes lined the wall behind the counter, with skeleton keys dangling from a hook in each box. She scanned the rooms and found one labeled *Maggie* on the bottom right. Touched that someone thought to change the name on the innkeeper's slot, she reached for the key and slipped it into her pocket.

Now to find her new room.

New room—new life—new everything.

A tiny thrill fluttered in her stomach at the idea of exploring the Inn. A doorway to the left of the front desk led to a simple sitting room with bookshelves and tables. She could envision guests reading or playing games. Perhaps sipping coffee, hot chocolate, and enjoying homemade cookies. Maggie made a mental note to add an inviting coffee nook to the space. She opened the only door in the room and found a collection of coats and snow boots. She'd have to clean those out to fit in some board games.

To the right of the front counter, the stairs led to the second floor, but she passed those, instead walking down a short hallway. A guest bathroom sat at the end of the corridor, and to its left was a small but efficient kitchen with a door that led to the basement. One look at the creepy, steep stairs, and she promptly closed the door.

To the right of the bathroom was a charming eating area. More wooden beams graced the ceiling, and large full-length windows covered the right side of the room. A magnificent view of the mountains and woods caught her eye, but she forced herself to turn away and continue investigating the Inn.

Maggie figured her room would be on the first floor, but perhaps it was upstairs. She made her way back down the hallway and to the mahogany staircase. Worn carpet graced each step. The best part of the entire stairway was what appeared to be a hand-carved railing. It was dusty, but Maggie couldn't resist running her fingers along the stunning craftsmanship.

At the top of the landing was a beautiful bay window and a cushioned seat, adorned with built-in bookcases on each side. But that's where the charm ended. Everywhere else had chipped paint or outdated wallpaper. The carpet was musty and worn thin from years of use. And the bedrooms weren't much better. Most had double beds with dark green and brown comforters and a hodgepodge of furniture. Two accommodations boasted king-size beds.

Some rooms shared a small bathroom, while the king suites— if you could call them that—had a sofa couch and a tiny kitchenette made up of a sink and microwave above.

A glimmer of silver from the sofa caught her eye. Was that a spring poking through the cushion?

Worry knotted her stomach. This was going to take more money than she'd been led to believe. Turnkey ready? Ha. What was she going to do? And how was she going to run this whole place by herself? She had planned to hire help and offer room and board as a salary bonus. But it looked like she was going to have to deplete most of her savings to bring the Inn up to industry standards.

A crackle and pop sounded from below. Was that the fire?

Maggie made her way back downstairs and grinned. Walter had indeed got the fire going. The chill in the room subsided, and with the glow of the fire, her excitement returned. Maggie could almost forget all the problems looming over her head.

"Miss Maggie, that old boiler is being stubborn. I couldn't get it going."

So, she could *almost* forget all her problems. *Please don't say it's going to cost a lot of money.*

"I need to go into town and get a few different parts. It may take me a day or two, but I promise I'll get it up and running."

"But it is fixable, right?"

Walter chuckled. "It's almost as old as I am, but I can get it working again. Don't worry." He nodded to the fireplace. "That should keep you warm enough until it's ready. The news isn't calling for more snow for another week or so."

Right in time for Christmas. Maggie smiled. A tiny flicker of hope sparked. "Thank you. I really appreciate you working on it."

"It's no problem at all. I'm just glad to see this old place up and running again. The Starlit Inn always made Christmas so special." Walter's face lit up with a grin. "The Starlit always had a Christmas activity planned. Cookie decorating, a toy drive, Christmas dinner. The whole community came out all month long."

"That seems like a tall order, but I'll definitely try." Maggie tried not to think about how much of a task it would be to restore the Inn's reputation.

Walter grew thoughtful for a moment and finally nodded. "Well, something tells me you're up for the challenge." He walked over and patted her shoulder. "I'm going to head to town and look for those parts. I'll come back by after I find them."

Tears threatened at his kind words, but she blinked them away. "Thank you."

"You bet." He moved to the door and, with a big tug, pulled it open. "I'll fix that, too, but in the meantime, make sure you lock it."

"I will."

The heavy front door firmly closed, and Maggie blew out a deep breath. Now what?

There was so much to do and so little time. But first, there was still the tiny matter of finding her bedroom. Surely it was in the Inn. It wouldn't be in another building, would it? She stuck her hands out closer to the fire and warmed them.

What if it was in the basement with the boiler?

Shaking her head, she dismissed that thought. Why would someone build this Inn and put the owner's room in the basement? That made no sense.

The most likely case was that she just missed the room upstairs. It probably wasn't labeled like the other rooms.

Satisfied, she turned her attention to another set of built-ins surrounding the fireplace. A mixture of hardback books and paperbacks lined the shelves, and Maggie couldn't wait to browse the titles.

A chain exactly like the ones on the room keys hung around a notch on the face of the shelf, about halfway down. Curious, Maggie reached for the chain to remove it, and a metal faceplate moved, revealing a keyhole.

No. It couldn't be.

Could it?

Maggie pulled the antique key from her pocket, inserted it, and turned. The locking mechanism clicked, and the bookcase gently swung open.

chapter two

ANGRY VOICES CAME from down the hallway, and Prince Alexander Maxwell rose from his desk and peeked out his door. His parents came into view, and he quietly shut it. Tonight was not the night to draw attention to himself.

At least they weren't angry with him this time.

Alexander didn't think they were. He strained to listen to their conversation, but they'd already moved inside their suite, and he could only make out muffled tones. He didn't envy the poor soul who was the subject of their argument. Having been on the receiving end of those lectures—he wouldn't even wish it on his older brother. Well, almost.

His brother, Silas, could probably benefit from getting knocked down a peg or two. As the eldest, he always seemed to do no wrong. He always said the right thing, did the right thing, and was adored by everyone in the castle.

And Alexander—well, he was the opposite of his brother in every way. Sighing, he walked back to his desk and reached for the silver picture frame. Five smiling faces looked up at him as if each one of them knew that the trip through the portal to Earth would be the last time they would ever be one cohesive family.

What he wouldn't give to go back to that day. To savor each moment of their spontaneous trip to celebrate Christmas away from the demands and responsibilities of an entire kingdom. It was the first—and only time—they'd ever left their castle.

Alexander pulled out his chair, sat down, and returned the picture to its spot on the desk. He couldn't look away from the magical winter wonderland in the picture. When was the last time he felt that happy?

His gaze turned to the fifth face in the picture. Blonde braids, red cheeks from the cold, and bright blue eyes. His sister, Lilibet, stood between Alexander and his brother, holding giant snowballs over each of their heads. A smile tugged at his lips at the memory. Neither one of them had known she planned to smash them on their heads, but someone at the Inn where they were staying had captured the moment. Off to the side, his parents stood, holding hands, anticipating the snowball fight.

And fight they did. They threw so many snowballs that each one of them was soaking wet and covered from head to toe in the white fluff.

Tears clouded his vision, so he shook off the memory. It hurt way too much to dwell on how happy and at peace he was the last time they were a complete, functional family.

A door slammed, and Alexander flinched. As Christmas neared, his parents grew more on edge. The unrest and violence in the outlying cities had only escalated since his sister's disappearance. Twelve years and no answers.

But this Christmas was different. While there had always been crime in the kingdom, it stayed closer to the bordering cities. It wasn't uncommon with the immigrants from their neighboring kingdoms to have skirmishes over land titles and trade. Except now, it was spilling over into the capital city.

Alexander didn't envy his parents or his brother, who would inherit the throne and all the turmoil.

Three soft taps on his door—his brother's signature knock—startled him out of his thoughts. "Come in."

His brother burst through the door, a frown on his face. "What did you do now?"

"What do you mean?"

Silas crossed his arms in front of his chest. "Don't say you can't hear them."

"The entire castle can hear them." Alexander sighed. "What's your point?"

"They were fine at dinner, so you must have done something."

Alexander stiffened, his brother's words stabbing him like a knife. "Nice. Thanks, Brother."

"Come on, you know it's true." A smile tugged at the corners of Silas's lips. "You know how they are. They seem to find fault with everything lately."

"So, you naturally assumed I would be the one they find fault with?"

"Forgive me." Silas's expression softened. "That came out all wrong. Of course, you're not *always* the cause of their ire."

"Oh, well, in *that* case—you're forgiven." Alexander leaned back in his chair. "Sorry to disappoint you, but it wasn't me this time."

"I was sort of hoping it was you, so I wouldn't have to prepare for whatever lecture they have planned for me tomorrow."

"Can't help you there."

Silas walked to his desk and sat on the corner. "What are we going to do, Alex?"

"I have no idea what *you* are going to do."

Annoyance flickered across Silas's face. "Really? You are going to put everything on my shoulders?"

Alex pointed to his brother. "Firstborn Prince."

"Funny."

"I'm serious. I can't change the birth order." Nor would he want to. He was perfectly fine with the way things were.

Silas jumped up and started pacing. "Stop it, Alex." His brother's tone changed from irritation to something else. Weariness, maybe? "For once in your life, can you please be serious? Stop hiding behind your humor and witty comebacks. Be the man I know you are."

He wasn't sure how to respond. His brother saw more than Alexander realized.

"Look, things are getting bad in the kingdom. Father doesn't want to admit it, but we will have to intervene soon."

Shocked, Alexander paused before answering. "Intervene? How?"

Silas frowned. "A show of force? War?" Silas rubbed the back of his neck. "I don't have the answers, but I know the level of crime is getting way out of hand."

"I'm sure Father—"

"Father isn't doing enough to stop it!" Silas threw up his hands, his fists clenched. Then he let out a deep sigh, running his hand over his face.

Alexander leaned back in his chair. Silas wasn't one to lose his temper, so perhaps matters of the kingdom were far worse than he was privy to. "What do you want me to do?"

"I want you to get serious about your role in the kingdom and help me."

"That's just it. I don't have a role." He shouldn't have to remind Silas of that fact.

"You are Prince Alexander Maxwell—"

"Second-born prince. Not Crown Prince." He got to his feet. "I don't have any say, any power, nor do I want it." The words came out harsher than he intended, but it was no less true. Having to be the one to carry the weight of the kingdom on his shoulders? No, thank you.

His brother took a step closer to him, his eyes narrowed. "Excuses. You have more say and power than you realize if only you would ..."

"What? Be like you?" Alexander crossed his arms in front of his chest. "There's not enough gold in the treasury."

Silas stepped back as if he'd slapped him. "Why are you so

bent on insulting your family's legacy? It's an honor to be in our position, to rule this kingdom."

"An honor?" He wanted to laugh. "It's brought nothing to our family but death, grief, and zero answers to show for it. Not to mention an entire population that resents us."

"You are not the only one who misses her and wants justice."

"Then why haven't we found the people responsible?" Alexander turned away from his brother and reached for the picture frame. "You realize the kingdom's struggled since Lilibet's disappearance. It's all connected somehow."

"Is that why you've stopped helping?" Concern lingered in Silas's eyes, and Alexander had to look away.

He set the frame back on the table. "All the investigating and dead ends have taken a toll. So much time has passed. I can't take any more false leads."

"Wait. You think she's actually gone? That she's ... that's why you've given up?"

His brother's accusation stung. No one in their family had ever said the words out loud. "Like it hasn't crossed your mind."

"I still have hope. But *you* ..." Silas cursed and balled his hands into fists.

Would his brother actually hit him? There was a part of Alexander that didn't blame his brother for wanting to. To give up hope for Lilibet's return was unforgiveable.

Instead of punching him, Silas relaxed his hands and looked at him with pity. Which was worse. Way worse. "You can't simply run away from your responsibilities, from who you are supposed to be."

Alexander's throat tightened, and the fight inside of him surrendered. He was tired of fighting and arguing. "What if I don't even know who I am anymore?"

His brother gripped both of his shoulders. "Then you let your family help you."

Alexander searched Silas's face—looking for any sign his

brother really understood what he was going through. "See, that's the problem. I don't know if you can."

Silas dropped his hands and sighed. "So, what are you going to do? Give up and run away?"

"Maybe I simply need some time away." His eyes drifted to the picture once more. Perhaps that was it. He couldn't change what happened to his sister, and he couldn't find those responsible, but he could go back to the last place where he was at peace.

Alexander went to his closet and pulled out a bag.

"Wait—what are you doing?"

"Taking some time to figure things out." He started pulling clothes from his closet.

"And where do you think you're going?"

Alexander pointed to the frame. His brother followed his gaze to the picture and then looked back at him, shaking his head. "You can't be serious, Alex. You can't just run away—"

The knife twisted a little more. Silas really had a way of hitting him with truth. For a moment, guilt weighed heavily upon him at the thought of leaving. He could stay. He *should* stay. But something tugged at him to go. He needed to do this.

"I know you think I'm running away, but I'm not. I need to do this, Silas." Alexander turned around to face his brother. "I wouldn't leave if I didn't think you were capable and what the kingdom really needs. If you care about me at all, you'll give me some time."

His brother stared at him for a few moments before finally nodding and turning for the door. "You'll need the key to the portal. And some money."

"Do you know where it is?"

"In Father's study." Silas opened his mouth as if he was going to say something else, but then turned to the door.

"Thanks, Silas." He emphasized the words, hoping his brother could understand how much he needed this break.

Silas turned the doorknob and pulled it open, but didn't look back. "The thing is, if you run away from your problems and shut out everyone, then you'll always be running, Alex."

chapter
three

MAGGIE TURNED OVER—AGAIN—AND braced for the inevitable resistance of her foot gliding across the sheets. Is this what it had come to, sleeping in socks? Yuck. Maggie pulled the covers tighter and drew her feet closer to her body. Her fuzzy socks weren't helping to keep the cold from her toes and did nothing but distract her from sleeping.

She had been so excited to finally find her room and unpack some of her belongings. The queen-sized bed was pushed up against the far wall, with a desk and dresser taking up the opposite side. The small room had a homey feel she was sure she could make the most of.

Now, she wasn't so sure.

About one in the morning, she gave up having the door closed and left it open, hoping the warmth from the fireplace would heat her room. But it didn't help. A brutal, cold draft blew in from around the window, and her quilt wasn't thick enough to ward off the chill.

Light poked through the blinds, and Maggie pulled the blanket over her head, hoping she could trick her brain into thinking it wasn't daylight. Not quite long enough, the blanket bunched up to her face, exposing her feet—fuzzy socks and all.

Ugh. It was no use. She threw back the covers and sat up,

reaching for her phone. It was cold in her palm. Climbing out of bed, she rushed on tiptoes to grab jeans and a hoodie. She needed to add a space heater and flannel pajamas to her ever-growing shopping list.

The fire in the lobby had slowly died to almost nothing, but after a few tries, a warm blaze roared to life again. Once she could finally feel her fingers, she made her way to the kitchen and opened her cooler. She removed a carton of eggs and then rummaged through the drawers until she found a spatula and a pan.

Luckily, she thought ahead and also brought a jar of peanut butter, jelly, and bread with her to the Inn yesterday. She could make a fried egg sandwich and find a store after Walter stopped by.

Once she finished breakfast and the dishes were put away, Maggie set out to make a list. According to the lawyer, her first guests were scheduled to arrive in three weeks. Not near enough time in the grand scheme of things. They would no doubt take one look at this place and head in the other direction. And she wouldn't blame them.

How did she think she could pull this off?

Get it together, Maggie. You can do this. She'd start with the basic necessities and go from there.

She squared her shoulders and dug through the front lobby desk until she found scrap paper and a pen.

1. *Heat*
2. *Groceries*
3. *Cleaning*
4. *Wash Bedding*

There. That wasn't so bad. Maggie set the pen down and leaned back to study her list. She only needed some heat, sustenance, and a thorough cleaning. A little TLC would go a long way to making the Inn homier. Walter was taking care of the heat, so she could concentrate on the rest of the list. No problem. Satisfied, she laid the list back on the counter. "I've got this. What could go wrong?"

Outside on the porch, wood creaked, followed by something snapping. A loud shout came seconds later. Was that Walter's voice? Maggie hurried to the front door and yanked it open.

"What in the world?"

Walter looked up at her, face red. "Looks like you had a rotten step. My foot sank all the way to the ground, and I lost my balance."

She reached down to help him up. "Are you hurt?"

"Just my pride." He laughed. "At least, I think." He slowly rolled his ankle, and Maggie felt him flinch beneath her hands.

"Okay, maybe I tweaked my ankle a bit."

"Come on, let's get you inside and check it out."

"I think I'll be fine." Walter took a step forward and then fell again.

"Let me help." She rushed to his side and caught him. "Easy does it." Maggie assisted him through the front door, into the lobby, and eased him into a chair.

"Thank you, Miss Maggie." He sighed. "I'll be fine. We must get your boiler fixed. That's more important."

"You're not going anywhere until we can take a look at your ankle." She kneeled in front of him. "Let's get this boot off."

Maggie helped him slip his foot out of the work boot and gently pulled down his sock. It was a little puffy and red but didn't look too bad. She sighed in relief. "Let me get you some ibuprofen and see if I can find an ice pack."

"Thanks." He pulled his cell phone out of his pocket. "I'll call my crew and tell them to head this way now. I'd planned on getting the boiler done first, but I'll have them come now to finish the archway."

Nodding, she went to her room, grabbed the ibuprofen from her purse, and headed to the kitchen. She tugged on the freezer door—no ice packs. A few ice cubes stuffed into a Ziploc baggie, and she had a makeshift cold pack.

She waited until Walter finished the phone call. "Here you go." She handed him the medicine and a glass of water. "This should help the swelling."

"Thank you, but I'm fine."

Maggie pulled over another chair to prop his foot up. "Well, your puffy ankle says otherwise."

He frowned but placed the ice on his ankle. "I'll ice it until my guys get here."

She stuffed down a laugh and nodded. "Sounds good." Walking back to the desk, she picked up the pen and put a few question marks beside "heat" and added "fix porch stairs." The newest addition to her list was out of her element of expertise. She looked at Walter to ask if they could fix that as well, but she didn't know if the Inn's budget could handle that added expenditure.

She'd have to get back to the lawyer about the financial records. Her personal accounts had dwindled at the expense of moving here. She managed to sell a few pieces of bigger furniture from her apartment and had a tiny nest egg in her savings, but the shipping of her belongings dipped into both.

Groceries and cleaning supplies. Maggie would need both, and that was at least a place to start. "Walter?"

The older man looked up from his phone. "Yeah?"

"Will you be okay here for a little while? I need to go to the grocery and stock up on a few things."

"Of course. Not a problem at all."

"Thanks." She went to her room to grab her purse and keys. "I'll be back in a little while."

Walter shifted in his chair to look at her. "Don't worry, we'll get everything fixed. Even those stairs."

Maggie tucked a strand of hair behind her ear and let out a sigh. She had given up everything—her life in Kentucky, her teaching job, and what few friends she could count on her fingers.

For what? A "supernatural" Inn that was supposed to be the start of a brand-new adventure.

She'd let the lure of a family she'd never had the opportunity to meet convince her to sink all her funds to move to the Starlit. Now, the Starlit and all of its problems might end up sinking *her*.

Maggie pulled the door shut only to watch it pop back open. She grasped the doorknob and forcefully pulled it shut. Now, if only she could successfully stop the restlessness from creeping back in that caused her to end up on the Starlit's doorstep in the first place.

chapter
four

THE MIDNIGHT STREETS of the capital city, Pax, were eerily quiet. The air was humid and warm, and sweat beaded across Alexander's forehead. He pulled his black hood over his head anyway. He didn't want to take a chance on being recognized, whether by castle guards or citizens.

Both lurked in the shadows of tall buildings and alleyways.

Lately, it seemed the weather was just as unpredictable as the people. As the city became more unsteady, so did the weather, growing warm and humid one day and cool and rainy the next.

Alexander knew that feeling all too well.

A hard thump hit him from behind, and his backpack fell from his shoulder.

"My apologies!"

He turned in time to catch a young child taking off in the opposite direction.

"Shouldn't you be at home and in bed?" He called after the boy, but of course, there was no reply. Where were this kid's parents? Didn't they realize how unsafe the streets were at night?

Adjusting his pack, he shook his head and strode to the city's outer gates. If he remembered correctly, the portal was several miles past the gates, nestled in the forest.

There were better methods of getting to the portal, but

Alexander didn't want to draw any attention. A vehicle would be too noticeable, especially a royal car. And a horse, while affordable for most of the kingdom's residents, wasn't something he could just leave at the portal.

Once he was outside the city gates, he pulled back his coat sleeve to check the time, but his wrist was bare.

The little runt stole his watch.

Sighing, Alexander crossed the road to the woods. Without his watch, he could only guess at the time. If he kept a steady pace, he should be at the Inn by sunrise. His memory was a little fuzzy on the details of how the world and time worked at the Inn, but it seemed to be several hours ahead. So, he should arrive by late morning.

The path from the road grew thicker the farther he trekked into the forest, and Alexander had to pay extra attention to the rocky terrain. He didn't remember it being this overgrown when he last traveled to the portal, but his family hadn't been back since that trip either. Not since they couldn't find Lilibet. No one in their family felt like taking a vacation without her.

And here he was, abandoning his family and running away.

"It's not like that," he whispered to the forest. But no one was there to care.

He simply needed some peace and quiet. Some time to clear his head. But he doubted his parents would see it that way. Especially since he snuck out without talking to them first. He left a note, a cowardly thing to do. He shook off the thought for now. It was done, and he didn't want to go back. Not yet.

A stone chimney rose up in the distance, and Alexander picked up his pace. Excitement grew with each step.

However, when the small cottage, completely overrun with weeds and vines, came into view, his hope sank. Alexander vaguely remembered guards posted at the portal to keep away any passersby, but obviously no one had been stationed there in many years.

Were his parents unconcerned about someone accessing the

portal? Perhaps they figured a simple lock would prevent a break-in.

He slid off his pack and dug in it until he found his knife. It was a last-minute decision to bring it, and now he was glad he did. He cut away vines and brush from the front door until he could slide his father's key in and push it open. It barely budged.

Cutting more foliage away, he pried it open a little more.

"Oh, man."

The door scraped across the wood floor. Dust and dirt clung to the air. He sucked in a breath and squeezed through the doorway, dragging his pack, shutting and locking the door behind him.

He placed the key and chain back around his neck and surveyed the room. It was small but served its purpose. A fireplace for warmth, table and chairs, and small kitchen nook. He headed to the back, where two bedrooms framed a bathroom in between. His destination was to the right, the portal room, empty except for a stone pillar in the center. It glowed, casting a glimmering light across the floor and walls.

Alexander's throat tightened. A rush of joy and then grief flooded his mind and heart. How could an item bring back such a mixture of emotions? All he had were happy memories here.

He rubbed his eyes. "You can do this, Alex. There's no turning back now."

Squaring his shoulders, Alexander reached out a shaky hand, touched the granite, and the cottage disappeared.

chapter
five

ALEXANDER TOOK a moment to get his bearings and let his eyes focus. In mere seconds, the old stone cottage vanished, replaced by a thick forest. Cold air slapped him in the face—stinging his eyes—but he looked up and grinned. A stone archway stood above him with a wooden sign hanging down. Taking a step backward, he looked again to read the sign.

The Starlit Inn

He made it.

Tightening his hold on his backpack, he trudged up the long, winding driveway. Trees lined both sides of the asphalt, which had seen better days. He dodged potholes as he climbed to the top of the hill. With each step, his excitement grew. A trip into town would be on the list, though. He pulled his jacket tighter and looked down at his shoes. Leather. The thin soles wouldn't keep him very warm here. He needed some boots and a heavier coat.

Blending in was a must. While he packed mostly cotton shirts and denim pants, he did not know what the current styles were in the mountains of Virginia. Wasn't that what this place was called? It wasn't like his kingdom kept up with the latest news on Earth —let alone, America.

The royal family had exclusive access to this beautiful place, at least as far as his family knew. If only it would snow. Then he could really sit back and clear his head.

Wait—*this* was the Starlit Inn? Alexander halted at the top of the hill and took a harder look at the building before him.

Peeling paint, debris around the building, and broken stairs?

What happened? A moment of panic hit. What if they weren't even open? Then what would he do? He'd have to find somewhere else to stay or sulk back to the kingdom. Neither one was a preferable option.

Two vehicles were parked in front of the Inn—a square automobile with round headlights and a van with the words *W. Construction* on the side. Alexander approached the van to get a better look, and sure enough, there were all sorts of tools inside. Perhaps they were open but doing some renovations.

He could deal with that. Climbing the stairs, he dodged the gaping hole, intending to try the doorknob, but the door already stood slightly ajar. He pushed it open.

"Hello?" Alexander stuck his head through the doorway. He didn't see anyone nearby, so he fully entered the lobby to wait.

The lobby matched his memories, but now it lacked Christmas decorations. Dirt covered every surface, and the whole place seemed worn and sagging. A toolbox lay open on the counter, but nothing else seemed out of place.

"Anyone here?" He called out again and approached the counter to see if there was some type of bell or something. Nothing.

What should he do now? Alexander didn't want to walk around and end up scaring someone. There was an open door off the lobby, so he went to check it out and found no one. It was just a bedroom with an unmade bed and a large suitcase open on top of it.

"Hello?" A man's voice called out from the lobby area. Alexander turned back to find a man in a uniform, holding some sort of device in his hands.

"Good afternoon." Alexander nodded to the man and turned toward the counter. Maybe he was another guest.

"I'm here with your boxes."

Alexander turned back to the man, but he was looking at the device. "Boxes?"

"Yeah, the delivery you scheduled. Where do you want them?" He looked up. "There's a lot."

"I'm sorry, there's been a mistake. I'm not the owner."

The man sighed. "If I don't deliver them now, then we'll have to reschedule another time, and we are getting really booked for Christmas." The guy gestured around the room. "This is the Starlit Inn?"

"Yes ..."

"Then there's no mistake." He handed over the device. "Sign here."

Alexander accepted the weird device and looked down at the screen, but there wasn't a pen. "With what?"

"Just use your finger."

"Oh." Alexander scribbled his name and immediately wanted to try again. "It looks awful."

"They always do." The man grabbed the device back and headed for the door. "So, unload them in here?"

Alexander was committed now. He shrugged. "Sure."

The man nodded and slipped out the door. It slammed shut but then popped back open. The door must be broken, which explained why it was open when he arrived. Alexander slid off his backpack, placing it in one of the armchairs, and went to examine the latch.

Sure enough, the plate was jutting out, causing the door not to latch all the way. He rummaged through the toolbox on the counter until he found a screwdriver that would work and went to fix the plate.

"Oh, thank you so much!"

Alexander looked up, nearly dropping the screwdriver. A young woman stood behind him, grinning. Her hair was a deep burgundy, but it was her eyes that drew him in immediately. Ocean blue and warm—they reminded him of the waters back home.

He finally found his voice. "You're welcome."

"Walter said you guys would get to that, but I didn't expect it today." She walked behind the counter and reached for something behind it. It was a small rectangle with a screen that lit up when she touched it.

"Did I hear someone else in here?" She looked up from whatever she was holding.

Who was Walter? The van flashed back into his mind. He must be the construction man. "Yes, your packages are here. The guy is getting them now."

"My belongings are here?" Her face lit up. "Finally, a little bit of good news."

Alexander finished tightening the last screw and tested the door. It latched and stayed closed. "There. All better."

"Thank you." A trilling tone came from the small device in her hands, and she did something to turn it off. "That means dinner is almost ready." She started to leave but turned back around. "I know it's not your job, but would you mind helping bring in the boxes? I'm afraid I have a lot of them, but I will be back in a minute to help."

Did she think he worked for this Walter? He looked down at the screwdriver in his hand and wanted to laugh. It was a logical conclusion.

He started to introduce himself, but she had disappeared. Sighing, he placed the tool back in the box and turned around to open the door in time to assist the deliveryman carrying two boxes stacked on top of each other.

"Here, let me help." He reached for the top box and placed it on the lobby floor, close to the outer wall. "Watch your step."

The man chuckled. "That's a lawsuit waiting to happen."

Lawsuit? Whatever the guy meant, Alexander surmised it wasn't a good thing. He followed the man out to the truck, and the two of them fell into a steady rhythm of hauling the boxes inside. Several of them were incredibly heavy and took both men to move them.

By the time the last box was stacked inside, Alexander's heart raced, and he'd worked up a sweat. It was a nice change to exert physical effort. He never got to do anything at home without a servant stopping him from finishing a task.

"Oh, you're already finished? That was quick." The woman was back. She waved her hand for him to follow her. "I hope you're hungry."

Was she ever going to let him respond to anything she said? He bit back a chuckle and nodded. "Don't I need to check in first?"

"Check in? Oh, you mean with Walter?" She continued down the hallway.

"No, I meant—" He stopped. The poor girl was already on a mission, bringing out the food. Two places were set on one of the dining room tables. The food smelled amazing, and his stomach rumbled. The last substantial meal he'd had was before he left the castle.

"I hope you like lasagna." She disappeared into the kitchen again and then brought out a basket of bread.

She took a seat and scooped up a serving onto her plate. "Don't worry about Walter. I've already taken him and the other man a plate. He wouldn't stop long enough to join us."

"I'm sorry. I think there's been some confusion." Alexander walked toward the table. "I'm not with Walter. I'm here to check in as a guest."

The woman choked on her bite and coughed, her face turning bright red. She jerked to her feet, and her fork hit the floor. "You're not with Walter and his crew?"

Alexander sighed, hoping she wouldn't be upset and refuse the room. It certainly wasn't his intention to mislead her, but he couldn't pass up the opportunity to do something not linked to his royal title. He could get used to the feeling of helping—and to actually being needed by someone.

Alexander shook his head. "I was hoping to get a room and stay for a little while."

"But we aren't even open yet!"

"The door was unlocked, and I assumed ..." It was Alexander's turn to be embarrassed. "Which now makes sense since it was broken."

"Ugh, I'm so embarrassed." She covered her face. "My first guest ever, and I made you work!"

"It's not a problem. I was happy to help."

"Well, Mister ..." She got to her feet and held out her hand.

He reached for hers to shake it, remembering his father doing the same all those years ago. He was determined to start over and this time get off on the right foot. "Alexander Maxwell." Her hand was warm and fit perfectly in his. He found himself not wanting to let go.

"Maggie Benson." She stated her name, letting her hand linger in his longer than normal. A slow smile came across her face, but it was her gaze that drew him in.

"And I'm Walter."

chapter six

MAGGIE'S FACE BURNED. She yanked her hand away from the handsome stranger and turned around to find Walter and his employee standing behind her, empty plates in hand. The older man raised an eyebrow while the younger man fought back a grin.

"Walter, this is Alexander Maxwell. The Starlit Inn's first guest under the new ownership."

The older gentleman shuffled closer, favoring his bad leg. "Nice to meet you, Alexander." He gestured to the man beside him. "This is Carson."

She nodded, placing her hands in her back pockets and avoiding Walter's gaze.

"It's nice to meet you both."

"So, you're here to stay at the Inn?" Walter set his plate on the table and eyed the guest up and down.

Maggie couldn't miss Walter's protective tone. She glanced at the younger man, who caught her gaze and shook his head, slightly laughing. Evidently, he hadn't missed it either.

"Yes. I had the pleasure of staying here with my family when I was about twelve. I've wanted to visit again for a while now."

"Well, welcome back." Walter eyed the man for a few more moments before turning to her. "Miss Maggie, the boiler is fixed."

"It is?" Maggie couldn't help but clap her hands and hug the old man. "Thank you so much."

He chuckled and patted her back. "It's me who should thank you for the lasagna. Some of the best I've ever had."

Maggie pulled away in time to see him point a finger at Carson. "Now, don't you go and tell my wife that."

"Your secret is safe with me, sir." Carson grinned. Turning to Maggie, he added, "It was fantastic. Thank you."

"I'm so thankful." She took a deep, relieved breath. "That takes such a load off my shoulders."

"Happy to help." Walter nodded. "The news alerted that the snow's coming earlier than predicted, so I can sleep now knowing you'll be warm."

"How bad is it going to be?" Maggie had been through some cold winters but hadn't really experienced snowstorms before. A mixture of excitement and worry settled over her.

"Several inches. The main roads in town should be okay. The road department has already been salting the roads. But it's the side roads that can cause you trouble. If you have to go out, go slow. Your Jeep should be able to handle it."

Her throat tightened. Maggie hadn't had anyone looking out for her in a long time. "I will. Thank you."

"We'll see ourselves out. You two enjoy your dinner." He paused at the doorway. "After the storm, I'll call you about getting those stairs fixed."

"Sounds good."

Maggie turned back to Alexander, suddenly feeling very self-conscious. It was one thing when she thought he was a worker, but altogether different now that he was a guest. She must look like a mess. Maggie spent most of the afternoon cleaning the kitchen and putting away the groceries she bought. She had dirt and grime on her jeans, and she didn't even want to see what her hair looked like. She ran a hand over her to her ponytail.

She gestured to the table. "Should we go ahead and eat?"

"Sounds good to me. It smells amazing."

Maggie took her seat across from him and cut up her pasta. "How long will you need a room?"

While she wasn't ready for guests, she couldn't afford to turn him away now that he was here. Perhaps he was the answer to her prayer—the help needed to fund the renovations. How much should she charge? And what if he thought it was too much for the current state of the Inn? She thought she had time to figure out these things before she officially opened.

"I'm not sure. I do not have a departure date." Alexander took a bite, and his eyes widened. "Walter was right. This is great."

"Thanks." Maggie took a drink. "It's actually the only thing I can make really well."

"Oh, really?"

"Yeah, I'm not much of a cook."

Alexander gestured to the food and raised an eyebrow. "I don't believe it."

"You will once you have my food again." Maybe she shouldn't have said that. Not exactly a selling point to a guest. "I mean, I haven't hired a cook yet for the Inn."

"Ah. I see."

Alexander looked around, and she tried to see it from a guest's perspective. She sighed, reaching for a piece of garlic bread.

"I'm sure my unexpected arrival has put undue stress on your plans. I can look into other arrangements."

"No!" Maggie cleared her throat. "I mean, I would love for you to stay if you don't mind that the Inn is in—" She tried to come up with an accurate description. "A transition phase."

"Hence the boiler's new state."

Maggie started to reply, but then noticed his grin. He was teasing her. She relaxed a little. "I actually arrived a few days ago myself."

"Really?"

"At Thanksgiving, I learned I inherited the Starlit. Imagine my surprise when I got here and saw it in this state."

He leaned back in his chair and took another look around. "But that's exciting. A new adventure for you."

"Yes, it is." Maggie sat up a little straighter. "It just needs some TLC."

Alexander reached for the bread. "And evidently a chef, because I don't think you can serve this every day."

"Well, do you cook?"

"I might." Alexander took a sip from his glass and leaned forward. "Are you hiring?"

Maggie pushed her plate away and placed her arms on the table. "Depends. Are you any good?"

He leaned forward, lowering his voice to a whisper. "You haven't lived until you've tried my pancakes."

Her pulse skyrocketed. What was wrong with her? She was flirting with a complete stranger. But there was something about him. She cleared her throat and sat back. "Well, how about you make them for me in the morning, and we can discuss it further?"

"That sounds like a plan."

"Great." Maggie stood. "We should probably get you a room."

Alexander gathered their plates. "How about I wash, and you dry?"

"Oh, that's okay. You're a guest. You don't have to help." She took the plates from him and carried them to the kitchen.

"I don't mind at all." He entered behind her, carrying the lasagna dish and bread bowl.

Maggie bit her lip. "Well, you just might."

Alexander set them on the counter and sighed. "And why is that?"

"Because we're going to have to clean your room and wash your linens first." Maggie closed her eyes, waiting for him to come to his senses and decide to leave.

Silence filled the room, and she slowly opened her eyes in time to see him burst into laughter.

"Well, I guess we'd better get started."

chapter
seven

"I HAVE to hand it to you. These are good." Maggie waved her hand and bowed—Alexander stiffened, but forced himself to relax.

Alexander poured another batch of pancake mix into the skillet. "I'm glad you like them." He couldn't help but smile. It'd been a long time since he'd been free to work in a kitchen without the threat of hearing about it later from his parents.

"They only need two things." Maggie hopped down from the counter and rummaged through the pantry until she brought out two items. "Peanut butter and chocolate chips."

"On pancakes?" Scrunching his nose, he flipped the pancake. They had chocolate in the kingdom, but peanut butter? He'd never heard of such a thing.

"Don't knock it until you try it." She grabbed a knife and smoothed the brown goop on top of the pancake. Afterward, she sprinkled small teardrop-shaped chocolates all over. With a fork, she stabbed a bite of the pancake and held it out to him. "Try it."

Reluctantly, he accepted the utensil and raised it to his nose to smell. He wasn't surprised that all he could smell was sweetness. "The smell makes my teeth hurt."

Maggie rolled her eyes. "Don't you mean it makes your mouth water?"

Here goes nothing. He took a bite before he could change his mind. It was thick and creamy, but surprisingly, all the flavors blended together nicely. "Hmm. Not bad."

Maggie rolled her eyes. "Not bad? It's heavenly."

He had to swallow a second time. "Can you hand me some milk?"

"Sure." She reached for the jug and slid it his way. Was peanut butter supposed to be this thick? He tried clearing his throat, but the sticky material clung to the roof of his mouth. He poured himself a glass and downed it all in one gulp.

"Thirsty?"

"I can't seem to get that bite to go down." He coughed and then turned off the stove's burner and poured another glass. "Is it hot in here?"

"Are you all right? Your face is red."

Now that she mentioned it, his face tingled. He lifted his hand to his cheeks and noticed red bumps swelling on his arm.

"Alexander, are you allergic to peanut butter?" Maggie reached for his arm and pushed back his sleeve.

The bumps were trailing up his arm.

"Alexander?" Her voice rose in alarm.

"I ... don't ... know. I've never had it before." Allergic? He didn't have any allergies that he was aware of, and it was something that his family kept a strict eye on, as his brother was allergic to insect stings.

"Come on. We're going to the hospital." Maggie grabbed his arm and hurried him through the kitchen and down the hall to the lobby.

"Grab your coat." She dashed from the room into the bedroom that he had noticed the day before and came out with a pink bottle of liquid and a purse. "Drink some of this."

"What is it?"

"An antihistamine. Should help ward off some of the reaction until we get to the hospital."

He took a swig and nearly gagged. "This is awful."

"Alexander, come on." She gave him a push through the door and slammed it behind him, nearly knocking him over to get to her vehicle.

Wet drops hit his face, and he looked up to see snowflakes falling. Was this the storm that Walter mentioned? If so, they really shouldn't leave right now.

"What are you doing? Get in!" Maggie already had the Jeep running as he hurried over to the other side and climbed in. It wasn't that different from the vehicles in his kingdom, but the steering wheel was in the wrong spot, and this car had more gadgets than theirs.

"How are you feeling?" Maggie looked at him briefly as she sped down the driveway to the main road.

"I think I'm okay."

"I can't believe this," she murmured. "First day with a guest and I nearly killed him."

"Wait—I'm going to die?" Alexander faked an alarmed tone and then laughed when she glared in his direction.

"Not funny."

She was cute when she got mad. The thought caught him slightly off guard, but he continued. "Oh, come on. It was a little bit funny."

Maggie sped down several roads, the tires squealing a few times before the town loomed in the distance. Okay, so maybe he shouldn't have teased her. She was obviously distressed.

"Take another drink." She nodded toward the disgusting little bottle he still held in his hand.

"Don't you think I've had enough?"

She eyed him quickly, returned her gaze to the road, and firmly pressed her lips together. "It's children's medicine, so drink."

"What are you so worried about? I'm just a tad itchy."

Maggie reached over and flipped a flap above his head. It was a mirror. Alexander nearly yelled at the creature staring back at him.

His face was a mixture of red, angry blotches and very swollen lips. "What did you do to me?" Leaning closer, his heart thudded faster. "You really *are* trying to kill me!"

"I'm sorry! You should have said you can't have peanut butter!"

He matched her frantic tone. "I didn't know I couldn't!"

"Really? Who hasn't tried peanut butter?" Maggie reached down, pushed something on the dashboard that clicked, and sped up. "Peanut butter is one of the biggest food allergies there are!"

"Why are you yelling at me?" Alexander turned the bottle of medicine upside down and chugged it.

"I'm sorry. I don't know what else to do." She turned the Jeep hard and skidded to a stop in front of a large concrete building. "Come on."

He unbuckled and staggered after her, his thoughts a little foggy. Was it a result of the allergy? Shaking his head, he followed her through the doors that opened on their own.

Woah. I wonder if we can get doors like that at the castle?

"We need help!" Maggie called out, running ahead of him. An older lady in a blue uniform came around the desk. "He's having some sort of reaction to food—maybe peanut butter."

The woman frowned. "Did he use an auto injector?"

Alexander tried to sit down but nearly missed the chair, and Maggie rushed back toward him. "We didn't know he was allergic!"

The nurse yelled for someone else, and before he knew what was happening, they had him in a small room on a bed.

"What about Maggie?" He pointed back in the direction they came.

"Is she family?" The nurse asked, wiping his arm with a pungent liquid.

"No."

"Then she'll have to wait outside for now. They will have her get your paperwork started."

Paperwork? Hopefully, they would accept the Inn's information. He could never say where he was really from. Two more people entered the room, carrying a bag of liquid, and—was that a needle? Alexander leaned back in the bed and closed his eyes. He'd never handled needles well.

A few pokes and prods later, he struggled to stay awake. Whatever they'd given him was making it very difficult to concentrate. The nurse did something to the bed, and it started reclining.

She adjusted the pillow under his head. "Would you like a warm blanket?"

"That sounds wovely ... lovely."

The nurse chuckled and left the room, bringing back the blanket, another pillow, and Maggie.

"Will he be all right?" Maggie came to the side of the bed. Concern lingered in her expression. He wanted to tell her not to worry, that he was feeling great, but he couldn't quite get the words to form. Instead, he reached out and patted her hand.

She must have mistaken his intentions, because she entwined her fingers through his.

"I think we have the reaction under control now, but the doctor will be in to see him in a little bit." The nurse settled the warm blanket over him, and he closed his eyes. Maybe a nap would do him good.

"The medicine is going to make him very tired."

Alexander opened his eyes and tried to focus on what the nurse was saying. He missed the last part, but Maggie replied, "Thank you," and pulled up a chair beside his bed, never letting go of his hand.

"I'm so sorry, Alexander."

"It's okkkayy." *Wait. That didn't sound right.*

"Rest. We'll talk later."

He turned his head to her and smiled. "Yeah. Talk ... later." His eyelids drooped. "About ... you ... tried to kill me."

chapter
eight

MAGGIE REALLY HAD to stop asking what else was going to go wrong. She rubbed her eyes and pulled her robe shut, making her way to the kitchen. The Inn was still quiet. They arrived back late last night, so Alexander must still be in his room sleeping off his allergic reaction to the peanut butter fiasco, and once again, Maggie couldn't sleep, so she was up way too early.

Maybe once she ate, she could get her thoughts in order and figure out what needed to be done. She pulled a bowl down from the cabinet, opened an oatmeal pack, and dumped it in. After putting it in the microwave, she grabbed the orange juice from the fridge.

It was days like this—when everything that could go wrong did—she wished she had someone to talk to. Friends from college drifted away once graduation hit, and then coworkers only wanted to talk about her behind her back.

And family? Well, her only family left—after her parents passed away—just gave her the Starlit. The microwave beeped. She carefully pulled out the bowl and reached for the syrup container.

"Please, no more pancakes today."

Alexander stood in the kitchen, his brown hair sticking up a little from sleep. Her heart fluttered, and she nearly dropped the bottle of maple syrup. "No pancakes today."

He reached around her to grab a mug. "Coffee?"

"I haven't made any, but I can."

"No worries. I think I can figure it out." He flashed her a smile, and she had to turn back to her oatmeal to keep from staring at his lips. *Get a grip, Maggie. You barely know him.*

She carried her breakfast to a table in the dining room, heat burning her cheeks. Alexander came out several minutes later, holding a plate of eggs and toast.

Maggie winced and set her bowl down. She should have been the one making him breakfast. He was the guest.

"I hope you don't mind that I just helped myself."

"Not at all." She sighed. "I should have offered to make something—I didn't think. I'm just glad you don't mind cooking until I find someone."

"I don't mind at all. It's nice being able to make food for myself for once."

What did that mean? She picked up her juice and took a drink. "Do you normally have people make it for you?"

Alexander's gaze met hers before quickly glancing away. "Well, my family does."

He finished the rest of his eggs in silence and rose from the table. He took his dishes with him. Was he embarrassed to admit that? Whatever the case, he obviously didn't mean for it to slip. A knot settled in her stomach. She couldn't tell by the simple clothes he wore, but she imagined he was like her—trying to make his way in the world. She never assumed he was rich. He probably had a trust fund.

And she offered him a job!

Well, it was a joke—flirtation, really. They were both joking around about it, so it didn't really count, did it? Regardless, she felt like an idiot. And she was worried about charging him too much.

"So, what's on the agenda today?"

Startled, she spilled her drink in her lap.

Alexander frowned, reaching for a napkin. "Sorry, I didn't mean to alarm you."

"It's okay. I need to get dressed, anyway." She wiped the juice from her robe. "I, for one, need to clean the rest of the rooms. And I need to bring in some more wood from the shed in case we lose power."

His brows furrowed. "Oh, right. The storm. I forgot it started snowing on us when we left yesterday."

"Well, you were sort of sleepy from all the medicine."

"Yeah, I was." He groaned. "Not my finest moment."

Maggie collected the dishes and went back to the kitchen, Alexander following her. She eyed the dishwasher and the sink before ultimately filling the sink with hot, soapy water and letting the dishes sink to the bottom. There were only a few dishes, and for some reason, the dishwasher gave her pause.

Probably a good thing.

Alexander joined her at the sink and picked up a dish towel. "Did you have to help me inside last night?"

"Yeah. You kept trying to stay outside on the porch. Said you wanted to watch the snow fall even though it was freezing, and you forgot your coat when we left."

"Well, in my defense, I had a panicked woman screaming at me to hurry and drink this awful concoction."

She passed him the last utensil. "That awful concoction probably saved you from having a worse reaction."

"True." He flashed her a grin, and her stomach fluttered. Charm and charisma oozed from this guy, and usually, she could see right through those types and never gave them the time of day. Except she couldn't ignore that she was drawn to him.

"Thank you, Maggie, really." He reached over and squeezed her hand.

He didn't have to thank her. If it wasn't for her, he wouldn't have been sick in the first place. Embarrassed, she pulled her hand from his. "You don't have to thank me."

Alexander slowly pulled his hand back, started to say

something, but then looked like he changed his mind. "How about I go bring in some firewood?"

Maggie put the last dish away and shook her head. "You don't have to do that. You're a guest. Remember?"

"Technically, I am. But you said you'd hire me, so I guess that makes me your employee now."

Ah, so he remembered their flirtatious agreement. Maggie squashed down her joy at that realization and hurried to come up with some type of excuse for why this wouldn't work. She needed him to be a guest.

Perhaps she needed to be honest with him. It wasn't easy when she knew he probably never had to work a day in his life for anything.

"I know I said that, but the truth is, I'd rather you be a guest." She slammed the cabinet door harder than she meant to, frustrated at herself for getting into this situation. Maggie needed this Inn to be successful, and she didn't need any distractions.

"Oh—if that's—"

Maggie left the kitchen and called over her shoulder. "I mean, I don't have any guests here yet—well, besides you—and there are so many repairs that need to be made that I wasn't expecting." Once she started speaking, the words poured out. "I'm not sure how I'm going to be able to do this."

"Maggie—"

She ignored him and waved her hands. "And I've sort of spent my nest egg, so to speak, so unless you're willing to exchange room and board for work, then—"

Alexander reached out and gently grabbed her shoulders. "Maggie, take a deep breath and slow down a little."

"Sorry—"

"Maggie—"

She clamped her mouth shut.

"Deep breath."

Rolling her eyes, she did as he asked but made it a point to be extra loud about it.

"Feel better?"

"Sure."

He dropped his hands and chuckled. "I've never seen anyone talk so fast and so animatedly before. I can't keep up with you."

Embarrassed, she nodded. "I've heard that before."

"Well, what I was going to say was that I'm thankful that you let me stay, even though the Inn isn't officially open yet. And I want to show you my gratitude by helping out around here." Alexander's half-smile lit up his eyes.

Oh, dear. Concentrate, Maggie.

"I wasn't asking for anything in return."

"Oh." Well, she couldn't stop making a mess out of everything. If she were Alexander, she would have already checked out and found another place to stay.

"That's very kind of you. I could use all the help I can get." She gestured all around them. "As you can see."

"Well, it's settled then. You get to boss me around." He gave her that grin as before. The one that sent butterflies fluttering in her stomach. Ugh. She kept alternating between wanting to wipe that smirk off his face or ask him to smile again.

Frustrated, she left the dining room. Before she entered her room, Maggie took a chance to look over her shoulder, and sure enough, Alexander was already slipping on his coat and heading for the door.

"Alexander, where are your gloves and boots?"

"I haven't made it to the store to purchase them yet." He pointed outside. "I almost died, and there's a snowstorm."

What was she getting herself into? She sighed. "You can't go out there without gloves and boots. Look in that closet inside the game room. I think I saw some supplies the previous owner left."

"Will do."

"Oh, and Alex?"

He turned around, his eyebrow raised at his shortened name.

"You can't keep using the fact that you were mostly dead as an excuse for everything."

chapter
nine

FOR THE FIRST time since arriving at the Starlit Inn, Maggie actually got a full night's rest. In fact, she slept in, missing breakfast time altogether. But Alexander had food still warming for her in the oven.

She ate alone, enjoying the quiet and watching the snow fall and pile up outside the dining room window. It glistened off the trees, and she had the sudden urge to curl up on the couch with a book. But that wouldn't get the Inn ready for her next guest.

Sighing, she finished her breakfast, washed her dishes, and headed back to the lobby. The boxes Alexander brought in still lined the wall, but at least she had made some headway. Her room was beginning to look like hers. A bedspread now graced the four-poster bed, its blue and yellow quilt brightening up the space. Clothes filled the closet and the small dresser, which was way over capacity and had a hard time closing. Her books lined the bookshelf in the game room, and her toiletries took up space in the tiny bathroom that adjoined her room.

"You're up."

Maggie set a box on her bed and turned around to find Alexander leaning against the doorway. Her breath caught in her throat. Hair tousled, stubble on his cheeks, and that grin—he really needed to stop smiling at her like that—caused her to lose all her words.

"Maggie?"

Shaking her head, she opened the box and quickly skimmed the contents before replying. "Yes, sorry. Just trying to decide where to put everything."

"Ah." He moved away from the door and joined her. "I can't relate. I've never picked up my whole life and moved before."

"Really?" That surprised her. What must that be like to have roots?

"Yeah, my family has always lived in the same place."

"That actually sounds really nice."

"It can be." He reached into the box and pulled out a stuffed animal. "What in the world is this?"

She grabbed it from his hands. "This is Mr. Wolf." Maggie averted her eyes. "I got him when I was a kid, and he's been with me ever since."

"I can tell. He's missing an eye."

She stroked the fur around the animal's face. The poor wolf had been through it over the years but had served its purpose well. "He can't help it. He's had a hard life."

"Has he now?" Alexander raised an eyebrow. "I must know more."

Maggie laughed and tried to fluff the poor creature back out, but the stuffing didn't cooperate. The animal was almost flat. "For one, he's a good sleep companion. See?"

"Mr. Wolf is definitely skinny. Have you been starving him?"

She rolled her eyes and set him on her bed. "Ha-ha. He has been well loved."

Alexander nodded, his gaze turning thoughtful, and his voice wavered. "I see that. My sister had something similar."

"Had?" Maggie sat on the bed and pushed the box out of the way. Suddenly, she didn't like where this conversation was going.

Alexander sat on the corner of the mattress and sighed. "My

sister Lilibet had a doll. Blonde curly hair, blue eyes, green dress. It was made to match her."

"How adorable."

"It was. She was like you and carried it around everywhere." He got up from the bed and cleared his throat. "Well, I think I'm going to tackle the rooms. Which room would you like me to work on first?"

Obviously, he'd changed the subject. Maggie took a second to catch up, not wanting the conversation to end yet. "Um, I'm going to keep unpacking, so if you want to take an inventory of how many rooms have which size beds, and what items in each room are broken or obviously need to be replaced, that would be great?"

Alexander clapped his hands. "Sounds good. Where would I find paper?"

"Check the counter in the lobby. I haven't had a chance to go through all the drawers yet."

"Will do."

Maggie watched him leave and stared at the doorway for a moment. There was such sadness when he talked about his sister that she knew something awful must have happened. She reached for Mr. Wolf and placed him on top of her dresser. Maggie didn't have the heart to put him back in the box with the rest of her childhood belongings.

But where to put the box? Maggie surveyed the room and dropped the box on the closet floor. The opposite side of the wood plank sprang up.

Ugh. Broken floors? Go figure.

Maggie kneeled down to place the floor plank back in its spot, but something below the wood caught her eye. She moved the box out of the closet, pulled the board up, and gasped. There, in the floor, was a stack of leather journals.

Sticking her hand in the dark crevice, she cringed as her fingers went through a sticky spiderweb. Maggie quickly pulled out the journals and wiped her hand on her jeans. A trail of dirt smeared across her leg. She ignored it, praying there weren't any spiders attached to the web.

The journal on top was leather-bound, with tattered edges on the pages. The others were all different colors and styles, so there wasn't any common theme among them. She got up from the floor, closed her bedroom door, and got comfortable on the bed.

She flipped open the first journal. There wasn't a name inscribed on the inside, but it looked like the entries were all dated and had the same initials at the end—"H.B." She turned to the last entry. It was dated 2012 and written in a messy cursive. As if this H.B. had been in a hurry.

> January 2012
>
> I've held on as long as I can, but I can't put it off any longer. I'm tired and too old to continue operating the Starlit. I'd hoped to find someone to carry on in my place, but when it came down to signing over papers, I couldn't do it. This place is very special.
>
> There's too much history and magic to leave the Inn to a complete stranger. Perhaps I should have tried harder to settle down and marry, to have children. I should have tried harder to reconcile the family. But life happened, and all I have to show for it is a lot of "should haves."
>
> The truth is: this place HAS to stay in the family. No one else can take care of it like the Bensons.
>
> So, I'm heading to my sister's to convince her to take over. She'd never wanted to help before, but I can't give up. I won't give up until the Starlit has a Benson family caretaker to take my place.
>
> Wish me luck ...
>
> -HB-

Maggie flipped through the remaining pages, but they were all blank. What happened to H.B.? Did the sister take over? And why didn't they leave it to Rose? After all, she was supposedly her cousin. Was her mom the sister this H.B. spoke about? Was this why Maggie didn't know her extended family?

She went back to the beginning and skimmed the first few entries. They were random tales from taking over the Inn and the many different people who walked through the door.

But a few entries later, something caught her eye. She started, turned back to the beginning of the entry, and read it out loud.

It's finally happening!

I've been waiting for it to be my turn. For something magical to happen while I'm running the Starlit, and it finally has.

My guests checked in on a late Saturday evening. Two businessmen who had a meeting scheduled in town for Monday morning. They were kind and kept mostly to themselves, but I could tell they were stressed. From what I could figure out from their conversations, the meeting would either make or break their company.

The next day, they had an argument, and one man checked out, taking the car and leaving the other man stranded. It turns out that's not all he took. The man who left stole the presentation and depleted their business account.

The man left behind was devastated.

I helped him the best I could. Gave him a ride into town so he could arrange a way to get home. But something else happened while we were waiting.

The company he had the meeting with—the

OWNER CAME BACK TO THE STARLIT AND HIRED HIM ON THE SPOT! WALTER AND I STILL DON'T KNOW HOW HE FOUND OUT ABOUT THE ENTIRE ORDEAL. I TOLD HIM IT WOULDN'T BE LONG BEFORE WALTER WORKS HIS WAY UP AND OWNS THAT CONSTRUCTION COMPANY.

Maggie closed the journal. It couldn't be. Walter? The old man who came and helped her? What a small world. She put that book aside and reached for another one.

Hours later, Maggie shut the last journal and rubbed her eyes. Each journal was from a different owner throughout the Starlit Inn's history. Each one filled with strange incidents. But there was one thing each of the journal owners had in common—they fully believed that the Inn was supernatural. Things happened here that couldn't be explained. Goosebumps rose on her arms, and she rubbed them.

What in the world had she signed up for?

chapter
ten

"WHAT'S THE DAMAGE?"

Alexander joined Maggie in the small room off the lobby. She was cleaning out the same closet where he had found the gloves and boots. She had her dark hair braided down her back, but a few strands fell along her cheek.

What would it feel like to brush them back?

He shook his head, clearing the thought from his mind. "Ten rooms—all different types."

What had she called them before? Queen- and king-size beds? Alexander wanted to laugh when she first said it, but held it in.

"The mattresses are really worn with metal poking out through most of them."

Maggie closed her eyes. "Please tell me we have at least one room with a mattress that's in decent shape?"

He looked down at his notes. "Actually, two. The largest room that has the microwave and a very large tub, and room ..." He turned his paper over. "Nine has a queen-size bed."

"Okay, so two rooms with okay mattresses?" She sighed. "That's doable. The first guests are a couple and a baby. I can put them in the queen room. But we are going to need a crib. What else?"

Alexander looked back at the list. She would not like what else he had to say. "It looks like you're going to need new carpet in most of the rooms. It's worn thin and stained in some places. Several pieces of furniture are wobbly."

Maggie's eyes widened in disbelief. "What am I going to do?" She stepped away from the closet and started pacing. "Okay, I can figure this out. I'll go to consignment and thrift stores. Surely I can find some furniture that isn't too expensive. The bed linens can be laundered, and they'll be okay until I can afford to replace them."

Alexander watched helplessly, unsure of what to say—or when—the more she paced, the more her speech intensified.

"The carpet will be tricky. But it wasn't that bad. I'll rent a shampooer and maybe get some area rugs." She turned toward Alexander. "Bright curtains and rugs, and a few well-placed pieces of decor, and it will be all right ..."

Her words cut off as she sank into a small couch. "I mean, I'll spruce up each room as I go, right?"

Her bright blue eyes gazed up at him with such hope, he felt bad for having to bring her his next set of news.

"What's happening right now?" She gestured to his face. "I don't like that look."

Frowning, he lowered the clipboard. "The bathroom closest to those two rooms has some type of leak."

"Of course it does!" She leaned back on the couch and closed her eyes.

"Maggie, I'm sorry, but I'm going to help you figure it out."

"How bad is it?"

He rubbed the back of his neck. "The faucet sprays water when you turn it on."

"Okay, so we need a new faucet. Can't be that hard to replace, right?" She sat up and shrugged her shoulders. "We'll just YouTube it."

"YouTube?"

She raised her eyebrow. Oh, no. He slipped up again. There

was so much of this world that was like his, making it hard to remember to be careful about the things that weren't.

"Wait, you're not anti-social media, are you?" She pulled out the rectangular device again. When he didn't respond, she continued, "You should really download the app on your phone. You can learn how to do just about anything on there."

Time to panic. Alexander scrambled to come up with something. "I don't have one."

Maggie got to her feet. "Wait—seriously?" She crossed her arms. "Wow. That's impressive. I don't know anyone who doesn't have a cell phone. You don't want your family or friends to be able to reach you?

Okay, it was starting to make sense. A *Ringer.* Pax had technology—well, the families that could afford it did. But word of mouth, apprenticeships, and books passed down knowledge. Only the courtiers and some wealthy merchants had Ringers. And a household wouldn't have more than one—maybe two, if they were lucky.

"Kind of the purpose of this holiday." He tried to cover his slipup with a laugh. "I needed some peace and quiet."

"And here I am, messing up your vacation." She sighed. "I'm sorry, Alexander."

"Don't apologize. I'm kind of partial to this Inn."

"Oh really? Why is that?"

"I think I mentioned my family stayed here when I was a kid. But it was Christmas, and it was ..." He tried to come up with a word that described the wonder he felt at all the snow, good food, and beautiful decorations he'd never seen before. "I guess you could say it was magical."

Maggie's face went blank as if he said something outrageous again, but she quickly recovered before going back to her task in the closet. "That sounds like a wonderful memory. Um, have you checked the pictures in the dining room? Maybe you can find your family's portrait on the wall."

Did he say something wrong? Alexander waited a few

moments, but Maggie remained focused on stacking games on the shelves. The lights flickered and then shut off, throwing the entire Inn into darkness.

Maggie groaned and must have done something to her Ringer because a light started shining from it. Annoyance mixed with resignation filled her voice. "There goes the power."

chapter
eleven

LUCKILY, Maggie already had candles and lanterns set aside in case the storm caused a power outage, so now, she was camped out in the lobby with the warm fire and a cozy blanket. The snap and crackle of the wood, mixed with the warmth from the flames, brought a calming touch to the Starlit. And at least it hid the warmth in her cheeks each time Alexander smiled her way.

Alexander sat beside her on the floor, roasting a marshmallow. It was one more thing that he'd never heard of—who'd never had a s'more before? Another item to add to her ever-growing list of things she was learning about him. The only thing she could come up with was that his parents must really hate sugary treats.

"Here you go," he said, passing the marshmallow to her. She assembled the ensemble of chocolate and graham crackers on her plate, keeping one for herself and passing him the other.

Maggie couldn't wait to watch him try it. "You're going to love it."

"That's what you said about the pancake."

"That was not my fault. And I'm sorry you can't have peanut butter."

He shrugged his shoulders. "I haven't missed it this long."

"True." Maggie took a bite of the gooey delicacy and leaned back against the chair. "Mmm."

Alexander shook his head but finally took a bite. Maggie watched until a smile broke out on his face. "Okay, this is good."

"Told you."

They ate in silence for a while until Alexander reached for the bag of marshmallows. "You want another one?"

"Yes, please."

"Did I hear you say you inherited the Inn?" Alexander skewered two more marshmallows with the roasting stick and hovered them over the fire.

"Yeah, a distant relative I never met before left it to me in her will."

"And it didn't go to your parents?"

Maggie waited for the familiar stab of pain to hit when someone asked about her parents, but the ache wasn't as sharp this time. "They passed away when I was in college."

"Oh, I'm sorry." His face softened, and so did his tone. "Losing a loved one is hard."

"It is." She tucked the blanket around her. "You sound like you know how that feels."

The marshmallows caught on fire, and Alexander blew them out. "My sister."

"Oh, Alex."

"She disappeared when I was twelve. Just months after visiting the Starlit." He pulled something from under the chair beside him. "I found this after you mentioned I should look for a picture."

Five smiling faces grinned up at her—a regal-looking couple and three children, two boys and a girl. All standing in what had to be the Starlit Inn's lobby under a giant Christmas tree. "Your family?"

Alexander nodded. "My parents, Winston and Beatrice, me on the left, my brother Silas on the right, and Lilibet in the middle."

"She's beautiful. And she looks so happy."

"She was." Alexander cleared his throat. "Lilibet was always smiling and laughing. And she loved practical jokes. She was the glue that held us all together and helped us get along. No one could stay mad at her."

Maggie had to work to clear her throat. The way Alexander spoke of her, she knew something horrible must have happened. "Did they ever find her?"

Pain flickered across his face as he turned his gaze toward the fire. "Her body has never been recovered, nor do we know who is responsible."

Tears pricked the corners of Maggie's eyes as her heart ached for him. "I don't know what to say. That's horrible."

He passed her the marshmallows. "That's part of why I'm here." He set the roasting stick aside while she finished assembling his s'more. "My family is still searching, and I'm—"

Alexander's gaze met hers, and the brokenness in his eyes made her want to wrap her arms around him. "I'm tired of leads going nowhere."

"They can't fault you for that. It's understandable."

His eyes narrowed. "Perhaps you should tell them that."

Maggie hesitated, not sure how to respond.

"Like I said, she was the glue." He rubbed his face and sat a little straighter. "Okay, that's enough about me. Tell me more about you."

Maggie nearly choked on her snack. "Me? I'm boring."

He raised an eyebrow. "I highly doubt that."

"Let's see. I'm twenty-four years old, broke, and restless ... I guess that's the best word." Maggie reached for her mug. "I graduated from college and landed a job in my field, but it didn't make me as happy as I thought it would, you know?"

Alexander nodded. "What did you study?"

Maggie nearly rolled her eyes. "Childhood education." She held up her hand. "Don't get me wrong—I love kids." She grinned. "But spending so much time with *other* people's children, not so much." She covered her face with her blanket. "Does that make me a terrible person?"

"No, of course not." Alexander chuckled. "And just think, if you stayed, then you wouldn't have this." He swept his arm all around, his eyes lighting up in excitement.

"Yes, an old, worn Inn that needs more work than I can give."

He reached over and placed his hand on hers. "Well, you've got me now."

Maggie's breath caught, and silence filled the room. She couldn't be sure, but Alexander seemed to lean forward, and Maggie caught herself doing the same.

"Well, you know, since I'm staying and helping, that is."

Was he going to kiss her? Maggie leaned a little closer, and Alexander's gaze flickered to her lips. A log cracked, and sparks flew out of the fireplace, breaking the moment. Alexander turned to check the fire. Maggie leaned back against the seat once more, clearing her throat. "I'll take all the help I can get."

chapter
twelve

ALEXANDER AWOKE to the lobby lights shining on his face and the ceiling fan spinning. The power was back on. He turned over, his back sore from falling asleep on the floor. Maggie was still asleep on the other side of the room. A strand of hair fell across her face, and she had her hands tucked under her cheek.

Why didn't you kiss her last night? Alexander sighed. He was an idiot. He had to fix that—if she gave him another chance.

Not wanting to wake her, he slowly got up and folded his blanket, leaving it on one of the chairs. After their talk last night, he wanted to do something extra nice for her, and he knew what it would be.

He went back upstairs, past the guest rooms and toward the corner at the end of the hall. A rope hung down. He gently tugged, and a ladder came down with the door. Maggie mentioned her guests would be arriving a few days before Christmas. He might as well get the Inn decorated.

He climbed the stairs to the attic and searched for items that resembled the decor from the last time he visited the Inn. They didn't celebrate Christmas the same way at home—no Christmas trees, lights, or ornaments. Each city in the kingdom had its own traditions and holidays.

There were presents, though. Something simple, handmade,

and usually only given to immediate family members. There would be a meal—whatever the family could afford, whether it was a meat dish and sides or simply bread and cheese.

Dirt and grime caked the attic floor, and cobwebs hung from the rafters, but Alexander forged ahead. The decorations had to be up here. The first few boxes were random pieces of clothing and decor. But nothing jumped out at him for something that Maggie could use for the guest rooms. Passing those, he headed to the back of the attic, where red and green plastic bins were stacked on top of each other.

Success.

He picked up the first and stacked each closer to the stairs so he could bring them down faster. As he placed the last one, an opened box caught the corner of his eye.

Braided yarn resembling blonde hair hung over the side.

Alexander would have dropped the tote of decorations if he hadn't already set it down. Pulse racing, he slowly stepped toward the box.

It couldn't be.

But yet—there it was. Lilibet's doll.

Tears pooled in his eyes as he lifted the doll out of the box. It was dirty but exactly the same as he remembered. Blonde braids, blue embroidered eyes, and a green dress.

Oh, Lilibet. What is this doing here?

Was this why he wanted to come back here so badly? Was he meant to find her doll? Nothing made sense anymore. Dizziness washed over him, and he had to sit down. The memories, the despair, Lilibet's disappearance. It all swirled around inside of him until he couldn't breathe.

"Alexander, are you up there?"

Maggie's voice called up to him, but he couldn't form any words to answer.

Footsteps sounded on the creaky stairs, and then she was there, hair falling out of her braid and sleep lingering in her eyes. She was beautiful.

"What are you doing up here?" She kneeled beside him. "What is that? Wait—"

"Lilibet's doll." Somehow, he managed to choke out the words.

"Oh." Maggie laid her hand on his arm, and her touch sent a spark throughout him.

"I didn't even know she was missing this." He glanced over at her and immediately wished he hadn't. Tears shimmered in her eyes. Her sympathy brought on a whole new wave of pain.

"She must have left it when you guys stayed here?" Maggie brushed a tear from her cheek.

Alexander nodded. "That's the only thing that makes sense."

"I'm so sorry." She shook her head. "I feel like I've been saying that a lot, but I am truly sorry you and your family are going through this."

"Thank you." He wiped his eyes. "Oddly, the doll helps, though. Just holding this makes me feel closer to her. Does that sound stupid?"

"No, of course not." She squeezed his arm and lifted her hand away. Immediately, he missed her touch. "Would you like a few minutes alone? I can make us some breakfast."

"No, that's okay." He cleared his throat. "I don't feel like being alone right now."

She gave him a small smile. "Then how about I keep you company while *you* make breakfast?"

He chuckled. "Pancakes?"

"With bacon?"

The cute, teasing look on her face made him want to give her whatever she asked. He shook his head. What was wrong with him? He barely knew her. And he had the sneaking suspicion that once she knew him, she wouldn't want anything to do with him. He should tell her everything and see what happened. But if he confessed where he was from—she would think he was crazy.

And he wouldn't blame her one bit.

"Sure." He followed her down the stairs and through the

hallway. "I'm going to drop this off in my room, and I'll meet you there."

"Okay." Maggie reached out and squeezed his arm. "Take your time."

Alexander opened his door and placed Lilibet's doll on the desk next to his backpack. When he returned home—whenever that might be—he'd return it home where it belonged.

Except he didn't know if he belonged there as well.

chapter
thirteen

A FEW DAYS PASSED, and the snow had finally melted. Maggie pulled a piece of paper from the supply cabinet under the lobby counter and started making another list. She needed to go into town to find a crib and the other small pieces of furniture for the two least-offending rooms. After that, Maggie would tackle one room at a time until they were all fixed.

Then she'd move on to sprucing up the rest of the Inn.

"Hello, Miss Maggie." A head poked through the front door, and Walter stepped through, carrying a toolbox and a round pie plate.

"Walter, how are you?"

"Oh, I'm fine. Just here to fix the porch stairs."

She opened her mouth to protest, but Walter cut her off. "Now, there will be no objections. You need these stairs fixed, and I'm going to do it."

"Walter, I can't afford—"

"You're not listening." He held up his hand. "This repair is on me. I'm the one who fell through."

"I don't think that's how it works."

"Well, it is around here. Besides, this Inn is special."

The journal entry about Walter flashed back into her mind. She smiled. "Well, I appreciate it so much."

"Oh, this"—Walter thrust the pie plate toward Maggie—"is from my wife as a thank-you for the delicious lasagna you sent home with me."

"That's so sweet of her." Maggie took the pie and peeled back the aluminum foil. Apple. Her favorite. "It smells amazing."

"It tastes amazing too." Walter chuckled. "You should visit her diner. She really wants to meet you. Bring what's-his-name with you, if he's still here."

"Alexander. And yes, he's still here. Actually, he's been helping me get this place ready."

"Hmm. Does he have any carpentry skills?" Walter sighed. "If he hangs around for the long term, I could probably find a spot for him on my crew."

"That's very kind of you. I'll pass it along."

"Good." The older man nodded and pointed toward the door. "If you need me, me and my guys will be out here."

Maggie raised the pie up and grinned. "Thank you."

"Any time."

Maggie watched him leave, and she took the pie to the kitchen to cut a slice. Her list could wait a few more minutes.

She rounded the corner and nearly collided with Alexander, who was coming down the stairs. His arms reached out and caught her before she fell, but the pie toppled out of her hands.

"Are you all right—"

"Is the pie all right—"

His arms around her sent a thrill of excitement. Alexander released her and laughed. "You crashed into me, and you're worried about pie?"

Maggie sighed, missing his embrace. She scrambled to get a hold of her thoughts. She bent down and retrieved the pie from the ground—still intact. "Don't tell me you've never had pie?"

"I can assure you, my lady, that I've had lots of pie. My favorite is peach."

"Well, I have an apple pie here courtesy of Walter's wife." She continued on down the hall. "Come on, I'll cut you a slice too."

He nodded. "Well, that seems fair, since you nearly ran me over."

"I think it was *you* who ran into *me*."

Alexander waved his hand in the air. "Details."

Maggie laughed and placed the pie on the kitchen counter. She pulled back the foil. Bits of crust were broken, but that seemed to be the brunt of the damage. "It looks good to me."

Alexander handed her plates and silverware as she cut two pieces, slid one to Alexander, and sat to enjoy her slice.

"Okay, this was worth running into you." Alexander teased, scooping up another bite on his fork.

"Totally." Maggie placed her fork on the plate. "Do you want to come with me to town? I thought we could get some things for the guest rooms. I also want to visit the diner. Walter's wife runs it."

"Sure. I thought I'd start going through those Christmas bins, but going into town sounds more enjoyable."

She finished her dessert and pushed her plate back. "You just want more pie."

"Possibly."

"Hey, before we go, there was something I wanted to talk to you about." Maggie bit her lip, waiting for his reaction. She couldn't stop thinking about those journals, and then seeing Walter today brought everything back again.

"Of course." He stacked both of their plates and placed them in the sink.

"I found something really odd in my room." She hopped up on the counter to sit.

Alexander's eyes gleamed. "Don't tell me—you found a trunk of gold and now you're rich."

"If only." She sighed. "No, it was a stack of old journals."

"Really?" Alaxander filled the sink with soapy water.

"If I tell you, you promise you won't laugh?"

He held up his hand. "I promise."

She quickly told him about the journal entries and the story about Walter. He listened to the whole thing without interrupting. Finally, a strange expression crept onto his face.

"Forget it." She jumped down from the counter. "It's silly. Forget I said anything."

"No, don't." He reached out his hand and stopped her from leaving. "You threw me off for a moment. Please, I want to know more about it."

Maggie crossed her arms. "You do?"

He dropped his hand. "It's exciting, though, to have documented stories from the previous owners."

"True. The journals made it sound like this place has some sort of supernatural abilities. But that's insane, right? It's just a house."

Alexander tilted his head to the side, as if he was debating on what to say. "I've heard of much weirder things before."

Maggie nearly snorted. "Yeah, but who really believes those stories?" She shuddered. "At least it's not haunted. I don't want to inherit a haunted Inn."

"That's definitely the type of supernatural happenings you *don't* want." Alexander's tone was amused, but something else lurked underneath as well. Like he had his own secret to share.

Maggie waited for him to continue, but he stayed silent and washed the plates. She reached for a towel to dry them, unsure if she should ask if he'd elaborate. "I don't think the guests care if I inherited a supernatural Inn." Maggie sighed. "We might as well get started on that shopping list. I could use a distraction."

Alexander nodded. "Lead the way, my lady."

chapter
fourteen

ALEXANDER WAS GOING to fix this faucet, that much was certain. Even if it took him all day. He opened the box they bought while they were in town and laid out all the parts. Between the instructions and the video Maggie showed him—on something she called a laptop—surely, he'd be fine.

He reached for a wrench and took the handle off the sink. As soon as he lifted it, a burst of water sprayed the entire front of his shirt.

"Did you turn the water off?" Maggie called from the doorway before rushing to his side. He covered the spout with his hands, trying to stop the rush of water.

"Obviously, I forgot that part."

Maggie opened the cabinet doors and must have found the valve, because the water suddenly ceased.

He stepped back, drenched. If only his parents could see him now. They would no doubt have a loud, hearty laugh at his expense. Just like Maggie was trying hard not to do.

"It's okay, you can laugh."

"I'm sorry—it's not funny." She forced her grin to flatten, widening her eyes, but finally burst into a fit of giggles.

"Yep, laugh it up."

She turned serious. "I'm sorry. I'm good now."

He crossed his arms. "You sure?"

Maggie nodded. Her gaze traveled to just above his eyes, and she shook her head. "No, I can't help it. You should see your hair."

"I can imagine. I can feel it dripping." He ran a hand through it, trying to squeeze out the water.

"Here." Maggie grabbed a towel from the rack and passed it over. "Why don't you get cleaned up, and I'll order something from the diner? You look like you could use a break from kitchen duty."

"That sounds good, but I'm buying." After their shopping spree to fix up the two guest rooms, he knew she had to be feeling the strain of those purchases.

"Even better." She grinned and disappeared down the hall.

"Don't forget the pie!" He called out.

"Already a step ahead of you!"

After a dry outfit, he went back to the bathroom to mop up the water. This faucet would not get the best of him. He brought Maggie's laptop with him this time and followed it step-by-step. About an hour and tons of frustration later, he stepped back, relieved.

It was fixed, and it worked properly. No more leaks.

He went to find Maggie to tell her the good news, but she was pacing back and forth in the dining room, talking to someone on her phone. Not wanting to interrupt, Alexander headed to the lobby. There was still the matter of decorating for Christmas. He might as well get started.

"Hello, I have your lunch order." A sweet, melodic voice came from behind him, and he turned to a young woman holding a bag.

Alexander dropped the box of ornaments. Glass shattered as a few of them fell from the box and hit the floor.

It couldn't be.

"Lilibet?"

The girl's eyes widened, and she gasped. Her hair had

darkened some in the years since he'd seen her last, but she had the same blue eyes and freckles across her nose.

"Alex?"

He took a step toward her, tears clogging his throat. "Yeah, it's me."

She dropped the bag of food on the chair next to her and ran to wrap her arms around him. "I can't believe you're here."

Tears soaked his shirt, but he didn't care. His sister was at the Starlit. He'd found her.

Lilibet pulled back and searched his face. "I tried so hard to come home, but the portal never worked." She raised a shaking hand to wipe her tears. "I think I need to sit down."

Alexander moved with her to take a seat, trying to figure out what she meant. "What do you mean, it wasn't working? How did you end up in this world?"

"I came back to the portal after our vacation because I left my doll at the Inn. Do you remember her?" Her big blue eyes glistened as she waited for him to answer. After all this time, his sister had been right here.

Alexander nodded. He was about to tell her he had found the doll, but she hurried on.

"Mother and Father wouldn't take me back to look for her, and you know how stubborn I can be—well, I came back. But when I arrived, there wasn't anyone around. The Inn was closed."

"Then why didn't you come back home?"

"I was going to, but a thunderstorm came, and I waited it out and tried to get into the Inn to search for the doll." Her eyes filled. "When the storm was over, I went back to the archway, but it wouldn't work."

"And you've been stuck here ever since?" Alexander rubbed a hand over his face. This was too much. All the years they spent looking and tracking down criminals, trying to find out who had taken her, and she was right here the whole time.

"Yes. I stayed here for a couple of days, but a nice lady came to check the property and found me. They placed me in foster care, and once I turned eighteen, I started working at the diner."

"I can't believe this. We've been searching for so long, but never thought you'd be here. If I had even thought it was a possibility, I would have come sooner. I wouldn't have given up —" He stopped, not wanting to admit that he'd given up hope of finding her.

Understanding dawned on her face, and she looked away. "None of this is your fault."

"I shouldn't have stopped looking." His voice broke. "Lilibet ... I should have tried harder."

Her head snapped up at his confession. "No, I shouldn't have come here alone. But I was young and stupid. I wanted to prove to you and Silas I was just as brave and adventurous as you two." She reached for his hand. "But this is not your fault, Alex. I know you did everything you could have to find me. I'm so sorry you had to carry this burden."

His family, Maggie, practically anyone else could tell him the same thing, and he never would have believed them. But to have Lilibet forgive him—tell him it wasn't his fault—a sob broke free, and Alexander felt her arms wrap around his shoulders.

The carefully built wall Alexander had crafted to survive all the grief and pain crumbled in an instant, leaving in its wake an emotional cloud of dust that he couldn't see a way out of.

chapter
fifteen

MAGGIE EYED the dishwasher with suspicion. She needed to see if it would work, but she was afraid to push the start button.

Once the Inn was fully operational, they would need the commercial dishwasher to keep up. She'd been mulling the decision over for days and decided the best thing would be to start with offering breakfast. They weren't that far from town—and after having an amazing lunch at the diner with Alexander, she wanted to throw business their way. After all, she wouldn't have made it this far without Walter.

Or Alexander.

She smiled at the thought of his name. In such a short amount of time, he had become such a big part of her life. She couldn't imagine him not being at the Inn.

Squaring her shoulders, she reached out and pushed the start button—and waited.

The machine started, making normal-ish sounds. She held her breath, waiting for something catastrophic to happen.

Except the pre-wash cycle continued, with no water leaks.

"Thank you." Maggie sighed in relief. She didn't think she could take one more thing going wrong.

"Maggie!"

She whirled around, finding Alexander behind her. His eyes were glassy, as if he'd been upset.

"What's wrong?"

"Lilibet's here."

"What?" What in the world was happening? Maggie listened in confusion as Alexander explained how she'd arrived on the Inn's doorstep with their food, that she worked at the diner, and how she'd been in their town since she'd been lost.

Happy tears threatened to spill for their reunion, but Maggie had to stop him from going further. "Wait, can you say that again?"

Alexander ran a hand over his face. "My name is Prince Alexander Maxwell, and I'm from the Kingdom of Pax."

What he was saying didn't make any sense. Maggie crossed her arms. "You're telling me you're a prince from another world, and you arrived through a portal?"

"Yes, I know it sounds crazy—"

"You think?" Maggie backed up, needing to put some distance between them. She needed to get her thoughts in order and try to find some rational explanation.

There had to be a sane, logical answer. Did Alexander think this was funny? Who would joke around about something like this? Except when she looked up at him, his face was completely serious.

"I wish I could explain." He paused and searched the room with desperation, and then his eyes lit up. "Come with me."

Maggie's heart raced. "What?"

"I'm taking Lilibet home. My family needs to know she's alive." He took a couple of steps toward Maggie and reached for her hand. "Come with me. Then you can see everything I'm telling you is true."

Oh, how she wanted to believe him—but what he was claiming was impossible, and he knew it. The journals flashed in her mind, and she jerked her hand out of his.

"This can't be real. It's impossible."

He sighed. "I assure you, it is possible."

Maggie wanted to believe him, and the journals hinted at all kinds of supernatural circumstances happening at the Inn. Reading them was one thing, but to entertain the stories as truth? That was entirely different. "If you're trying to just mess with me ..."

Alexander looked stunned. "I would *never* do that."

A small seed of doubt crept in at his words. She searched his sky-blue eyes, looking for any trace he was telling the truth.

"I came through the portal with my parents long ago—you have the picture hanging up here. And I wanted to get away from everything at home and come back to the one place I remember being happy."

"Then why didn't Lilibet go back?"

"She said a storm hit. And you mentioned Walter fixed the archway the day I arrived. It must have been damaged in the storm, and somehow that broke the connection to our realm."

Maggie bit her lip, debating his words. His reasoning made sense, but the whole thing was incredible. How could he honestly want her to believe there was a magical portal on her property?

"Maggie, dear, the Starlit Inn is a magical place where anything can happen." Her cousin's words were so serious that Rose obviously believed what she claimed.

"Why didn't you tell me about the portal and who you really were when I told you about the journals?"

Alexander raised an eyebrow. "Would you have believed me then?"

"I don't know."

Alexander sighed. "And do you believe me now?" He sounded so sad, and Maggie wanted to agree to restore their friendship—relationship—whatever they were, back to what it was before all of this happened.

"I don't know." It was the truth, but she could see the effect it had on him. "But I want to."

A spark of hope lit his face. "So, you'll come with us?"

Was she seriously considering going with him? She'd have to be back before her guests arrived, and there was so much to do to get ready. Her heart and mind were both desperately trying to win out over the other. Maggie's heart wanted to follow him, but her mind was screaming this wasn't real.

Except—her cousin's word, the journals, even Walter's story, and how helpful he'd been to her when she didn't do anything to warrant his loyalty—all pointed to trusting Alexander.

Maggie unfolded her arms and rubbed her face. She wanted to trust him.

"Maggie?" Alexander stepped closer and reached for her hand again. "Will you come with me?"

Maggie's heart raced so fast she felt like it was going to burst. But she nodded. "Yes. I'll go with you."

chapter **sixteen**

IT DIDN'T TAKE LONG for Maggie to pack a bag and wait for Alexander to meet her in the lobby.

"Lilibet should be back any minute. Are you ready?"

"All packed." Maggie held up her bag and nervously looked away. This whole thing was awkward, and she didn't quite know what to say. Evidently, Alexander didn't either because he nodded.

The door opened, and a young woman entered. She smiled when she saw Alexander.

"Maggie, this is Lilibet."

"It's nice to meet you." Lilibet turned her smile toward Maggie, and she could instantly see the resemblance to Alexander. That made her feel a bit better about the whole thing.

Conversation was quiet after Maggie locked the Inn, and they made their way down the driveway to the archway. Big, bright stars twinkled above them, and the chilly air played with tendrils of her hair. The Starlit Inn's sign gently swayed back and forth. It was cold, but overall, a beautiful night.

"I'm suddenly nervous." Lilibet shook her head. "It's silly, I know."

"It's not. A lot of time has passed." Alexander dug around in his backpack and pulled out her doll. "I found this in the attic.

Maggie said it must have been in some sort of Lost and Found bin."

Lilibet's eyes brightened. "I can't believe you found it." She took the doll and ran a hand over it. "This thing has caused so much trouble."

"Well, the important thing is you're coming home."

"And just how does that happen?" Alexander and Lilibet both turned to stare as Maggie's question came out harsher than she intended.

Alexander sighed and said, "There's a group of stones with a symbol on them. We place our hand in the right spot."

Maggie raised an eyebrow. "And how did you figure that out?"

"My parents showed us. It's a royal secret that's been passed down throughout each generation."

Maggie narrowed her eyes, but she said nothing else as Alexander moved to stand below the archway. He held out his hand for his sister, and she took it.

Lilibet turned toward Maggie and did the same. "Take my hand and don't let go."

Maggie hesitated, but Lilibet's encouraging smile made her take a step forward and clasp her palm.

Alexander grinned and reached out toward the archway. "Okay, here we go." He placed his palm against the stones, and the ground vibrated, distorting everything around Maggie. Lilibet squeezed Maggie's hand, and Maggie gritted her teeth as everything around her disappeared.

Suddenly, they were standing in a small, stone room with a large pillar in the center.

"We made it!" Lilibet let go of her hand and wrapped her arms around her brother. "I can't believe it."

Neither could Maggie. She took a moment to smooth her hair and get her bearings. Her stomach teetered on the edge of losing its contents.

"Are you all right?" Alexander spoke softly behind Maggie,

and she turned around. Excitement spread across his red cheeks and sparkled in his eyes.

Still, she could tell he was trying to subdue it.

"I'm fine."

"Come on, let's get to the castle." Alexander held out his hand, and she hesitated before sliding her fingers through his.

He led them out the front of the stone cottage, holding vines and brush to the side so they could each exit through the door. The air was much warmer here, and Maggie lifted her face to the warm sun.

Lilibet talked the entire way through the forest, asking questions about their brother and parents. Every now and then Alexander would look over and give her an encouraging smile, but he didn't let go of her hand.

Perhaps he was just as nervous as she was about meeting his family.

After they hiked for a few hours, Maggie could make out the outline of a large building ahead. Wooden gates surrounded the perimeter, and as the path from the forest changed to a dirt road, small houses appeared on both sides of the road.

When they came to a stop at the top of the hill, Maggie froze. It was indeed a castle. Deep down, she had doubted the castle existed. Her head spun, and she reached over and grabbed Alexander's arm with her other hand. He stopped and pulled her close. "What's wrong?"

"This can't be real." She whispered. "Where are we?"

"This is my home." Alexander's tone sounded confused.

"There's a castle in front of us." She looked down at her clothes and tried to imagine what his parents would think of her. "Your parents are a king and a queen."

Her heart raced as reality finally snapped into place in front of her. "For some reason, I thought we'd get here, and it wouldn't be true. Because this *can't* be real."

Maggie wanted to run back to the portal and go home. To go back to reality. She waved her hand toward Alexander and then gestured to herself. "You're a prince, and I'm not dressed right to meet royalty."

"Maggie, honey, breathe." His voice was calm, soothing, and she felt him kiss the top of her forehead. "It's going to be fine."

He'd never called her that before, but hearing those words calmed her down. It was sweet and right somehow. She leaned into him, taking a deep breath. When she moved, she caught Lilibet grinning at their embrace. Her cheeks warmed, and she had to look away. Somehow, flirting and teasing each other had changed into something more. Her feelings for Alexander snuck up on her and caught her by surprise. And his sister was a witness to it.

After Alexander exchanged a few words with the guards, there was a flurry of activity as Alexander and Lilibet entered the palace. Maggie followed behind them in awe.

Servants, dressed in different shades of green, stared as they passed by. Vaulted ceilings, sculptures, and elegant flower arrangements drew her attention. Maggie tried to study each one, taking in the opulence of the great room, but she didn't know what to focus on first.

It was as if she stepped into the pages of a fairy-tale book she'd read as a child.

How could any of this be possible?

They walked through the public areas of the castle toward what she assumed was the family's private quarters because fewer servants and people were visible.

Alexander led her to a beautifully decorated, expansive room with couches and tables and a marble fireplace.

A maidservant entered and bowed to Alexander and then Lilibet. "Your rooms are being prepared, Your Highnesses. I'll take your bags." The servant's gaze swung to Maggie and back to Alexander, confusion on her face.

"Maggie will need a room as well."

"Of course, Your Highness." The girl curtsied and took Maggie's bag.

"Alexander, the guards said Lilibet was here!" Decked out in gold and deep shades of blue, a man and woman rushed into the room. A smile broke out across Alexander's face, and he moved to the side, pulling Maggie with him.

"Mother," Lilibet whispered, rubbing her palms on the side of her jeans. Alexander squeezed her hand before letting go and hurrying to his sister's side and gently ushering her forward.

"Oh, Lilibet." The queen's voice broke as she held out her arms, and that was all it took for Lilibet to run to her parents. Maggie stepped back to allow them more room and privacy. They embraced, and moments later, another man entered. He was taller than Alexander but had the same shade of dark brown hair they all shared.

The man must have been Alexander's brother, Silas. They shared another round of tears and hugs with his family, and the room grew quieter.

Alexander left his family and strode back to her. "I want you to meet my family."

Maggie shook her head. "This is your moment."

"Please." His eyes pleaded with her to follow him, and Maggie found herself following in step beside him.

"Mother, Father, this is Maggie. She's the new owner of the Starlit Inn."

"Hello, dear." The queen was elegant and slender, and her dark brown hair had wisps of gray around her temples. The woman's critical green eyes narrowed as she looked Maggie up and down. She wished the floor could open up and swallow her whole.

"It's nice to meet you." Maggie finally found her voice but was unsure what to do next. Should she curtsy? She started to clumsily bow when Alexander's arm went around her waist.

"Well, looks like we have a lot of catching up to do, don't we, Son?" The king chuckled. "And you're just in time for dinner."

Dinner? With the whole royal family. On the first night they were all back together again? She tugged Alexander's arm, and he stopped, turning to face her.

"I think I'm going to sit this one out." Maggie didn't want to impose.

"Why?"

She lowered her voice. "I think you need some alone time with your family."

"We'll send a tray up to your room."

Maggie didn't realize the queen had drifted closer to them. She let go of Alexander's arm and stiffened at the queen's tone. It didn't leave any room for negotiation.

"Come along, Alexander."

Alexander's brow furrowed, but he nodded to his mother and asked for a servant to take Maggie to her room. "I'm sure this will take a while, but I will come check in with you after."

"Of course."

He hesitated, clearly not wanting to leave her alone.

"I'm not going anywhere." She gave him a gentle push. "Unless your parents get rid of me." She meant it as a joke, and Alexander laughed, but there was something else lingering in his expression. Was that worry?

"Follow me, Miss ..." The servant's interruption made Alexander frown.

"Lady Maggie." Alexander corrected and leaned down to whisper in her ear. "I'll explain later."

chapter
seventeen

ALEXANDER HAD to find Maggie and talk to her alone. He couldn't imagine what she was thinking—or how she was handling being in an entirely different world than her own.

He dressed quickly and splashed cold water on his face. The entire family had been up almost all night, talking and getting reacquainted with Lilibet. It seemed as if no one wanted to leave and go to bed, as if she would disappear again.

If he was lucky, everyone would still be asleep, and he could talk to Maggie without the prying eyes of his family. Alexander left his room, taking time to softly close his door and make his way down the hall to the guest rooms. He knocked on her door and waited.

"Alexander." She opened the door, smiling. His breath caught in his throat.

Maggie wore a purple velvet gown, with her hair pulled back in waves of curls. Her face flushed, and he realized he was staring.

"Your servants insisted I wear this, and another one came and fixed my hair." Maggie sighed and gestured inside her room. "There's an entire closet full of dresses that just happen to be in my size."

"The work of my mother." He cleared his throat. "Part of why I wanted to talk to you. Are you hungry?"

"Starved."

"Let's have breakfast on the patio."

"That sounds nice."

Alexander waited while she closed the door, and he led the way along the hall and down a series of stairs to the common areas of the castle. Servants stopped and stared, but then went back to their work. Alexander and Maggie would be the highlight of the castle's gossip.

The dining room was empty, and Alexander sighed with relief. No one was up yet.

"Good morning, Your Highness."

"Morning, Carlton." He gave the man a smile. He was one of Alexander's favorite servants. "Lady Maggie and I will have breakfast on the patio. Alone."

The man nodded. "Of course, Your Highness. I will do my best to make sure you're not disturbed."

Carlton led them past the dining room and to the outdoor patio table. "Enjoy, Your Highness."

"Thank you, Carlton." Alexander pulled a chair out for Maggie and then sat across from her. She said nothing while two more servants brought a tray of dishes and cutlery.

"How did you sleep?" Alexander asked once they were alone again.

Maggie raised her eyebrow. "That's what you want to ask me?"

"I'm sorry. I don't know what to say. I'm sure all of this is a little …" He struggled to find the right description.

"Crazy? Insane?" She leaned forward, lowered her voice, and gestured to her outfit. "Too much?"

"I know, and I'm sorry. There wasn't any time to prepare you, and would you have believed me, anyway?"

She seemed to think over his words. "No, I wouldn't. I'm still not sure if I believe everything I'm seeing."

"I know it can be a little jarring."

"A little?" She sighed. "So why are they dressing me up and making me a lady?" Her face scrunched, and she laughed. "That didn't sound—you know what I mean."

Carlton entered the patio, carrying a tray of food. He set it down in the center of the table. Fresh fruit, bacon, eggs, and biscuits filled the serving platter.

"Do you need anything else, sir?"

"No, thank you, Carlton."

Carlton bowed and turned toward Maggie, nodding in her direction. "Lady Maggie."

She smiled back at the man. "Thank you. It all looks lovely."

Carlton's face went blank for a second before a pleased smile came across his wrinkled lips.

"I think you just made a friend," Alexander said, waiting for Maggie to take what she wanted from the platter.

"Almost everyone has been so kind to me."

Ah. He knew who she was talking about. "I apologize about last night. My mother can be a little overbearing."

"It wasn't my place to intrude at dinner anyway. I was surprised, I guess, by what happened this morning."

"What do you mean?"

"The servants brought the dresses, and when I politely said I was fine, that I didn't need them, they said the Queen had insisted they do what they could to make me look like a lady while I was here, however brief that may be."

Alexander nearly dropped his fork. "Oh, no. Part of why I wanted to see you alone this morning was to explain the Lady Maggie title."

He set his fork down and pushed his plate back. "We've always kept the portal a secret—if everyone knew, then who knows who would try to go through or what would happen?"

"Makes sense."

"So, we had to come up with a cover story for your arrival. And if you're a friend of mine, then you must be a courtier."

"Ah. Hence, the Lady Maggie and the dresses." She nodded. "Of course. I didn't even think about that."

"Still doesn't excuse my mother's behavior. She's always made it known her children would only ..." How could he put it nicely? "Court someone of noble ranking."

Maggie coughed and reached for her glass, taking a long drink. "Court? As in ..." She gestured back and forth between them. "We are together?"

"You have to understand. Customs here are much different than your world. I brought you here, held your hand—they could only assume we were together."

"Did you tell them we are together?"

Alexander's heart picked up speed. How was he supposed to answer that question? He didn't know when exactly it happened. Maybe it was that first day in the Inn, when she had to take him to the emergency room, but he was falling for her.

Did she feel the same thing about him?

And even if she did, Maggie would have to go back to meet her first guests.

Everything was happening too fast. Had they still been at the Starlit Inn, they could take their friendship slowly and see what developed, but here, with the pressure of his family, the kingdom —expectations were so different. It sort of escalated everything. He wanted her to reveal how she felt about him, but not like this.

"I didn't get to talk to them about that. It wouldn't be fair when you and I haven't ever talked about our relationship."

A smile broke across her face. "That's a relief." He must have looked sad because she backpedaled. "I mean, I'm not exactly a princess."

Alexander's eyes met her gaze. "You are to me."

He watched Maggie's expression, but she just stared back at him. Worried he pressed the matter too quickly, he stood, walked around to her side of the table, and held out his hand. "How about I show you around and give you a tour of the kingdom?"

Maggie nodded, placing her hand in his. Alexander tucked her hand in the crook of his arm and headed for the castle's gardens. He may have shocked her with his declaration, but it was true. He was one hundred percent sure how he felt about Maggie.

Now, if only he could untangle the mess he made fleeing the castle and his family. *But some messes take a lot longer to sort out.*

chapter
eighteen

ALEXANDER BECAME a dutiful and exuberant tour guide. Almost a week had gone by since Maggie arrived at the castle. After that first night and defining breakfast with Alexander, she finally fell into an easy and relaxing routine.

The kingdom was beautiful, and the people were mostly kind. Curious, but kind. It was as if Alexander was trying to make her feel welcome while also giving Lilibet time alone with their parents.

Maggie couldn't imagine how hard that was for them all. So much time had passed, and they would have to get to know each other all over again.

No matter what the two of them did, whether it was sightseeing, having a picnic, or playing games with Silas and Lilibet, Maggie still couldn't get their conversation at breakfast out of her head. They hadn't talked more about defining their relationship, but she took advantage of every moment to get to know Alex even more.

She needed this time to sort out her feelings and was coming to a quick realization—she had fallen hard. Fallen hard for a prince, and for the past week, she'd pretended she was a princess.

However, Maggie could dress in all the pretty clothes, wear

the jewelry, and say the right things, but it wouldn't change the truth.

She didn't belong here.

Tears filled her eyes at the thought, and she ran a hand down the soft fabric of her dress. The satin blue ball gown sparkled in the evening light, and she took a moment to admire herself in the mirror.

A part of her wanted to stay here with Alexander, and she was afraid of how easy that decision to stay would be. But what about the Inn? What about her life? Could she really turn her back on everything she'd ever known?

She stared in the mirror until she couldn't stand to look at herself anymore. There wasn't any use keeping up this charade. Maggie wasn't a princess. No matter how much Alexander said she was to him.

Maggie pulled her phone out of her bag—it didn't work here, but she could roughly figure out the date. Her stomach roiled at the realization that she only had two days before her first guests were to arrive. That was it. Her time was up.

It was time to go home.

Rubbing the back of her neck, she tried to ward off the tension that had settled between her shoulders. It wasn't working.

"Are you ready, Lady Maggie?" A servant poked her head into her bedroom, something she had yet to grow comfortable with.

"Yes, Sofia. Thank you."

Maggie gave herself one more look in the mirror and followed the maid down to the ballroom.

Courtiers from across the kingdom would be in attendance, and Maggie had to put her best acting talents to use. She didn't need any distractions, and she didn't want to take away from the momentous occasion of celebrating Lilibet's homecoming.

The palms of her hands itched, but she didn't want to wipe them off on the beautiful gown. Why did she realize she had to leave on the night of Lilibet's ball? Why couldn't she stay in her bubble of denial a little longer?

It didn't take long for her to find Alexander standing with his brother and sister. His face lit up when he saw her, and he made his way over to greet her.

Alexander reached for her hand and lifted it to his lips. "You look beautiful."

"Thank you." Her voice teetered on the edge of breaking, so she tried to cover it up. "You don't look too bad yourself."

"Something's wrong." He searched her face, and she had to blink and look away. He was beginning to know her all too well. "Why don't we go for a walk?"

Maggie nodded, and he offered his arm for her to hold. Every now and then someone would stop them, and Alexander had to make small talk. With each interruption, Maggie fought to get her feelings back in check.

Finally, they were out the doors and walking the path through the gardens.

"You're leaving, aren't you?" Alexander's smile had vanished, and his eyes glistened. The jovial glint she'd come to get used to was now gone.

Maggie halted. "I have to go back."

He sighed. "I knew it was coming, I just—"

"Hoped I would stay?"

"Well—there was a part of me that hoped all of this would convince you to stay."

Tears filled her eyes. "There's a part of me that wants to stay—*with you.*"

Alexander reached for her hands and drew her close. "I don't want you to go." His gaze trailed down her face to her lips, and he leaned toward her, his lips inches from hers.

Maggie wanted to lean into his kiss, and it took everything she had to refrain. "I don't belong here, Alex. I'm sorry, I can't."

Confusion and hurt flashed across Alexander's face. He stepped back, releasing her and taking all the warmth with him.

"Don't do this, Maggie. We don't have to rush anything." He shifted his weight back and forth as if he was trying to decide to run or stay and fight for them. "I admit that I don't have all the details worked out, but I do know that I want to be with you. We can figure the rest out."

"And how would this work?" Her heart ached. She hated hurting him. "I can't stay here, and you can't come with me."

His eyes lit up. "Why not?"

Maggie scrambled to come up with something. She didn't expect him to come with her. "I can't take you away from your family—from Lilibet." His face fell at her words, and she knew the pain it would cause his whole family if he left. "You just got her back."

"There has to be some solution." He closed the gap between them and pulled her into his arms, placing a kiss on her forehead. "There's a reason why I met you."

She closed her eyes, savoring the feel of his lips on her head. She whispered, "Maybe it was simply to bring back your sister."

Alexander pulled back to look at her, his eyes begging her to deny it. "You don't really believe that, do you?"

Maggie reached up on her tiptoes and planted a kiss on his cheek. "I think I might."

Alexander moved out of her reach, and she desperately wanted to take it all back. But what good would it do? It would work out the same way. He had his world, and she had hers.

He ran a hand through his hair and let out a long breath. "I don't think you mean it." He paced for a moment and then faced her. "I think you are too scared. You've always been alone, and now, instead of letting yourself be happy, you're pushing me away because it's easier than figuring all of this out."

All the breath left her lungs.

Alexander waited for her to respond, but she didn't know how. He finally gave her a curt nod and bowed. "I'll take your silence as your answer." His voice wavered. "But I want you to know that you're making a mistake."

"Alexander—I'm so sorry." The words hurt, but she couldn't be the one to pull him away from his family. It wasn't right.

"I'll have a guard escort you to the portal." He bowed. "If you'll excuse me."

chapter
nineteen

"WHERE'S MAGGIE?"

Alexander took his spot at the table and placed his napkin across his lap. Lilibet and Silas were already there, but his parents hadn't made it down to breakfast yet. "She went home after the ball."

"What?" Lilibet gasped. "Why?"

"She had to go back to get ready for her guests at the Inn." Alexander reached for a pancake, pulling it onto his plate and wishing he was back at the Inn making breakfast for Maggie.

Silas filled his plate and then passed the pancakes to Lilibet. "I'm sorry. We all figured you were going to announce your engagement at any moment. I've never seen you so smitten before."

Alexander reached for the maple syrup. "Hilarious."

Silas set the syrup down with a *thud*. "Wait—did she turn you down?"

Lilibet shushed Silas. "Leave him alone. He is obviously upset."

"I'm fine. No need to worry." Alexander sighed. "And no, she didn't turn me down because I didn't ask."

Lilibet leaned back in her chair and frowned. "I'm confused."

Alexander poured a glass of milk. "She made it clear we come from two *very* different worlds."

"So, what?" Lilibet's voice turned annoyed. "So have I, frankly. You seem to forget I've lived in both places."

"None of us have forgotten that," Silas said, looking back and forth between each of them. "And we are so happy to have you home. Where you belong."

"And I'm happy to be back, but honestly, Alex, did you tell her you loved her?"

"No, I didn't." Alexander could feel the heat on his cheeks. "She didn't exactly give me the opportunity when she was the one running away."

The look on Maggie's face when he left her standing in the garden flashed across his mind.

They could have found a solution together. Alexander couldn't imagine not having her in his life. It was too painful to think about. He might have walked away, but she ran away first. She didn't even give them a chance to work it out.

As if I haven't ever run away before.

"Do you blame her?" Lilibet pushed her plate back and crossed her arms on the table. "It's not exactly easy for someone to start over in a new place, especially a world of royalty and ball gowns."

"And didn't you say she turned her world upside down by taking over the Inn?" Silas asked quietly.

"And Mother wasn't exactly welcoming to her." Alexander told them what she had said to the servants.

Lilibet reached across the table and grabbed his hand. "Go and tell her how you truly feel. Tell her you love her, Alex."

"I did. Sort of—"

Lilibet tilted her head to the side. "Did you say the words, Alexander?"

"I can't ask her to give up the Inn, just like she couldn't ask me to leave my family." He squeezed her hand. "To leave you."

Lilibet let go of his hand and stood, throwing her napkin on the table. "Alexander Maxwell, that is the dumbest thing I've ever heard you say." She wagged her finger at him. "And you've said some really stupid things."

Silas laughed but tried to cover his smile with his hand.

"Lilibet—" He gaped at her outburst.

"I'm home." She squared her shoulders. "You found me and brought me back, and I'm very thankful to you for that. But don't think I'm not going back there whenever I want. I have friends—a whole life that I know doesn't include you all—but that doesn't mean it is any less valuable or special to me."

"No one said—"

She held up her hand to stop him. "What I'm saying is, why do you think you have to stay here or there? Why can't you have both?"

"She has a point." Mother walked into the room and placed her arm around Lilibet's waist. Alexander and Silas got to their feet as their father joined them at the table.

"We've had long talks with Lilibet, and we agree with her." Father gave his daughter a smile. "We know that Lilibet's life in that other world has not been easy. And at times, it was very hard." His father cleared his throat. "But she's also had good times. And we can't ask her to give up that part of her life just because we didn't play a part in it."

Alexander had to work to clear his throat as well. He'd never heard his father give such a warm speech. "What are you trying to say?"

"I'm sorry for treating Maggie so harshly, Son," Mother added. "And I'm sorry I waited until she left to tell you. Lilibet has our blessing to come and go as she needs, and if you need that too—we will not stand in your way. We only want you both—all of our children—to be happy."

Alexander didn't know what to say.

"I think the words you are looking for are, 'see you later.'" Lilibet grinned. "Go win your princess. We'll be here when you get back."

chapter
twenty

MAGGIE unplugged the vacuum and surveyed her handiwork. The guest room wasn't stunning, but it was homey and warm. She wrapped the cord around the handle and dragged it out into the hallway closet. Maggie hesitated outside Alexander's room before quickly shutting the door and moving on. She didn't have the heart to change his room over. Not yet.

Maggie went downstairs to mark the rooms off her list. The kitchen was stocked with food, the dining room tables had new tablecloths and centerpieces, and the game room was stocked with a fully operational coffee bar and board games.

The Starlit Inn was as ready as she could get it in the time allotted.

Except, the Christmas decorations were still sitting in the boxes Alexander brought down from the attic. Maggie hadn't had the heart to put them up when she returned.

But neither could she let her guests come to the Inn without some Christmas cheer. The tree would have to wait, as she wanted to get a live one. But she could decorate the mantel and hang up lights. Maybe put some candles in the windows.

Maggie grabbed her phone and turned on a Christmas playlist. Music always seemed to brighten her mood.

This time, it just made her sad.

The Starlit Inn was supposed to be a magical place, so why didn't that magic work for her? Why bring Alexander into her life only for her to end up feeling more alone?

Except Lilibet was home. And that seemed like a miracle. If getting Lilibet home was what was supposed to happen, then she would move into the Starlit and meet Alexander all over again.

Two hours later, the lobby and other common areas twinkled with lights, garland, and snowflakes. Satisfied, she made a mug of hot chocolate and pulled out the new leather journal she'd bought. She might as well start telling her story at the Starlit Inn.

The front door opened. Maggie glanced at her phone to check the time. Who would need a room this late?

"Excuse me, Miss. I was wondering if you already gave my room away?"

"Alexander!" Maggie's heart nearly thudded out of her chest. "What are you doing here?"

"You didn't answer my question." He tried to maintain his seriousness, but a smile tugged at the corners of his mouth.

"No, I haven't given away your room."

"Good." He leaned against the counter. "Then I would like to extend my stay."

"We've already been through this. I can't take you away from your family—from your home."

He nodded and came around the counter, turning her toward him. "For a long time, I felt so out of place, so restless. That's partly why I left my family and came to your Inn. But then, I met you."

"What are you saying? I don't understand." Maggie put her hands in her back pockets, trying to keep from simply flinging herself into his arms.

"Maggie, I came here because I thought the Starlit was the only place I'd ever felt peace." He reached out and tucked a stray strand of hair behind her ear. "But now I know peace isn't found in just a single place or memory—it can also be found in one's family, one's faith—with the one you love."

Alexander reached for her waist and drew her closer. "What I'm saying is—I love you, Maggie. And it doesn't matter that I'm royalty and you're not. Or that we're from two different worlds."

Maggie held her breath as he leaned closer.

"It doesn't matter if we stay here, or go back to my kingdom, or travel between the two regularly. All that matters is that we're together. We'll figure out the rest."

She didn't wait for him to close the distance between them. Instead, she reached up and wrapped her arms around his head, pulling his lips to hers.

When they pulled away, Alexander whispered, "Okay, now I'm really not going anywhere."

"Not even if you have to fix every faucet in this entire Inn?"

"Nope."

"And not even if the entire Inn falls apart—which in its current state, it just might?"

Alexander shook his head, leaned down, and kissed her again. "I'll still be here. I'm never walking away again."

"What if I accidentally try to kill you again?" Maggie teased, wrapping her arms around him once more. "Who knows what other allergies you may have?"

"It's a chance I'm willing to take."

"I was hoping you'd say that."

Alexander grinned. "You were?"

"Yeah. Because I love you too."

The End

acknowledgments

Thank you to Brett, Dawn, and Jennifer for asking me to join in on this collection. I had a great time working with you all and dreaming up the Starlit Inn. Thank you to the Expanse Books and Scrivenings Press family—I'm so thankful for you all!

Thank you to everyone who helped me through this entire process. Whether you helped me with the plot, critiqued, read, or offered encouragement, it means the world to me. I couldn't do it without you.

And a huge thank-you to my readers. I hope you enjoy this new adventure with Maggie and Alexander!

about the author

 Erin R. Howard is the award-winning fantasy author of *Window of Time* and the Acquisitions Editor for Expanse Books, an imprint of Scrivenings Press. Her other titles include *The Kalila Chronicles* (YA urban fantasy) and *The Gates of Deceit* (dystopian) series.

When she's not writing or editing, Erin loves playing video games with her husband, watching movies with her children, and fueling her many craft addictions. Erin has a Creative Writing degree and is a member of Realm Makers, RagTag Writers, and Once Upon a Page. She resides in Western Kentucky with her husband and three children.

Asunder

Brett Armstrong

Asunder is dedicated to the glory of God,
Who gives us a sure hope eternal in the heavens to which we look
forward.

chapter one

"I'LL KILL YOU," Naomi snapped. Her eyes fixed on James O'Connell so heatedly, he could feel the exposed skin on his neck warm.

Hand hovering in the air, he dithered. Those were the only three words the woman had spoken in more than an hour. On some level, he knew she wasn't kidding.

His hand shot forward on impulse and silenced the drivel of the least interesting segment in the history of broadcast radio. He flipped to a local station, and immediately the cabin was filled with the notes of "All I Want for Christmas Is You." James smirked. Naomi used to love that song. He remembered their first Christmas together, her singing it to him with a hairbrush. The whole song.

"Ugh, you're impossible," she accused. "I needed to hear that for work."

"You're on vacation," he reminded her tersely, his eyes never leaving the road ahead of them. "Relax, Nomi."

Waves of annoyance radiated off her like a sidewalk scorching under a summer sun. "You know I hate that nickname."

James just bounced his eyebrows. He was well aware of everything that irked his wife. He had called her "Nomi" from their very first date, a blind one, where she had been so reserved she mumbled her name, and he thought she was "Nomi." Some might find it an endearing and romantic nickname. Not Naomi. Not anymore.

She turned her gaze from him, her softly rounded face with its distinctly Mediterranean features taut with fury. If James's intent had been to wound and alienate her, mission accomplished.

What are you doing? You're supposed to be fixing things.

He started to reach for the radio to turn it back on, an overture of peace, but he stopped. He caught a glimpse of himself in the rearview mirror as he drove their SUV. His red hair was shaggy, and a scruffy beard grew thick and wild, instead of being neatly trimmed. Too pale skin contrasted with russet freckles. Dark circles adorned bloodshot eyes. Wrinkles were forming on his forehead. Weary. The man James saw in the mirror was weary and battered and bitter.

No. That phase of our relationship is over. If we're going to fix this thing, no caving in.

He caught her watching him out of the corner of her eye, anticipating him to do just that. To cave. To bow to her every wish.

Too bad for you, Nomi.

He returned both hands to the wheel. Was it his imagination, or had she just winced? She definitely scooted in the seat as far from him as possible.

The effect was huge, even if there wasn't much room to escape each other in the cramped confines of the vehicle. Her sleek black curls stirred as she looked away, tanned arms crossed over her chest. The silky blue-green dress she wore was too tight for her comfort, and she was wearing more makeup and jewelry than a road trip merited. Even after hours of driving, the faint scent of lavender and vanilla from her perfume lingered in the space between them. Naomi had come dressed for a date. Prepared to give this her best shot. Not practical, but passionate. That was definitely Nomi.

"Hey," he tried, his voice tight. "I just need to focus on the directions. We've only been to Treehouse Grove once."

"Maybe once was too much."

At least that's what James thought he heard her mutter. Pain radiated from deep within, and he knew the sting of that wound would be hard to overlook. The last time they had been to Treehouse Grove was on their honeymoon.

"Right, well, we can't be more than an hour away," he stated, more to himself than to her.

"It's more than an hour away," she challenged. "You always try to do that—make things less than they are."

Okay ...

James fixed his eyes on the road. More than two minutes of silence passed between them. He hated the charged quiet and all that it implied, but it was a struggle to rein in the torrent of heated retorts he wanted to lob.

"And then you have nothing to say. I'm so sick of it!"

You're "sick of it"? You've got to be kidding me!

"Still nothing 'real' to say?" Naomi pressed.

Whenever their fights came to this point, it felt like his mind and body set all power to shields. Every hatch battened, every door braced for attack. All he wanted was for it to end. To be able to take a single breath of free, clear air. For both of them to just drop whatever the latest dustup was over. That never happened, though. Hence, this trip. Struggling to resuscitate the desiccated corpse of their marriage. Why had he ever thought there was any point in trying?

"Pull over," Naomi demanded. Her brown eyes had cooled her expression, betraying complete exasperation. "I'm done. We just need to sign the papers."

The back of James's neck prickled at the mention of the formal divorce documents in an innocuous folder in the back seat. Try as he might to bury the vile thing under a stack of luggage, it had been looming over them both the entire trip.

"No. Dr. Peterson said to—"

"He said to see if this trip sparked anything. Well, it did. The last bridge just turned to ash, James. It's over. *We're* over."

James wasn't able to hide the fear, the desperation in his eyes. The emotionless gaze she leveled back at him was as icy as the snow mounded on either side of the road.

Lord, please, no! Please, fix this!

Naomi wore an incredulous look and pointed to the side of the road. "I said pull over!"

The hauntingly beautiful melody of "O Holy Night" began playing. His favorite Christmas carol. This couldn't be it. Not right now.

"What will we tell our families? I mean, Christmas is in a few days. This will blindside them. They'll be devastated!"

Naomi gave him a muted look of something verging on pity. "My baba won't be. He always said you were wrong for me."

James's heart felt ready to implode. He couldn't breathe. Over the radio, the song echoed to him, *"A thrill of hope, the weary world rejoices, for yonder breaks a new glorious morn ..."*

It was too much. Each note of this song about hope and joy was a painful barb. The holidays were becoming an unrecognizable debris field from his life, crashing nose-first. Weary he could relate to—he had to stop. To breathe. To think.

His eyes darted around the road ahead, desperate. What caught his attention was an off-ramp that led over and up onto a wooded hill alongside the highway. It was probably an overlook. He could stop, get out, remember how to breathe.

Without a warning or hesitation, he jerked the wheel, and the SUV bounced off the highway, skidding as it took the off-ramp too fast for a dry day, much less a wintery slush-slicked one.

"What are you doing, you maniac?" Naomi screeched, her knuckles white from bracing herself against the violent twists and turns as the road cut back and forth up the hill and into a still more heavily wooded area that eventually became a gravel road, which terminated in a clearing.

A series of sharp jolts rocked their SUV as he had to slam on the brakes to stop in time. The added bumps launched Naomi into a series of curses for his incompetence and questions about his sanity. Maybe both were appropriate, but if he felt anything beyond the deadening of his heart, it was that there was something here. Something he needed to see.

chapter
two

AS SOON AS he cut the engine, all his resolve dissolved. A hotel of some kind loomed before them. An inn? A lodge? Was this a chalet? Whatever it was, it was quaint. And kind of pathetic. James had dimly noted they had passed under a wooden sign and stone arch of some kind that said, "Welcome to the Starlit—something."

The Starlit—whatever—was a large, weather-battered log cabin-style building. All around, the verdant fir and spruce of the trip up gave way to the mangled bare branches of dozens of deciduous trees, long dormant, and a few evergreens that looked ready to die.

What a hideous place.

"Are you insane?" Naomi bellowed from beside him. "You could've gotten us killed!"

"I need to get out," he huffed. "Take a break."

Naomi rolled her eyes. "Yeah, go crash on a couch to avoid things. Your go-to move."

When he didn't respond and just stared out the windshield to an invisible point well beyond a thousand yards distant, Naomi's tone softened. "If we need to stay a bit, we can. I need to call and cancel our other reservations, anyway. Not that we'll get any refund this close to our check-in date."

James rested his chin on the steering wheel. Some other Christmas song droned in the background. Every inch of him was completely numb. He tilted his head toward the lodge. A faint trail of smoke issued from a couple of chimneys along its length.

Naomi cleared her throat. "So, are you ready to sign?"

He looked at her as if she were speaking another language. And she might as well have been. What had driven him up to this place? It was such a bizarre impulse. Maybe fight-or-flight had kicked in, and he had flown here? To what end? He and Naomi didn't even have *Breakfast at Tiffany's* between them anymore—though they might've if he'd ever agreed to watch anything she wanted to in the past four years.

No. She was right. They were done. Completely over. He was so hollow inside.

His voice echoed the emptiness. "Let's just stop here for the night. In the morning, we can head back and sign them at your lawyer's office."

"Here? Are you serious? There's no way—"

He opened his door, got out of the vehicle, slung on a backpack, and stumble-marched off without waiting to hear her answer. Numbness, shell shock, whatever this insensate sensation was that consumed him—the only thing that registered was how very tired he felt and how bitterly cold it was outside.

Under his weight, the stairs up to the Starlit whatever-it-was cried out in wooden terror, threatening to shatter with each step. A strong breeze gusted past him and blew open the front door, smacking it against the wooden face of the building enough times to make it clear that neither the hinges nor door latch were worth anything.

Inside the lodge, a crackling fire's warmth emanating from a great hearth at the back of its foyer area did little to pierce the frigid chill gripping him. It didn't help the room with its high, beamed ceilings, which looked like it had such potential—thirty years ago. Like a zombie, James stumbled up to the desk he presumed to be for checking in. "We need a room for the night," he informed the attendant before she could even react to his arrival.

"Two rooms, actually," Naomi amended softly from behind him.

If James could feel anything, that latest figurative barb in his back would've stung deeply.

"Um, well," the attendant fumbled. She was a girl in her twenties with burgundy hair. Serious worry lines embedded her brow. Apparently, the clear lack of other guests about wasn't granting her any added peace. "We only have one room usable right now—nine. It's got a king-size bed, though. It's our version of a ... honeymoon suite ..." Her rising cheerfulness melted like the snow clinging to James's boots. "I'm sorry," she added quickly, giving a little shrug as if she sensed the tension between them.

When James just stared blankly back at her, Naomi spoke up, her voice ragged as if she was choking back some deep-seated emotion. "We'll take it. Thank you."

The girl, Maggie, James read on her nametag, held onto the old-time room key, staring at it pensively. Whatever thoughts or second thoughts she was having about giving them this room only served to weary James.

A princely looking man strode into the reception area carrying some impressive Christmas decorations. In one swift movement, he bent down and kissed Maggie on the cheek. "Honey, I brought a few more things from home to decorate with."

"Alexander!" Maggie cried in surprise.

The look that passed between the pair before the man realized they had an audience broke through James's numbness to deliver a deep stab of agony in his chest. He didn't dare look at Naomi to see what she made of Maggie and Alexander's tender moment. The very kind of moment they would never have again. He snatched the brassy key from Maggie.

"Hey!" she called out.

James ignored her and staggered off toward their room. By the time he found it and stepped inside, Naomi was right behind him, chiding, "What is wrong with you? You've gone nuts or something!"

Some lights were already on in the room, but they only dimly lit the space. He hoped she couldn't see the tear tracing down his cheek when he whirled to face her. "It sounds like you already know what's wrong with me. I'm nuts. I must be, because what— I care that our marriage is over?

"Yeah, that must be it. I must be bonkers, because I'm not made out of ice like you!"

Up until that last bit, Naomi looked abashed. Perhaps even moved. But the moment his volley hit, the battle was on. "I guess it would seem that way to an immature twelve-year-old. Some of us have to think, plan, face the hard truths."

He tossed the backpack he hadn't even realized he'd slid on into the corner of the room. It crashed into a nickel-finished lamp beside the silky sheeted bed, nearly knocking it over. "'Have to think'? Right, you're the adult. Which, to most people, would translate as snobbish and boring. You used to be adventurous. Have dreams. Now all you do is penny-pinch and complain."

"Maybe if you were more mature and didn't mess up all the time—" She closed her eyes and groaned. "See, this is exactly why we should've signed the papers by now. By last week."

Slinging himself onto the bed, he rubbed away fresh tears while facing away from her. Then put his arms behind his head in the most petulant display of nonchalance he could manage. James sneered at her. "If you knew we were so over, then why did you even agree to try this? We could've saved the gas and hours of misery for us both."

Again, he thought he saw her wince. She took a moment, as if rebuilding her ramparts, and opened her mouth to say something. But didn't. For once, Naomi had no retort. No insult or criticism or passive-aggressive comment. After a minute passed, she more quietly commented, "Get off. The bed is mine."

James bolted upright and started to challenge her claim, to sting her in kind for the caustic burn he'd just taken from being forced out of their bed. He had thought she would at least want one last night beside each other, one last memory of closeness to end things. But no. She truly was done. The hollowness in him deepened. He eyed a plush couch with an ottoman in the opposite corner of the room. "All right." He shuffled over and dropped onto it heavily. "Happy?"

There was a tightness around her eyes that he read as, "No." But she managed to choke out, "Yeah."

A moment later she stalked into the bathroom and shut the door. It was a long time, maybe thirty minutes or more, before she came out again. James wondered what she was doing in there, but he couldn't bring himself to move, as if he'd been frozen to the chair.

As soon as she emerged, he broke free of enough ice to ask, "Are you okay?"

Naomi stiffened, keeping her back to him. She switched off the remaining light in the room before calling out, "I'm going to bed early. Night."

"Night," he replied. As his eyes adjusted to the darker room, he couldn't help noticing the way she was on the bed, facing away from him, curled into a ball. She had the whole bed to herself, but was definitely on her side. Was that a sign? That she hadn't fully removed the space he fit into in her heart, either?

He started to say something. But no. She had been clear. She was done. So, he had to be as well. Besides, she hadn't bothered changing into pajamas or even getting under the blanket, as if she was too exhausted with life and with him to be burdened by one more thing.

Turning in the chair and propping his legs on the ottoman, James stared at the darkened room, heavy with its quiet. A single square window looked out onto the dying grove of trees that lacked even a covering of snow to pretty them up. The walls didn't have any special papering, nor did they take advantage of the rustic charm of the wood used for construction. If anything, they looked blank, as though they had been covered over in the hopes of something better being done, only to have been abandoned. It was a somewhat depressing room for a couple looking for a "magical" place to start their life together.

The irony was just one more blow to bear. Though he guessed this room hadn't always been a honeymoon suite. There was another door on the opposite wall from where they'd entered as though the room adjoined another. Who would want that on their honeymoon?

Of course, who was he to say anything? Memories came unbidden of their own idyllic honeymoon, filled with laughter, smiles, and adventure. A somewhat younger Naomi, her long dark hair pulled back, ready to face anything. Her brown eyes warm, inviting, like a good coffee. So full of energy and life. Not at all like the hard brown stones which had weighed heavily on him for so long. How was she such a different person? Did she change, or had he just never known the real her? It all played through his mind as he sat there, memory after memory tallied in the scales, but he couldn't resolve the question that most needed answering for him.

How did we end up here? Bitter. Jaded. Hopeless.

When he heard Naomi snoring, he sighed and closed his eyes. It was time to set aside his fruitless quest for fixing or even understanding the mess that was their marriage. Better to try to get some sleep. He'd need the energy to face the worst day of his life.

chapter
three

A SHIVER RAN down James's frame, and he jerked awake. Looking around, it took a moment to place where he was. The hotel ... motel ... lodge thing. Except something was off about their room. It felt like he'd only been out for a few hours, so it must be deep in the night. That seemed right, because there was a faint sheen to the room as if everything was caressed by moonlight. James started to settle back in his chair to drift off again in a more comfortable position when a thought sent a fresh chill through him.

It's a new moon tonight.

Eyes open again, he also realized the light wasn't exactly like moonlight. Everything had a blue tinge to it now. Nothing in the room when they'd arrived was that color. He was up on his feet in an instant, looking around, suddenly uneasy. Searching, he found the source of the light. A metallic-looking door with blue light panels around its trim.

James rubbed his eyes. That couldn't be right. The metallic door was where the adjoining one he'd noted before drifting off had been. That entry was the nicest thing in the room, polished oak. Definitely not something out of a sci-fi flick.

"What is going on? Am I dreaming?" he muttered.

Twisting curls of icy vapor crept past the sills of his lips and drifted like a ghostly guide toward the glowing door.

Clenching his arms around himself, he understood at last why he'd shivered awake. "When did it get so cold in here?"

The condensed vapors told him nothing, passing once more across the room to the door before dissipating. Heading over to his backpack, he reached inside and pulled out a jacket he'd thought to pack and slipped it on. Rubbing his hands for warmth, he tried to turn on the lamp next to where his pack lay, but it was no use. It wouldn't come on.

Drat, I broke the thing. Naomi is going to love adding that to our bill.

Oh, that was right. There was no more them, theirs, or ours. He'd be likely paying solo for the casualty of his earlier fit.

"James?" Naomi asked groggily. She yawned. "What are you doing?"

"Nothing. Go back to sleep."

"What are you doing over there?" Naomi insisted, rising out of bed. She, like him, still had on her travel clothes, even her shoes. He almost chided her for going to bed with them on when he realized he was wearing his too.

Naomi shuddered in the cold. "Brr. Did you set the room's thermostat to zero or something?"

"Not everything that's wrong is my fault," he grumbled as he looked around for the thermostat, mostly annoyed at himself for not having thought about it.

He missed whatever snide retort Naomi had for him as he failed to find a thermostat anywhere. Or any signs of heating and cooling elements in the room. In fact, only now did the room's complete lack of windows, vents, or normal amenities of a hotel room register.

"What's with that door?" Naomi asked, scooting off the bed and shuddering as she came to stand beside James.

As if awaiting her notice, the metallic door slid aside with a pneumatic *whoosh*. "Just like a sci-fi flick," James mumbled to himself, his eyes wide on the dimly lit room the open door revealed.

"What are you going on about?" Naomi asked as she tucked behind her ears the wayward curls of her dark hair.

James held up a finger to delay answering and edged cautiously into the mysterious room. Inside, the walls were made of the same metallic material as the door, with bands of blue lighting running along the trim of the room. There were a few displays of some kind, but those were switched off, it seemed. At least until Naomi entered behind him, and the door they'd come through suddenly whooshed shut.

"Ah!" Naomi screeched and ran behind him, grabbing onto his arms like she had that time a raccoon had snuck into their first house. The monitors within the room switched on, and a strange, droning message, spoken by a masculine voice, played over them. But it kept cutting in and out as if the bandwidth was too low.

"James," Naomi asked, her voice tremulous. "What's going on?"

"I don't know," he whispered, his eyes darting from the mysterious displays to yet another door, like the first, on the opposite side of the room. It all felt strangely familiar, but equally alien.

He tried pushing and tugging at the door that had closed behind them. No good. It may as well have been welded shut. Glancing around the room, he snorted, seized by a need for levity. "Well, I don't think we're in—"

"If you say 'Kansas,' I'm going to sock you," she warned.

He shot her a withering look. "Relax, *Dorothy*, I was going to say the Inn."

"Well, duh," she sniped back and shouldered past him brusquely.

He grabbed her arm as she approached the new glowing steely door.

"Hey!" she grumbled, trying to wrench free.

"Hey, yourself," he retorted hotly. But he released her and

elaborated more earnestly, "Let me try first. Something is going on, and we don't know what's out there. Could be dangerous, okay?"

Naomi's eyes widened for an instant. She seemed thrown, her mouth opened as if to speak but never succeeding. After a moment, she gave a nod.

James swallowed his nerves, willing himself to move toward the bizarre door. It had no discernible handle. Nor did it slide away from his approach. He felt along it, its smooth surface revealing nothing to grab hold of for a release. The chill was so intense, it stole the warmth from his hand and instantly set it to aching. Pulling back, he yelped, "Yow!" He rubbed at his hands as his teeth chattered. "Was it supposed to get below zero here?"

She put one hand on her wide hip. "How am I supposed to know that? We weren't even supposed to be here!"

"Right." He rolled his eyes. "Try your phone then."

Demurer, she replied, "I don't have mine. It's still in the other room. How about you?"

"I should ..." he trailed off as his hand found nothing in his pants pocket. He was sure he'd still had it there when he drifted to sleep earlier. "No," he admitted at length. "Mine's not on me."

Swallowing back his discomfort and bracing himself for a scathing tirade from Naomi, he glanced her way. All he saw was her shivering as she gnawed at her lower lip. She always did the latter when she was scared.

"Let me try the door again," he offered. There was a different area on it now that he had touched it once. A section that was slightly darker near the door's middle. This time, as his hand passed over this spot, it lit up with the same blue light as shone in the room. The metal plate whisked aside faster than a blink. In the door's absence, a gust of the most frigid air he'd ever encountered burst into the little chamber, instantly chilling him through his coat.

A ferocious howl accompanied the icy winds now whipping

into the room. A swirl of white flakes carried along with them made it difficult to see.

"Close it!" Naomi screamed. "Close it!"

"I'm trying!" James bellowed as his numbed hands frantically worked over the doorframe. There was still nothing. No buttons, levers, releases, handles ... nothing!

He slipped to the other side from where the wind whipped in and realized too late that there was no flooring outside—just a five-or-so-foot drop-off. James scrambled to grab the doorframe, but the frosted exterior surface just slid past his freezing fingers, and he fell backward.

As he landed with a crunch of impacted snow, he groaned and looked up. Naomi had run to the doorway. "James!" she cried out.

"I'm okay," he called. "But watch out it's—"

The door started to shut behind Naomi. She yelped, windmilling her arms for just an instant before she had to hop out of its path to avoid being crushed.

James made it to his feet and extended his arms, partially catching her. They both went down hard into the snow.

He would've laid there longer to let the aches subside, but the snow dug into every gap in his clothing, needling him like relentless frozen claws. Naomi, who was on top of him, rolled over and struggled to her feet, clutching her hands and moaning. He joined her a moment later.

"What were you thinking, trying to catch me," she muttered through teeth that were already chattering.

He partially removed his jacket and draped it around them both, huddling close for warmth. "Sorry, thought I'd catch you like I did when you fell on our actual honeymoon. Remember?"

After a moment, he added with some chagrin, "Guess I'm not quite that guy anymore, huh?"

Her brows knit. Naomi stared up at him for a moment and then commented under her flash frozen breath, "Yeah, I guess that's a little of you and a little of me, huh?"

James looked at her for a moment. What did she mean by

that? Was that some kind of concession? Where was that kind of understanding coming from?

Naomi's eyes widened as she averted from returning his gaze and looked beyond him. "J-J-James ..."

He turned around to take in what she already had. If he could have given a low whistle or uttered a curse or cried out in panic or done anything other than tremble there beside her as they struggled to keep warm, he would have. And it would not have nearly approached the depth or expanse of the horror that now gripped him.

Stretching beyond them was a nightmarish landscape of ice and snow. Overhead, stony gray clouds roiled with the faintest hint of obscured light beyond them. Everything was frozen over as far as he could see. Hadn't the Inn they'd checked into been atop a hill and surrounded by tree-lined mountains overlooking the highway? Here, there was no sign of any vegetation or roads— only jagged icy spires and mountains of snow, amidst which peeked out little angular structures.

Even from this distance, he knew those were buildings. Just like he, in some strange intuitive way, understood without reservation that this was the sort of cold that, even fully clothed, they could only survive in for a handful of minutes. Minutes that were already racing past.

chapter
four

"OF COURSE, we're trapped outside in a blizzard," Naomi griped as they trudged along. "Great plan, getting us locked out of that rat's nest of an Inn. Wait, I'm sorry. You couldn't have planned this. Planning implies some thinking actually happened."

James stopped and glared down at Naomi, his hands clenched into fists. It was his forethought to have a jacket and his thoughtfulness to share it. Now he had to fight the urge to shove her into the snow drift and leave her to fend for herself.

Sounds of Naomi's whimpering as she shivered and the way she clenched her teeth mollified most of his cruel intentions. Instead, he grumbled, "Do you know how much time we've wasted? It was your thinking that led us to try to come around the building and go in the front. And also, your idea to try to find the car in all this."

That suitably chastened her, but just for a moment. "I didn't hear you coming up with anything better. Or anything at all!"

She had him there. Loath as he was to recall it, but he hadn't voiced his objections. What was he supposed to say? "No, I don't think that will work, because I'm not sure where we are anymore?" It was nonsense. Those buildings he thought he spotted had to be masses of trees blurred into an illusion of other structures by the snowstorm and his fatigue.

Fatigue. Yeah, they definitely needed to rest soon. This trek was quickly wearing him down, and he knew Naomi wasn't any more a model of fitness than him.

Ignoring her fuming—she'd apparently been laying on thicker to him than he'd realized—he scanned their surroundings. Assuming he wasn't crazy and factoring in that it didn't matter if he was, they weren't going to make it another five minutes out in this frigid weather. There was a dark shape just ahead they could make for and possibly reach.

"Argh! You're not even listening to me, are you?" Naomi accused. "You never do. You're like a huge rock all the time. Never hearing or saying anything."

James felt a tightness in his arm and the thrum of his pulse in his neck. She always did this to him. Made him feel like the whole world was collapsing down on him. Of course, he didn't respond. Did she want to hear that he thought she was a hypocrite? Accusing him of being checked out while she spent hours on her phone and took as much overtime for her law firm as she could?

Which only doubled his guilt, considering the state of his career. Or rather, his *lack* of career. No. She didn't want to hear that, because it led to shouting fights instead of just anxiety-laden snipe fests like this. The standard plan was to take it, because getting past it, getting back to that place where he wasn't walking over broken glass with every thought or action, was crucial. Delaying it was like refusing to break the water's surface well after running out of air. The silence she hated was a survival mechanism for him.

"You owe me something. Anything after going rogue and bringing us here," she insisted.

Stiffening, James took several slow breaths, the cloud of vapor curling around him like a dragon's smoke before it would blast its fire to incinerate its foes. "How about you listen for a change, Naomi? I've kept my peace for years because I was trying to be loving. To not say the first hurtful things that came to mind. I thought I was being a good husband. Building us up instead of tearing us down.

"And I'm so oblivious. You weren't in a relationship with me. This was a war for you, and you've been besieging me for way too long. I'm happy to march my armies out to have a real battle, if you want one."

Naomi's brows furrowed. "Don't be so dramatic. I'm not some kind of monster for wanting you to use your degree and get a job. Or take my side. Or be at all present in what I thought was *the* relationship of my life."

James regarded her warily. Waiting for the sting of barbs and arrows to strike him. None came, and her tone sounded dangerously ... sincere? Full of candor?

"That's what I thought, too, I guess—"

"You guess what?" Naomi prompted, then followed his gaze and gasped. A dark amorphous shape materialized out of the blizzard. Was it heading toward them?

"Let's keep walking. We can talk more once we're back inside."

She rolled her eyes but motioned him to lead on.

And he did lead on and on and on until he couldn't feel his hands or his feet anymore. And still farther on to when the strident ache and sharp stabs of cold were over. For a brief moment, he was relieved, but something in the back of his mind told him this was a bad sign.

It was made no better by the fact they had been walking for what seemed like an hour without encountering anyone or anything except more snow and ice and a horizon dark, foreboding, and utterly unfamiliar.

Turning back to check on Naomi, he saw that her walk had become listless and wandering. She wasn't coping with the cold at all.

She's getting drowsy.

His own thoughts were foggy, which he again understood to

be a bad sign. Going to sleep right now, no matter how heavy they felt, no matter how good it would be to rest, would be disastrous.

We'll die if we stop.

Which is exactly what Naomi did. She reeled off their agreed path and dropped to the ground, her knees together and her hands in the snow like she was a schoolgirl playing with the flowers in a meadow.

"Naomi, n-no," James insisted. His voice sounded distant to him. Small and pitiful in the swirling flakes and perpetual twilight. He dropped down beside her and shook her arms. There wasn't a response, which sent a jolt of fear through him that helped to unthaw his thoughts a bit. He rubbed her arms vigorously. "Come on, Nomi, come on. Don't go to sleep. We have to keep moving."

"Tired," she replied breathily. "Going to rest."

"No, no. We can't," he insisted. "We'll freeze to death if we stop."

"Mm-hmm."

She had that quality to her voice when she was super drowsy and already nodding off. At some point in their life together, he had found it cute and endearing. Right now, it was terrifying.

He tugged on her, but she was too heavy for him to haul to her feet, particularly because she was dead weight right now. If they were both as fit as when they first met, then maybe, but they were both dozens of pounds and years of sedentary life from then. Just like they seemed to be miles from help. Miles from hope.

Futile tugging lasted a minute longer before he dropped to his knees. This was it. He couldn't move her on his own, and he wouldn't risk leaving her to be buried in this white vortex even to try to find help. They were going to die of exposure, here, tonight.

What a terrible way to celebrate Christmas. Almost as silly as them getting a divorce. He loved Nomi. Why would they do that?

James looked up into the continuous drift of flakes. The hardened sky above, baleful, unnoticing of their plight.

Please, Lord. You see us here, dying. Help?

No sound of trumpeting agreement or splitting of the sky. No sudden burst of warming rays and enrapture in a balmy breeze. As his gaze drifted down, he saw a dark blur on the horizon from the direction they had come. Hadn't he noticed it and dismissed it before?

James rubbed his wife's arms for a minute or so longer. Then stopped. His arms were too heavy now. As much as he wanted to keep trying, which was honestly a hard thing to muster through his dazed, drifting thoughts, as inscrutable as the sky and as flighty as the snowflakes. No point in it. Sometime, someone would find the two great lumps of their bodies and bring them back. Maybe not until spring.

He closed his eyes.

Yeah. Spring.

A sudden sharp pain radiated from his back and with it a rush of heat that carried so many aches it choked out the cry building in James's throat. His heart raced, and he was on his feet in an instant. He whirled around to find someone standing there in the hazy swirl of snow. Silent, unmoving, as if evaluating a project. The person held a device from which a small cartridge dropped.

"Whoo, are you?" James asked, suddenly much more aware of the cold that he shivered.

Wait—why was he shivering?

The cold. The snow. He recalled them now. As well as accepting they were going to die of exposure. He remembered his last prayer for help.

"Help," he repeated to himself. And then, as if suddenly coming to a brilliant conclusion, he spun to Naomi and shook her still body, and he yelped to the stranger, "Help!"

The dark, heavily coated figure dropped to one knee, assessed Naomi's quickly purpling face, and adjusted something on his device. An instant later, he pushed James out of the way and pressed the device to Naomi's back. There was a sharp click, and he backed away.

Suddenly, Naomi burst up from her seated position, almost tumbling over. Her voice squeaked as she squalled about the cold.

James burst out laughing and sobbing and grabbed her in a hug. She pushed him away and stared at him, her eyes still somewhat unfocused. It took a moment, but once they resolved back to the moment, she smiled and hugged him back. "We're not dead!"

"Still here!" he agreed.

"For now," a gruff voice replied, though there was a lilt to it. As of surprise. "The adrenal burst won't last much longer. Follow me."

Without any further word, the dark figure trudged off.

chapter
five

THEIR MYSTERIOUS RESCUER halted in front of a shapeless mass of white snow that James knew they had passed by long before. Or perhaps only minutes ago. The fuzziness of thought induced by nearly freezing to death made even the seconds before being on the move again like pursuing a wraith in a London fog.

Even so, James didn't hold it against himself for missing this haven. It was only visible after the snow slid aside with a metallic whir. From within emanated the same unnatural blue light he and Naomi had encountered earlier. The sense that something beyond his grasp was transpiring fell heavily on him. He knew it had landed on Naomi as well because they'd held tight to each other all the way to this place, and he felt the tremor run through her as they entered after their unnamed rescuer.

Behind them, the door slid shut and clicked. An unsettling sound, given they had no idea where they were or who they were with, though it would be difficult to miss the biting cold. Now that warmth was washing over their bodies and fighting to dispel the cold that had sunk its claws deep into their flesh, James didn't know if he could ever bring himself to go back out.

Blue lines that emitted a matching spectrum of light ran the length of the walls, which were otherwise a dull metallic box, with a few pieces of oddly futuristic-looking furniture that emphasized rounded shapes and bright seats.

Without addressing them, their host stalked off toward a door out of the room. James called out. "W-wait. Th-thank you for … helping us."

If the other person so much as blinked, James couldn't tell. He was wearing what looked like polarized lens goggles and a cowl that covered his mouth.

"I'm James, and she's Naomi."

The stranger cocked his head without a word. He looked again, as if evaluating them. Maybe he thought they were out of their heads.

At length he answered. "Svikull."

Meandering over to a wall, Svikull waved his hand in front of it, and a blue light outlined the shape of a drawer before it slid out. From it, Svikull pulled a pair of large red blankets.

Carrying them over, he abruptly stopped several feet back from James and Naomi. Tossing them to the couple, he instructed, "Stay in here. I will return shortly."

As Svikull exited through another automated sliding door at the room's back, a shudder ran through James's frame. He clung ferociously to the red blanket draped over him. It felt much like wool but had an odd aromatic scent to it, unlike anything he could recall.

"Do you wanna talk about what was going on with you when we arrived at the Inn?" Naomi asked pointedly. Her teeth were chattering as she clung to her own blanket.

"You want to talk about that … here?" He gestured to the sparsely decorated and still quite frigid room they sat in.

Naomi shrugged. "Why not? I'd rather not go down the rabbit hole of trying to figure out where we are right now."

That he could understand. "Yeah. I thought we were in a dream at first. If only, right?"

Naomi nodded enthusiastically. "Same! I mean, I thought that until I saw that you were still here."

"Ouch."

Naomi's eyes widened with surprise. "Oh, no, I didn't mean it like—"

"It's okay. It's what we do to each other."

That time, he definitely saw Naomi wince. He hadn't been meaning to land a punch on her. He had been so matter-of-fact in saying it. Thinking back now, a sizable share of the verbal spiky traps being placed in front of them were laid by him. "Hey, at least this will make for a great story at the family Christmas party in a few days," he offered.

Naomi's countenance fell further. "James, there isn't going to be a party. We're getting a divorce."

Oh, right. Of course.

Silence, heavy and thick as the frozen buildup outside—and just as chilly—fell on them. It lasted every pain-filled second until Svikull came through the door.

Their rescuer glanced at each of them in turn, seeming to perceive the tension that had set in since he left. If he had thoughts about it, he did not share them. Instead, he rubbed his hands together for warmth, stomped across the room, and dropped into a seat opposite James and Naomi, staring at them.

After several seconds without saying a word, Naomi shot James a look that said, "Well, ask him something."

James hadn't the faintest clue what to say. Did she really believe they had somehow accidentally locked themselves out of their Inn room?

When he failed to step up as she desired, she gave her patented sigh of frustration and asked, "Did you find a way back into the Inn?"

Svikull tilted his head and regarded her, almost as if he wondered if she was insane.

"Look, we appreciate you getting us out of the snow and warmed up, but you need to take us back to our Inn. Right now."

"I cannot do that," Svikull responded in his heavy, accented voice, so bereft of emotional warmth he might have been carved from ice himself.

Naomi shot James a worried look. He had been grateful for the rescue, but he'd seen enough horror films to know things aren't always what they seemed, and it was moments like this when things usually took a dark turn.

"Why not?" James prompted, keeping his tone firm but still within the congenial zone. Hopefully not setting off their potentially unhinged host.

"Because I don't have the proper equipment here," he replied, still devoid of inflection to his words.

"Oh." the tension drained from Naomi's shoulders. "Can you take us back in the morning? We can't be too far from it."

"You are incredibly far from it by my estimation. And though you will no doubt dispute it, the hour is only slightly past noon. Which is to your good fortune. If it were night, you would both have died long before I reached you."

Concern knitted Naomi's brow again. "What are you talking about? It's so dark out there. It has to be before four in the morning still."

"On your world, perhaps."

James felt a familiar jolt of terror trace down his spine. The very kind that indicated a dream's descent into a nightmare. Except he knew he wasn't dreaming. And it was the peak of insanity, but in that moment, he could only think with great regret that Naomi hated horror stories.

A little tremor ran down the length of her blanket as if confirming his worry. "Listen, Mr. Svikull," she began, her voice taking on the higher pitch it always had when she was stressed. "I don't know what kind of game you're playing here, but—"

Svikull stood abruptly. "Perhaps I should do the talking for now."

The tone he delivered it in was deadpan and resolute. James watched Naomi lean back as if physically restrained by the esoteric man's words.

If this induced any sensation of pleasure or perplexed him at all, Svikull persisted in revealing no emotions. He merely stalked over to a largely blank wall and waved his hand at it. Immediately, it shimmered, and a moving picture appeared. Unlike a TV, the image wasn't on a screen—it was in the air a few inches above the surface he'd waved at.

James couldn't see where the image was projected from. He leaned forward, his heart rate picking up. Svikull was moving his gloved hands quickly in the air, and the video changed to a menu of options onto which he motioned, selecting a quick series of characters without needing a keyboard. The video changed again, this time to a view of space. None of it stood out to James as recognizable. Space was something he knew well, but identifying things at a glance like this was tricky.

Their host gestured to a cluster of stars. The video zoomed in and held position briefly. James almost commented on how realistically it depicted the solar system, except it only had five planets orbiting the sun. One planet was close enough and of the right size to be the Earth, but on here, it looked like it was carved from smooth marble. A bleak swirl of gray and white. "This is Vonlaus," Svikull stated. He swiped again, and the image zoomed into the planet, which looked still worse up close, a miserable icy landscape dominated by unforgiving clouds. As the display continued to close on a location, Svikull crossed his arms over his chest and looked squarely at James and Naomi.

A sickening sensation hit James as he noticed a building by a snowbank that looked eerily familiar. He felt Naomi reach for and grab his hand. Her brown eyes were fixed on the still-adjusting position being displayed. He gave her hand a gentle squeeze as it stopped abruptly over a building and circled it in red.

"You are right here," Svikull informed them.

James blinked as he stared at the glowing display. This couldn't be real. One hundred percent, unequivocally, this must be a dream. It simply wasn't possible.

As if to offer a counterpoint, his hands began throbbing as they finally warmed enough for sensation to fully return.

Okay, so this definitely feels real. But it can't be! People don't just—

"I don't know what kind of sick prank you're pulling, James." Naomi jerked her hand from his. "People don't just drop off the Earth and onto other planets by going through a door at an inn. This cruel ... whatever it is ... it's done."

James was on his feet in an instant, heat flooding his cheeks with shame and anger. "You think *I* did this?" He looked around them and gestured. "You've got to be kidding me!"

"You know how much I love science fiction stories. I know you haven't forgotten our first date. This is your parting shot, isn't it?"

Yeah, he did know she loved sci-fi. And he most certainly remembered that first awkward outing where they'd been pushed together by friends hoping to aid fate. It had gone miserably until they were walking down the street away from the restaurant they'd been to. What was it? ... Antonio's! Just before they were going to go their separate ways, she raised her hand and splayed her fingers. "Live long and prosper."

He had gaped at her in surprise. Nomi had snickered and then burst out laughing. "So, you like *Star Trek* too?"

"Uh-huh." He pointed to himself as if communicating to her across languages. "Trekkie."

She had nodded appreciatively. "Well, then, I guess we have something to talk about at last."

That was an understatement. They both gushed about their favorite sci-fi stories for the next hour. Eventually, James suggested they head to a nearby movie theater to catch a late showing of *Passengers*. After that, everything was a montage of growing together in every way to the tune of a romantic ballad. Until it wasn't.

So, yeah. He remembered her love of sci-fi. And he resented her for tarnishing that first treasured memory of their love. "I would tell you to go somewhere hot, Nomi, but I guess us freezing in this icy opposite suits just as well."

Naomi gasped. Never, ever in their relationship had either of them openly wished evil on the other. They had both grown up in church, been married in a church, and stopped attending church together soon after being married. The last bit aside, he knew they both believed in Christ. In Heaven. In Hell. It made what he'd said about as cruel and final a dismissal as he could leverage.

"You don't mean that," she murmured, her arms wrapping tighter around herself. She'd never looked so vulnerable before. Like a single, further harsh word would shatter her.

He started to deliver that last hammering blow to break her. To destroy her like she had just destroyed him when she tore down the last pillar supporting the crumbling mess that was them. "You ..."

He couldn't do it. As much as he hungered for it—for the bittersweet savor of revenge and scoring the final hit rather than waiting in fear to be its recipient—he couldn't do it. His faith, malnourished and neglected as it was, wouldn't allow it. And the look of hurt, of fear in her eyes—he couldn't let anyone or anything make that worse. Not even himself. Especially not with the fear of almost losing her still raw on the periphery of his memory. "No. I don't mean it," he said at last. Resigning himself to whatever counterattack would come.

None did. Naomi just seemed to settle down into a pensive silence.

"Ahem," their forgotten audience, Svikull, spoke up. "I do not know what places you speak of, but this *is* Vonlaus. I can tell neither of you is from here. I can also, unfortunately, discern you did not arrive here by choice."

James shot Naomi a look. She held his gaze for half a second, and he could tell she wanted to demand that answer from him and challenge his assertion that this wasn't a hoax. She let her gaze drop and resumed her brooding. He sighed and said, "No. We didn't. What is, er, where is Vonlaus exactly? We're supposed to be near, um ..."

"Bethel," Naomi supplied. "The town nearest was Bethel, Virginia."

"You clearly have ... things to work out. Not the least of which being accepting that you have passed from your world of Bethel-Virginia to Vonlaus."

Naomi stirred from her stupor and rolled her eyes. "I'm still not buying it. If you're really an alien, then how do we even understand what you're saying?"

Svikull chuffed and stood. He retrieved something from another hidden compartment that seemed to materialize from the wall. Gesturing toward them with the unopened cylinder, he explained, "You are the ones not on your own world. It is a mystery that our languages would be so similar. Though hardly so great a one as how you came to be here without intending it. It's beyond coincidence ..." His voice trailed off and he dropped to be half seated on the edge of a table. Without elaborating, he popped the top of the cylinder and removed his headwear and protective gear for the cold. He took a sip from the cylinder.

James felt every inch of his skin tingling with fresh dread. Svikull's shoulder-length hair was a shade of white, platinum blond perhaps, as was his long but thin facial hair. All of which could almost pass for normal. Except his face was pale, almost translucent, with an ever-so-faint blue tint. Dark red flushes extended up on each side of his face well beyond his cheeks. This wasn't albinism—James knew someone with that condition. It was as if every molecule of melanin in Svikull's body had withered to nothing. He was hideous and incredible to behold. Try as he might, James couldn't stop staring.

The fixation had not gone unnoticed. Head cocked to the side, Svikull's dark, purple eyes held fast to James for several seconds before he gloated, "Believe me now, hmm? Good, because you should take the next words I speak to heart. By coming here, you have both guaranteed your deaths."

chapter six

"IS THAT A THREAT?" Naomi was on the edge of her seat, her voice fiery as if ready for a fight. But James knew her, and the rest of her body said flight was her first plan.

"An inescapable reality," Svikull corrected, his posture completely relaxed as if being threatened by a fly instead of a large woman from another planet.

He held his hand up in deferral. "Again, not a personal threat from me. Vonlaus is a world gripped by a cataclysm so great that there is no chance of escaping death. It is only a matter of time before this world ends."

James watched the display of the snowy landscape, recalling the depth of the cold outside. Was he referring to that? Was the entire planet frozen rather than just this region?

As if he sensed James's thoughts, Svikull gestured calmly for Naomi to resettle in her seat. He waited until she did so, with reluctance, before further clarifying. "This world is dying. As you have noticed, almost no stellar rays make it through the atmospheric obfuscation, and the planet is slowly freezing to death in perpetual winter.

"It was not always so for Vonlaus. Some of us remember when the world was warm. Once upon a time, we Vonlas enjoyed the feel of grass and liquid water, the sensation of basking in summer radiance, the smell of a thousand varieties of flowers in bloom, and the taste of sweet berries and hardy grain. One could hear the sound of children's laughter as they ran through fields kicking about a ball ..."

It took several moments for Svikull to return to himself. James thought if he were human, the look on his face would be called "haunted." But it wasn't possible to know if expressions translated perfectly across species—and yeah, though he hadn't consciously decided until that moment, he believed Svikull. Believed they were on another planet, a dying one. It was something in the air, some instinct deep in his bones that told him they were so very far from the world on which he and Naomi belonged.

Naomi, too, seemed to be working through her feelings on the matter. No doubt in part because of the comment about kids. She wanted very badly at the start of their marriage to have a family, and he had talked her into waiting. Always deferring it to next year or after such and such event. At some point, she quit bringing it up, and he let it lie fallow.

Perhaps he was being too inward-focused. When he glanced at her, she seemed deep in thought, and she hadn't pestered Svikull for more details. They were two species from different worlds meeting for the first time. What were the chances they were all hung up on talking about children laughing?

"How did your world become this way?" James asked, surprising himself as the first to break the silence.

"No one is fully certain. It was preceded by climatic instability and tectonic activity, but what cinched our fate was a failed attempt to mass evacuate the planet once it became clear Vonlas across the planet faced extinction. An engineer's misguided attempt to create a more favorable launch window led to a disastrous chain of events that compounded our woes."

Svikull drew in a raspy breath, his gaunt face twitching for an instant from stoic to pain-filled and back again. "And now the government that backed that fool's ambitions has us all in a stranglehold. Forcing us to watch as our people shrivel and die from lack of proper nutrition and vitamins provided by our primary star's rays. We are withering day by day, as you can see. Yet they will not let us try the one thing that could rescue us from our torturous demise!"

His tone had heated. The hottest in temper and fervor since James had met him.

"That's awful," James said, not sure what else he could say.

Naomi found a more purposeful comment first. "That is tragic for you and your people. You say there's something that could deliver your world from this?"

"No, nothing will deliver Vonlaus. It is lost," Svikull countered, almost snarling. "But the Vonla race ... something can be done to relieve their suffering. Our suffering."

The aggressive edge to Svikull's tone set off a dozen internal alarms for James. Though what would he expect someone to sound like when trapped on a dying planet? James had only shared in that fate for hours, and it had already brought him to the brink of death and exposed every raw nerve between him and Naomi.

"You want us to ask you what can be done," Naomi observed, her own voice betraying her hesitancy. She eyed James, whether for support or in continued suspicion of some sort of collusion, he couldn't tell.

Svikull's thin face drew still tighter around the eyes. "You have keen insights. My wife had that trait. My daughter did as well."

Had. Meaning, Svikull had lost them. Suddenly, that bitter edge made more sense.

"Do you believe in fate, Naomi of Bethel-Virginia?"

The intensity with which he asked it seemed to take Naomi aback. Her eyes flicked to James, and her cheeks reddened. "I used to," she said, and her gaze fell to the floor.

Before the sting could fully register for James, Svikull had picked up the tattered thread. "Understandable. Perhaps it is only a phenomenal coincidence, but you have both dropped out of another world at the moment I—and my people—most need it.

"I was an engineer by trade, specializing in aeronautics, and I believe I have created a device that could deliver all of us from the miserable end ahead for us."

James's interest was piqued now. "Really? I'm a nuclear physicist—"

"You never held a single job in that field," Naomi pointed out sharply and then bit down on her lip as if she had just missed catching the words before they escaped her mouth.

For his part, Svikull looked only mildly annoyed, as though he was lecturing and had caught two students passing a note. "Wonderful. Then you will be even more help in my endeavor. Though for now, my chief concern is that I need additional power to test my design. We utilize geothermal energy for our power, vast amounts harvested from the still-hot core of our world, but the government is rationing selfishly. It's controlled from within a government facility, and I cannot redirect the power on my own ..."

It took a few seconds for James to register what was being proposed. "Wait, you want us ... *us* ... to help you break into someplace and steal the power?"

"Liberate it," Svikull clarified, a slight tilt to his lip that was a somewhat distant cousin of a smile.

"But we're complete strangers and not even from this world," Naomi protested. "This doesn't make any sense."

"Doesn't it? You dropped out of your world of plenty and peace into my world of harsher realities. Our people are crushed by leaders who willingly ignore the heart-rending suffering which I—which *we*—are forced to endure.

"Our hopeless march toward extinction has one solution, and when I began this day, I had no allies. Will you not at least consider helping me save what few Vonlas remain from the cruelest fate imaginable?"

Wow. When he puts it like that ...

"I ... I don't know. How could we possibly help you? I mean, look at us. We almost died out there and ... well, do other Vonlas look like you? Because there are some noticeable differences between us if they do."

Naomi gestured to her pronounced silhouette and James's, and then to her soft olive-skinned face, which made Svikull's complexion look like clear Saran Wrap stretched tight. Pale as James was, even he looked well-sunned compared to Svikull.

"Ah, but that only makes this all the more perfect," Svikull crowed. "Me, they may anticipate, but other minds, other bodies, from other worlds—that, they could never guard against."

Naomi shot James a wide-eyed look that told him, *Do something*.

This was usually when James folded. Deferred or disengaged himself altogether. The urge to just stare at the ground and hope he woke up from all of this was so strong. But there was a pull, faint and insistent, that told him it couldn't be that way this time.

"Listen, Svikull," he began, searching for the most ingratiating mode he could find. "We're grateful for you rescuing us, taking us in." He gestured to Naomi and saw in her enthusiastic nod and relieved eyes that he was following the line she wanted him to take.

"But we're not spies or revolutionaries on our world, and this is —"

"An impossible situation you've been thrust into, and I'm asking you to jump immediately into yet another?" Svikull sounded almost wistful, as though he had already seen this movie and hoped it ended a different way, all the same. "Indeed. It isn't fair. My time, and yours, is running out. I'll leave you to think and discuss the matter, but I must act with or without you. I lost everything I love to the wretched fiends holding the one hope of freedom for my world. On my own, I'm certain to fail, but my world has one hope, and until you each arrived in it, that hope was too thin to dare lean on. Now ... now it is real. This is impossible and madness, yes, but hope is sometimes the maddest reality we can and must embrace to survive."

James gaped. What in the world was he supposed to say to all that? He looked over at Naomi, and her brows knit. She wanted something of him again. They were so far out of sync, he had no clue what. There had been a time when they could've said exactly what the other was thinking, but they were as far from then as they were from Earth.

James sighed. "Can you give us a few minutes to digest this?"

The phrasing seemed foreign to Svikull, but he was only thrown for a moment. "Of course. I need to make my preparations anyway. I leave this evening for my mission and for the doom or deliverance of my people."

With that, he nodded to them each and left the room through one of the sliding doors. James wasn't able to catch much of what lay beyond the door, besides a bare hallway leading to a couple of other doors.

The instant the metallic door hissed shut, Naomi groaned. "James, what are you thinking? 'Give us a few minutes to digest this.'" Her tone as she repeated his words was in a mocking imitation of his voice. "What is there to digest?"

Wheeling to defend, James shook his head. "I don't know, maybe I'm crazy for wanting us to survive this impending apocalypse, not to mention all the Vonlas."

"Vonlas? What even is that?"

"I think it's Svikull's people—"

"I know that. I'm not dumb."

"I didn't say you were!"

"Yeah, well you might be, if you buy into all this. Even if I believed we were on another world, which I don't, by the way, but even if I did, this Svikull is clearly hiding something."

"Oh, like you can just read a complete stranger from another planet."

She put her hands on her hips. That usually meant James was about to get hit hard. "Yeah, he's a stranger who's got you gobbling his every word. And I've gotten pretty good at figuring out when people have secrets from trying to read you."

"Me?" James pointed to himself, as if she could mean anyone else. "What secrets?"

"I know you've been talking to your family again," Naomi said, her voice hot with accusation. "Regularly."

That stopped him. Every fiber of him tensed, and any semblance of peace evaporated under the scorching heat of dread. "Oh. I didn't realize you knew."

It was all he could think to say, and he was pretty sure he would've been better off if he jumped outside and let the frigid temperatures claim him.

"Yeah, I figured," Naomi replied, her voice taking on her sarcastic tone that scoured him so often.

James braced himself for the litany of wrongs to begin, but she just drew in a breath and shut her eyes. When she opened them, her brown eyes seemed to be calmer, if resolved. "I'm not mentioning it to start a fight. It's why I agreed to come on this stupid trip in the first place. Why I thought we had a chance."

Naomi paused, and a flicker of concern passed over her face. He guessed it was because he may have looked like he was a victim of electrocution. "What?"

She tucked some of the dark curls of her hair behind an ear. "Well, I overheard you on the phone with your dad a few months back. He talked you into getting me Little Shell, even though you hate them."

"The turtle? I don't—" he started to protest. A pointed look from her stopped him. "You're right," he admitted with a sigh. "Why did that make a difference?"

"Because it was the first time, in a long time, that I could tell how you feel about me. If you were willing to get me something you hated, probably guessing I'd show him more affection than you ..." she said this wincing, no doubt because he had unintentionally cocked his head to the side as if to say, *Ain't that the truth?*

She persevered. "Then I could tell you did still love, or at least cared about, me. Genuinely."

Naomi reached out a hand, so slowly, so cautiously, it was like she was afraid the slightest rude movement might shatter it.

He reached out with equal care and took the precious offering in his own. "That's all it took?" he asked softly, sincerely.

She nodded, her eyes on their interlaced fingers, hers still sporting her wedding ring. "Svikull is right about one thing. Sometimes it only takes something small to keep hope alive. And a little hope to survive."

"Yeah," he replied, his voice breaking before he could steady it. "I think you're right."

A part of James stirred, and he let Naomi's hand drop. "Okay, so you're right. I have been talking to them. I guess I never gave up on spanning the gulf between the most important people in my life ..."

Naomi's expression had softened significantly, though his sudden retreat hardened her by several degrees. Her ire and intimacy had morphed into something more akin to exasperation. "You're a sucker for lost causes, James. And you're trying to drag us both into a new one."

Until a moment ago, he hadn't wondered about whether she thought his attempt to save their marriage was a lost cause. Where she stood on that previously was painfully clear. Was it still?

James felt that inward stirring and had to push on. "Listen, I ... I know this is crazy, but I almost lost you out there. Like, really lost you. I watched the life draining from your eyes, Naomi. And I get that it's crazy, but if there's any chance I can keep that from happening again, any shot at all to get us out of this mess, I'm taking it. I still believe that things happen for a reason, and this— you have to admit that either this is a fever dream or we've been placed here 'for such a time as this.'"

She sighed. "You're using the *Book of Esther* against me?"

"It's still your favorite, right?"

"Favorite Bible book, yes," she confirmed grudgingly. "Of all the things for you to remember." She rubbed the bridge of her nose as if staving off a headache. "Ugh, fine. Fine. We—I can't believe I'm saying this—we help. Svikull."

James hadn't realized before that moment that he'd been arguing in favor of Svikull's plan precisely. At least not consciously. There had been something more abstract, more expansive, he felt, because hearing her acquiesce to aiding Svikull, he almost backpedaled. But Naomi hadn't consented lightly, and if he didn't take it now, whatever else he had been aiming at would be lost with it. So, he was going all in with Svikull.

"All right," he replied quietly. "Then it's decided. We're in this together?"

Instinctively, he reached out his hand to her. Immediate regret gripped him, because he knew that after he minutes ago squelched their most intimate moment in months, he could expect the viper of rejection was about to venomously latch onto his hand.

Naomi was slow about it, but she took his hand.

"I guess so," she answered.

chapter
seven

ALTHOUGH HE HAD PLANNED to launch his raid that night, Svikull listened to reason and delayed long enough to properly work James and Naomi into the scheme. In the four days since agreeing to participate, James had become steadily more uncertain about Svikull's earnestness. Something was off, and though each day made James more and more confident that he and Naomi had truly been transported to another world, it was the inverse for Svikull's credibility. He was furtive and dour, which of themselves weren't necessarily signs of deception, but every time James tried to strike up a conversation about the nature and details of his interstellar transport meant to whisk them all safely away, Svikull cut him off. Belittled his understanding. Dismissed his concerns.

Naomi, on the other hand, was quite taken now with his stories about Svikull's wife and daughter. The tragedy of it all and the nobility of Svikull's suffering and determination against all odds struck a chord deep within her. One that James hadn't heard in her voice and mannerisms for a long time. The way she intuitively found and responded to the empathetic needs of others was a part of her he had always respected and treasured. At this point, she was fully beguiled by Svikull's wistful recollections of his daughter running through meadows long gone and wishing on stars now invisible, and even her complaints about the damp, heavy summer air.

Lugging the sleek silvery bag of tools Svikull needed, James dropped to one knee and peered around the building's corner. Like all of Vonlaus's structures James had seen, the research facility with the component they needed was a gray island amidst the white sea of frozen flakes. Though this building didn't have the faint blue glow around its doors or trim, indicating it had power and was emitting the now-familiar artificial light necessary to sustain life. A nagging concern that something was off rankled James.

There was no point dwelling on it. Naomi was on board for a change, and if he doubled back now, he'd only complicate their predicament because there was no way she would forgive him after he fought for them to work with Svikull in the first place.

Extracting his short-range comm, he did as Svikull instructed and removed it from the weatherproof casing, dialed out to Svikull, and then slipped it inside his hood to rest against his cheek. The device was incredibly thin, but his borrowed outfit was so snug in fit that the comm created an awkward bulge that, within seconds, allowed the cold to bite his face with frigid ferocity. "I'm in place."

"Confirmed. I'm moving in now. Naomi is in the agreed spot for extraction."

"Understood." James had to fight a sigh. Having his wife act as a getaway driver wasn't something he'd ever expected to experience. It was by far the safest job of the heist. Even so, it felt like his heart was being held hostage in the vehicle with her. Something he definitely couldn't tell Naomi. She didn't want his love, even if he was starting to realize he had never truly stopped loving her. Probably never would.

"Focus, James," Svikull chided from James's left. He had snuck up to join James as planned. His device for accessing the facility was in hand and already being applied.

As the device hummed and projected some graphics and an

interface, he thought it looked like he was correct—the building had only what appeared to be enough power being supplied to keep it from totally icing over. "Are you sure we're in the right place?" James asked. "I thought you said this was a heavily protected government facility?"

Svikull didn't bother looking up as he continued to work at changing some settings on his device. "I did. Protection looks different on Vonlaus. You can't have guards out in this cold all the time. But it can be under heavy surveillance and ..."

The door powered up and slid open. "Now we have five minutes to get in and out before we're captured, tortured, and executed."

He slapped James on the arm, hard enough to be felt through the thick padding. "Shall we?" His tone almost singsong, at least as close as Svikull's perpetual stoicism allowed.

As soon as they entered the structure, a warning tingle crept up the nape of James's neck. Within the building was a wide and open room, which they entered on a gantry that would lower down to the heart of the space. There, all the machinery and structures analogous to a power substation, if with the streamlined Vonla style, were located, along with the holographic displays they utilized.

"Are you sure we're in the right place?" James asked again as they descended to the ground floor via an open lift. "This doesn't look like the government warehouse you described."

The lift groaned to a halt on the desired level, which made James think there might still be more below this floor. Svikull stepped off and headed toward a display with a terminal and commented over his shoulder, "I never said it was a warehouse. You assumed that on your own. I said it was a government facility with a part I need.

"Now be useful and go access that terminal on the opposite side of the room."

Scowling, James started the trek over to where he was directed. He glanced over his shoulder once to check on Svikull and found him hurriedly interacting with the display. He knew what he was doing. Whatever that was, exactly.

James was five or so feet from the terminal, which was about sixty yards from where they entered, when he heard a keening sound echoing overhead. Soon it was joined by a like chorus. They weren't familiar tones, but they were close enough to Earth versions that, coupled with flashing red lights, James recognized them. "Alarms? What did you ..."

Svikull wasn't at his console. In fact, he was nowhere to be seen at all.

"Svikull?" James shouted over the growing din. "Where are you?"

If the Vonla answered, James couldn't hear it. He ran to where Svikull had been working and tried to access the console by touching the display. The display wavered and then an even louder alarm blared. On the display, symbols appeared that weren't familiar to James. What he could discern was that they were separated into three groups of two and then followed by a longer string of uninterrupted symbols, and those on the end were cycling through the same characters over and over. Meanwhile, the other duos would change just before the ending characters reset.

Icy fear, more painfully frigid than any winds outside, chilled James's heart and froze him in place.

It's a countdown!

To what? Was there ever a good reason for a countdown like this? Certainly not in the movies, and doubtful with secretive Svikull suddenly absent.

A whirring sound filtered into the alarms. James turned to find Svikull. He was on the lift rising up to the entry point.

"Hey!" Finding the ability to move fumblingly restored, James charged over to the lift. "Wait, where are you going?"

Svikull nodded. "Time to leave. Best hurry."

There was no catching the lift, and James held no illusions about performing an action hero leap and managing to hang onto the platform all the way up. In the silvery platform's absence, he could see that the building did indeed stretch deeper into the planet's surface. The levels he could make out from here were also bathed in flashing red lights.

Overhead, the lift clicked into its spot at the room's entry. James licked his chapped lips and watched like an expectant puppy. The lift didn't head back down. Svikull hadn't sent it back for him.

"Oh, come on!"

He looked back at the display with the countdown and grimaced. Who knew how long was left or what it meant. Whatever it indicated, it was enough to send Svikull slithering off at super speed.

James examined the lift control display, and his hand shook as he tried to sort out what any of it said. The Vonlas may have spoken a language that perfectly mirrored English, but their symbols for letters and numbers were completely different.

James yelped in frustration and tugged at his hair.

Come on, hold it together. They have the same words as us. So, this has to say something that you can understand. It's like solving a cryptogram.

James wasn't bad at them. In fact, he only took a few precious seconds to deduce which symbols to touch to bring the lift back down. The instant it was, he jumped on it and began the agonizingly slow ascent. He watched the display as he went up, recognizing that there was maybe a minute left before every digit on the countdown became the equivalent of zero.

The lift jarred him as it reached the end of its ascent, and he stumbled to the door. It was jammed open already, and frigid air swirled inside. Barreling through the entry passage and out into the perpetual Vonlaus midnight, he stumbled and slogged through the deep snow, his breathing ragged and his heart hammering so hard he was sure he was about to have a coronary event.

At his back, he felt a slight tug, and then there was a loud *boom*. He was flung forward and slammed onto the harder-packed and frozen snow, skidding for a few feet. Groaning, James lay there until his heart and breathing had slowed enough to feel them under control again.

He fought to sit up, wishing for better-toned abdominal muscles and hoping he wasn't concussed. His ears rang a little, but it was the faint warmth coming from the direction of the building that concerned him most.

Sure enough, a golden-orange blaze crackled up into the sky, casting an otherworldly glow on the contours of the icy landscape all around. Light caught on currently falling flakes, twinkling like the stars no one would ever see from the Vonlaus surface again. It was kind of beautiful.

And it was absolutely terrible.

What had Svikull done? What had he helped him do?

There was a muted crunching from behind him, and James whirled around to find a collection of thickly adorned but uniformly arranged and adorned figures surrounding him. They held spherical devices in their hands.

"Um, hello there. I'm—"

One of the figures stepped forward and tossed up the sphere. It landed a few inches from James. He stared at the distinctly silver surface with its blue light trim and saw his reflection in it. Including his grimace of terror as the bolts of electricity arced off its surface and shocked him until all went black.

chapter eight

VOICES FLOATED AROUND JAMES, invisible and of a timbre not within the human range. He couldn't understand them rightly. His hands were trembling. Was he ... dead? All was dark now, but he knew that he only needed to open his eyes and things would be much brighter. In fact, through his eyelids he knew it would really be too bright. Could he be in heaven?

He didn't dare entertain the other possibility. Sure, he wasn't ardently faithful, but he was faithful. A follower of Christ. At least he believed he was. Right? Suddenly, he felt very unprepared to open his eyes and see the Creator of the universe looking down on him, every secret and every failing naked before Him.

The longer he kept his eyes shut, the more he noticed strange smells that were vaguely evocative of familiar ones and began to register other sounds. A faint, repetitive hiss and whoosh. A steady, if at times unpredictable, thump. At some point, he would have to open his eyes and trust his Savior had carried him past his faults and failings. And he had failed. A lot. Especially when it came to Naomi.

Naomi.

Her face and name hit him hard. Was she okay? Did she make it out? He recalled she was supposed to just be waiting for them to return. Waiting until ... just before the explosion and ... whatever had happened that left him weightless and then nothing.

"Oh, Lord, please let her have gotten away safely."

The sound of his own voice startled him. Why had he said that aloud instead of in his thoughts? Had he been speaking all his thoughts aloud this whole time? That would make sense if he had passed on to be with the Lord. What use would there be in hiding anything from Him?

He let his eyes flutter open, and as expected, the light was overwhelming. But to his surprise, he adjusted pretty quickly, at least enough to know that he was just under a bright light, not in the presence of the Lord's light, which by all accounts was felt as much as seen. Other sensations crept in. Cold, dull aches from injuries and ... restraints. Something held his arms down at the wrists and his legs at the ankles.

He struggled against them, and instead of feeling the resistance of leather, he felt the sharp bite of an electric shock.

"Ow!" he squalled.

He turned his head, and the thudding noise from earlier intensified. He could see he was in a very white room with a large dark window looking in. James could make out his reflection in it. He was completely naked and lying flat on a table. As if he were in an exam room—only he knew this wasn't Earth, and he understood now he had been knocked out earlier by some kind of device after the explosion. Which meant he wasn't in Heaven. He was still on Vonlaus, which was more like the opposite of Heaven.

"Inspector, the sedatives have worn off, and he's awake." The voice came from beyond the bright light.

"Did he say anything under the suggestive serum's effects?" someone with a distinctly feminine, if somewhat cold, voice inquired.

"Minimal. Some reflections on the hereafter life that might be of interest to our clergy and philosophers. Though he did slip in a mention of hoping a 'she' was safe."

"And I can question him, now?" The female speaker pressed.

"Yes, but be careful, Inspector. The genetic exam confirmed he isn't Vonla."

"What do you mean?"

"Well, I, um, I suppose I'm telling you he's an alien species. Tread carefully. We don't know what he's capable of."

Retreating footsteps sounded from the metallic floor. The bright lights faded and redirected. In their absence was a face. The Vonla woman's hair was that same platinum blonde as Svikull's and if it hadn't been done up into a bun on the back of her head, it likely would be just as straight and fall well past her shoulders. Her face was sharp, and she had large purplish eyes and lips, which complemented the almost bruised-looking redness of her cheeks. They were near translucent, like Svikull's, if a shade cloudier and bluer.

On Earth, she would be tall for a woman and thin, wearing a dark, close-fitted gray and cerulean uniform with a luminescent badge. It was reminiscent of Earth's thermal adaptive workout wear. This must be the indoor uniform for after shedding the heavy coat. There was no sign of a weapon or other devices on her person, so she probably wasn't planning to torture him. Though her stern expression and the way her eyes bored into him were unnerving enough.

James swallowed hard in the ongoing silence. Her eyebrow ticked when he did, as if his discomfort alone told her something important. The embarrassment of being naked in front of a woman who wasn't his wife finally registered as his initial panic fell dormant in the absence of anything to agitate it. At least, until he noticed she was eyeing a display just outside his view that no doubt had his vital statistics, including heart rate, available.

"You're lost, aren't you?" The female inspector concluded at last.

"Well"—he cleared his throat before continuring—"I don't know where I am if that's what you mean."

"It isn't, and you know that." Her eyes were hard, dark amethyst, imprisoning him in their hold without hope of escape.

"How do you—"

"I'm Chief Inspector Tristwe. It will suffice for you to know that I've already gleaned nearly every bit of information I need from you."

"I'm—"

"In your species, middle-aged range and overweight, even for your height. You're self-conscious about your body, but not aloof or self-absorbed. You assessed and questioned your environment quickly, including searching me for signs of weapons, so I would gather you are intelligent. Your combat performance was poor and lacked any of the hallmarks of formalized training. Ergo, you aren't a soldier. Your apprehension slipping into ease even as I, a member of a species and sex not your own, examined you suggests you understand your predicament but don't believe you've committed any moral transgressions, though you must understand there was a legal infraction because you attempted to flee the site of the attack.

"You were colluding with a known terrorist, but he did not give you even a rudimentary explanation of how our weapons for incapacitation function, nor did he hesitate to leave you behind. Therefore, you aren't a scout of an invasion nor even a full party to Svikull's crimes, thus you must be somehow lost and stranded here. Although your acquisition of our language, with its own unique accent, indicates that you have been here or in communication with Svikull for quite some time. Which brings me to the one thing about you which I haven't yet elucidated—why you are aiding Svikull."

"I was going to say my name is James," he offered with a winsome smile. It was short-lived. His deflection felt rather pathetic next to her exhaustive analysis, much of which was frighteningly insightful.

Inspector Tristwe rolled her eyes. "Clever. I know you want to get back to the female of your species. What is her relation to you?"

James swallowed uncomfortably. For a moment, he wondered

how to play this. He had never been in legal trouble before, so he wasn't sure what to say and what to keep to himself. After everything Svikull had told them about the government's seditious and Orwellian agenda, he had to tread carefully. Even if she didn't have a weapon on her, too little from him, and they'd likely kill him outright. Too much, and they might find Naomi.

Cooperate as much as possible and conceal only what is necessary for Naomi and Svikull's sakes. No stone walls, but no matter what, I can't give them up.

"It doesn't matter," he decided upon as his answer, giving his voice a cryptic edge.

She crossed her arms at the waist and leaned against a wall. "Really, because your pulse quickened when I mentioned her. I think she's important to you. Perhaps a relative?"

The inspector glanced up at where his heart reading must be. He tried to look but couldn't see. This wasn't good. How was he supposed to control his heart rate? They could do that in spy movies, to beat lie detectors, right?

"Hmm, a sister?" Cocking her head, Inspector Tristwe seemed dissatisfied. "Not a sibling. A daughter, maybe?"

"Do I look that old?" he countered, a nervous laugh edging his words.

That earned a grin from his interrogator. "Ah, she's your mate. What we would call, a wife."

James's heart sank. Not bothering to hide it, his face fell into complete dejection. He'd lasted what, thirty seconds with one of the most important bits of truth he could hold onto.

"Is she involved in Svikull's plans?"

The question jerked James off the morose coaster of his emotions and dropped him squarely into fear. "What plans?"

"Hmm, perhaps you don't know the plan. Is your wife the head of the family? Of this mission?"

A dozen responses passed through his head, some snarky, some vague. He tried to catch one he liked, like a bear snatching a salmon out of a stream. No luck. "What plans?"

"Did she bring both of you here? Hatch this treacherous plot with Svikull?"

He winced away from the accusation. "Naomi is a good person. She'd never ..."

Inspector Tristwe's eyebrows both raised. "So, *Naomi* wouldn't plan anything bad? Would she go along with it to protect you?"

Not again! He'd given away another detail.

"Would she? Do anything to protect you?"

That was such a loaded question. Did Naomi even care that he'd been taken? It might make things more convenient for her this way. For him to be dead or as good as dead, trapped on this giant snowball. She could start over, have a new life, new love. Man, did that ever hurt to think about. Which was strange given that not that long ago—

The investigator slammed her fist against the metallic paneling of the wall. The clang echoed through the room. "Focus, alien!"

His eyes fixed onto her deep purple ones. Rather than shudder as he expected, his jaw set. His brows furrowed. No. He would not give her an inch. Not one tidbit more that could hurt Naomi.

"The question of what life exists beyond our planet having been answered should be one of the greatest things the Vonlas all across our planet should ever face. But the attack you participated in tonight with Svikull could mean the end of our civilization, so your options are down to two—talk or die."

There it was, the ultimatum bolded, underlined, and in all caps. There was no way he was walking out of this in one piece. Not if he hoped to keep Naomi safe. In spite of all the harsh words and passive-aggressive nonsense that had passed between them, there wasn't a world near or far where he could bear her being hurt because of him. Funny that he had to travel to another planet to realize it. Funny or tragic. Too bad he'd squandered so much time he had with the woman who proved to be his star-crossed love. Naomi deserved more, better.

His throat was tight as he spoke, and he had to really fight to get the words out, but he finally managed to say, "I can't give you what you want."

Her arms crossed again. Inspector Tristwe scowled at him. "You really love her," she asserted, almost accusing him.

Huh. That charge he was actually guilty of. And oh, did it sting to realize that in this moment, he still loved Naomi. He *still* loved Naomi. He still *loved* Naomi. He still loved *Naomi*. No matter how he turned it, appraised it, parsed it, it all came back to a truth that rang so deep within that there was no turning from it. But embracing it was like grabbing a red-hot iron—there was no avoiding a serious burn.

After a full minute of delivering the most withering stare James had ever endured—including from angry Naomi—Inspector Tristwe's entire expression snapped to neutral. "Very well. Perhaps, I am handling this wrongly. You are the first of another species to visit Vonlaus, and, by appearances, you are peaceable, intelligent, and capable of love. A better course to understand one another may be to dialogue in a freer, friendlier setting.

"Would you be willing to take a walk with me?"

James eyed her as though she were offering to hand him a viper. "'Freer,' as in no restraints? What if I choose to take advantage of that freedom and leave our chat?"

She shrugged. "That is your right as a sapient being. In fact, I would encourage you to do so if you'll also be good enough to lead me straight to Svikull." She gave a little bounce of her shoulders to accompany a thin smile.

So, not so free. Just a new environment to analyze me and my reactions.

As much as it seemed like a spider inviting a fly for a visit in her web, James felt like he had to take it. Here, he had no chance of escape. Out there, elsewhere ... who knew? The odds were at least not zero, even if just barely.

"Well, in that case," he began, noting the faint lift of Tristwe's left eyebrow. "Do I at least get to wear some clothes for our stroll?"

For a moment, his response threw her, and he even saw her eyes flicker to take in his current state as if for the first time. She didn't blush, of course, but it was enough to know she wasn't fully a robot.

"Of course. I will return your clothes. We no longer make outfits of your size on Vonlaus ..."

The way she trailed off, it was ambiguous as to whether that was a dig and calling him overweight or a wistful commentary on how emaciated both she and Svikull appeared. Which seemed to be exactly how she wanted to keep him—uncertain and off-balance.

James put on his most winsome smile and said, "Thanks, Tristy. I'm in."

The inspector's eyes narrowed by a fraction, revealing as much of how nonplussed she was about his impromptu nickname for her as she seemed able. He imagined it had earned him a little chink of respect in her stoic armor. After all, he really was intelligent, and he would make sure they sparred in her little match until there was no possibility left that Inspector Tristwe could find Naomi and keep her from escaping this nightmare.

Undoing the restraints holding him in place by tapping a panel, Inspector Tristwe walked over to the room's exit. "This way, James."

chapter
nine

JAMES HELD his hand over the light in the corridor. He hadn't noticed before, but a strangely pleasant sensation accompanied doing so. Almost like basking in the sun's rays when winter gave way to spring. But it was more than that because the more he looked at the light, the more amazed at it he became. He didn't need to blink while staring directly into it. Didn't feel the anxiety that had been building in him for almost an hour since being given his clothes and allowed to follow Inspector Tristwe out of the Vonlaus police headquarters.

"Don't stare too long," the inspector instructed as she approached him. She was signing something onto a projected document before collapsing the portable holographic display and stopping beside him. "Those lights give us key vitamins that our primary star once provided. With most plant and animal life on Vonlaus extinct, it's the only way for us to survive. Though it also damages our ability to properly metabolize our food and degrades our melanin. She gestured to her extra-slim physique and near-translucent skin. "Also, stare too long and they burn your retinas without you realizing it."

James blinked and backed away, taking stock of the Vonla inspector. "Are you serious? What's keeping you alive is slowly killing you too?"

She shrugged. "Perhaps. Or perhaps I'm engaging in a bit of hazing.

"Welcome to Vonlaus," she added in almost sugar-sweet tone, at least as close as it came for any Vonlas he'd met.

"Cool, another great reason to trust you Vonlas," he mumbled under his breath, rolling his eyes.

"Careful with the profanity," she chided.

"What? What did I say?" He looked aghast.

"You're on a planet that is literally freezing to death. Which word would you guess?"

"Oh." His cheeks grew hot and reddened.

That ghost of a smile worked its way onto her lips again.

"You know, you're awfully convivial after threatening me and acting like I'm a terrorist," he observed.

The inspector nodded. "I have my reasons." She gestured for him to follow her. "Try to keep up and don't stare back at any Vonlas we encounter."

Five steps into the trek, they passed two other inspectors, and James immediately had difficulties with heeding her order. Both Vonlas had openly gaped at him. Their near skeletal faces with their platinum hair that should have been beards but looked more like ghastly piercings were hard to ignore. They were what his mind conjured when he heard the word goblins, and he only hoped they weren't as malevolent.

"Eyes forward," the inspector insisted.

She hadn't even looked back at him. Though need she have? Could she have access to a video feed of the hall or some other surveillance happening? Malevolent or not, the two Vonlas he'd met so far were both certainly manipulative.

"You're still digging information out of me. Aren't you? You're just using a carrot instead of stick."

Inspector Tristwe glanced over her shoulder and shrugged. "Am I?"

That was all she said until they came to a rather large stretch of completely bland wall. "Here we are," she announced.

"Okay." He looked around for any sign of significance to the spot.

"Hmm." The inspector tapped her palm to the wall. A cerulean line highlighted the rectangular shape of a door, which slid aside.

His guide and guard motioned him inside a large but rather bland room. Nothing visibly adorned its floors, walls, or ceilings. A single pair of Vonlas, a man and woman, were standing near the room's back. Both eyed him with slack jaws and wide purple-tinted eyes.

"Official police business," Tristwe informed them.

The pair took a few moments but gradually meandered to the exit, gawking at James every moment of the trip. Behind him, he heard the door whoosh shut and click.

Probably locked in.

"Welcome to the Vonlaus Archives and Museum," Tristwe announced.

"You're kidding." He could get the Vonlas being depressed, but this was a bit extreme, commemorating the void of frozen wasteland outside by making an empty room here.

When he didn't move any farther into the room, the inspector cleared her throat and pointed to a spot in the middle. That didn't exactly make him hurry, but he complied. Whether it atomized him or froze him into a decorative statue, it didn't matter. Perhaps if he complied just enough, it would allow him to slow them up in other ways.

The instant he reached the room's center, a circle of blue highlighted around him, and the walls all around lit with holographic projections of pulsating lights. A voice, clearer and more emotionally resonant than any Vonlas he'd heard so far, proclaimed, "Welcome ... newcomer, to the Vonlaus Archives. What resource would you like to access?"

"Special investigator override, 01202510," the inspector commented. "Global tour compilation."

The pulsating blue lights faded, and the chipper voice responded, "Override acknowledged. Accessing archival footage."

A moment later, a meadow of peculiar purple flowers rose up around James. Insects, or so he presumed, flitted about along with avians and small mammal-like animals. Unique in physiology, but not so much that an analog of a bunny and some robins wouldn't fit. A strong wind cut across the meadow, sending all the grass swaying in a dance not unlike ones he'd seen on Earth.

The wind seemed to carry him away and into the air, sailing over a vast evergreen forest with rich jade-decked timbers that soared into the sky as he and the wind raced up rocky mountain slopes, which eventually became snowcapped. James expected it would then usher them to their current icy wasteland. Instead, like a roller coaster, it whooshed them back down and across a vast desert covered in gloriously colored stone canyons with a river cutting through it. They cruised over the canyon and back into what eventually became a verdant jungle filled with exotic-looking flora and fauna, all zipping past until the tour reached an enormous ocean.

He visually skimmed the pristine blue waters with vibrant coral formations visible in the depths below until he skidded to a stop on an island. There, he was brought to the summit of a mountain overlooking an archipelago, dotted with cities connected by bridges and tunnels that radiated a luminosity not unlike what he saw any time something lit up in the ice bunkers he'd been in. Except the colors were all brighter. He wasn't actually there, but the warmth of the sunlight was obvious in the sheen on the water and the sounds of sea spray and gull-like birds calling. All of it together evoked such a sensation of sylvan splendor, he wondered if the Vonlas had somehow infiltrated his memories of Earth and were plying at him with them. Especially once it ghosted him through the streets of the city, which, though futuristic with more robotic elements and things that no earthly city held—flying cars, elevators that worked without gears, and motorized pathways—the diversity of people, their attire, and their vitality were so rich and varied.

"The western hemisphere of Vonlaus, with a tour of Grexyn City," the computerized tour guide announced. "As they appeared five years ago."

Hmm, that's about the time Naomi and I got married.

"You are here," the guide added as it pulled him past the sprawling city to another island. An unspoiled paradise. Night had fallen, and the vast array of stars and cosmic wonders were on display. Though just as foreign as when Svikull had shown them to him, James was even more awed at this view. It was breathtakingly beautiful, every bit as much as when Naomi and he had seen a similar display on Earth while hiking in Grand Teton National Park early in their marriage.

You are here ...

He tried to speak but covered his mouth, unable to coerce anything coherent to come. By compulsion, James reached out toward the display, as if to try to push Vonlaus away from the nightmarish ruin he saw now to the earlier vibrance. He yearned for that more halcyon era of the planet. The warmth of sun and gentle embrace of breezes winding through the trees. The sound of water rushing to the sands and retreating in their playful game —so reminiscent of Earth. It was a peculiar homesickness that had beset him, and he couldn't quite place it. Why and from where did this longing originate? How had these images of an alien world so thoroughly impacted him? They had leeched beneath his skin and into his bones within minutes.

Inspector Tristwe clucked her tongue. "You wonder how such splendor became a desolation? Don't you?" The inspector's tone reverberated with a dark humor. A bitter cynicism, born of an injury that one could not bear to face fully for the misery of how bad it has become. It was a pain James well understood, if not on the same scale.

She continued, "I'm sure there were signs along the way. Maybe if we had listened more, we could have turned things around. If only we had taken more care to pay attention along the way, we would have realized something was going terribly wrong. But it is difficult to hear with the drone of day-to-day living and all its demands. Society and its trajectory have a gravity of their own that is almost irresistible, dragging us forward, even into perils we did not see coming.

"By the time we understood where we were, it was too late. Our desperate attempt to correct our situation only served to exacerbate our suffering. Perhaps fatally ..."

It was said with such finality, James had the chilling sensation that Inspector Tristwe, and perhaps by extension the Vonlas collectively, had processed through the grief of the demise of their species to the point of acceptance. At least all of them except for Svikull.

Even as the thought entered his consciousness, it rang hollow. No, something more was off with Svikull. He struck James as someone on a very different path. Which only deepened his unease, because here he was standing a foot away from a representative of the government Svikull claimed was willfully condemning their people to death, and in spite of the acceptance, he recognized the silver-sweet scintillation of hope in Tristwe's words.

"Why have you shown me this?" James croaked, too shaken to care how tremulous he sounded.

The inspector crossed her arms over her chest. "That is a fair question." She glanced up at the ceiling.

"Is it not enough that we are two like species communicating with one another face-to-face after existing for millennia without any comprehension of the other's existence? To have you, our first visitor, understand my people's sorrow and character?"

From that vantage, it did seem reasonable. If not for the other earlier moments of rigid inquiry and inspection. "You're still trying to pry information from me about Svikull and what he's planning."

A slight tick in the inspector's cheek was confirmation

enough. Even so, it wasn't as if she was deceiving him. It was almost like a parent lovingly leading a child to confess to a misdeed of which they were already fully aware.

"I suppose my most burning questions do revolve around Svikull. Though I'm certainly interested in discovering why you came to our world in the first place. And how."

James scowled, unable to help it. He was the rope in a tug of war. Part of him stridently defied sharing his priceless morsels of information that could doom his wife. Another part of him felt an increasing dread that perhaps the greatest danger lay in leaving her with the enigmatic and treacherous Svikull.

All the events of the past days played over and over in his mind from different angles, interpreted and reinterpreted in his vain war of attrition to make a decision. Which, of all things, was something Naomi didn't like about him. His indecisiveness. How many times had she railed against his inability to choose dinner, choose a movie, choose a job, choose a home, choose when to try for a family, choose anything and everything?

All at once, he blurted out, "I don't know. It sounds unbelievable, but we just suddenly appeared here."

He gritted his teeth, wrestling with himself over what he wanted to say next. An incredible rush of triumph flooded his veins. Without intending, he had chosen a side. Chosen who to believe in this alien world, and there was zero percent chance he'd properly weighed the consequences. But it was too late for that now. "Which is why Svikull was able to recruit us so readily. He promised he could get us back to our home if we helped him."

It was several painfully quiet seconds before Tristwe spoke again. "What did Svikull tell you about our planet and race?"

James licked his lip, knowing still that if he shared even a word more, there was a good chance he was going to be giving Svikull over to the government he had decried, which by proxy meant giving over Naomi. "He, uh, told us, there was an experiment gone wrong."

She huffed out, a little derisive snort. "Of course, that was the final blow, but that was only after all seemed lost and we were desperate for any solution. I don't think any of us remembers what led to that point. A thousand decisions, actions, inactions—all adding themselves to the scales that tipped us into disaster."

For some reason, though vaguer, that explanation sat better with James. Felt more honest. "So, Svikull was telling the truth about the experiment and its outcome?"

"Without a review of his precise words, I cannot say for certain. Knowing him, if there was anything he would speak truthfully about, it's that event."

James looked at the display screen for a moment, weighing his next words carefully. "The government—it isn't opposing his attempt to create the machine to get everyone off Vonlaus, is it? It's not just because the power it needs is in such high demand."

That got Tristwe to turn to face him. "He told you he's trying to power a transport?"

James nodded.

A twitch of Tristwe's cheek told him that didn't sit well at all. The news had saddened her. Her entire bearing was folded in as though she had just received a punch to the abdomen. Betrayed. Haunted. Embittered. All these ghosted through her expression in differing degrees before she managed to get ahold of herself. She cleared her throat, reapplying her sterile mask. But there were cracks in it, and James had little doubt that with the right pressure, not only would the facade crumble, but she would too.

When her eyes returned to him, they weren't hard, no longer those of an interrogator. This wasn't just a matter of security for her. It was personal.

Tristwe's voice caught a bit as she said, "I think I know his plan. The building you helped him break into was a substation in the power grid. With it down, our power will be routed through a particularly vulnerable node in the grid. If he takes down that node, with it goes the generators for heating our structures."

That was sharing a lot with him. Trusting James more than he would've expected her to. For the life of him, he couldn't see the angle behind it. "Won't that cause everyone, to uh ..."

"Yes, all of the remaining infrastructure, civil spaces, and homes on Vonlaus will freeze. We will all die. That is his plan." She ran a hand through her hair, evidently forgetting it was in a bun at the back, and undid a few strands in the process. "He has given up hope. This is him ending our pain."

A sickening feeling in James's stomach, building since the alternative narrative began, intensified. It rang with a peal of truth Svikull's had lacked. Either Tristwe was a fantastic liar or Svikull was a poor one.

James banged his fist against his leg with anxious energy, his gaze shifting from the display to Tristwe and back again. There was no way to get out of what he had to do, even if he was only about 70 percent sure it was the right thing to do. "Inspector Tristwe," he began. Judging from her reaction to him using her name, he could continue. "I want to help you stop Svikull."

She leaned back from him, once more the investigator. "You trust my account over his?"

He nodded.

"Good. Very good." Tristwe's taut face pulled tighter around the eyes. She had appeared emotionless a moment before and now hid nothing. "You must understand how extraordinary what I'm about to offer is, and it is only appropriate in these extraordinary times. You may accompany me to the location at which I anticipate finding Svikull. There you may restrain your mate while I address ... Svikull."

The pause was so sudden and pregnant with significance that James almost asked after it. Something about the Vonla's expression stopped him, though. Drawing in a breath, he steadied himself. "Thank you for that opportunity and your trust. I have to ask, if Svikull is doing this as a ... a mercy killing, and your people are slowly, inexorably dying, why stop him?"

Tristwe's eyes widened for an instant before she slipped back into a more schooled expression than before. "I had profiled you as a being of theistic beliefs that define existential realities for you. What we might call 'spirituality.' Perhaps I have erred regarding that, as this may not seem a sensible answer." She pursed her lips, her formality and composure slipping once more. "We fight on, because sometimes it only takes something small to keep hope alive. And a little hope to survive."

James could tell he must be gaping by the hardening of her gaze and stern set of her mouth. The brief glowing spot in her armor, hot with sincere emotion, conviction, was buried beneath cold steel once again. "Perhaps it is best if I do not bring you after all."

"No, no. I, uh—" He had to pause to work some moisture to his mouth and wrangle his erratic heart and thoughts. "I won't betray your trust or your estimation of me."

She nodded curtly. "I will have you prepped for departure. Svikull has a significant head start and has been eager for this since we lost ..." The hurt and heat within her gaze all made so much more sense. It was his own ire he recognized in her. A scorned lover. Bitter. Brokenhearted. But not yet beyond hoping. Which meant they could all be in a lot of trouble when everything went down.

"We leave within an hour," she said hurriedly and strode off.

chapter
ten

A SHUDDER RAN through the hull of the transport, and the faint blue lights flickered off and on again. James rapped his fingers on the armrest of the seat he was strapped into. That was the fourth time the vessel had seemed like it was going to die on them.

Directly across from him, Inspector Tristwe cocked her head and arched a brow. "I told you already, the farther from the warm zone we get, the more strain it places on the transport's systems. It takes significant amounts of energy to maintain hovering over incongruous terrain. Without even factoring in the thermal disparity dampening within as the temperatures plunge around us."

He offered a wan smile. "I'm more of a theoretical physicist. Applied stuff is um, too bumpy for me. Usually."

The hull of the transport groaned as it rocked again.

Tristwe didn't even blink as they were both nearly shaken out of their seats, held in place only by their sturdy harnesses. "I suppose I could guess that from prior behaviors. It appears your love for your mate is pushing you into abnormal behaviors."

"Yeah," was all James could say. Inside him was far more molten, shifting and churning, compared to the frozen fixedness outside. It was as if every step he'd taken since getting to Vonlaus had pushed him further and further into the realization that he'd been foolish and running from the truth about how deeply he still cared for Naomi. How irrecoverable the damaged wreckage of him would be if they really ended things, whether here in such operatic and unbelievable circumstances or back on Earth in the polished rigidity of a divorce proceeding.

"If it would be of aid to you," Tristwe spoke up, barely shifting in her seat once the transport stabilized more, "You may recite an invocation for divine aid."

James forced himself to loosen his grip on his seat. He was past embarrassment over how tight his voice sounded when he spoke. "I should say a prayer?"

Tristwe splayed her thumbs. "If I was correct in assessing your species to have such a proclivity."

He closed his eyes. "Um, yes. We, uh, well, I do specifically." To even his surprise, he chuckled.

"You find humor in piety? Or are you being derisive and think Vonlas have no sense of it themselves?"

Holding his hands up in deferral, James shook his head. "No offense intended. It's just, I realized that my wife and I have been here long enough that it's Christmas. Er, a holiday with particular spiritual significance to uh, humans with 'such a proclivity.'" More solemnly, he added, "Humans like me."

"Interesting," Tristwe commented with a lilt of genuineness to her voice. "The practice had lapsed long before Vonlaus's ruination. But still longer ago, Vonla celebrated a spiritual holiday at this time of year as well ..."

The way she trailed off clued James in that there was something more to the coincidence. "What did you celebrate?"

Her brows knit for an instant. "Light. The promise of the Creator overcoming the darkness to make all things new."

"Oh." The tension in James's body relaxed as he settled back into his seat. A shiver not born of Vonlaus's cold raced down his arms and back. "I suppose ours is as well. Except the Creator already came and began making all things new. Those of us who believe in Him, call Him Jesus. And we call the holiday Christmas because we celebrate His coming, the Christ or 'anointed one.'"

There was a flash of something in Tristwe's eyes. It was hard to place. Yearning, perhaps? "How marvelous it must it be to live on a world where hope is realized. Do you think He will make new even this world?"

That threw James for a moment. "Oh, well, I suppose so. He came once to show everyone the path to a renewed relationship with the Creator, but He's also giving everyone time to choose whether or not to embrace that gift. When He returns, I think even Vonlaus will be made new."

"Hope with the earnest of its fulfillment given ..." Tristwe cleared her throat needlessly. "We should talk more on this. Later."

"Okay." James found a new mixture of emotions besetting him. Joy and anxiousness vied with one another for the chief spot in his heart. "Good to know you're optimistic about our chances. You know that there will be a later."

The transport rocked. Presuming they lived to the end of this, they could talk about the "good news for all people." A phrase that suddenly held new meaning for James as he sat across from the resident of another world.

A particularly jarring bounce hit them, and James banged his head on the roofing of the transport. Wincing as he rubbed at the impact spot, the pain briefly eclipsed the simmering spiritual sunrise he was experiencing, and he grumbled, "Doesn't your pilot have any sense? Or do they not mind tossing the *alien* around at the expense of your team?"

Tristwe's eyes drifted to the flooring of the transport. A twitch of her cheek's muscles, which James realized was her *tell*, sent a fresh boil of anxiety through him. "Inspector?"

Settling her hands neatly in her lap, she leveled a firm gaze on him. "The pilot has no prejudices, because it is a program. I did not tell you in advance—there are no others on this mission. There is no time for procedure and protocol. Nor sorting through the sensitivities of interspecies diplomacy. It has to be us, only us, if Svikull is to be stopped in time and kept from ..."

She let her words trail off, adding nothing more. Her eyes were on him but melted from ice into chilly night seas. James could tell the simple completion to her sentence would be to keep Svikull from "killing us all." But he didn't think Inspector Tristwe would struggle with that, which only further deepened his unvoiced conviction that shortly they would both be in a very personal and precarious position to try to save not only the planet, but specifically those they loved.

chapter
eleven

TZZT. The little device Inspector Tristwe applied made a peculiar chirp as it overrode the door controls. A side entry to the compound, half snow-submerged, slid aside. Carefully, she slipped in, barely dislodging any snow, even in her bulky snowsuit. Beyond was a room lit by the familiar blue lighting and wall patterning that was only slightly more interesting than the other drab fare of the rest of Vonlaus.

Shivering after the long trek from where they had landed the transport—because she had insisted it would keep Svikull from detecting them too soon—James tried to be as agile. And failed. Miserably. He consoled himself that even if he had been in any kind of decent shape, he wasn't as adapted to this cold environment or as small as Tristwe. It didn't help him absolve his guilt about looking like a whale running aground into the base. For those miserable seconds, though, he was emotionally buoyed because self-deprecation felt so much better than the self-loathing that he was responsible for Naomi being in danger. If he hadn't told her they could trust Svikull, maybe they wouldn't be here now. And definitely, if he hadn't swerved onto the path to the Starlit Inn, they wouldn't be on Vonlaus at all.

Why did I take that turn, anyway?

"Hello, Vonlaus to James," Tristwe commented, waving a

hand in front of his face. Her whispering had gone up a few decibels and was in the decidedly annoyed range. "Do you want to get lost and botch this entire mission?"

His default defenses kicked in. "Guess so. How am I doing?"

Tristwe glowered at him, not unlike Naomi. "We must move quickly. I would hate to spare your mate the bountiful gift of your company a moment longer."

Yup, sarcasm is definitely a universal language.

"Sorry, I'm on your six."

"I beg your pardon?"

He rubbed the bridge of his nose. "Just an expression to say I'm following behind you." This whole Venn diagram of phrases and words in common and difference between Vonla speech and English was giving him a headache.

No, his head hurt, but it wasn't just figuratively. It really hurt. "Ahh, what's going on?"

Tristwe was holding her head and grimacing. "Sonic attack. He knows we are here—or expected we would come. We have to get out of the emitter's range."

Without bothering to see if he really listened this time, the inspector took off at a full sprint down a corridor ahead of them. Only his longer strides and better nutrition gave James any hope of keeping up. By the time Tristwe skidded to a halt in an open room with three enormous displays on the walls, James was doubled over, wheezing and wishing he had some snow from the outside to cool the searing pain in his lungs.

Definitely ... hitting ... the gym if we make it ...

After less than a minute, Tristwe lowered her hands from where she'd locked them behind her head like a true runner and had her breathing evened out. She studied the room they were in for several seconds. "This isn't good," she muttered.

James tried to respond but only managed to half rise up and fumble after her on legs less firm than gelatin. He noticed Tristwe wasn't engaging the displays like normal. Her hands were pressed up against the screens, and she was craning her long neck in either direction.

"Wait, those are just windows. Not fancy high-tech holographic monitors?"

Tristwe rolled her eyes. "Holographic displays are hardly advanced technology. And yes, this building was constructed ... before Vonlaus became so disastrous. Windows were fairly common architectural features."

"Oh, why did they stop—"

"Later. We have a problem," she cut him off, backing away from the window she was near to try another.

"What's that?" James asked, finally straightening up and catching his breath. Mostly.

"The attack led us to the central observation room. Each of these other rooms once held computer hardware that was utilized in the failed attempt to rectify Vonlaus's plight. This room was a command center to coordinate the other three."

Giving the room a more thorough assessment and noting the collecting dust, James shrugged. "I don't get it. It looks like the computers haven't been in here for some time."

"Exactly. None of the hardware should have been moved from here," Tristwe said, her voice in the register of a sleuth puzzling through a clue that didn't fit.

"Well, we could—"

Clang.

Both James and Tristwe whipped their heads toward one of the rooms. Only James's heart hammered with the heat and intensity of a rocket taking off. Naomi was in one of the other rooms, rubbing her knee she had just banged on a low railing. In her hands, she tremulously held some sort of projectile weapon. One like the Vonlas used to capture him.

"Naomi!" He didn't even hesitate, putting his former pace to shame. He bolted for the door to the room with his wife and had it open before Tristwe could stop him. He only slowed as he bungled over a chair he hadn't seen and went down to the floor. It definitely left a bruise.

"Ah!" Naomi screeched, and the air sizzled over James's head.

He glanced back at the wall and saw a scorched ring where he had been the moment before.

"Stay there, or I'll shoot again!" Naomi yelled. James could see the faint tremor in her legs as she stood poised to make good on her threat. She was up on a walkway above him, but not high enough to have a clear shot, thankfully.

"Naomi, don't shoot. It's me, James." He lifted his hands slowly, palms out for her to see, and rose to his feet slower than he'd possibly ever moved in his life.

Halfway through standing up, he heard Naomi gasp. "James! But I thought ... Svikull told me the government had killed you!"

Of course he did. That pretty much settled the score in James's mind on which Vonla he should have trusted. He'd been right to side with Tristwe. Tristwe, who at that precise moment burst from the other side of the room with her weapon drawn. "Drop it. Drop your weapon now!"

Naomi fumbled as she backed away for cover but didn't loosen her clear death grip on the plasma gun.

Tristwe snapped again in her authoritarian voice, "By the authority of the Vonlaus Investigative Bureau, you will drop your weapon and surrender to arrest!"

"James, watch out!" Naomi yelled. "They followed you!"

This was a nightmare. Naomi was going to get herself killed, and if there was anything left of James after losing her, he bet she was just a good enough shot to wound Tristwe and guarantee no one was left to stop Svikull. He had to do something and fast.

"Wait, stop!" James flung himself between the two women, his body shielding each from the other's fire. His body was tensed for one or both of them to rend him through.

Both women hesitated, long enough for him to face his wife. "Nomi, please, you have to listen. This is Inspector Tristwe. She's here to help. Svikull tricked us."

As soon as he said the nickname, James regretted it. Though as he watched Naomi, the crazed resolve in her eyes softened. He could see she was struggling to process everything. There had been a sincerity and tender quality to his voice as he'd used the pet name he hadn't had in a long time. He could understand why she had come to hate it. A montage of instances in which he'd used it, many recently, flashed through his thoughts like a slide reel. In each, there had been a petulant point to its delivery. As if it were pejorative instead of a pet name. And, of course, he had chosen to drop it now, in perhaps the most charged and confusing moment of their lives.

"Nomi," he repeated, not having to force the compassion, the depth of feeling for her. "He lied to us. There is no machine to transport us to our world or any other. That's why he tried to get rid of me at the warehouse. I had been asking him questions, doubting what he was telling us.

"I was right to be suspicious. He's not redirecting enough power to save everyone—he's going to shut down the power to all buildings left on the planet. Once it's out, everything and everyone on Vonlaus will freeze solid. Including us."

Naomi lowered the plasma rifle, her hand shaking. She drifted down some stairs to stand directly in front of James, shaking her head. "No. He couldn't ... he ... wh—why?"

Taking cautious steps, James watched until her gaze drifted up to hold his. Moist with welling tears, she focused as if coming to the eye of the emotional storm besetting her. From experience, he knew she was listening now. "He gave up hope. Like me." His voice cracked, and he knew he wouldn't be able to say anything else. Why did he have to fall apart at a moment like this?

Tears freely slid down Naomi's round cheeks, and she stared hard at him for several seconds longer. The projectile weapon shook as she wavered between believing or blasting him. Inspector Tristwe shifted anxiously behind James, no doubt agitated that he was delaying them from stopping Svikull to try to rescue his soon-to-be ex-wife.

Naomi sucked in a breath and collapsed forward. His arms reflexively received her, pulling her close in a tight, sheltering embrace. There she sobbed into his chest, and he felt the ferocity of her grip on him, her reliance. It shattered through the wall against words his fear had been building up.

"I thought you were gone. That I'd really lost you."

"It'll be all right," he soothed.

She pulled back and asked, "How? How can this be all right?"

Those eyes that had drawn him in from their first date were wide with a desperate need for something, anything, that could validate his words. His own heart's thumping filled his ears. He felt ready to burst from the tension. Only one thing came to his mind, and he knew she would challenge it. Probably reject it, but it was welling up in him like an underground aquifer piercing ground parched to dust for so long it could barely contain the water bubbling up to the surface. "Sometimes it only takes something small to keep hope alive. And a little hope to survive."

Naomi's eyes impossibly widened still further as if he had shocked her with a taser. A maelstrom of emotions raged within her expression. Fear, confusion, annoyance, and, unless he imagined it, happiness. "How does that help?" she asked, barely above a whisper.

James nodded thoughtfully. Fair question and one he didn't have an answer to ... or did he? As if the slats of an optometrist's phoropter had clicked from the blurriest to the clearest lens, he saw it. "I guess, in spite of all we've done to and put each other through, you're what I brought with me from our world that feels warm in the midst of this unbearable cold. One thing that feels true amidst the deception and scheming we've been drawn into. So, please, just trust me now.

"And above all, you know, Svikull was right about one thing. All of this can't be a coincidence. I think—no, I *know*—God is with us, whatever happens next."

Wonder shimmered in her eyes. "It's been a long time since I heard anything like that from you. Years."

He nodded. "It's been a long time since I should have said that and so many other things." Glancing up and catching Tristwe giving him a look that said she was ready to blast them both, he added, "And there are many more things I could have and should have said along the way. I promise, if we manage to stop Svikull, I'll tell you them all. Beginning with how very sorry I am—"

"Touching as this may be," Tristwe interrupted, "I need your mate to drop her weapon or I will have to atomize you both." Her voice sounded strained past the point of breaking.

Naomi stared at James, her eyes searching him as she had so many times before. Not with criticality or skepticism. This time, there was a tenderness, a vulnerability long absent. She laid down the plasma weapon and took James's hand. "I'm with you."

For the first time in a long while, James felt like he could breathe again. He beamed a smile at Naomi, crazy as it was, given their circumstances. Deep inside, he felt he'd gotten her back. And he couldn't begin to frame what that meant to him.

Tristwe shouldered past them. "Then let's get going," she barked.

A zing cut through the air, and a scorched sizzle rose from the flooring in front them. "Actually," Svikull called out from the walkway above them. "None of you are going anywhere."

chapter
twelve

TRISTWE HUNCHED OVER, gripping her right arm just above the wrist. Her weapon had already clattered to the floor.

"My apologies, dear," Svikull called out to her with all the warmth of the ice outside. "Our last meeting was less than cordial, so it seems prudent to relieve you of temptation to act rashly."

Through gritted teeth, she snapped, "Is it rash to stop a madman from murdering hundreds of innocents?"

"Innocents? None of us are truly innocent. Not even our rotund friends from another planet. Our choices landed us all here, so you might as well abandon your self-righteous posturing.

"After all, I'm about to end the suffering of our entire civilization."

"You're really planning to kill everyone?" Naomi asked, crestfallen. "You lied to us!"

Svikull shrugged. "See things as you wish. I promised to get you off Vonlaus. Soon, you will be beyond the mortal bounds. Thus, my promise will be kept."

He cocked his head and evaluated her. She was still in James's embrace, shaking with rage or fear or both.

"You aliens should be thanking me," Svikull said with a disgusted sneer. "You're both plump and healthy now, but after a few months on Vonlaus, I'm sure you would look more like us. Wraiths. Echoes of who we were and doomed to vanish entirely."

"Like your daughter? You want us to all die like her?" James asked impulsively and immediately regretted it.

Svikull leveled the plasma weapon at him. "Do. Not. Dare disrespect her memory!"

"He isn't the one tarnishing Synnove's memory, Svikull. We witnessed her passing from here, and instead of leaving it hallowed and a memorial like the rest of us, you've turned it into a weapon!" Tristwe's words went from a painful murmur to an anguished scream. "She would be terrified of what her father has become!"

Svikull whirled and pointed the weapon at Tristwe. He jogged down the stairs and jammed the barrel directly into her chest. "What *I* have become? Look at you, serving those beasts who allowed my daughter to die from an ill-conceived scheme to escape. There is no escape! You are like a desperate mongrel too dumb to see it is being beaten by masters who will never love it."

James caught a flicker of a glance aimed at him before Tristwe pushed back against the barrel of the weapon with her chest. "She was our daughter. *Ours*. And you talk as if only you know what loss is. I lost you both that day."

Svikull took one step back, his cheeks twitching as he seemed to struggle to respond.

James's throat tightened, and his heart pounded. It was now or never. Tristwe had Svikull's full attention.

He wished the moment were like a movie or novel where he would heroically sweep over, disarm the bad guy, and in one slick move render him unconscious. This wasn't like that. He hesitated a half-second too long. James knew that as soon as he took his first clumsy, heavy step. But it was too late to turn back. He was committed.

So, he charged Svikull and caught the butt of the weapon on his jaw as the Vonla whipped around to face the sudden threat.

Pain exploded from the impact spot, blurring his vision.

This is it. The end.

But it wasn't. His vision cleared, and he saw that Svikull was just as mortal as him. The movement had put him off balance. The maniac was forced to stabilize himself and then deliver another like blow to Tristwe as she surged at him.

She went down, hard. Svikull hadn't pulled his punch, so to speak, for his estranged wife. It was plain on his face as he looked at her on the floor, bleeding and dazed. Svikull was crestfallen, his mouth agape at what he'd just done. For all his crazed talk, there was still a person, a being capable of love and remorse, and maybe, just maybe, a person who could be reasoned with and pulled back from the brink.

"Svikull," James began and ducked as the other man turned on him, his eyes wild.

"You caused this, bloated brute!"

Szzt.

"Argh!" Svikull dropped to a knee as a blast from across the room seared his calf.

James whipped around to see Naomi, trembling as she held the plasma weapon.

Her eyes were wide on him. "James!" she called out.

He reached a hand toward her before movement beside him caught his eye. Svikull was rising up and leveling his weapon at Naomi. Dread was all her face registered, paralyzed by it.

"No!"

Without hesitation, he leaped at the weapon.

Szzt.

This time, pain unlike anything James had ever experienced flooded every neural pathway. His whole mind screamed. Hitting the ground without bracing himself barely registered as his shoulder screeched like a choral of hate-filled harpies.

The only thing that he understood through the pain was Naomi crouching beside him. "James! James!" She wailed between sobs.

"Nomi," he managed to grind out through clenched teeth. He shot her a crooked grin before it twisted back into a grimace.

She snorted a tear-laden laugh and rocked him until he yelped in pain from it. Something else bothered him, something beyond the pain. Something that mattered enough to break through his wife's soothing crooning that he was going to be okay.

"Svikull?" he asked and forced himself up on one elbow.

Naomi's tear-streaked eyes took a second to refocus, and he swiped away the flood of them. "He, uh, you knocked him into the railing for the stairs, and then he ran off."

She glanced back across the room. "His blast hit you and knocked down my blaster-thingy."

"Blaster-thingy ... you're going to have ... to turn in your nerd card."

"Ooh," she sighed in a frustrated way. "Don't joke right now."

But he could tell that was exactly what she needed. It was an incredible sensation to know and give his wife what she needed instead of constantly dreading any interaction with her.

If the pain wasn't so sobering, he could've been lost in the moment. "We ... have to get ... up." James struggled to force his untoned abdominals to haul him up while moving his shoulder as little as possible. He floundered at first.

"Are you sure you should move?" Naomi asked, even as she worked to help him up.

James glanced toward Inspector Tristwe. She was sprawled where she fell, still motionless. There was no one left to save Vonlaus but them.

"We have ... yowww—"

"To stop Svikull," Naomi finished.

As soon as he got on his feet, she grabbed his face in her hands. "Whatever happens, I still love you. You must know that I still love you."

And he almost replied the same but his words were cut off as her lips smashed into his in their first kiss in ... he couldn't even remember how long. Especially since this kiss was the kind that was good enough to convince his brain the pain didn't matter. Time. Space. Not so important. Naomi mattered.

The kiss wasn't long enough, but it couldn't be.

"I know where he's headed," Naomi said breathily, her cheeks rosy and her tone a bit conspiratorial, like they'd snuck a kiss under the high school bleachers instead of here on the knife's edge of death. "I helped Svikull set up the machines. He is going there."

James almost asked how she could know that for sure, but thought better of it. Naomi trusted him, and he would do the same for her. He draped an arm around her, and they ran—or what they could manage—together up the stairs and onto the walkway, following the mad Vonla's path. They had to get to him before he enacted his scheme, and amidst all the tragedies and evil that would befall Vonlaus, he and Naomi would lose what they'd just gained.

chapter
thirteen

THE CLOSER THEY came to the epicenter of Svikull's plan the more apparent his intentions became. Large bundles of cables protruded from the walls and ceiling where the smooth paneling lining the corridor had been removed or smashed in to allow the massive conduits to snake through. Svikull had been working toward this for some time. It blunted the edge to James's ire for him, knowing the Vonla had labored in isolation, bent on this insane vendetta. He had to be stopped, but surely there was something of him left to salvage.

Naomi slowed and stopped. She whispered, "We're almost there. Around that corner is the hall with the room. It's big but a mess of computers and cables. Kind of like your office at home."

He shot her a mock amused look. It was hard not to smile even with what was on the line. Normally, a comment like that from Naomi felt barbed, intended to injure. This felt more like a playful nudge, meant to draw him closer rather than push him away.

"So, not much room to maneuver?" He realized he was smiling because she arched a brow at him. A wan smile tugged at her lips for an instant.

"Not much. He knows we're coming, so we need a plan."

James frowned. "Is he still armed?"

She shrugged. "I don't know. I just saw him running off in this direction. I was too worried about you ..."

As if set off by her mention of it, the pain in his shoulder began to force itself back into his consciousness. He must have been riding an adrenaline high, and he was coming down from it fast. He winced, knowing he needed to assess his injury, but from the blackened edges he could glimpse of the wound, he really didn't want to see it yet. If the past was any indicator, he'd probably crumple once he did.

"You follow me in. I'll distract him, and then you shut down whatever device he's using."

"That's a terrible idea. If he's armed, he'll blow you away!"

"Maybe, but it means he won't be able to stop you."

She put a hand on her hip. "Do you really think I'm going to let you sacrifice yourself right after I got you back? Besides, you're the tech-savvy physicist."

James thought about it for a moment and said, "It would be better for everyone if you do it. You're brilliant and have seen him put his device together. Right now, with my injury, I'm not much good for more than deadweight."

She put her hand on his chest over his heart. "No! Don't ever say that about yourself."

He took her hand and kissed it. Even though it stung just shifting his arm that much. "I'll be sure to have you elaborate on how great you think I am later. For now ... we have to move. We'll try to be stealthy, but mostly, this is how it has to go."

Without waiting for her to agree, he shuffled around the corner. Right away, he saw things looked just as she described. They were out of time. Wrenching loose of her support, James pushed himself to move faster, smoother.

He hurdled the first round of cords and darted across another tangle before Svikull heard and turned to face him.

Szzt.

The shot was wide and scorched the wall at James's left only inches away. He flung himself to the floor to dodge another. That one hit the wall back in the hallway.

"Ahh!" Naomi cried out.

James was back on his feet and charging forward. It was a mistake.

Svikull was back on him, and James managed to bash the weapon aside in time to have a second searing blast devastate his already injured arm and shoulder.

He crumpled. Everything blurred in and out of focus. Even with it, he knew Svikull had pointed the weapon at his head.

"That's far enough, Naomi. Unless you'd like to see your mate rendered a smoking lump."

James was relieved to see Naomi had brought her plasma weapon. He had completely forgotten about it. She was good with details like that, one of a dozen things he should've been giving her more credit for over the years. His relief evaporated in an instant when she lowered the plasma weapon.

"Please, don't hurt him."

James tensed. If Svikull moved so much as a fraction to shoot her, he would tear the spindly Vonla apart. Or at least make his best effort at it.

To James's surprise, Svikull just nodded. "Very well. So long as you both behave for another eighty seconds, I will not shoot him."

"Eighty seconds?" Both James and Naomi repeated inquisitively.

"Mm hmm," Svikull affirmed, a smarmy twang to the sound.

James glanced at the display behind him. The symbols he recognized from the substation Svikull destroyed were flashing by.

Oh, no! Whatever he's going to do to bring down the power grid is set to start at the end of the timer!

That meant they had sixty-five seconds left.

"Svikull, listen to me, please, don't do this. It's not too late to—"

"No worries. While not as simple as shooting you, our deaths will not be from freezing to death. You, my compatriots, shall join me in a more dramatic end."

As much as James expected the frothing madman to be exultant in this moment, he thought the Vonla sounded almost pensive. "If you have regrets, you should stop this. Pause. Think about what you're doing and why," James urged.

He caught a look of urgency from Naomi. She clearly wanted to raise her weapon but couldn't while he was pinned down like this.

He tried shifting, but Svikull's barrel tracked him.

"You have seen Vonlaus for days. Little of the world is left, and what remains is slowly desiccating. Soon, all that will be left is a dead sphere of ice. Why prolong the suffering?"

"There is more than you're considering. Vonlaus isn't only pain and death," James protested, desperately trying to find a way to get to the controls as the seconds sped past. Forty left to go.

"Existing isn't the same thing as living. What is there left to live for?"

"What about love?" Naomi's gaze focused on James.

"Such a saccharine sweet sentiment, but my Synnove is gone. And, well, you saw how my mate greeted me earlier—with a weapon aimed to kill. With good reason. It was my foolish plan to improve the launch favorability that doomed our daughter and all aboard to die. I guaranteed that none will ever survive this world's demise."

James sucked in a sharp breath. Svikull caused all of this, or at least he blamed himself for it all.

Twenty-five seconds left.

He stopped trying to find a way around Svikull. "There's hope. You still have hope this isn't the end for your people, as long as you have breath in you. And if not hope for this life, then for life beyond with the Creator."

Svikull sneered, "You are so predictable you—"

Fifteen seconds left.

James leapt at Svikull and received the hammering blow he

expected from the plasma weapon's frame. As he crumpled, he saw Svikull turn to fire on Naomi with cat-like agility and speed.

Szzt.

With a gurgle and a thud, Svikull dropped beside James. He looked past his body to see Tristwe standing beside Naomi. The inspector favored her injured arm, but from the slight crackle in the room, he realized she had only stunned Svikull.

Five seconds left.

Rolling to the base of the apparatus, there was no time to evaluate the setup or think of options. James gripped the bundle of cables going directly to the display and jerked with all his might.

SZZZZZ.

He didn't even feel the impact of being thrown against the wall. In fact, there was very little he could still feel. Doing experiments with electrical equipment, he had, of course, been shocked before, but this was in a whole other class. A fatal one.

Naomi was beside him before he could even strain to see her. His arms were trembling, and he wondered if he was convulsing. It was difficult to hold his focus, and he knew he had to get his last words out before the dark overtook him.

It was hard to hear her, but he thought that Naomi was crying and saying his name. "Did we ...?" he managed to get out.

She looked up at Tristwe for confirmation and then nodded.

"Good ... you're safe ... good."

There was that knitting of her brows that said she didn't buy a word he said. Even with her curly strands of hair falling in her face and her eyes bleary with tears, he recognized it.

"Hope ... you have ... a little ... can ... survive. Find ... a ... way ... home ..."

chapter
fourteen

JAMES JERKED UPRIGHT AND COUGHED. His heart thudded in his chest as if he'd just survived the running of the bulls. He'd definitely had a scare and had almost died!

Rubbing his face, he swung his legs around to dangle over the side of ... the couch. He tapped his feet on the floor and found them on wooden boards. The sharp sting in his feet after a few seconds told him they were quite cold. In fact, he felt the whole room was frigid.

That makes sense, Vonlaus is very cold.

No, his eyes were beginning to focus now. He wasn't on Vonlaus. This place he was in, it was from a lifetime ago. What was it ... the Lit ... the, uh, the Starlit Inn. That was it. He was back in the Inn and had just woken up. How had he gotten here again?

Rolling his shoulders, he found there weren't any sharp pains from his plasma injury and no scars or aches at all that he could deduce from the electric shock, which should have killed him. How was he back on Earth and healed up with no memory of the in-between?

There was a faint groaning sound from the bed in the room. Leaning to peer over at it, his heartbeat picked up faster. Naomi! She was safe, too, and sleeping, if fitfully, on the bed.

Across the room, a little gust of icy air swirled and encircled James. He saw the door that he once thought adjoined another room was open and the frigid night air was creeping inside along with a light dusting of snowflakes.

Testing himself, he stood without any trouble—well, any more trouble than ever—and closed tightly before locking it. As he backed away from the door, he began to weave all the disparate strands together.

Wait. We were both sleeping. So that was ... just a dream?

He exhaled a sigh, letting the tension flow out of him. Just a dream. No Vonlaus. No crazy Svikull. No icy, certain doom. No ... his stomach tightened and twisted.

No, no, no!

If that was all just a dream, then everything he had experienced, including his reconciliation with and renewed love for Naomi, had just been imagined. His eyes held fast to her sleeping form, which had stilled now, and she was lightly dozing, casting off the occasional snore as she did every night.

It was so much worse than just having imagined it. He felt like a man who walked a thousand miles only to find that he'd arrived back where he started. Every fiber of his being coursed with undeniable love and desire for Naomi, but if it was all a dream, then she hadn't been through any of it. When she woke in a few hours, she'd still hate him. Still want to divorce him, and when they left, it would be to part permanently.

James had never wished for and yearned so much to be wrong. That this was the dream, him standing here in this defunct little lodge in the middle of nowhere. Why couldn't this be a dream and he awaken back on Vonlaus, facing an inevitable, protracted death with the Vonlas? Because, on that world, in that reality, he had Naomi's love again. He knew that there was no reconciling for her, no explaining what he'd experienced. It would sound insane to her, like he was being desperate. And he was.

He tugged at the ruddy strands of his sweat-soaked hair and dropped onto the couch. What could he do? How was he supposed to fix this? Worse, how was he supposed to live with it? This was far worse than a nightmare, because there was no waking up. This was reality. The hopeless reality he and Naomi had made for themselves.

Svikull wasn't crazy. This must have been what he was feeling. There's nothing left. Just a miserable wait for the end.

Sitting on the couch, head in his hands, James sulked that way for several minutes. He lifted his head and watched the slow rise and fall of Naomi's side as she slept. It had all seemed so perfectly orchestrated, like it was meant to be. Divinely appointed.

A shiver not of cold but sudden wonder and realization ran through James. Maybe it was all still divinely prepared, not for both of them, but just for him. Maybe, this had been the sort of classic *Christmas Carol*-esque scenario in all the stories. It felt a bit reductionist to view it that way. It was more profound than suddenly valuing Christmas and having hearty friendships, or even valuing his family and life more. He had been on the verge of some real change. Things had stirred in his heart that hadn't been removed from the dusty inner sanctums where they'd languished and desiccated for years. Not just his love for Naomi, but his sense of himself. A sense of worth, of being able to care for them both and to act, even boldly, when needed.

Eclipsing it all had been that moment when he'd inadvertently become an interstellar missionary, encapsulating the message of Christmas for a person who had never had the slightest chance of hearing it. Hope, eternal hope—he'd tasted the first familiar draughts of it, like the first breaths of air after being submerged in water.

He rubbed his hands together and tapped his foot. It had felt so good to look beyond his circumstances for a time and remember *"the substance of things hoped for and the evidence of things not seen"* was not dead in him—its pulse had become so faint, but had quickened.

Naomi wouldn't understand all of this. It was true. How could he convey that in one night, one dream, God had taken the chaos and disillusionment and brought order and beauty within for him? She might very well reject him even more forcefully, but with genuine, irrepressible hope in him, he couldn't bear the notion of not trying once more to keep from being torn asunder from his wife. It was a faint hope, but hadn't she told him in the dream that was enough to survive? Enough to nurse their sickly love back to health now that he would stop shunning the Great Physician and would no longer be actively sabotaging them both, drawing closer instead of pulling away from her?

It wouldn't be easy. Naomi would still wound him and be skeptical—if she gave him another chance. But there was no denying it. He had to try. Svikull wasn't crazy, but he was wrong. There was still hope, and it was worth fighting to hold onto that warmth.

chapter
fifteen

JAMES TOOK a breath and opened the door he'd just unlocked. Pocketing the old-fashioned key, he bent, picked up the tray he'd laid down, and slipped into the room again. Morning had done much to beautify their surroundings for him, though they were still admittedly humble.

She's awake.

His heart revved in his chest. Naomi was sitting upright on her bed, combing out kinks from her curly black hair, her thoughtful eyes fixed more than a thousand yards in the distance. He got all the way up to standing beside her bed without her noticing. Not until he cleared his throat.

She looked up at him, conflict in the set of her mouth. "Yes?"

"I, uh, got you breakfast in bed."

"What?"

"I know how much you like it. Turns out Alexander made your favorites this morning. There's some bacon and French toast. He even put the powdered sugar on it. Oh, and there's Aztec cocoa for us both."

"Xocolatl? But you hate spicy food and especially that."

Naomi had him there, and her lip was curled in an incredulous look that made it seem like the precipice of her spurning his overtures was dangerously close ahead. He focused on laying the tray down next to her without spilling or knocking anything over.

"It's not my favorite," he admitted. "But it's been a long time since you've had it, so—"

"Actually, I have it every couple of weeks," she replied, taking an appreciative sip from her mug, all the same. "There's a café near work that sells it—and French toast."

That was news, and at one time, he might've let it derail or deter him. Not today. Not anymore. "Ah, well, it's still been quite some time since we drank it together."

"Mm-hmm," she agreed, eyeing him as she lifted the mug to her lips with both hands.

James took a sip and managed to only grimace a little. "It's an acquired taste I'm willing to spend some time to get."

"Hmm," was all Naomi offered in reply before closing her eyes, mouthing a silent prayer, and then digging into the breakfast he'd brought her.

They sat in silence for the rest of the meal, which Naomi took an extra-long time to finish. At the end of it, she looked down at the blanket over her legs. "You put this on me when I was cold last night. Didn't you?"

He put his arms behind his back and flashed an innocent smile. "Oh, um, yeah. You looked like you were getting pretty chilled there."

She returned an absent nod. "Thank you," she murmured.

"You're welcome." He cleared the tray and dishes. "I'll take these back to their kitchen."

"You aren't just going to sit them down and not worry about them until later, or you know, never?"

"Ha ha, yeah, okay, I guess I deserve that. I'll just be a second."

When he got out to the hall, he raised his eyes and prayed. "Lord, it's in Your hands. You can turn ashes into something beautiful. I definitely need you to intervene now and make what I can't of us."

It took a couple minutes to get the dishes sorted out and get back to the room. Once he did, he slipped back inside and saw Naomi's broadly curved silhouette highlighted by the light streaming in through the door that opened to the outside.

"Hey, I'm back," he called to her.

She glanced wistfully outside once more and then closed the door and came back over to the bed. Tapping a place beside her on it, she offered, "Care to sit together?"

"Yup." James's voice pitch warbled, betraying his enthusiasm. He tried to rein himself in and ended up sitting down so slowly he could feel the weight of his awkwardness crushing the life out of his plans to fix things with his wife.

"Are you okay?" she asked. Thankfully, before he could answer with a reply that would make the case against his sanity airtight, she added, "You've never gotten up early in the morning. Ever."

That was true and forced a laugh out of him that helped to neutralize his nerves. "Yeah, it's kind of rough. But I guess I hadn't realized what I was missing out on. You know, how special my morning could be."

"Hmm," she replied, her expression hard to read.

After a few minutes of sitting together, James cleared his throat. "So, speaking of meaningful mornings, while I was getting you breakfast, I also noticed that there's a sturdy old sleigh outside. Maggie—you know the owner and front desk clerk—uh, she said we could use it."

"You hate sleds and sleigh riding."

The way she had said it, it almost sounded like a question. Somehow, he felt certain he needed to be 100 percent open and truthful with her right now. Even for embarrassing things. "I know, but you love it, and I wanted to make this morning ... about you."

She regarded him with what could best be described as caution. She took in a slow, deep breath. Running her tongue over her teeth, she shrugged suddenly. "Why are you going to all this trouble? You're still going to sign the divorce papers, aren't you?"

James sucked in a sharp breath. It was the first time she'd said that awful word since he'd woken from his dream. It nearly smashed him to bits. He bolstered himself against the sudden swell in emotions. "Honestly, I don't want to anymore.

"And before it upsets you, just please. Hear me out. I know I've made mistakes and been a less-than-stellar husband."

Her brows twitched with agitation, so he barreled ahead. "Awful, okay, I know, I'm an awful husband. But last night we ... I ..." This was so difficult. How was he supposed to explain what the dream meant to him? What it could mean for them. "I did a lot of thinking and recalled something you told me once. 'Sometimes it only takes something small to keep hope alive. And a little hope to survive.'"

His wife blinked at him, her mouth slightly open as if trying to form a question but unable to find the proper words. As the silence lingered, it struck him, she had only said those words in the dream. Not in person. Which meant he probably sounded completely nuts to her right now, and she was debating whether to run.

"I mean ... it's just ... I want to be a different man. I *am* different and will continue to be. I still love you and—"

Naomi held up a hand to stop him.

"Please, Naomi, please, I can't—"

"James, stop!" Her voice was low and firm.

He nodded and laced his fingers tightly together in his lap. This was it. The end. One last blow to end it all. He tensed, bracing himself for the final sundering strike.

Naomi averted her gaze, gnawing on her lower lip for several seconds. There was a glassiness to her eyes. Dread swelled inside James, threatening to burst the cork of his respectful silence.

She still wasn't looking at him when she spoke softly, almost as if she wasn't sure she wanted him to hear her. "I was afraid you only believed that while we were on Vonlaus."

"Vonlaus?" Shock twisted his face into a portrait of confusion worthy of an Edvard Munch painting. Had he heard her correctly?

Cheeks reddening, Naomi scowled. "Never mind, it's nothing. I just—"

He grabbed her hands in his. They were trembling—whether it was his or hers or both that were shaking, he couldn't tell. "Wait, no. Vonlaus, I remember. I woke up here and thought it was just a dream."

Naomi's head bobbed faster than he thought possible. "I did too. I don't know how we got out of Svikull's compound, and you were hurt, and I thought ..."

"It was real," he said. "Whatever it was, it was real." James pulled back for a second. "Right? It was real? All of it?"

She considered this for a moment, her brows knitted and then smoothed. "All of it that matters," she concluded. A smile more beautiful than any he could recall played on her lips. "I don't know how. Just that what God put together, He made sure we didn't put asunder."

In that instant, hope was made blazingly real in James's heart. He leaned forward and wrapped his arms around his wife as though he'd never let go again. He kissed her, his heart in a riot, not of chaotic emotion, but gratefulness. There was a lot he didn't understand, couldn't properly frame with words, and might never be able to do so. What he understood: God indeed had granted them a wonder at the Starlit Inn.

acknowledgments

It is not a stretch to say that without my wife, whom I love dearly, this story would not have come together as it did. The initial seed of this story and its ultimate twist were inspired by those rare and brief moments when we were not on okay terms with each other. Rarely lasting more than a night—but that pain of waking from a dream in which things weren't that way between us to find the gulf still there ... that heartache and contrast between what I had "experienced" and the reality I woke to has been with me as a story conceit for years. It always lacked something more, though, something to contextualize it and give it meaning. For that, I have to thank my publisher, Linda Fulkerson, and my fellow writers in this collection.

This collection, its symbolism, and the positive and collaborative effort of writing the collection made the story come to life in a way that I had always wanted to see it.

Thank you to you as well, dear reader. Without you, none of us would be able to share these stories laid on our hearts. Your support, encouragement, and excitement for these stories allow us to keep writing and finding a publishing home for them.

Above all, thank You to the Lord. His patience with me is proved over and over again, and His faithful love never ends. But He gives greater grace, and I get to be a part of composing stories He inspires in me. I'm still an insufficient utensil for His art, but I treasure being used and seeing what He makes with me.

about the author

Brett Armstrong has been exploring other worlds as a writer since age nine. Years later, he still writes, but now invites others along on his excursions. He's shown readers haunting, deep historical fiction (*Destitutio Quod Remissio*), scary-real dystopian sci-fi (*Tomorrow's Edge* series), and layered, sweeping epic fantasy (*Quest of Fire*). Every story is a journey of discovery and an attempt to be a brush in the Master Artist's hand. Through dark, despair, light, joy, and everything in between, the end is always meant to leave his fellow literary explorers with wonder and hope. Always busy with a new story, he also enjoys drawing, gardening, and spending time with his wife and son.

keeper of the stars

dawn ford

To Erin, Jennifer, and Brett. Thank you for letting me tag along on this novella journey.

chapter
one

Star Date 75, in the Earth year 2135
Mars Sector Nine
Genesis Colony
Starlighter Star Station One

VENUS BOLT'S boots echoed as she ran down the hallway in Sector Five, the aluminum composite making her movements loud despite their insulating nature. Even with the space suit and helmet on, she could hear the thunking footfalls clearly. Her grandfather's words chased her like a monster on her heels. *"Save yourself. You know what to do."*

Tears trickled down her heated cheeks as she blasted across the familiar path. Her grandfather would be gone by now, floating among the stars. His treason charges, all lies, cooked up by Commander Ridenour, her space colony's self-elected and corrupt cyborg leader.

Humans, the commander insisted, were weak vessels. He'd augmented himself early in his career, slowly leaving his humanity behind. Too late, their sector realized his plans to eradicate the very humans that built the Genesis Colony.

The hallway went on for what seemed like forever to Venus's frayed nerves. It had been years since she'd come this way. Light glowed from red emergency beacons that ran along the gray walls. A few remained dark, a result of the Commander's orders. He didn't need light to see with his advanced-vision eye implants.

Venus's foot caught a loose tile, and she stopped. She bent over the silica-coated vent cover, which would lead to her destination and hopefully her freedom. Or her death. Her hands were damp as she muscled the square free. Dusty air spiraled around her face shield, glimmering in the dim light.

She'd spent much of her childhood in these vents, helping her grandfather with his maintenance job. A scientist by trade, he'd taken the only job left open when he'd entered the space program. He'd been brilliant but woefully unappreciated. Her heart fluttered at her loss. She hadn't stayed to watch them send her beloved grandfather to the stars from the safety of the vents.

Venus shook her head. She didn't have time to linger. One of the Commander's bots had spotted her sneaking between the barracks. It was only a matter of time before Ridenour found her. Her mission now was to make it to her grandfather's storage unit to access his Starlit Transporter stowed there.

Feet first, she slid into the vent, her vaporizer gun snagging on the side. Then her helmet caught. She grasped it tight and gave it a hard yank and fell sideways as it let loose. The oxygen tank dug into her back and side, but she needed it too much to let it go yet. Every molecule was necessary until she reached the storage area.

Carefully, she secured the thick tile back, grimacing as it screeched into place. Green symbols radiated from seventy-five-year-old phosphorescent paint illuminating the vents, lighting her way. Some things stood the test of time.

With a quick movement, she reached into her pocket and took out the piece she'd saved as a marker. It matched the chunk missing from the tile. Venus added the last of her sealing tape, reinforcing it. She wouldn't be going back.

Belly to the bottom of the duct, she crawled and tried to keep her breathing restrained. Shut down years ago due to population loss, this vented section of the station received no fresh air. That's why she needed the air tank. Sweat drenched the inside of her space suit, but she ignored it. She secured the face cover in place and flipped on the oxygen switch.

These vents had been her childhood playground. It wasn't so any longer. Her helmet, tanks, and larger adult size made the going difficult. She moved past the other inlets and ticked them off in her mind. At last, she made it to the one she needed—a thankfully larger chute leading down to the substation dock and storage area. Her heart thumped in her ears like the *whomp-whomp-whomp* that the station's massive ceiling fans made. Venus braced herself.

With hands firmly planted on the slick metal walls, she pushed herself forward and plunged down the chute. She plummeted and then landed on the section that angled at the end. Her gloves had been little help in slowing her descent.

At the bottom, her body tried to flip over itself, and her legs hit the other side of the wall. "Ow!" Her helmet muted her scream, but she clamped her lips closed. She couldn't chance the possibility of a sensor being live, alerting the Commander and his bots to her whereabouts.

Venus righted herself. She panted, getting dizzy from the low oxygen setting she'd placed on the tank. Like a fish out of water, she realized she'd used up the small supply, so she unsnapped the helmet, removing it and her suit. Gasping, the non-circulated air chilled her sweat-damp body, and she shivered. Couldn't be helped. The space suit was of no use to her now. She did, however, grab her vaporizer gun.

Security lights revealed the maintenance hall doorways. Each of the essential personnel had a small room to store their tools and necessary items to support and repair the station. All but one had a pin code security system attached to the outside wall. Without electricity, though, they wouldn't work. Her grandfather was a genius, after all.

She removed the antique key that they'd hidden in their quarters for years from her jumpsuit's pocket. Before her, at the last of the doors, an equally vintage lock secured her grandfather's storage unit. The key fit and the padlock opened easily.

Venus walked across the threshold, each of her boots' steps echoing, her body a shadow among the ghostly cloth-covered items. Oil and metal scented the brisk, stale air. Though the Commander's regime barricaded this area off, they hadn't completely shut it down because they needed access to the rooms to repair the bots. Thankfully, Ridenour hadn't understood the value of her grandfather's treasures. And here, there would be enough oxygen to do what she needed to do—or die trying.

The room was twice the size of their living compartment and stuffed full of all her grandfather's equipment and tools. She ran her hand across his astronautic engineer uniform, which hung from a hook inside the door. Though worn, it was as wrinkle-free as she remembered it. Her fingers lingered on the star insignia stitched on the chest. Two strides away, grime coated the top of a computer her grandfather tinkered on and secretly taught her school lessons.

She searched for the rounded frame of her grandfather's greatest inventions and found it at the center of the room. Dust clouded the air as she flung the cloth off it. The surface of the transporter was odd. It was convex, resembling a cut pie, with the slices overlapping each other in the center. Red bricks embedded the metal machine frame in an arch pattern. Cords ran from panels on the back of the unit to a GenerAC Pwr Flow generator. They'd used it a handful of times, sending objects like books or a piece of jewelry into it, but Grandfather wasn't brave enough to try anything alive.

Venus recalled his words after the coup as if he said them now. *"One day you might need to use the transporter. It's not powerful enough for two, but it can support you, my Venus. If it comes down to death by Ridenour's hand or stepping into the unknown, choose faith."* In him or the God he proclaimed waited on the other side, she wasn't sure.

She swallowed back grief. He'd always called her his joy. There was no joy left in her life now. But she could make him proud. She flipped the switches in order from memory and then turned the generator on. Its black display board lit up and hummed to life. *STRLT* glowed blue on the screen embedded in the bricks. The convex shield snicked open, revealing a mirrored round opening. The surface glimmered like liquid steel, moving as smoke.

Venus stared at the transporter, her watery eyes wide, her pulse racing. Beside the GenerAC Pwr Flow unit, she found her "bugout" bag, as her grandfather dubbed it. He'd used one when the plague hit, telling her it saved his life until making his way to the Starlit Space Station in some place called Bethel, Virginia. Embroidered on the canvas tote was the Starlit Station's logo. She ran a thumb over the raised threads and swiped a hand across her dewy eyes.

Heat radiated from the frame's surface, and the scent of the machine components warming made her choke. The generator hummed beneath her calloused palm as she leaned against it, waiting for it to fully power up. This was Plan A. If that failed, Plan B, staying and submitting to the Commander, was a fate worse than death.

She set her gun on the generator and hefted the bugout bag onto her back. It was lighter than the space uniform and oxygen tanks had been. She didn't need to look inside it. She recalled what she had packed. A plain change of worn clothes she'd pilfered beneath the supply monitor's nose. Along with the first aid and dried food items was an envelope of Earth money, something no one used on the Genesis Coloney, where digital tokens ruled.

A noise from outside the room caught her attention. The Commander's voice echoed, as did the beeps of the bots. The sound ricocheted off the bare hallway's walls.

Her heart leaped into her throat. She'd expected them, but not so soon. She stepped in front of the flowing silver surface of the mirror. Its meter showed a full charge. The bluish light brightening made her squint. The surface's radius was large enough to step through. She aimed the gun at the open door as she stepped one foot in, and cold enveloped her leg. The surface crackled, but there was no pain thanks to the subatomic particle stabilizer. She pulled her leg free, unsure, but it was intact. An object had to be fully engulfed before the molecular fragmentation was engaged.

The Commander's voice boomed, ordering his machine army to search every inch of the storage area for her. They were getting closer. Their eye beams lit up the open storage doorway, flashing a menacing yellow. She should've thought to close the door. It was too late for that now.

Air caught in her lungs, but her determination overruled her doubts. Scenery flickered across the surface like an image on a computer screen and then disappeared. It had happened before when they'd sent her grandfather's journals into space. With a heavy gulp, Venus stepped into the mirror, the backpack steadying her as she moved.

Intent on escaping without one of the Commander's bots following her, she lifted the gun and aimed at the generator as she stepped inside onto a plank attached to the transporter's frame. Sparks flew as her shot hit the power source dead center. The subsequent explosion hit her in the gut and made her ears ring. It propelled her backward as light burst from the laser's impact and the fragmentation engaged. She fell into nothingness.

chapter
two

COLD AND PAIN penetrated Venus's consciousness at the same time. Had they run out of oxygen in Sector Two again? But it wasn't her chest that ached—it was her back and head.

With a snort, she woke, jerking sideways and gasping for air that was easier to inhale than she expected. She choked, then blinked at the brightness that surrounded her.

White mounds as far as the eye could see, with things protruding from them. She closed her eyes, wishing for the blurriness to go away. Had the starship exploded? But, no. She was alive and could breathe.

Venus rubbed her eyes and glanced again. "Trees?" she mumbled groggily, recalling her grandfather's computer lessons. "How?" Her breath clouded in front of her face. Her stomach dipped and churned. "Where am I?"

Familiar-looking red bricks arched over her. She blinked. Though the bricks resembled the transporter's frame, there was no convex surface. It was simply an open-air arch. Where had the transporter sent her?

She dragged a hand through her matted hair and over the spot on the back of her head that throbbed. Another thought brought a new panic. Was she dead? Her grandfather had told her there was something beyond death to look forward to. Yet, if she were dead, would she be in so much pain?

Noises filtered through the confusion once her fear died down, and slowly the cold overtook her wariness. If she wasn't dead, what was she? *Where* was she?

Her grandfather had left a dying planet behind after virus warfare had unleashed a worldwide plague upon Earth. Space travel with self-sustaining stations had launched shortly before Earth fell, and so he'd shuttled to Mars Sector Nine using his credentials as a scientist. If she'd been transported to Earth in real time, sixty years after the evacuation, would there be any healthy life remaining?

An animal of some kind dropped onto a tree's limb and chittered at her. Her heart jumped, and she slapped a hand to her chest. "Not a bot," she murmured as a reassurance. But what was it?

She closed her eyes and fought to remain calm. The last thing she remembered was ... what? Her heart pounded in her chest double time until the memory came to her. The Commander sentenced her grandfather to death when he'd been found sabotaging the lab records after the bots had detected her. She'd fled and made it to his workspace. Her memories all fell back into place, along with the explosion after she'd shot the generator.

Venus ran a shaking hand across her middle, where the energy rebound hit her, but she wasn't bleeding. The creature in the tree screamed at her one last time and darted away, knocking condensation from the limb onto her head. The slush was cold and wet.

"Hey!" she yelled and wiped a hand across her short hair. "What is this stuff?"

The transporter obviously worked, but this place wasn't anything she was used to. It wasn't even something she could conjure in her mind. All she'd ever known was the metal space station. Even the Garden Sector didn't come close to what she was looking at. There, anemic plants grew along narrow plots with sun lamps and water spigots above them.

She eyed the trees, the freezing white mounds on the ground, and the wide-open sky. "The sky *is* blue," she muttered and couldn't help the note of wonder in her voice. Her grandfather's memories and his computer's grainy photos hadn't prepared her for the reality.

Venus blew out a foggy breath and stood. Her legs were weak, and she teetered into a frost-covered limb. Her jumper was waterproof, so the moisture dripped down the slick material without soaking it through. The chill traveled through the fabric, though, and shivers wracked her body. She needed to find shelter.

Her bag rested a few steps from where she'd landed. A huge rip split the side open. She grabbed it, searching the contents. Her clothes were missing. She found the bundle of money, some first aid items, and a freeze-dried meal pouch, one of four she'd packed. The other three packets were missing. Although she was hungry, she'd need water and a heating source to rehydrate the food. She set the packet aside.

The bag wasn't a complete loss, just the few contents, so she piled the items back inside and wrapped it with a compression bandage to keep it closed. Venus shuddered against the icy air and set out away from the brick arch. Her footsteps sank into the mounds as she tried to recall the name of the frozen particles of water. It took a moment for the term to come to mind—snow. Her grandfather had loved winter with the abundant snow and all the activities he used to perform in it.

She stopped, her chest heaving, her heart aching for him, but also with a new concern. Was she safe here? Was the air and snow toxic? Had she catapulted herself to a dead planet? Would that be worse than the space station? No. She'd take a dying world over the Commander and his bots any day.

Noises broke through her hysteria. Voices. "People," Venus muttered. She quickened her pace, working through the blanket of snow and around a thicket of flora that poked above the white. She followed the sounds. At last, she broke through and stopped, staring.

A massive building rose against the snowy background, a stunning wooden establishment. Her grandfather had salvaged a carved wooden sign that the Commander had confiscated after the coup. It had been a rare item, her grandfather said. Trees, such as the ones she'd walked through, couldn't grow successfully in space. At least not on their colony. First, because of the sheer amount of area they needed to grow. Second, because they'd used up too many resources to make them thrive, like light, nutrients, and water.

The brown exterior of this structure gleamed against the light. Snow piles on the floor—ground, she corrected herself mentally—reflected in the glass windows. She craned her neck and stared at the sun in the sky, something she'd only seen from a distance in the perpetual dark expanse of space. She blinked away the etched image the bright ball left on her corneas and grinned.

Venus walked closer to the building, inspecting the logs. They were smooth to the touch, cold.

"Hello?" a woman said.

Venus screamed, jumped, and spun around, all at the same time. She readied to run, though her legs wobbled. A flood rushed to her ears as her heart raced to catch up with her fright. Then she realized the woman wasn't trying to capture her but was asking her a question.

She was taller than Venus, older, wearing a warm-looking coat and boots. Venus didn't think she was as old as her grandfather had been, having celebrated his eighty-sixth birthday not so long ago. But her gray hair and crinkles around her eyes pointed to a woman in her sixties, possibly older. Her eyes were kind, bringing a certain beauty to her aged face. There were no signs of a plague or illness. She seemed healthy.

The woman's smile faltered at Venus's awkward hesitation.

"I'm so sorry. I didn't mean to startle you. Are you one of our visitors?" Her words were smooth, not gruff, like she was used to.

"Visitor?" Venus repeated and cringed. She knew what the word meant. She tucked her pack behind her elbows against her back awkwardly.

"Of the Starlit Inn." The woman waved an arm to encompass the wooden building and the surrounding area. "It's embroidered on your bag, though I don't recognize the logo."

Venus squinted at her, trying to comprehend what she meant. Then it hit her. The stitching on the canvas. "Oh," she said, her voice cracking. Her mouth was dry. She cleared her throat. "Yes. Starlit Station." Her grandfather mentioned the station was defunct shortly after he'd arrived at the Genesis Colony. As far as his understanding went, no one survived the plague.

The woman sent her a confused look, which cleared as fast as it appeared. "I see. You must be one of *those* visitors. I'm the owner, Maggie Benson. I've been away for a while, so my apologies for not greeting you yet." Her eyes narrowed at Venus's discomfort. "Has your stay been comfortable, Miss—?"

"Venus. I—I've only just arrived."

Maggie clapped her hands. "Excellent. Then let's get you registered."

Venus followed several steps behind Maggie, who led her around the building to a different side. There, a set of double glass doors automatically opened upon their arrival.

She studied them as she walked through. They didn't creak like the space station's old metal doors did. The doors jerked back into the wall when she touched them. Curious. It wasn't something she'd expected from a wooden building.

Logs lined the walls on the inside as well. The red squares on the floor gleamed, making the space warm. The color made her smile. She was so used to white, gray, and black as the only hues.

She stared at the large room. A few people relaxed around a blazing fire on cushioned seats. A well-decorated tree sparkled with lights to one side of the sitting area, a silver gleaming star topping it high above the main floor. Music, *real music*, drifted above the drone of voices. It had been years since she'd heard anything so lovely.

"Coming?" Maggie asked, a wide grin on her face. She held out an arm in welcome and invitation, pointing to a partitioned section where two people typed away at a computer similar to the one her grandfather had. Something trilled, and one of the uniformed people picked up a device, held it to their ear, and spoke into it.

"Um—okay." Venus stumbled over her words. She glanced around, searching for places she might hide if it came to that. Old habits died hard. But one thing she needed to know right away. "What year is it?" she asked, eying the incredible building. Everything she saw overwhelmed her, from the melodious sounds to the scent of fresh air and the cheery colors. It was everything and more than her grandfather's descriptions could paint in her mind.

Several emotions flashed across Maggie's face. Her smile faltered before clicking back in place. She took a moment before speaking. "It's the Christmas season. December 15, 2060."

Venus's sight dimmed, and she stumbled. *Seventy-five years?* How had she traveled back so far in the past? She gulped.

Maggie put her arm around Venus's shoulders. "Breathe. It will all be okay. You're in the right place, I promise."

Venus allowed the woman to lead her while she blindly fought back alarm and incredulity. A side glance at Maggie's calm face gave her enough strength to pull herself together. Her grandfather had been correct. His transporter worked. She wished she could've traveled with him, though. He always maintained there would never be enough power for more than one person to use it at a time. And after the Commander had taken him, there had been no way to rescue him.

She shook off the thoughts and emotions, something she was used to doing, having watched the Commander destroy the colony for too many years.

Venus's surroundings slowly came back to her. The elegant room with framed pictures and decorated side tables was charming—idyllic. Nothing on the space station, where bare rooms and metal ruled, looked like this. This place was warm and alluring. Venus stood back while Maggie approached the two uniformed people behind the half wall.

Someone bumped into Venus's arm. "I'm so sorry. My suitcase isn't cooperating." A distracted man muttered without looking at her directly.

She stared at him, not saying anything.

When he glanced up, his gaze transfixed her. He had the most beautiful pair of blue eyes she'd ever witnessed. His smile was just as handsome. "My apologies. I'm running late and wasn't looking." He bowed and took off, his suitcase's wheel wobbling, sending the bag sideways again.

Maggie patted her arm as she greeted a woman on the right, bringing Venus's attention from the man back to her. The other man still spoke into the device held to his ear while he tapped on the keyboard.

Venus's attention wandered, though the man was no longer in view, and she missed what the two women spoke about. Her mind spun. Maybe she was unconscious, and this was all a dream. However, she'd never be able to come up with something so grand in her wildest imagination. She definitely wouldn't dream up such a good-looking man.

"Venus?"

"I'm sorry. What?" she asked dumbly. Inwardly, she cringed at her awkwardness. She needed to gather her wits. Her survival depended on it.

Maggie's light laugh was not condescending. "You've traveled a long way. One time, Alexander and I went on a long journey into the wild—well, out camping, and when we got back here, it took me a while to reacclimate myself." Her gaze was keen, intuitive. Somehow, Maggie knew more than she showed.

Venus swallowed what little spit she had in her mouth. "Reacclimate. Yes."

"Put her in Suite 315," Maggie told the younger woman behind the computer, handing her a card. "Charge this and add any other expenditure she has while staying here to it." Her smile was serene but brooked no argument.

Realizing what the woman was doing, Venus slid the bag off her shoulders to get the money she'd packed. "I have payment."

The woman handed Maggie the card back. "It's already been paid for. Enjoy your stay, my dear. Now, I must run. Never a dull moment." In a flash, Maggie was gone, striding down the hall and around a corner.

"Here's your key to the room." The desk woman spoke to Venus, garnering her attention. A badge on the woman's shirt read Stella. She smiled. "Suite 315. Internet code is there." A painted fingernail tapped the card cover. "Elevators are that way." She pointed down the hall and to the left—the opposite way that Maggie went. "If you have any questions at all, dial the front desk."

Venus took the plastic card with holder and gave the woman a questioning glance. Stella repeated what she'd just said, with an added "follow the signs on the wall to find your room."

Venus didn't ask for clarification. Though not well educated, her grandfather's training kicked in. *If you find yourself in a different place, act like the locals. Blend in. Don't act confused or it will make them too curious.* "Thank you," she mumbled.

From what she gathered, she needed to find the elevators. She'd used them once upon a time on the space station before they'd shut down the loading dock. She understood the term. Her mind was far too scattered to take everything in fully. She moved away, and a couple with their children stepped up to be helped by Stella. The young boy sent her a shy grin, which reminded her so much of her grandfather's crooked smile that she had to turn away.

"I can do this," she whispered to herself as she walked past the sitting area with its bright fireplace and the fancy tree stacked full of colorful decorations. Finding a room to stay in couldn't be that difficult. It had been her job on the station, finding places to hide. She clutched her bag to her chest and made her way to the elevator.

chapter
three

VENUS ENTERED the elevator with several others, the music from the main entry room muting as the group entered. She tried to make herself as small as possible in the back of the square space.

"Floors?" asked a perky woman in a fluffy white and pink coat and matching pants. She glanced at Venus's card, pressed the number three, and smiled.

"Are you an alien?" she asked.

"That's an offensive term to use. And if she were a visitor from another country, she mightn't understand your question," said a frowning man to her right. His mustache twitched.

Venus knew from her grandfather's lessons that she'd be an "alien" to Earthlings, people born on Earth. She'd been born on the space station, so Venus nodded but said nothing.

The doors shut, and the elevator's slight jerk startled Venus. It was moving up, not sideways like the station's elevators. A ding sounded when it started, and Venus glanced at the blinking number one and clutched the metal handrail. It felt familiar in her hand.

"She's obviously not from around here. Just look at her pale skin and spiky haircut. And those clothes. Aren't they the newest look out of Paris? Maybe she's from Europe." The woman's smile was warm despite her insulting words. "She probably doesn't know English." She smiled at Venus again.

Fit in, Venus told herself. She nodded back at the woman, who was oblivious to her unease. It wouldn't do to argue with anyone when Venus didn't know what rules she'd break or how they punished people here. Another ding and the elevator shifted. She clutched the handrail tighter. The blinking number changed to two.

The door opened, and the others got off. Venus took a deep breath, relishing the ease with which she inhaled despite the fear clutching her chest. With a swish, the door shut behind them, leaving Venus alone on the elevator. Floor three blinked, the elevator dinged, and the doors opened again. She stepped off.

The wall signs pointed her to the left and down the hall. Each door had a number beside it. Pictures decorated the spaces between rooms, and overhead lights bathed the area in a warm glow. It was silent except for an errant voice leaking from behind the walls. She reached the door that had 315 beside it and glanced at the card. How did it work?

She touched the door and found it to be locked. Stepping back, Venus surveyed the square on the handle. There weren't any instructions in sight. She set her bag on the floor and put a hand on her hip.

"Need help?"

Venus jerked in surprise and found an elderly gentleman in a neat shirt and slacks walking down the hallway. His dark skin and facial features reminded her of her grandfather. Her grandfather, though, had a full head of gray hair while this man was bald, his skin and age spots shining beneath the lights. Something in his gentle brown eyes drew her to him. "Yes, please."

He took her card and held it up. "When I was younger, they had keys. Now they use these infernal cards. Half the time they don't work. You need to put this end down the slot with the strip at the back." He pointed to the side with triangle arrows on it and the long black stripe. "Then pull it out quick to get the green light to come on." A small green light flashed below the handle. He twisted it and opened the door for her. "And there you go." He handed her the card back. "Let the front desk know if you have trouble. They'll get you another card." His voice was low and warm, a balm to her raw soul.

She blinked back tears. "Thank you."

"Anytime. May God bless you." He grinned, nodded, and continued his jaunt down the hallway and into a different room.

Venus stood for a second longer but turned her attention to her room. Rustic wood boards framed a large living space with a couch, cushioned chairs, television, and a fireplace. In front of a large window stood another decorated tree, like the one in the entryway. Lights blinked merrily from the limbs. A small kitchen area with a refrigerator opened up to her left. The space was incredible. But where was the bed?

The door closed by itself when she let it go. It slid shut with a click, shutting out the world beyond it. Venus's knees buckled, and she collapsed to the floor. Trembling, she allowed the grief and shock to sink in now that no one was there to watch her break down. The two reminders of her beloved grandfather had been a stab to her heart.

She'd left him behind. Left her entire world behind. She was a stranger in a strange land. It had sounded like a better option on the station. And deep down, she knew it was. But nothing here was the same. Like a falling star, her blazing path through the darkness ended in the light, burning her out even as she landed safely. But how would she survive without her grandfather to help her?

She curled around her bag and wept.

After her tears had dried, Venus gathered her wits about her and explored the suite. It was triple the size of her grandfather's barracks and much larger than her hiding spaces among the station's inner walls that she kept to most of the time. The bedroom was around the kitchen, past a dining table, and through another doorway. Beside the enormous bed and through another doorway was the bathroom. A single bathroom, not the dormitory ones on the station. It was decadent.

The outdoorsy decor was welcoming and warm, and every surface sparkled. She tossed her bag on the bed, relishing a good night's sleep in an actual bed, not on pilfered rags in a vent. But later. She was too hyped up to try now.

Back in the main area, a basket of food sat in the middle of the table. It held two muffins, two packs of microwave popcorn, and two individually wrapped packs of chocolate chip cookies. Beside it was another container with tea bags and coffee pods, along with sugar, salt, and pepper packets. The popcorn fascinated her the most. She knew of corn but had never heard of a popping corn.

Venus took everything out and then put it back exactly as it was originally. Was it for her or was it simply a decoration, like the adorned trees?

She left it behind to inspect the kitchen and then the living area. A wide window overlooked a patio area below with tables, chairs, and a brick fireplace. Someone had shoveled snow from the space, which sat in piles around the edges, leaving the furniture clean. It was very cozy and appealing. She spun in a circle. "This is all for me?" She'd never had so much room before. A binder on the table explained how to use the television, the electric fireplace, and everything in the kitchen. Luckily, she understood mechanics enough to work the antique appliances.

A thump resounded from the bedroom area.

Startled, Venus stood in place for a few seconds to catch her breath. Then she carefully made her way back to the bedroom where the sound originated. Possibly her bag had fallen off the bed. Sunlight shone in from the bedroom window to reveal her bag still on the bed.

However, on the floor was a black book. It had fallen with its spine to the floor and lay open. She picked it up and read a highlighted section, *"Ephesians 2:19, Consequently, you are no longer foreigners and strangers, but fellow citizens with God's people and also members of his household."*

Venus dropped the book like it stung her. It fell back to the floor, the pages askew beneath it. The title of the book on the front made chills rush across her skin. *Holy Bible.* Her grandfather had owned this book a long time ago. It was the first experiment they'd tossed into the transporter when she'd been too little to know the dangers of having a machine that could collapse time and space.

She hugged herself as she studied the innocent-looking book. Could it be? She stooped to pick it up and looked inside the cover. Her grandfather's name, Joseph R. Bolt, was elegantly written above her name, Venus Bolt, which she had penned in her childish scrawl.

"How?" A sob escaped her as she hugged the book like she wished she could hold her grandfather once again.

A knock sounded from the other room.

Venus wiped her face dry. She placed the book on the side table and walked to the entry door.

Another knock. "Room service."

Her grandfather used to tease the residents on Genesis Colony that he was "room service" when he'd fix something. She opened the door to a man in a uniform with a cart full of covered trays. His name tag read *Reggie*.

She glanced down the hallway both ways. "Can I help you?"

"Compliments from the owner. Mrs. Maggie hopes you enjoy her picks and that you find your accommodations acceptable," Reggie said as he handed her a tray full of food and covered drinks.

"Oh." She took the tray from him. "Please give her my thanks." Venus heard her grandfather's voice in her head as she spoke. It was something he would've said. Reggie nodded and wheeled the cart back toward the elevators.

She carried the tray over to the table and set it down. She

noticed a card tucked beneath a ceramic mug. Venus plucked it out and read it. "Please forgive me for assuming you needed a pick-me-up. Call me if you need anything." Below the note was a number.

Venus had heard of phones, of course. The old-timers on the station would talk about the good old days where telephones would always come up in conversation. They had a comms box for speaking room to room on the station and an overhead comms unit the Commander used to order them about.

She shook her head to rid herself of the painful memories. The food smelled delicious. Her stomach gurgled in anticipation, and she sat down to enjoy it. She lifted the lid and found a bowl of creamy-looking soup, a sandwich, and a pickle spear. The chunky soup steamed, so Venus bit into the sandwich instead. She groaned with pleasure. "I don't know what I did to deserve this."

Before she knew it, she'd finished the meal, including the lettuce leaf placed beneath the pickle. Venus couldn't remember when she'd had so much to eat, and dehydrated food certainly didn't taste this good. Her stomach bulged, almost painfully so, but she didn't regret it. She moaned as she stood and went to the bedroom to lie down. Sated, she was drowsy, and the bed was incredibly soft and, best of all, warm. With a deep sigh, Venus sank beneath the fluffy, red and white checked comforter and immediately fell to sleep.

chapter
four

BRIGHT MORNING SUNLIGHT woke Venus the next morning. Startled, she jumped out of bed before she realized the glare wasn't flashing emergency lights. Her heart thudded uncomfortably in her chest, and she sat back down on the warm spot she'd just vacated.

She wasn't on the station. It was safe here. It took a moment to sink in.

Hands on her head, she waited for the panic to die down before heading to the bathroom. She used the soap provided in the shower and cleaned up, appreciating the hot water and the thick, fluffy towels when drying off. A search of the storage units revealed a hair dryer. It was a luxury. Her grandfather had built a dryer from errant pieces from the station when she'd been a child with long hair. She plugged it in and relished the heated, blowing air drying her spiky brown hair. Cut close to her scalp to hide her identity, it didn't take long to dry.

A glance at her clothes revealed how dingy they were next to the gleaming room. That, along with the cold weather, assured her she needed something more consequential to wear. She put the jumpsuit back on, along with her boots.

Her grandfather's planning had ensured she had cash, but she wasn't completely sure how that worked. He had explained to her long ago that tokens worked differently than cash. Money wasn't status-based, with complicated levels of transactional exchanges. Should she try to call Maggie? The binder did not explain how to *dial* a number when there clearly wasn't any sort of dial on the instrument that she could find. She preferred to speak to Maggie in person, anyway.

Venus tucked the card in her jumpsuit's pocket and took a few of the bills out of the cash to stash them beside the card. With a deep breath, she opened the door and headed back out into the great unknown.

Emptiness greeted her in the hallway. Silence followed her to the elevators. She pushed the only button on the wall, the down button, as she'd seen others do the night before. It took a couple of minutes, but the elevator arrived, the beeping sound now familiar. She entered, and the doors shut. Nothing happened.

With a start, Venus realized she needed to push the numbered button on the side panel. She braced herself against the handrail when it jerked into motion. Music spilled in when the door opened to the entry area. People milled around the sitting area and fireplace, talking and enjoying refreshments. She put on her brave face and stepped off the elevator.

Scents of food drifted in the air, teasing her with tantalizing aromas. Venus stopped to take in the area, which she hadn't had the presence of mind to pay attention to when she arrived. Photos lined the walls, depicting the Starlit Inn through the years. Many changes had transpired as the pictures flowed down the wall, including a renovation adding a second and third floor to the original Inn. One photo depicted a younger Maggie smiling brightly. Venus couldn't believe the state of the Inn, which had been around for decades.

Each photo showed a progression of betterment and technology improvements, unlike the Starlighter Star Station One. The station had only been operational for seventy-five years, fifteen years before the plague, and it had been falling apart since

Ridenour had assumed control. Maggie was a caretaker, like Venus's grandfather had been.

Turning from the photos, Venus followed another short hallway where a cafeteria opened up. Several groups sat around tables, conversing and having breakfast. A bright light glowed from overhead bulbs, bringing a cheerful vibe to the area.

"Good morning." A young girl in a uniform smiled at her. "I'm Amber. The buffet is open for another half hour. Coffee and drinks are on your right. Hot food is in the center, with the cold to your left. Let me know if you need anything."

Venus stared at her. She'd never eaten in the cafeteria on the station. She was used to rations and her grandfather pocketing extra portions for her.

"Do you have a question?" Amber asked, her brow furrowed.

The mantra, fit in, echoed in her mind. "Do I pay?"

Amber shook her head. "It's included with your stay here at the Starlit Inn. Enjoy."

All of it? Venus made a wide circle around the stations, speechless at so many choices. So much food. She watched as others came, filled their plates, and left. There were even a few who came back for seconds, something unheard of on the station. She made her move, taking a little of everything. Since most all the adults visited the coffee machine endlessly, she tried that as well.

The milk was heavenly, differing from the tasteless, rehydrated dry powder she was used to. It was especially delightful in the coffee, toning down the strong flavor. Everything was delicious, and Venus only stopped when she couldn't eat another bite without bursting.

Sitting alone at the table at the back allowed her to blend into the wall and afforded her the luxury of watching others. No one seemed to pay much attention to her, which she was grateful for. The people all spoke with smoother syllables, their words coming out quickly. Since she'd arrived at the Inn, she'd spoken more than she normally did to anyone except her grandfather. Her breath caught at the thought of him. How could she have forgotten?

"Excuse me, may I join you?" a deep voice asked.

Venus glanced up to see the older gentleman who'd helped her unlock the door to her room. Swallowing back her sorrow, she plastered on a smile and nodded.

Amber had cleared her table and was making a circuitous path around the dining room, cleaning other tables.

"I don't know about you, but I hate eating alone. Luckily, I got in line just before they started breaking it down," he said. He set his tray on the tabletop. He'd piled his plate high with eggs, sausage, and biscuits with gravy. Had she not been painfully full, it would've still been tempting for her to go back again. "By the way, I owe you an apology. I didn't introduce myself yesterday. My name is Michael Vincent."

Venus glanced at his outstretched hand, recalling the gesture from her childhood. She gingerly placed her hand in his. "I'm Venus Bolt."

He bowed over his food and silently murmured.

She couldn't help but stare at him.

A sheepish smile traveled across one side of his lips. "Sorry, I pray blessings on my meals. At my age, it's the only thing keeping me alive." His laugh was infectious.

They sat in companionable silence as Michael ate. Venus was unsure what subject to broach with him. He was neat and clean, leaving no dregs of gravy behind. He ate almost as quickly as Venus had, finishing mere minutes later. Then, with a satisfied sigh, he sat back and sipped his black coffee.

"So, Venus Bolt. I detect an accent. Possibly Eastern European mixed with some American. Where does your family hail from?" His brown eyes were kind and open.

What could she tell him? Did she say she was from another time and a different place? Her grandfather had been in North America when he'd joined the Starlit Station. She never paid much attention to Earth geography or history, though. There'd never been a reason to know it.

Amber stopped to clear Michael's dishes. After she left, Venus answered in the most honest way she knew how. "I'm not from here. I come from a great distance. Where do you *hail* from?" She reused his turn of phrase, hoping to mimic him well enough to not seem as alien as she truly was.

"From the South. I've moved a lot in my life. Was in the service, so we, my wife and kids, traveled all around thanks to my assignments. When I retired from the military, I became involved with a civilian space program here in Bethel."

That piqued her curiosity. "What space program?" The Starlit Space Station had been the biggest operational station working in the northern American hemisphere when her grandfather evacuated. However, she wasn't aware it had been around for so long.

"We were mostly involved with satellites and ground-to-air communications. I was more of a grunt worker than anything, though I know there were some top-secret goings on. It wasn't something I dirtied my hands in." Michael took another sip of his steaming coffee. "How about you? What kind of work have you done?"

Venus's throat closed. She coughed to keep from choking.

"Oh dear, I didn't mean to upset you." Michael's hand covered her clenched fingers.

She shook her head. "I followed my grandfather into maintenance. He just—" Did she tell a stranger about her grandfather's situation? No, that was unacceptable. She swallowed back coffee flavored spit. "Died."

"I'm so sorry for your loss. It's always hard losing someone around the holiday season. Christmas especially. Do you have other family to celebrate with?" His gentle words stung, though she knew he didn't mean them to.

"No. Grandfather was my only family." She used one of her extra napkins and wiped the moisture from her eyes.

"That makes it doubly hard." He let out a deep breath. "This is my first Christmas without my beloved wife, Sheila. Oh, but she loved to decorate. We'd moved into a retirement village a couple of years ago, downsizing from our last home, where we raised our youngest son." He chuckled. "I had to build a small shack for Sheila to house her holiday containers." Michael lowered his head. "I miss her so much."

Venus's heart ached for him. "I'm so sorry. But you have your sons, right?"

He sniffed and gave her a sad smile. "They're both gone as well. My youngest died when he followed my example and went into the service. He died seven years ago in the line of duty. My older son lost his battle with cancer when he was eleven."

She sat back in her chair, staggered by his loss.

"But God." Michael's face cleared and a sedate smile creased his worn face. "I wouldn't have made it through any of that had I not known Jesus. He gave me the strength, and continues every day, to know this world is not the last place I'll see my family."

Venus's mind spun. Her space station had been another world, separate from Earth. "In what other world will you see them again?"

"Have you not heard? God sent his Son Jesus, Who died on a cross so you can have eternal life. Believe in Him, and your sins can be forgiven. Then you, too, will share in that paradise." Michael's face lit up, the sadness leaving his eyes.

Her grandfather's lessons from her early years whispered through her mind. He'd talk of God and Jesus in such exuberant terms. She longed to speak to him one more time. Ask him about this other place.

Another thought entered her mind. "How do you get to this world? Is there a portal to it?"

A thoughtful expression crossed Michael's face. "Not unless you count death as the portal to Heaven. But, no. The only way is through Jesus."

chapter
five

VENUS APPROACHED the front desk after Michael left to go skiing, wanting to inquire where she could do some clothes shopping. Two new people worked behind the desks, which was a relief since they wouldn't know how awkward she'd been when she arrived yesterday.

A middle-aged woman glanced up, her colorful jewelry standing out against the Starlit Inn's navy blue uniform. A friendly, though detached, smile spread across her bright red lips. "How can I help you?"

"I need to shop. Where would that be possible? How do I get there?" Heat pricked her scalp, but she powered past her hesitant insecurity. She needed warmer clothes, and allowing herself to cower at her new circumstances would get her nowhere.

"I can call for a driver or you can wait to take our van into town. They make stops every half an hour at the Visitor's Center. It's within walking distance of the various tourist destinations throughout town. The van will be here"—she glanced at a clock on the wall—"in ten minutes. You can wait inside or on a bench outside. It's free. Of course, a driver would cost you a small fee." The woman spoke as if from memory, having said this enough times to not have to think about it before speaking.

Venus flexed her hands to relieve her stress. "I'll wait for the van."

The woman nodded toward the glass double doors as a trilling ring broke out. "It's a white van with the Inn's name on the side. It's hard to miss. Enjoy your shopping." She picked up the receiver dismissively.

Since she had to wait, Venus wandered over to the fireplace, now devoid of any guests sitting around it. Piped music filled the silence, broken by the crackling of the fire. Upon closer inspection, she realized it wasn't a real log and fire. They'd had a couple of fires on the space station. With no means of escaping, it had terrified anyone close by. This wasn't anything like that.

She bent to study the fire closer and reached out a hand toward the glass enclosure. It exuded heat, the flames a simulation. The wonders of Earth didn't cease. A screech broke the quiet. A dark blue transport van parked outside of the front doors. Venus hurried to get to it before it departed again. Exhaust clogged the air, reminding Venus of working on the colony.

The door of the van folded open, and an overweight man smiled down at her. "Welcome. I'm going to take a quick break, only a couple of minutes, and I'll be back again to take you to the Center."

Venus entered and found a seat in the middle to sit and wait for the driver to return. The rumble of the van beneath her brought a fresh wave of anxiety. She flipped her room key over and over in her hands. Warm air circulated around the inside of the vehicle, helping to ease some of her stress. A few others entered the van and distractedly found their own seats. Finally, the driver returned, shut the door, and put the van into gear.

She braced herself, supposing it would be like the elevator and surprise her. The van bounced and, with a muted squeak, moved. The motion made her scramble to remain sitting, but no one else reacted to the movement. She concentrated on the seat in front of her, and before she knew it, the brakes squealed again and the van slowed to a stop.

All the riders stood, so she followed their example. In an orderly fashion, they disembarked.

Outside of the van, Venus studied her surroundings. Brick buildings lined a paved road. Decorative lights in snowflake shapes ran above the streets, attached to poles along the sidewalks. Music streamed out of speakers attached to the snowflake lights. The riders walked off in different directions, confusing her. Which way should she go?

"If you go that way, you'll find more bargain stores and mom-and-pop eateries." The driver appeared next to her. His voice was good-natured, like he was used to making friends everywhere he went. He pointed to their right, where Venus spied smaller shops. "Down that way are the more trendy tourist stores and pricier restaurants." He pointed left. "Pick your poison."

A joke? She nodded, unsure. However, his tone hinted favorably toward the bargain area. "Thank you."

A bright sun glittered off painted windows, depicting seasonal greetings along the walkway. Like the food in the cafeteria that morning, it was all overwhelming. They'd had one place on the station to receive new items—the commissary. Everything she owned, her grandfather had found for her or she'd taken extras from other colony residents. She'd never purchased anything in her life. For a moment, panic bloomed, and she hoped she brought enough Earth cash to cover what she needed.

With that thought, she entered the first clothing store she came across.

Four hours later, and Venus had traversed both sides of Bethel and had made an astonishing discovery—her grandfather had been well-off according to Earth standards. Each bill was a hundred of Earth's dollars, and she was now the proud owner of a new wardrobe.

The driver snickered at her when he opened the folding door. "I see you found what you were looking for?"

"Your world has too many options." She bit the inside of her cheek after the slip, her tongue having grown loose in conversing with several store employees. But the driver didn't seem to notice. Possibly, he also thought she was an "alien" and didn't fully understand the language.

"My wife has the same problem. Why buy one shirt you love when you can get it in every color?" He reached out for her bags. "Here, let me help you."

Taken aback, she released the bigger of the bags, which contained shoes, and allowed him to put them behind his seat.

———

Later that evening, as the sun sank below the horizon, Venus finished organizing the clothes and accessories she had purchased. Her mind still whirred at the ease with which she made the exchanges. She chose a soft blue sweater the saleswoman told her went beautifully with her alabaster skin and dark hair. It was warm and comfortable, unlike the thin polypropylene jumpsuit.

Her thoughts turned to her grandfather and what his life must've been like before the plague hit. He'd been her age when he'd left for Mars Sector Nine and Genesis Colony. He'd lived his entire childhood on an Earth that was embroiled in political strife on all continents. Famine, war, and disease were rampant.

Venus sat on the cushioned lounge chair and watched the burning orange ball of light disappear into deep hues of purple and blue until the forest beyond the Inn swallowed the sun completely.

Her grandfather had mentioned how he thought the station would be his sanctuary from all the upheaval and lunacy of humanity. She hugged a pillow to her chest to realize the colony had been just as sinister.

How did one reconcile the darkness of humanity with the kindness like she'd experienced today with the driver and with Michael sharing breakfast with her? She needed her grandfather to help her make sense of everything.

Thunk!

Venus jumped at the sudden noise. It was a repeat of the previous evening and the Bible. Slowly, she rose and went to the bedroom. The Bible remained on the nightstand. However, there was another book on the floor, spine down and pages spread open. This wasn't a printed book, but more like a notebook with pages full of handwriting.

She glanced around but found nothing to explain how a strange book that hadn't been there ten minutes before was there now. "But I searched the entire room when I put away my clothes," she muttered, her chest tight.

Ghosts? Being a scientist, her grandfather didn't believe in them when the others would tell tales. He'd claimed there was always an explanation for everything. Even God.

She turned on the bedroom light before creeping closer to the book. The handwriting looked familiar. A step nearer verified what her mind said couldn't be happening. It was one of her grandfather's journals. She reached out but hesitated, drawing her hand back to her chest. "How?" Her voice came out choked.

It couldn't be! But it was.

Carefully, she flipped the book over, revealing the doodles her grandfather had made on the cover. Mathematical equations. Scientific symbols. And his name in large letters on the top right-hand side. She turned it over to find the stick person she'd drawn on the back one day when he wasn't watching her close enough. Tears slid down her face and dripped onto the carpet. "I can't believe it."

She cradled it to her chest as she rocked back and forth, her mind and heart warring with the validity of the occurrence. "Stop it," she growled at herself. "If you can travel millions of miles through a transporter, so can books."

Venus took the journal to the living space to read. Was there a clue in the books? Venus started on page one, where her grandfather had journaled his theory of using quantum physics, distal and proximal space, and black matter, pertaining to collapsing distance in space travel. She stared at the book. "I don't understand a word of that." She flipped through a small section where her grandfather had created graphs and drawn scientific calculation images. The neat penmanship ended a tenth of the way through the journal.

"April 1, 2073," she read the haphazardly scrawled heading. *"Not an April Fool's Joke! This is the Day the Earth Died."* Venus frowned. "What's that supposed to mean?"

Shaking her head, she read on about the plague—MRS6L— its consequences, and how he made his way from MIT where he worked in Cambridge, Massachusetts, to Bethel, Virginia, traveling via a cargo ship. He'd transported what equipment he could move with him and traveled a week down the coastline to get to the Starlit Station, where the only functional space station was situated. *"The fires are everywhere. It's anarchy. The plague-ridden die, and the unaffected aren't to be trusted. Everyone is out for themselves, their own safety. It looks like the end of civilization as I know it."*

Venus sat back and pondered her grandfather's journey to Bethel and her experience since she'd transported to Earth. Earth before and after the plague were two different worlds, just as the space station differed immensely from Earth. She glanced out the window at the dark sky. This Bethel was not the one he knew.

Shortly after her grandfather had settled in Bethel, the United States fell. *"Not for lack of resources,"* she read his notes. *"The government gave up and, like the population, put their own safety above the good of the whole. What a fool's folly! I'll take my chances in the stars where technology and innovation have joined to form a new sanctuary. There, I'll pursue the ultimate experiment by folding black matter and energy while in space. It will put H. G. Wells to shame."*

"Who was H. G. Wells?" she murmured, reading on. More calculations and paragraphs full of complicated and confusing writing filled the pages.

She flipped through, searching for anything that made sense again. On the last page, she found a note from her grandfather.

"Today, God has given me a reason to live again. My joy. I'm naming her Venus after my granny."

Her pulse quickened. He'd only spoken to her once about the day he'd found her in the lab. An accident had killed the lab tech, and her grandfather had gone to make repairs to a digital radiography machine. He'd told her once that his faith in life and God had restarted that day.

He'd hidden her in his quarters, sneaking her around the space colony in unobtrusive places when he had maintenance duty, and it had worked until the coup. That was the day grandfather cut her hair and told her not to speak unless it was to him. "Act mute, and if they find you, they'll leave you alone," he'd told her.

Her heart ached with longing. For the first time since coming to Earth, it grew hard to breathe. She bowed her head. Grandfather had been a fit man for his age, almost ninety. He'd stayed fit for her. But now she saw a younger version of him in the pages. He had been bright and optimistic before leaving Earth. The colony had worn him down. It had worn her down too.

With sadness clogging her throat, she turned to the last page and the final paragraph. His penmanship differed, as if he'd written it in a hurry. *"So, despite my discouraged state, I still trust in God, the Keeper of the Stars. I pray this journal finds its way to the one who needs it the most."*

Venus didn't know science or quantum physics, but somehow the journal had done exactly what her grandfather had wanted. It had landed in her hands.

chapter
six

THE NEXT MORNING, Venus was excited to head down for breakfast. She hoped to find Michael there. However he was nowhere to be found. Her meal passed along with two more cups of the aromatic coffee. Her stomach was full to overflowing when she decided it was time to explore the Inn's property.

Venus stopped at the front desk, where a new front desk clerk typed away on the computer. "Hello. I was wondering if there are any activities to do around the Inn?"

The uniformed woman without a name tag handed her a pamphlet. "This is a list of the local tourist attractions." She unfolded the colorful pages. "There are several ski resorts you can visit, along with a Christmas Cocoa and Cookies tour."

Her head swam from so many options.

"The Christmas Cocoa and Cookies tour is what I came for." A voice came from behind her.

Venus moved to the side to see who had spoken. It was the man who had bumped into her. Not frazzled this time, he wore a long overcoat, jeans, and boots. A knit hat matching the coat sat atop brunet hair, which curled over the hat's brim. His piercing eyes held her in their grasp before letting her go to glance at the front desk woman, who smiled warmly back at him.

"Sorry, I didn't mean to interrupt. It's just I'm in town with a group of teenagers I'm supposed to entertain. That tour you mentioned is on a hayrack ride, isn't it?" His smile was genuine and easy. Attractive.

Venus danced from foot to foot as her heart fluttered at meeting him again.

"Yes. They have blankets for the goers to use if it gets too cold or it snows. My sister and her family usually rent it once a season, and they love it." The clerk's wide smile showed her interest in him.

Venus glanced down at herself, self-consciously. The clothes she wore were all the new ones from the shopping trip she'd taken yesterday. The colorful array had made her happy, though she now realized they didn't match like this man's outfit. Glancing up, she realized no one was as boldly dressed as she was. She'd need to make a note for future purchases to be more deliberate with the color choices.

She wrapped her arms around her middle, scrunching the polyester jacket she wore. The knit hat with its fuzzy ball on top itched against her scalp.

The man swung his glance at her. He was young—around her same age—if she had to guess. "We'll be going tonight. It's a small group, but I'm sure we have room for one more if you want to join us."

Her tongue froze inside her mouth, and she ended up stuttering instead of speaking smoothly like the other Earthlings. "O-okay." Warmth spread from the center of her being.

"I'll leave a message at the front desk here for you—" He stopped and waited, his amber eyes sparkling.

The front desk woman frowned at her.

She realized he was asking for her name. "Oh, Venus Bolt."

"Nice to meet you, Venus Bolt. I'm Jeremiah Hunter, but my friends call me Jeremy. Now, I must go or I'll be late. See you later." He left in a swirl of cologne-scented air that made the hair rise on the back of her arms. She caught herself staring long after he was gone. Heat flushed her cheeks, and she rushed outside to let the cold air cool them down.

What just happened?

"Ah, there you are, Venus. I'm sorry I was late for breakfast today."

Venus glanced up to find Michael. She couldn't help but to smile. "It wasn't the same without you."

He stood behind her and just outside of the double glass doors, pulling black leather gloves over his hands. They matched the leather jacket he wore. The coat had an Army patch sewn over his heart, and several other patches lined the sleeves.

He grunted a laugh. "Quieter is my guess. I must say how lovely you look today in that outfit. Reminds me of my wife Sheila's fashion. She was bold and daring in her choices. Her wardrobe was rich with different colors and patterns." His eyes glittered before he blinked, and the moisture was gone. "So, what are your plans for the day?"

Venus warmed with his compliment. She looked around, wringing her hands encapsulated in gloves she bought yesterday. "I'm not sure. I was hoping to explore." She glanced into the distance as if she could find the answer in the snow-covered trees.

"There's a group of us taking a van ride through the countryside, you know, visiting all the local artisans' shops. You could join us if you want to."

As he spoke, a group of people, both men and women, came through the door. Everyone was bundled up in warm jackets, boots, hats, and gloves. Their conversation and laughter filled the air.

Venus stepped aside, a rare pulse of excitement rushing through her. She wanted to go out. Doing so alone was intimidating. And lonely. She'd been lonely a long time and had always wished for a chance to join the groups on the station. Venus was determined to take advantage of it. "Thank you. I think I will."

Hours later and as the sun lowered in the sky, Venus entered the cargo van first while the others lingered outside the chocolate shop, finishing their hot cocoas. She rested her head back against the van's chilled window. Though it was cool outside, it had been a sunny day with little wind, making it warm—especially with the arctic zone jacket she wore. She'd scrapped it earlier to keep from melting.

A few of the others on the tour entered the bus and found seats. They were all nice, but some spoke in a language she didn't understand. She smiled and closed her eyes to rest.

"May I join you?" Michael's voice drifted over the din of other voices.

She opened her eyes and scooted over. "Sure."

"It's going to take me a week to work off the calories I ate today," he said as he sat down. "Did you have a good time?"

She rearranged the hem of her coat. "I did. Thank you for inviting me."

He nudged her on the shoulder. "Still a little sad about your grandfather?"

Venus sighed and glanced out the window. "A little. I know he'd want me to be happy. I just wish he were here with us. He loved winter and snow."

"He's here in spirit. Those we love never truly leave us."

She nodded as if she agreed.

"But?"

She glanced back at Michael. "He sacrificed so much for me. I don't know that I deserve this." She waved her hand, choked up. He'd died trying to hide her from the Commander. It should've been him here on Earth, enjoying what had once been his—a healthy Earth full of things to enjoy.

"I see. You know, none of us deserve many of the things that happen to us in life, be they good or bad. It's what we do with our lives that matters. If we shine a light on others, lifting them up instead of tearing them down, it can make a difference in the lives around us."

Venus sniffed away the tears wanting to fall. "How do you do it?"

"Do what?"

"How do you stay so positive after losing everything you have?" She shifted in her seat, uncomfortable. "Today was lovely. But I keep going back to thoughts about him. And it always makes me sad. I know he'd want me to be happy. What I don't know is how to get there."

Michael patted her hand that clasped her gloves. "One of my wife's favorite scriptures is found in Proverbs, 'a joyful heart is good medicine but a crushed spirit dries up your bones.' Joy is not a feeling—it's a choice to find the things worthy in life and focus on them. Like our friendship. You've brought me much joy since we met in the hallway and you couldn't open your door. I still grieve, but I allow the joys of the day to ease the pain, and slowly, ever so slowly, joy becomes more than a choice. It is a lens through which I view life."

Venus thought about Michael's words later that afternoon, after they'd returned to the Starlit Inn, and she readied herself for another adventure with Jeremy and his group.

"Choose joy," she told her reflection in the mirror. On her face, brown spots formed across her cheeks. She ran a hand across them. "Freckles," she muttered, recalling her grandfather's term for them. He'd had some, though his skin had been almost as brown as her hair.

She'd only spent two days in the sun, and already Earth was changing her. Venus put the soft red sweater over her head, and her short hair crackled with static. She rushed to smooth it down, before remembering she wasn't on a station where static was dangerous. "Not used to washing it so often," she muttered. She pulled on a pair of insulated, black snow pants. She was glad for the warmth. The wind had picked up after she'd arrived back at the Inn. And since Michael had explained what a hayrack ride was, she knew she'd need to wear the warmest options she'd bought.

She jammed her gloves into her pockets, donned her knit hat, and took off for the lobby several minutes early to ensure she wouldn't be late.

The lobby was full of teenagers not much younger than Venus. However, they couldn't be more different from her. They were boisterous, playful, and animated. They bounced around from place to place, talking and laughing in a carefree manner.

Venus glanced around and fought the urge to head back up to her room. Right at the moment her anxiety level was at its peak, she saw Jeremy come in through the front doors. His glance went through the crowd straight to her. His smile unleashed a warmth, and her heart skipped a beat. She smiled shyly back, unzipping her coat to let out the sudden heat building inside of it.

Jeremy waved his arms and let out a piercing whistle. "Pipe down, everyone."

Sounds of voices died, though a few of the teenagers continued joking with each other.

"They canceled the event tonight due to high winds. The storm they forecasted has dipped south to include us." Groans echoed. "It can't be helped. You'll have to call your parents or guardians to get a ride home. Starlit Inn's owner has graciously offered us the use of the common room to wait until you get picked up. That means you're on your best behavior!" He yelled the last part as everyone moved out from the fireplace area to the cafeteria.

Several of the kids pulled out rectangle devices. Like the front desk man, they spoke into them. Venus watched them curiously, wondering about the gadget, though knowing they were some sort of portable comms unit.

"Venus." Jeremy appeared at her side. He smelled of the

outside and the cologne he'd been wearing from before. "I'm so sorry we had to cancel the hayrack ride. Do you need to call your parents?"

An abrupt befuddlement brought on by his nearness made her mind glitch. "My parents?" she asked, confused.

His smile was warm and welcoming, showing no signs that he caught her awkwardness. "Are you staying here at the Inn with family? You can join us in the common room if they don't mind. The group is perfectly safe."

"I—have no family."

A blank look crossed his face. "Oh. I'm so sorry."

One of the young teenage girls interrupted to ask Jeremy a question.

Too curious to leave yet, Venus walked off toward where the group was reforming in the cafeteria area. A video of someone dressed in a red and white fuzzy suit played on the television along the back wall. She stared at it, recalling her grandfather's video files he'd shown her on his computer. This screen, however, was clear and bright, not disrupted with signal strikes, as with the computers on the station because of its RPS, radio isotopic core. She watched it for several minutes, transfixed.

"Hey." Jeremy broke her out of her wonderment. "I'm sorry about what I said before. I didn't realize."

She blinked at him. Oh, right. His comment about her parents. "I had a grandfather, but he died recently. I'm here on my own."

His forehead wrinkled. "On your own. How old are you?"

She wasn't sure what age had to do with anything. "I'm twenty."

The lines on his forehead disappeared. "Oh. You look younger. I thought—" His lips pressed together. "Never mind." He was silent for a minute as they both watched the television.

"So how old are you?" Venus asked, thinking it a socially necessary question.

He grinned. "Twenty-three." The screen switched to a

snowball fight. Three boys crumpled up napkins and tossed them around mimicking the scene, spurring Jeremy to break up the mock fight.

"My apologies. Usually they're better behaved."

She snickered, recalling witnessing actual fights between the cadets and the colony residents. They'd been violent, and she'd been glad to watch them from the safety of the vent systems she hid inside. "I've seen much worse."

Another rambunctious encounter broke out with four teens sitting around one of the dining tables. Jeremy mumbled another apology before storming off to attend to it.

The small group grew as Jeremy wrangled the restless kids, and parents showed up. Jeremy's attention focused on matching everyone and marking everyone as safely passed to parents.

Though she wanted to stay and talk with Jeremy, it turned unruly. After several moments of trying to blend in with the background, Venus slipped out to head back to her room. Though she craved being with people, she was still unused to noisy encounters.

Wind batted against the windows when she let the door slide shut behind her. She stripped off her coat and hat and made her way over to the binder to re-familiarize herself with the remotes. That done, she turned on the TV and, gathering a blanket, sat back to enjoy the spectacle of cable television.

chapter
seven

VENUS WOKE the next morning on the couch, the small blanket having fallen to the floor. Orange sunlight poured in from the windows. Curiously, the television was off. She didn't remember shutting it off.

Yawning, the last thing she remembered was watching a show where you could buy items and get them shipped to you in time for Christmas. Space had pirates who moved between starships and colonies who traded goods. But it was unheard-of to order something and have it shipped to you within days.

Earthlings didn't realize how good they had it. Which made her wonder once again at how they had destroyed themselves so carelessly. Greed and power, her grandfather had declared. Still, her mind couldn't fathom it.

Venus readied and headed down to breakfast in a new outfit. It was a decadent feeling to wear different clothes each day. A few tables were open, the rest full of families and couples happily eating to the piped-in music she learned from the previous evening was Christmas tunes.

She listened to the words of the songs as she ate, slower this time to not eat so much as to give herself a stomachache again. Since food was readily available, there wasn't a reason to gorge

269

herself as if the next meal wouldn't come. Her second cup of milk and sugar-laced coffee was halfway finished by the time Michael strolled into the room, eyeing the food.

She smiled and then froze. Jeremy accompanied him.

A laughing Jeremy joined Michael, and soon they both had full plates. Michael gazed around to search for an empty chair when their gazes locked.

A zing flew through her body. Her table only had one other chair, so she didn't anticipate the men sitting with her, though they headed her way. Since she'd finished, Venus piled everything on the tray and prepared to leave so they could have her table.

Michael reached her before she stood. "Don't leave. We'll just pull another chair over." He motioned to Jeremy, who grinned at her.

Her breath caught in her chest. What was it about this man that made her react this way? It was as if she held a live wire every time he was around. "Oh. Okay."

Jeremy stopped a young boy on his way to get a third chair and pointed at them. Her heart thudded hard in her chest. Had she done something wrong?

The boy came over and took Venus's dirty tray piled with dishes with a distracted smile and an "I'll get those out of your way."

Venus relaxed and took a bracing sip of her coffee, wondering how long it would take to acclimate herself as Maggie had mentioned on her first day there.

Michael made himself comfortable immediately and sat patiently, waiting for Jeremy to slide a chair over from another table that wasn't being used. When Jeremy finally settled in, he and Michael both bowed their heads.

Jeremy spoke. "Lord, fill us today with Your grace. Bless the hands that prepared the food, the owner of this fine Inn, and all who are staying within its walls. Amen."

"Amen," Michael said before he dug into his mound of food.

"Good to see you again," Jeremy said to Venus. "I'm sorry last night was such a bust. Then all the parents showed up at the same time. It was a bit chaotic." His chuckle was light, with a dash of embarrassment.

Unsure of what to say, and with her insides vibrating at sitting beside him, Venus sent him a noncommittal smile.

Unfazed, Jeremy talked while he ate. "The group is getting together to go skiing later this morning. You could come with if you have nothing else to do."

"Skiing?" Venus glanced from Jeremy to Michael. Michael had mentioned the word before, but she hadn't asked him what it meant.

Jeremy stopped with his fork halfway to his mouth. "Have you never skied the slopes?"

"I don't think Venus is from around here, though I never found out where you were from." He sipped his black coffee, a keen eye on her.

Her scalp pricked. Her mind raced to find something that wouldn't implicate her as an alien. "Not from around here. I was raised on a station far away." She gestured with her arm up. "This is the first time I've seen snow."

"You can't be from Canada, then," Jeremy replied, laughing.

"Sounds like an Army brat to me." Michael misread her comment but turned the conversation toward his memories of skiing with his late wife and his sons.

Venus was relieved to have the attention off her. She would need to come up with some kind of adequate response, however, if she were to have friends. Everyone was so curious here.

"So, Venus, I—we could show you some of the basics if you want," Jeremy said, breaking her from her thoughts.

She shook her head. "Basics?"

"Of skiing. We leave in half an hour if you want to try. A few of the other teens have never skied either, so you'll be in good company." Jeremy smiled.

Venus glanced at Michael, who said, "I'll be gone, meeting some old friends who are in the area."

She could either go along with Jeremy and the kids or stay and watch more television. Though she'd enjoyed last night, she didn't relish hiding behind walls, waiting for life to happen. "Okay. I'll meet you back in the lobby?"

Jeremy's blue eyes sparkled while a wide smile creased his handsome face. "See you in a few." He strode off with his tray, handing it to the boy who had picked up Venus's earlier.

"That's how it's done," Michael spoke over his steaming cup.

"How what's done?" Venus studied his half-teasing expression, the rush of being near Jeremy dying back.

"That's how you continue on after loss." He set the cup back down and squeezed the hand she had wrapped around her own cup. "You live, heartache and all. And you find small pieces of joy to keep the fire in your heart going."

An hour and a half into the ski trip, Venus sat at an outside table, sipping hot cocoa. A space heater glowed from beside the wrought-iron table. Her legs and arms ached from trying to maintain her balance on the beginner's slope.

"Hey." Joe, the boy she'd met at the front desk on her first day at the Inn, sat next to her. He was a younger cousin of a member of Jeremy's teen group—Anthony, the boy who started the napkin snowball fight.

"What happened to you?" she asked, staring at the bandage on his forehead.

"Somebody ran me over and their ski caught me." He rubbed the space next to the large adhesive bandage. "It's not bad, but my ma will not be happy if I come back home all black and blue."

Something in the tone and cadence to his speech made her chest twinge with a familiarity. "I'm sorry. Does it hurt?"

He frowned. "Yeah. A little. Jeremy told me to wait here with you. They're on their last trip down and will be back shortly." Breath huffed out of his nose, his nostrils flaring like her grandfather's would when he would get angry.

She studied him curiously. "Do you want some hot cocoa?"

He puckered his lips. "I don't have any money."

An urge to take care of him overwhelmed her. "Wait here. I'll be right back." Venus hurried inside the coffee shop and ordered a hot cocoa deluxe with extra whipped topping and had them warm up a square of cherry coffee cake to go with it. She kept an eye on Joe as she waited for her order, unsure how old he was. He was scrawny, as if he was already struggling to catch up with his growth. Her guess was that he was ten or eleven.

She smiled at the cashier when the order was complete and rushed back outside. "Here you go!" Powdered sugar spilled from the plate as she set down the items.

His dark brown eyes widened, and his lips twitched at the corners. "Is this all for me?"

"Just for you. Enjoy." She smiled as he reached for the fork and dug into the oozy cherry filling.

"This is delicious. Thank you."

Venus relaxed back in the cushioned seat, savoring the moment. Michael had talked about lifting others up, and she had to admit it felt great to make the boy smile. Joe had been the first out of the van when they arrived and the first to swish down the slope. He obviously loved skiing. And even though she hadn't figured out how to work the skis without tangling them and falling, being out among other people enjoying themselves had energized her.

Their companionable silence ended when Joe finished the coffee cake. "How come you're not out there with everyone else?" He held the foam cup in his hands, breathing in the steam coming from the lid's opening.

"This is my first time skiing." She leaned closer to him. "I wasn't very good at it."

He giggled. "I wasn't very good when my dad taught me a few

years ago, either. But I like a challenge. Figuring out things is what I do best."

The tilt of his head and the way his lips formed his words were so familiar to her. "Oh, is that so? What do you like to do the most, then?"

"I'm good at math, and I like science. Dad says I could get into a big college when I get older if I apply myself now." He pulled out the rectangle comm device. "I got some photos on my phone of an experiment I've been working on." The screen lit up, and he flipped through to find an image. He held it up and showed her. "This is my anti-matter gun."

The photo was of a large drawing of a gun. Around the image were various equations and annotations.

Venus's heart tripped. These were like her grandfather's journal. Maybe all scientific equations looked alike on Earth. She smiled at him. "That looks complicated. I was never very good at science." It was true enough. Her grandfather hadn't had enough time to teach her much, though he'd taught her all about maintaining the space colony's various equipment.

"Dad said I can't make one in real life, though. We don't have access to the components to make a real blaster." He lowered his phone and shut the screen off. "But one day I will. I'm going to make lots of inventions."

She studied his face, taking in every detail. "I don't doubt that you will."

Five of the teens from their group came over to them, their voices and laughter cutting off Venus and Joe's conversation. Before she knew it, the entire group had assembled and headed back to the van.

Venus waited back with Jeremy and Joe as the others piled into the vehicle.

Jeremy bumped her shoulder. "Well, today was a bust, but did you at least enjoy the hot cocoa?"

"It was good," Joe answered him, his face animated. "Ms. Venus bought me some and a cherry bar."

"Oh, she did? That was nice of Ms. Venus, wasn't it?" Jeremy grinned down at the young boy.

Venus said nothing as Joe and Jeremy bantered about their favorite desserts as they entered the van. The front seats were open, so she sat down. Joe sat next to her, and Jeremy sat behind the driver as they took off back to the Inn.

chapter
eight

THAT NIGHT, Venus woke several times to bad dreams. Images of her grandfather dogged her mind. She woke groggy and blurry-eyed. A dull glow lit the sky when she rose and slunk into the bathroom to take a bracing, cold shower to help her wake up.

Once finished and a bit more alert, she stood in front of the coffee machine. She took a minute to examine the electric appliance before she filled it with water and turned it on. Inserting the pod, she yawned and tried to recall the dreams that had haunted her sleep.

Something about her grandfather. She shook her head.

A blue light blazed on the machine, so she pushed the lid down on the pod as per the video she'd watched on how to use it. The machine screeched as steam and the bold scent of coffee filled the space. A smile crept across her face. This was one of a hundred reasons she was so thankful to not be in space any longer.

After adding the cream packet—something much more akin to the colony's dried milk than the liquid version from the cafeteria—and sugar, she made her way to the couch to watch the morning unfold.

Her thoughts kept turning back to her dreams and what they meant. She turned on the television and flipped through the channels. Nothing caught her attention. Lifting the remote, she turned it off out of frustration. Dregs remained in the bottom of her mug when she returned to her room and tidied it, the act of making her bed soothing to her frustrated mind.

A thump sounded in the living area, startling her. She rushed back to the room and found another book lying face open on the floor in front of the dark fireplace. Her eyes were riveted to the hand-written pages. This script wasn't the crisp writing from the other journal. She bent to retrieve it and stopped dead in her tracks. On the pages was a crude drawing of a gun—an anti-matter gun.

Blood rushed to her head, and she had to sit down. She slammed the book shut and searched the cover for a name.

Joe Bolt.

"Joe?" Venus rubbed her hand across the rough cardboard exterior. "Joe is short for Joseph like Jeremy is short for Jeremiah." Her words were breathy, her body shaking. Could it be true? Had she met her grandfather yesterday on the ski trip?

She tried to do the math in her head, but her mind wouldn't make sense of it. Venus dropped the notebook and yanked on her boots. Maybe, if she was lucky, he would come into the cafeteria.

Her fingers stilled. What would she say to him? *Hey, I'm from the future where you died saving my life?*

No, that wouldn't work. She'd scare him, and everyone would think she was crazy. Best-case scenario, everyone would figure out that she was a space alien. That was no good. She dropped back down onto the couch's cushions.

What was she to do with this knowledge? Instead of running down to the cafeteria, Venus picked the notebook up. With a deep breath, she opened it and read.

Though his notes were more childish, Joe had a keen mind. There were anecdotes about school, intermixed with questions on the nature of the universe. Someone with better writing had added scripture in the side notes, possibly one of his parents since the writing was much clearer.

One paragraph noted Psalm 19:1, *The heavens declare the*

glory of God; the skies proclaim the work of his hands. Joe wrote beside it, *I would love to fly among the stars, to see the starry hosts. Wouldn't it be grand to float into space? To find my home among the Keeper of the Stars?*

Venus's heart stopped. Her hands shook. Her chest ached as if an explosive had detonated in it. "Had he predicted his death years and a million miles away later?" Her mind stuttered at the thought.

Though her grandfather had been worried about her, he had not fought the Commander. He hadn't hidden from him, though he probably could have with his in-depth knowledge of the inner workings of the station. He'd gone peacefully.

She'd been terrified, but he hadn't feared for himself, just for her.

How could he be so fearless in the face of sure death?

And the answer came to her unbidden. Because he believed in this God of the universe. He sacrificed his life to save hers in the only way he could. He trusted in the Keeper of the Stars to keep her safe when she used his transporter. Her mission now was to make sure his sacrifice counted, that her life mattered.

Venus wasn't sure how to pray, but she gave it her best shot. "Thank You, God, for sending me here to meet with my grandfather one more time. To see him as he was before." She hugged Joe's journal to her chest.

Cold water from the kitchen sink cooled her red eyes before she went down to the cafeteria. She prayed for one more chance to spend time with the child version of her grandfather.

As soon as Venus stepped off the elevator, cold air swirled around her. No one lingered in the foyer. Though the fireplace blazed, it did little to warm the room. One front desk clerk manned the station, and they wore a heavy coat and a hat. The usual din of noise from the cafeteria was notably absent.

Venus stepped up to the half-wall, fighting off shivers. She should've worn her coat. "Why is it so cold?"

The girl looked at her with a long-suffering glance. "The main furnace broke, and our maintenance guy is out of town for the holidays. And the local company can't get out before Christmas. They're still filling orders from the storm from a week ago."

Her mind spun at the possibilities of what could be wrong. "Does anyone know what's wrong with it? Is it an easy fix?"

"Don't know," Maggie said as she strolled into the small reception area. "I'm not a repairman. Our usual guy is busy for the next couple of days and then will be out of town for the holiday."

"I do repairs," Venus said and then rushed to explain when Maggie focused on her. "I mean, on other kinds of machinery. But I could take a look for you."

"Why is it so cold down here?" A dark woman accompanying Joe and another dark man appeared from the direction of the cafeteria. She had Joe's eyes and smile, while the man had his hairline and lanky build. His parents?

Venus tried not to stare.

Maggie sighed and muttered quietly to the desk clerk. "We'll need to put a sign up." She smiled politely at Joe and his family, speaking louder. "Something's wrong with the furnace and we won't be able to get a repair person here until after Christmas."

Venus raised her hand. "I can look at the furnace." A thought crossed her mind, and she turned to Joe. "You're into building things. Would you like to come with me? See if we can figure it out?"

"Oh, no. You don't have to do that," Maggie said quickly, her hand fidgeting with her scarf.

Several others walked up to the front desk, each of them with the same question on their lips.

Venus spoke over the crowd. "It's what I know how to do. Please?"

Maggie pursed her lips but relented. "Fine. Come with me.

My maintenance man has some tools and spare parts, but I have no clue what's in there."

Venus glanced at Joe. "Coming?"

Joe twisted around to get permission. The two older versions of him nodded. "Just stay out of the way and don't touch anything you're not supposed to," the woman said.

Joe pumped his fist in the air. "Yes."

Venus was afraid her heart would burst. She would work alongside her grandfather once more. Though it wasn't the same as being with the eighty-six-year-old version of the man, she held it as a treasure in her heart.

Together, they followed Maggie down the hall. She led them to a locked room beyond the doors with titles on them, far from the center of the Inn itself. Gray paint covered the walls and concrete floor. Fluorescent light fixtures blinked into life above them.

Venus almost felt at home in the space and fought off a wave of melancholy.

"The tools are on the shelves over there." Maggie waved to a metal and plastic unit against the back wall. "You're sure you know what you're doing? I mean, it couldn't get much worse, but if you get hurt or—"

Venus put her hands up. "I've worked on active thermal control units and internal combustion parts that are turbocharged, along with radioisotope converted heating systems with plutonium cores. This is nothing compared to them. I'll see if I can fix it. If I can't, you're not out anything. Let me repay you for your kindness."

Maggie's eyes bulged at her declaration. With a nod, she left Venus and Joe in the bare room.

The furnace sat silent on a separate cement foundation. She gave it a cursory glance and then smiled at Joe. "Ready to dig in?"

He smiled, an act that spread warmth throughout Venus's chilled body.

"Okay. Go to the tool kit and find me a multi-tool screwdriver. We'll open this up and see what the issue is."

Joe raced to do as she requested, and together, they dug into the furnace's main panel.

Venus started with the simplest thing and worked her way through each component until she found the problem. "Here it is," she muttered to Joe. "Look here." She motioned for him to get closer. "The heat strip is fried."

"How do you fix that?" he asked, his eyes glowing in the harsh lighting.

"Needs a new one. I thought I saw spare parts on the shelf when you were shuffling around. See if you can find something that looks just like this, and we'll replace it." She leaned over and stretched. It had been days since she'd had to do any real work, and her back was reminding her of it.

She watched little Joe rummage through the boxes, searching for a part to match, and her heart twisted as melancholy filled her soul. It was bittersweet, working alongside the one who had taught her these very skills. Though she was the instructor now, not the apprentice.

"Found it." Joe lifted the part in the air and ran back to her.

"Well done," she said, taking it from him. Minutes went by as they worked to get the new heating strip in. That done, she removed the dirty filter and replaced it with a new one. She double-checked the condensation drain, explaining each step to Joe.

As an extra precaution, she double-checked the manual tucked inside a pocket taped to the machine to make sure there wasn't anything else she needed to do before she turned the unit back on. Satisfied, she put the manual back and smiled at Joe. "We're ready. I'll let you push the button to see if it starts again." She gestured to the panel.

Joe flipped the switch, and the furnace rattled into action. It whirred and quieted, the motor kicking in. "Wow!" Joe said, excitement oozing from him.

"Let's go tell Maggie the good news."

Minutes later, Venus and Joe entered the main hall to whistles and cheers. Warm air already circulated through the vents, rustling the tinsel on the Christmas tree.

Maggie hugged Venus. "Thank you so much. You earned your stay." She pulled back, and her eyes glimmered. Turning to Joe, she held out a fist. "Excellent job, Master Bolt. You'll make a terrific scientist someday."

Venus smiled, knowing that he indeed would. He would exceed anyone's expectations. She pushed away the thoughts of his life's successes getting shortened by an unanticipated plague that would happen in the years to come. This moment was too precious to let the future's bleak fate ruin it.

Joe took her hand and pulled her over to a group crowded around the fireplace. "Mom, Dad, this is Venus. She and I fixed the furnace."

"Venus?" the man asked. "That's my mother's name."

"It is?" Venus glanced at Joe.

"She's my favorite granny. Dad—" Joe filled his parents in on how they searched for the problem with the furnace.

Venus tuned them out. Her grandfather had named her after his favorite granny? Tears pricked her eyes, and she worked hard to listen to the animated boy talking nonstop while his parents waited and listened patiently to everything he said. Just like Joseph used to do for her.

By the time Joe finished, Venus's stomach gurgled.

"You'd better get something to eat. You deserve it for your hard work." Mrs. Bolt placed a gentle hand on her arm. "Thank you for including Joe. He's so smart but can be such a handful."

Venus's smile wobbled. "He was no trouble at all. In fact, he was quite helpful. Joe's an incredible boy."

"He is a blessing." Mr. Bolt directed Joe away from the fireplace. "And now we have to go get our bags. It's time to leave for your aunt's house for Christmas." His last words were directed to Joe, who groaned.

Venus's heart sank. "Oh, you're leaving? Now?"

Mrs. Bolt glanced up at the tree and swung her gaze around the room. "Usually, we don't stay at the Inn. My sister's house had a leak, and they had to do some repairs before we could all gather there. We might have to make this a yearly thing, though. We've enjoyed our stay here."

"And I met a new friend." Joe took her hand in his small one. His youthful face, so full of life and joy, filled her with so many emotions.

"The best of friends." Venus sucked back the grief as she gave him a bright smile.

"Well, goodbye, and you take care. Maybe we'll see you again sometime." Mr. Bolt said.

They waved and left the room.

Maggie walked over to her side. "Is it a coincidence that you have the same last name as my other guests?"

Venus stared after them. "No. Somehow it isn't."

Maggie shrugged and winked. "Perhaps this Inn is enchanted."

chapter
nine

VENUS SAT DOWN, a heaping plate full of breakfast food and two cups of cream and sugar-laced coffee filling her tray. She wavered between grief and elation at time spent with her grandfather again. And to have worked beside him one last time before he left was a miracle and a blessing.

"Well, good morning. I hear you are the toast of the Inn this morning." Michael, with his own tray full of breakfast items, sat down across from her.

"I had some help." Venus grinned to herself. "It was an easy fix."

"That's not what I heard." Jeremy sat down in the third chair. Since it was still cold in the main part of the Inn, many of the guests filled their plates and took them back to their warm rooms to eat. He glanced at her, his gaze searching. "You're only twenty years old and can service a large furnace at an Inn? That's amazing."

Venus shrugged and hedged. "My grandfather and I used to work on larger—more industrial—machinery. He taught me everything I know."

"Well, our church could use someone with your skills. The reason our youth group met here was because our own furnace is antiquated and we needed to install a new one. However, it's had its share of quirks and problems." He glanced up from his food. "Would you be willing to look at it? We'd pay you, of course."

Venus was speechless. She'd never been recognized for the work she'd done before. Naturally, since no one had ever known she was doing it. And because of that, she'd never been paid for her labor.

"Sounds like a good opportunity to me. I think your grandfather would be proud of you." Michael grinned at them, his eyes sparkling with mischief.

Joy filled her as Michael's words sank in. It wasn't something she thought she'd experience again. Being reunited with her grandfather, albeit as his younger self, allowed a piece of her heart to heal. It had been a sort of closure she hadn't expected.

"I can try." Venus said.

Michael nodded. "God works in mysterious ways."

Venus stifled a laugh. They didn't know the half of what God had done to work this mysterious miracle.

They finished eating, filling in the spaces with comfortable conversation. Venus agreed to meet Jeremy in the lobby later that afternoon to travel with him and Michael to fix the church's furnace.

She returned to her room with a lighter spirit and step. Inside, the space was much warmer than the Inn's first floor, though the furnace was working fine. Venus turned on the fireplace and gazed into the animated flickering flames, considering all that occurred that morning. She closed her eyes and savored the memories.

Slam!

Venus jerked upright on the couch. "What—"

On the wooden coffee table in front of her was another journal. The bracelet her grandfather had helped her make from wire, nuts, and bolts dangled from the middle pages. She glanced around the room, but there wasn't any kind of explanation to how the items she and her grandfather had placed in the transporter continued to show up in the room.

"It's probably a good thing we didn't send anything big

through," she muttered. "Though I was large and ended up by the front entry." She grabbed the journal. It was empty except for two paragraphs.

She read it aloud to herself. "Venus, if you're reading this, I am no longer. I've lived a good, long life. My Earth life was blessed with a loving family, and the end of my space life was filled with the blessing of you. I named you after my granny and a young woman who encouraged my curiosity, love of building, and making my inventions. Know I loved you and any sacrifice I made was a joy, not a burden. As James says in the Bible, '*Consider it pure joy, my brothers and sisters, whenever you face trials of many kinds, because you know that the testing of your faith produces perseverance. Let perseverance finish its work so that you may be mature and complete, not lacking anything.*'

"Fill this journal with your own adventures, Venus. Take each day as the miracle it is and don't grieve me too much. Life is too short and full of its own problems to do so. I remain forever your loving grandfather."

Venus rubbed a finger across where he'd signed his name, Joseph Bolt. Tears blurred her vision of the date, a year before Commander Ridenour's bots spotted her sneaking across sector two. She shook her head. "How did you know?"

She lifted the heavy metal bracelet, but it was too small to fit over her hand now. Soldered together, it would be impossible to wear unless she found tools to cut and splice it back together. Maybe she could recreate it into something sleeker, like the pieces she saw in the stores she visited. But she shook off that thought.

"Doesn't matter." She wrapped her hand around the crudely woven bracelet. "Nothing I could buy would compare to how precious this is."

She bowed her head. "Thank You, God, for bringing me here and bringing me back some joy. Help me to not take Grandfather's sacrifice for granted, but to live each day as a light to others."

287

chapter
ten

One year later

VENUS SAT on the couch in the Starlit Inn's foyer, package in hand. The paper wrapping crinkled as she fiddled with it, nervousness making butterflies dance in her stomach. Christmas music played through a wireless speaker that sat on the fireplace's mantel, hidden behind the decorated pine garland.

"You're going to wear out the paper if you keep that up," Jeremy said as he laid a hand on her knee. His beautiful blue eyes danced with humor.

"I can't help it." She handed him the present, thankful for his patience. It had been a tough year. Venus had needed to learn many things in order to function as a proper Earthling. And it had taken months before she'd been brave enough to tell Jeremy her story. At first, he didn't believe her. But she'd shown him the journals and bracelet, and he'd reluctantly believed her.

Since then, they'd grown close enough to start dating. It was hard for Venus to open up, but she was learning to. It didn't help that she couldn't tell most people the full truth of who she was. She settled on calling herself an emancipated alien. Most people assumed she was from Europe with her accent. Luckily, her hair had grown and her skin tanned, so she no longer looked alien.

The front glass doors opened, and Venus sat up to see who it was. She leaned back as an elderly couple entered and headed to the front desk.

Venus's legs bounced in nervous energy.

Jeremy laughed. The sound warmed her. "His cousin Anthony said they'd be here before five today. He'll be here."

"I know." She grabbed the package back from Jeremy and hugged it. "I hope he remembers me."

Jeremy sat against the couch's back and leaned against her. "Why wouldn't he remember you?"

"I don't know. I look different." She ran a hand through her long hair. "And he doesn't know I'm me, though I know he's my grandfather." She pursed her lips. She was rambling. "Too much caffeine." She rose from the couch and walked around the room, checking the empty cafeteria for the third time.

Maggie entered the foyer and squealed. "Venus! So good to see you. Are you here to stay?"

"I'm here to give this to Joe." She held out the journal she'd wrapped a month ago when she was still wavering on whether she should take her chances on meeting with Joe and his parents again. They'd mentioned coming back to the Inn before they'd left last year, but it wasn't until Jeremy asked Joe's cousin if the Bolts were returning for Christmas that her hope ramped into overdrive.

"How have you been?" Maggie's keen eyes saw too much.

Venus blew out a breath. "Good. I received my GED and am taking some college courses toward a bio-engineering degree with an emphasis on bio-warfare, thanks to Jeremy's encouragement and the church's sponsorship." She waved to Jeremy, who walked toward them.

"That's amazing. I'm so glad everything is working out for you. You're always welcome to stay here." Maggie squeezed her arm.

"Maybe in the future. It's still kind of crazy right now." She twisted the package in her hands.

"I understand. Well, I'm needed somewhere. I just had to say hi. You guys take care." Maggie strode off toward the elevators.

The glass doors swished open again, and Venus swung around. Joe's parents stepped in, pulling wheeled suitcases behind them. Venus grinned but waited before rushing over in greeting.

After a minute, Joe entered. He was taller than last year, his arms and legs a bit gangly for his young stature.

"It's him," Venus breathed out, the butterflies making a mad dash around in her stomach. She twisted and leaned into Jeremy's warm body.

He put his hands on her shoulders and stepped back. "Let's go say hello."

"Okay." Venus fought back the panic.

"Hey, Mom and Dad. It's Ms. Venus from last Christmas," Joe said as he strode toward her.

Venus waved, unable to speak.

"Hey, Joe," Jeremy said and reached out to shake the boy's hand. "It's good to see you again."

He narrowed a brown eye. "You too. Are you guys staying here this year?"

"Um, no. I just came to give you a gift." Venus stumbled over her words. She'd found the exact journal her grandfather had used and bought it immediately. She'd saved it, thinking she'd write in it, but she couldn't force herself to put a pen down on the pages. After careful consideration, she'd determined to find Joe and give it to him.

"Oh, isn't that nice?" Mrs. Bolt said as she joined her son. "What do you say?"

"Thank you. But, what's it for?"

Venus's hands shook as she gestured to him. "Open it and see."

Joe tore into the package, unconcerned with saving the paper. "A journal?" he asked. "I mean, it's nice and all. But—"

She rushed to explain. "You showed me your picture last year of the science experiment, the gun diagram. I thought if you document all your experiments and ideas, it might help you when you finally can make something."

Joe's face lit up. "Like an invention?"

"Yes, exactly." Venus grinned, hoping her enthusiasm wasn't too over-the-top.

"Oh, thanks!" He flipped through the pages, and Venus could almost see the thoughts spinning in his mind.

"Anyway, that's why we were here." Venus drifted off.

Mr. Bolt joined the other two and curled his arm around his wife's shoulders. "That was awful nice of you. I'm sure he'll use it." He tipped his hat to Venus and Jeremy. "Now, let's get settled in so we can go grab something to eat. I'm famished."

"Thanks again, Ms. Venus," Joe said as he followed his father.

"Have a blessed holiday," Mrs. Bolt said.

Venus waved at them, her shoulders drooping when they were out of sight.

"Disappointed?" Jeremy asked carefully.

She shook her head. "No. It's not as exciting as those game systems your teen group loves, Youth Pastor Hunter." She loved teasing him about his title. "But I know it will be an important part of his life."

Jeremy nudged her arm. "Like you were."

"Yes." She wiped her eyes with a knit glove.

"C'mon, star girl. You've got a final tomorrow to study for."

Venus groaned, but she wasn't dissatisfied. Like her grandfather's Bible and journals, she planned to show up out of the blue and occasionally give Joe something to encourage him. It would be her way of paying him back for saving her. "Okay. I'm ready."

With a last glance over her shoulder toward the elevators, Venus happily strode out the glass doors, arm in arm with her new beau, and stepped into her bright future.

THE END

acknowledgments

As a writer, I must thank God first and foremost for my storytelling gift. I'm so thankful for all of the support of friends and family, fellow writers, and readers who find anything interesting in the stories I write.

about the author

 Winner of the 2016 ACFW Genesis Award and Finalist in the 2023 Carol awards and 2024 & 2025 Realm Makers Realm awards, Dawn has been recognized for her published and non-published works.

As a child, Dawn often had her head in the clouds creating scenes and stories for anything and everything she came across. She believed there was magic everywhere, a sentiment she has never outgrown. Nature inspires her, and her love for the underdog and the unlikely hero colors much of what she writes.

Dawn adores anything Steampunk, is often distracted by shiny, pretty things, and her obsession with purses and shoes borders on hoarding. Dawn lives in Iowa with her husband, a chef and food service business owner.

A Quantum
Christmas

J. L. Burrows

To Robert E. Henley, you'll forever be missed.
Can't wait to see you again in heaven.

chapter
one

Research Findings

December 2325—Elshaddai's Mission Command

DYCE MUNROE TRUDGED into the Commissioner's waiting room and slid into one of the hard, white, Z-shaped chairs that left his lower back aching. His team did everything right. He rubbed his palms down his thighs. Still—called into Mission Command?

Why couldn't his team have taken out the enemy's tech before it took a young boy's life? A heavy sigh did nothing to ease the weight of his failed mission.

So, why was he here now? Holding his hand in front of him, he squeezed his aching fingers. He'd held his weapon at the ready for so long, carried the line with the best team—his team—but it still didn't matter.

Dyce folded his arms across his chest to still his nervous habit. A slip of a woman, the only other person in the waiting area, sat staring at the Commissioner's door. Curious. A silver pencil secured her twisted knot of black hair, exposing an earring dangling just above the spot where her sharp jawline met her slender throat. Her gaze caught his, and his brain dissolved into mush. His heart skipped.

She let out a tiny gasp as if she'd just discovered he was waiting with her, instantly dropping her gaze to her hands. Her cheeks flushed a pleasant pink. What thought brought such lovely color to her face? She now focused intently on the door handle of the Mission Commissioner's office.

Something about her, the way she carried her shoulders, the navy Research Team uniform resting on her small but strong frame, or the tilt of her head as if she were ready to take on the world ... He wasn't trying to stare, but he couldn't put his finger on a familiarity that drew him in like family or friendship or something so kindred it detonated the emptiness inside of him.

Dyce swallowed.

Strength didn't prepare him for the sensations rattling him, despite being trained with many generations of various weaponry known to date. His team—actually, all of MI12—didn't carry weapons of their own. They used anything and everything to neutralize a hostile. Hand-to-hand combat was his specialty. But with a glance, she'd made him weaker than the Nano2314 Virus.

Had he met her before?

She glanced his way again. Dark brown eyes searched his face. Lips pursed, she turned back to stare at the door.

The experience, however, left his heart racing.

What was hiding in those dark brown eyes? And why did something so strong seem to call him by name?

This woman sent thoughts he had no right to allow juddering around in him.

A desire to be safe enough to allow feelings of weakness flashed through him. On its heels, the crazy desire to feel comforted in her arms after a day like today, a place safe enough to be broken by the hard world, if only for a moment ... They were wild, dangerous thoughts he shouldn't even imagine.

But after a failed mission.

Warriors couldn't let their guard down. They stood strong

when others cowered, carried the weak when they couldn't make a way themselves, fought for the friends and family they had and the ones they'd lost. Defending the defenseless—the young boy's last expression passed like a ghost through Dyce's mind.

The woman refused to send her wayward gaze his direction again. Dyce let out a slight scoff, and her head inclined just barely toward him.

Was the young woman in trouble too?

If she were in trouble, Dyce would shield her and take the brunt of the Commissioner's ire. Clearly, whatever she'd done would never compare to what his team had failed to do. Either way, they needed to get on with whatever this was, so they both could get back to their lives. He needed to brief his team, meet up with psych, and get back on the field. Defending and protecting didn't happen all by itself.

Dyce stood, and the woman glanced at him. Her dark brown eyes widened a touch before she cast her heartwarming attention back to the door.

Skin prickling, Dyce smirked. *Fine. Be that way.* He didn't want to deal with her either. Whatever vibes she was giving off were obviously ... *Keep a clear head.* The Mission Commissioner would dispense with—whatever—and then Dyce would be out of this confounding room with this woman.

He marched up to the steel door and delivered three sharp knocks.

"Come in."

As Dyce twisted the knob, the Commissioner said, "Invite Dr. Stein in too."

Dyce took a deep breath and squared his shoulders. Though everything in him said *avoid, avoid, abort,* he turned to where her gaze waited for him. "I assume you are Dr. Stein."

The woman nodded. Somehow, she contracted into herself as she drew to standing, all the while shifting around Dyce as if to enter the room first.

Dyce put his hand on the doorknob. No way was she going in first. He pushed the door open—

Dr. Stein slipped in before Dyce's brain commanded his foot forward. A wash of lavender left him stunned on the spot.

And there! That was clear evidence that the woman was a threat to his ability to function. How was he supposed to protect her from the Commissioner if she charged ahead of him and left him at the door empty-handed?

Dyce cleared his throat and followed the faint hint of lavender. He stiffened his upper lip and decided right then to keep his distance so he could protect her with a clear head in case she needed him to hold off the Commissioner or anyone else.

He extrapolated scenarios that could explain being called into the Commissioner's office with Dr. Stein.

Nothing good came to mind.

———

Refusing to run like archaic instinct commanded, Ellery Stein slipped past the handsome, muscle-headed beast before he could take charge of the room and scramble a year and a half of her research. With confidence she didn't feel, she strode toward the Commissioner and took the closest chair.

Why was MI12 here, anyway? A tremble took root in her gut and the tips of her fingers. She crossed her legs and curled her hands on top.

Since the Commissioner assigned her to this project, she and her team of research assistants followed every potential historical trail they could put together. She finally delivered the results yesterday.

"Dr. Stein, thank you for sending me your report and attending this meeting." The Commissioner steepled his fingers in front of his ever-creased forehead above an expression that pivoted from gentle, as he glanced her way, to sharp and assessing when taking in Mr. MI12.

Ellery's stomach twisted into knots. Muscle Man better not be the elite soldier the Commissioner planned to pair her with on-the-field research plans. Even as the thought struck her, at least three plausible reasons for MI12 to be present at her meeting now flitted through her mind, and it was simple to select the strongest potential. With photographic memory, she easily envisioned the page she'd sent to the Commissioner. Clearly written was the request for a time travel research permit and an MI12 escort. Ellery let out a breath she'd been holding.

To think she worried about facing resistance to her requests. Was Muscle Man to be her escort? Just the thought sent a spark of warmth through her stomach, which was not a Lead Researcher's appropriate response. *This was ridiculous! I'm malfunctioning—and for what? A few shared glances?* She couldn't trust herself around a man who affected her so.

Her responsibility to her position had to come first.

Nodding in turn to Muscle Man, the Commissioner added, "Thank you for meeting us here, Munroe."

"Yes, sir." Muscle Man Munroe was not one for many words, it seemed. That worked to Ellery's advantage.

Ellery steered her focus away from Munroe's penetrating blue eyes. "Sir, as you know, I've spent the better part of a year and a half researching your assignment, and it's an incredible discovery."

"That's why I called you both here." The Commissioner picked up what Ellery assumed to be a printed copy of her report. "Your research request has been approved."

"I'm honored." Ellery frowned as her stomach dropped. With his stamp of approval, she was going to December 2025. Never had she ever truly imagined she'd get this far, yet—

"Dyce Munroe will be the MI12 who will protect you from danger as you both travel back in time." The Commissioner glanced over Ellery's report as if maybe he could understand her facts and figures.

Ellery twisted her lips to the side, refusing to let her eyes wander to Dyce Munroe. If her instincts were correct, this mission would require a team of researchers—not just herself and one MI12. "Thank you, sir. I was hoping to request—"

"For me to give my final sign-off on this, I'll need the precise date and location for your insertion point."

Ellery had hoped to keep this hard-fought-for intel to herself, but in order to travel back to the precise moment in the past she'd pinpointed, she'd have to share the exact information not only with the Commissioner but with Dyce Munroe as well.

Those blue eyes caught hers again, and it was like he saw through her, penetrating into her brain, reading her thoughts.

Her thoughts were classified.

"The intel was for our eyes only." And she wasn't interested in letting Blue Eyes into the operation.

The Commissioner leaned forward, chair creaking. "In order for Munroe to protect you on this mission, you'll bring him up to speed on your research and the parameters of your request."

Her stomach did a funny somersault at the word *mission*. "I understand. However, the dangers of that archaic time period are slim—nearly nothing. Maybe MI12 isn't necessary."

"It's protocol." The Commissioner turned to the second page of her report.

"I wasn't aware. Yes, sir."

When she had been researching safely behind her desk, she'd triple-checked the results before reporting her team's discovery. The twelve families' life trajectories, now traceable through specially curated AI tech, crossed paths in time and space, stepping from obscurity to prominence and longstanding leadership. Her heart might have burst out of her chest, except there was no scientific explanation for this shift in trajectory. The AI simply noted it, but she wanted to explore why that intersection caused such a shift. She needed to do more research, but going without her team and in the presence of Dyce Munroe was less than perfect.

The Commissioner needed her focused.

"Sir, may I speak?" His voice sent a shock through Ellery. It was deep and warm, comforting, despite his bitter tone.

Ellery forced her gaze to remain on the Commissioner and noted the flash of irritation in his expression.

"Speak."

"I'm not a babysitter. I don't do research. My team needs me now, especially after today's loss." Munroe stood at attention just past the corner of the Commissioner's desk. As he mentioned his loss, his whole body seemed to deflate.

A pang of compassion struck Ellery for his loss, but to call protecting her research babysitting—how dare he dismiss the one thing she'd worked her entire life for? *Babysit?* "This mission is more important than anything you've ever been party to."

Those consuming eyes locked on hers and dared her to look away. His entire frame leaned into his words as he said, "Look, I understand achieving the Historical Researcher Degree and joining the summative comprehension of human history compiled from the lost archives might make you think you are some kind of special—"

"Enough!" The Commissioner hit his desk with his meaty fist, sending Ellery jumping in her skin. "Munroe, you have orders. A break from the team might just be enough to refocus you."

Munroe didn't react.

Ellery took a deep breath. Was MI12 a rogue? Or worse, some kind of broken soldier?

"Commissioner, this mission is too important for it to double as a break for MI12." Ellery fought the spark of rage filling her cheeks with fiery heat. What good were ten years of specialized training in Elshaddai's elite school only to have her research ruined at the eleventh hour?

The Commissioner waved his hand as if to erase her words. "That is not up for debate. I know exactly how hard you've worked. It's the reason I selected you for this assignment almost two years ago. Don't let Munroe get under your skin."

Dyce scoffed, and Ellery bristled. This mission was paramount to understanding life trajectories, especially for their current leadership. Besides, she finished things. Hard things like research that cost her friendships and a huge chunk of her life.

She took a deep breath, remembering what she contained within herself. It was so important that it held a life of its own, drawing breath, requiring secrecy, demanding a life for a life. She'd combed through and committed to memory three hundred years' worth of video and AI recordings. So, a life for three lifetimes.

Something in Dyce Munroe's gaze shifted, and she realized she'd been staring. She flicked her eyes back under her will and to the Commissioner. "Yes, sir. We'll need to travel to the Starlit Inn, December 2025."

"I'll add that to the directive, sign, and send it up the chain for final approval. Both of you need to prepare yourselves. Time travel, as I'm sure you already know, Dr. Stein, is dangerous."

"We might get lost in the quantum time-travel space loop." She stretched her neck and pressed her glasses back up her nose.

Some risks were worth it.

The Commissioner nodded.

Munroe touched the Commissioner's desk. "I didn't sign on for that."

The Commissioner stood. "Young man, you signed on to serve the people of Elshaddai. As your Mission Commissioner, you'll do as I order. Is that clear?"

Munroe shifted, almost dissolving into a sort of mission-ready stance. "Sir, yes, sir."

Ellery stood, since the two men were. "Sir, with all due respect, maybe it would be best to select a member of MI12 who can not only protect me but also the research. Mr. Munroe clearly has no interest in preserving historical records or research of any kind, for that matter."

As Research Lead, Ellery would not let her team down by allowing anything to ruin this mission, which could potentially reveal the most important historical information gathered since the war on data, when a radical group's cyberattack took out all historical records over a hundred and fifty years ago.

Despite the gravity of her thoughts, her eyes wandered to MI12. Again.

"Munroe, will that be necessary?" The Commissioner sneered at the soldier.

"Sir, no, sir." Munroe cut a sharp glare at her before focusing back on the Commissioner.

Ellery couldn't read anything more from Dyce Munroe's expression.

In her research, they'd found the exact period when the twelve families of Elshaddai experienced an event so indelible it marked their future trajectories for leadership. An ancestor from each family had touched this one moment, possibly this one place, and their lives pivoted in a totally new direction.

Ellery and Dyce might get lost in the quantum time-travel space loop, but they might also discover something ... dare she say ... monumental?

A cornerstone moment that could influence everything going forward.

chapter two

Waiting for Takeoff

DYCE SWIPED his hand down his face as the Commissioner's expression allowed zero recourse. Ordered to go back in time. To a place called the Starlit Inn. With a Lead Researcher he knew nothing about. What about his team? His current mission?

His men and women were counting on him.

They needed time to heal, to come together and rebuild, to protect Elshaddai and its people. Not go gallivanting into the past for some loose thread no one cared about except the higher-ups and the strange researcher with the brown eyes that possessed the power to throw him for a loop. He turned for the Commissioner's door and stormed out.

He'd have to alert the team and put Tate in charge. Figure out a way to heal and regroup without being together.

Ellery wafted behind him in a nervous fret, her petite feet dancing across the tile in an uneven pattern of steps and trots.

Dyce fought a smile as he imagined her twining her hands together, cheeks blazing red.

"Munroe—"

He almost stilled at his name on her lips. But he caught

himself and charged forward, picking up his pace. There was nothing to say to the—he had to go prepare his team.

"Wait. I thought we—"

He rounded on her, drawing in a deep breath, ready to let her have it.

Wide-eyed, she radiated both a defiant, fiery courage and a mousy intelligence that seemed to fortify her, lifting her chin to meet his bulking frame without fear. "Look." She held both hands up. "I understand your orders. But I need to bring you up to speed before we're called into action, and we don't know when that will be."

Dyce cleared his throat. Dipped his chin once.

A bit of tension seemed to drop her shoulders an inch. "We need to go to the site."

"That order was clear."

"I mean now, in today's timeline. I need to collect some more data—"

"Shouldn't you have done that already?"

"I want to do it again, just to make sure everything is accounted for."

"You *do* have photographic memory. That's one of the requirements for your—"

"My position has accounted for all aspects of this project. That said, due diligence is always essential to securing a successful and accurate historical record."

Her eyes dashed to the left as if she were lying. Dyce narrowed his eyes and stepped closer, studying her. Her subtle movement back so perfectly mirrored his approach that he almost missed it. Would have, if he weren't trained to catch every detail of a suspect. And right now, he suspected her of a lot of things. First and foremost, ruining his chance at keeping his life his own, his team's future healing, and potentially the Commissioner's search for the past. Something almost disloyal or insecure radiated from her.

He forced his posture into one of nonchalance, radiating ease in the hopes she might relax and let her truth slip. "Fine. I'll stop by my team, deliver the news, and set up parameters for my absence. Then, I'll escort you to the location."

Her eyes skidded across his face, almost in disbelief, before she gave a single nod and waved a hand, indicating he should proceed. "Thank you."

Hating the odd affection swelling in his chest, Dyce ignored her appreciation and vowed once again to keep his head clear so his training could maintain their safety through whatever research nightmare she would drag him into.

Ellery shoved her glasses up her nose with a bit too much gusto. Why was Blue Eyes storming through the halls so fast? Sure, they were on a time limit, but launch would never be that night. These things took time, and he was difficult to keep up with.

Somehow, she had to complete her research without the lug in front of her. Nothing about him screamed thorough and diligent, let alone intelligent.

"You're awfully quiet." Dyce frowned. "Are you nervous about visiting my team?"

Ellery shook her head. Did he flex his muscles *every time* he opened the door to his HoverQuest? Of course, she was quiet. Ellery had so little experience with people outside her sphere of elite researchers and hand-selected Elshaddai graduates, she'd never had to work so hard to converse in her life. Normally, communication just flowed. One like-minded thought to another's. Instead, she'd chased him through the halls, breaking a sweat and rethinking her footwear for the day and mission.

"It's fine with me." He filled in the silence, pressing the icon to close her door for her. He rounded the vehicle, giving her a moment with her thoughts. But the blissful seconds ticked by before she'd even caught her breath. He took the pilot's seat, his knuckles turning white as they gripped the helm.

How upset was he that he was being ordered into the past? How furious would she be if someone interrupted her research and sent her out to do the bidding of another faction's career path? Her heart stumbled at the thought of being forced to shadow Munroe on one of his missions.

While Dyce navigated to the coordinates of his team headquarters, Ellery lost herself in hypothetical scenarios where the tables were turned and she shadowed Munroe.

Again, he opened her door and led the way, but this time, she didn't keep up.

He gave her an odd glance, hesitated as his gaze roved her face, but still the silence between them persisted as he stormed yet another hall, albeit slower, with furtive checks on her progress. Should she follow him in to meet with his team?

"When we get to my team, I'll introduce you, but let me do the talking." His jaw muscle jumped as if he expected a fight.

"Is there a place I could wait and work?"

Again, his eyes found hers, narrowed as if he suspected she were rogue and ready to take out his team, and then he gave a single slice of his chin to the left. "It's better if they see you. To them, you will represent the importance of my mission."

Ellery gave a single nod, swallowing her desire to isolate in a private locale.

They rounded a corner that dumped them into a large open space with MI12's teammates, mats, and machines that clanged and clattered. In the matter of a split second, the warm bodies stilled, the sound swallowed, and the room's focus pivoted to first land on Munroe with respect and then her with curiosity.

Just as quickly as the room's noise and activity died, it rose, and his team formed a semicircle around them.

"Team, this is Dr. Stein." Munroe delivered a succinct summary of the meeting with the Commissioner and their immediate shift in mission initiative.

Ellery expected him to introduce her to each member, but his attention never once deviated from his objective of updating his team and establishing the protocol for his absence. When he finished, he took a few questions. His voice shifted in timbre when he commanded them all to see the psychologist.

Munroe took a deep breath and squared his shoulders. "Don't let your guard down. With or without me at your command, you are responsible for the protection of Elshaddai. Our people count on your commitment, courage, and confidence." He shifted his stance and faced his next in command. "Tate, do what is right and lead by following your instinct. Don't try to be me. You've got this, and frankly, you've been ready for it for a long time."

Tate's chest swelled even as his cheeks reddened. He gave a single nod.

Without another word, Munroe spun on his heel and beat a path back to his HoverQuest. Inside, he bit out one word as a question. "Coordinates?"

Ellery hesitated. It was highly classified intel, but she'd been ordered to share it.

"The Commissioner told you to read me in." It was as if Dyce had read her thoughts. "I can't protect you if I don't know where you are, and I can't be on a team where I'm not trusted to lead you in the right direction."

Ellery trusted no one. She'd rather navigate this whole endeavor on her own. It was really an errant fear she might come across some beast in the past and would need muscle to fight it. Stupid, really. Somehow, she'd have to get MI12 back to his team and find an assistant who would make the risky trip to the past. That would be a better situation for all.

For now, in a breathy gust, Ellery complied with the Commissioner's orders and released her highly protected information as the muscle in Munroe's jaw jumped and quivered.

Now with her precious intel, the tension radiating from Dyce eased, and after a careless brush of his fingers, the HoverQuest spun and pierced the world outside, delivering them to the location at breakneck speed. She should tell him about her research. Bring him up to speed as ordered. But that wouldn't be necessary, because as soon as possible, the Commissioner would release him from the duty he clearly resented so much.

chapter
three

Underwhelming Importance

IT SHOULD HAVE LOOKED like something important. Dyce fought to keep an open mind, struggling to imagine this mission had even a hint of real importance. Instead, he faced a small boxy construction that declared its antiquity. The desolate surroundings of Ellery's coordinates within the protective government walls whispered of empty promises and wasted time, but another element floated in the air. Its almost undetectable nature slightly shifted the breeze. An unfamiliar scent filled its sigh.

Orders were orders. It didn't matter what he thought. He waited, arms across his chest, legs wide and ready. Ellery wasn't getting hurt on his watch, despite the lack of danger.

Ellery's cheeks turned an alluring pink as she struck off ahead of him, an unfamiliar gadget in her hand, words tumbling in mumbles from lips she often stopped and pursed.

The image of the boy resurfaced in Dyce's mind. If he failed the boy when he needed him most, what confidence could Dyce have in his ability to protect Ellery?

Her slender physique folded until her face was only a foot from the ground as she studied something hidden there.

Dyce had allowed too much space between them. A hostile could penetrate the government fortifications and take out one of their Lead Researchers in her prime, and it could all happen on Dyce's watch. His mouth went dry.

"What kind of intel requires your personal search of the premises? Shouldn't one of your assistants be out here braving the elements?" Dyce cleared his throat, trying to remove the ache from it.

Ellery twisted to face him, squinting before shaking her head. "With the importance of our pending mission, it's best if I don't rely on my team of assistants. The intel will be fresh in my mind. Just being here will allow me to recall every instance of this place wherever and whenever I am."

It was curious she didn't include him in wherever and whenever. "Did you find something?"

Her gaze shifted back to her research. "It's best if you remain by the gate. This area is under high-priority protection. There's no risk, and I work best on my own."

Frowning, Dyce retreated a few steps, but not back to the gate. She'd have to get over her work-on-her-own bit, because once they were in the past, they'd have to be a team, united. Their safety depended on that connection.

Fine. If she didn't want him near, he'd study the territory himself. He began a perimeter sweep, noting any potential hiding spots for an enemy. The location might be under surveillance now, but once they traveled to it in the past, there would be no telling what kind of environment they'd encounter.

"Did you say we're traveling to 2025?" he shouted over his shoulder.

A nearby scuffle of steps flurried toward him, and Dyce spun, prepared to drop the attacker.

Red-faced and huffing, Ellery charged at him like an adversary.

Dyce fought and lost to the surge of laughter that struck like a sniper.

"Are you laughing at me?" Ellery scoffed, kicked her toe into the dirt, winced, and then locked her furious eyes on him. "Do you even know what the word *confidential* means?" She spun away from him as if her battle shifted with the wind. "Of course you don't. You do as ordered—no thoughts necessary. This is why ..." Her voice dropped, and Dyce missed a few words. "Just can't." She whirled on him. "It doesn't matter." Her gaze fell to her gadget, and she swiped a few more times at it before she lifted calmer eyes to his. "I can't possibly finish this task with you shouting at me from across the location. I'm sure you'll get a printed report before the mission. That'll sufficiently update you about the details. Correct?"

Dyce gave her a single nod, as if moving too quickly might send her into another fit.

"Good. I don't require your assistance. Please let me complete my work in peace."

Oddly, Dyce's stomach tightened for no reason. He'd never enjoyed being dismissed, but this felt different, like a teammate dismissing him.

"Understood? I must do this before we go." She spoke to him as if he were simple-minded.

He fought the urge to frown at her, keeping his face calm. "Understood."

"Why don't you wait in the HoverQuest? I'll be another hour at most." Ellery turned, as if the conversation was over.

"No. I'll keep my peace, but understanding the layout is just as important to the mission's success as your research."

With a scoff, defiance passed over her expression before something hidden flitted there. "No more talking."

It was gone before Dyce could analyze it. "Fine by me."

She took a deep breath and turned back to her work.

Odd little thing.

Dyce couldn't shake the feeling that something incredibly important had just been decided, and he was now thrust on the outside of the upcoming mission, but feelings weren't facts, and missions weren't decided by fiery women who couldn't stand their protector. Oddly enough, though he laughed, her furious glare unnerved him even after she'd returned to her work. Such a strange woman with so much power in such a small frame.

His gaze wandered to her again, and he fought the spike of warmth that shot through him. Man, one failed mission and his whole body went haywire. He needed that session with the psychologist more than any of his teammates. He'd make that his top priority when they returned from 2025.

Moving to the rear of the facility, Dyce took in the steep drop that ended in a dry ravine. It was probably once a river, if their historians were correct about the landscape. He refused to glance at Ellery. They'd have to be certain to land in front of the location. Danger lurked in such a stark and sharp decline.

Dyce allowed his mind to soak in the angles of the terrain, the distance from the lowest dip to the facility, and tried to imagine what the land looked like past the formidable wall in their current timeline. He almost asked Ellery to join him in investigating it but remembered their intentional silence. He shook his head, rubbing a hand on his thigh.

He'd never escorted a researcher before. No amount of preparation could account for the innumerable potential scenarios. Without a team, no one to pick up his slack if he lost focus, they might be dead on impact.

Refusing to dwell on thoughts counter to his orders, he focused on how Ellery made him feel whenever she was close, and his temperature rose. He was in for some serious trouble on this mission.

Losing Munroe before the mission took off would be hard but not impossible. Ellery had already decided that Reese would be the best one to join her instead. She had a good mind for detail, and often they'd think and say the same thing. If something happened to one of them, the other could carry the mission through to the finish line. That was one hundred percent the priority.

What had come over her? She'd never charged up to someone like that before. And, oh! She wiped a stray hair from her forehead. She'd yelled—actually shouted at him. Warmth wrapped around her throat like a grip choking the life out of her. How could she ever meet his eyes again? Say another word to him without falling to pieces?

It didn't matter. She could and should do this on her own. Clearly, having him around ruined her ability to think with clarity.

Case in point. She was once again daydreaming and problem-solving the situation with Munroe instead of focusing on the task at hand. She couldn't even imagine what the mission would be like if she were already this distracted and volatile. The whole thing would be a flop.

His gaze seemed to pierce right through her, and that filled Ellery with all kinds of dread. No one. Not a single person in her life really knew her for who she was. She allowed her gaze to wander once again over the simple interior of the square foyer of the protected and rebuilt location she would soon visit in the past, something known as a two-story cabin from a time long gone. If anyone knew her like she knew this foyer, they'd discover she was only worth something because of her ability to remember massive amounts of material down to the finest detail. Researchers were born, not built. Good for one thing—their memories.

Ellery strategically moved through the building, down the hall, into the room meant for food consumption. Here she hesitated, imagining dining with Munroe, earning the same focus he'd given to his team as he debriefed them on their upcoming changes in protocol. His closeness with that team both frightened and allured her. Every member belonged, wholeheartedly.

If only.

When she needed people the most, they always abandoned

her. Stepping into one of the dwelling spaces, Ellery took in the musty air, studied the preserved environment, and hoped beyond all hope she'd be able to ditch the muscle maniac first. She moved into the next room, and then the next, readying herself in every way possible for the impossible.

A thrill started at the base of her skull and slid in a warm swath down her spine, wrapping like fingers around her until her whole body glowed in excitement at what was to come. She wasn't prone to emotion, but something about this place sparked life within her, a vivaciousness that consumed her mind and brought a wholeness she'd only experienced a handful of times in her lifetime.

Her communicator dinged—a soft sound, but so foreign in this nostalgic environment it took a minute for Ellery to place it.

The Commissioner's message read, Departure: 1800 hours.

Ellery's eyes blurred as she read the address and final parameters for the items she could take with her. Almost nothing. The capsule's intel, size, shape, and passenger requirements rolled by as Ellery scrolled.

It was real.

It was happening.

She glanced at the time. 1300 hours. She had to finish her examination. After sending a message to Reese, she completed her walk-through and headed out.

He was on his way as she stepped out. His eyes widened as they caught her. "The Commissioner's message?"

He didn't even know how to communicate. How did the Commissioner even think someone like Munroe would make a good protector for a researcher? "I'll need to secure a few things with my team and pack."

He nodded. "Meet on location at 1700 hours?"

"Sounds good." She'd convince Reese to join her, then go at 1600 hours and adjust the cockpit requirements to account for more items—their supplies were necessary to conduct a thorough examination of the time period.

She climbed into the HoverQuest, feeling pretty pleased with her plan.

It was important to not get attached to people, and with the responses he incited within her, she needed to keep her distance. Three hundred years should do it.

She smiled.

"What's funny?" He searched her face.

Her heart sank. How long had she been sitting there, him watching her, and the HoverQuest not moving? "Nothing."

He scoffed. "Clearly something's up. Was there more to your message?"

Ellery bit her cheek. How could she answer that? She hadn't seen his message. He was so not on her level. "No."

"Okay. Well, keep me in the loop. We're a team, and as such, you'll need to let me in on your plans. We don't have time to develop the synergy that would be best, but we can start by choosing not to see each other as enemies."

She couldn't help her gaze dashing to his sleek profile as he navigated the HoverQuest. Did he see her as his enemy? Did she see him that way?

"Fair enough," she finally replied, then swallowed back a retort about him first. "It's hard for me to work with others. A side effect of my profession."

"Well, teamwork makes the dream work."

"I've worked on a team. They can be cutthroat, unreliable, and often their self-motivation drives them in a direction that is not best for others."

"That's not the kind of team I'm talking about. Nothing competitive should be in a team. Ideally, it's a place you belong, perfect for you and you alone, somewhere you fit as uniquely you but also as a part of something bigger and stronger, allowing you to do things you never imagined possible."

His team sounded like the dream he mentioned earlier. It wasn't real. It probably was some kind of governmental propaganda he bought into to make himself feel better as a member and leader of a team. If only he could analyze and think for himself. Ellery studied the scenery outside whizzing by.

But when he pulled away to go home and pack, a bereftness swallowed her. His team might be fictional, but it was the type of story she silently craved.

Ellery needed to keep her head clear, and now with Munroe at a distance, she could execute her plans with her usual discipline and resourcefulness.

She sent another message to Reese. "Grab your sack and meet me at the Research HoverQuest."

chapter
four

Only an Hour

REESE TRAILED Ellery into the warehouse for mission launch, her heels clicking in a quicker staccato than Ellery's long legs pounded out, but after Reese agreed to help Ellery launch without Munroe, time was of the utmost importance. They'd tossed their sacks together and were back in a HoverQuest before 1400.

Ellery blew a stray strand of hair from her eyes and checked her watch again. Time was creeping by, but it was also racing away as her time in the present grew shorter by the second, and 1534 swept across the screen.

The Launch Team Commander stood a foot taller than her as he walked his team through the setup for the upcoming time travel. "Nidge, set the credel-meter to zero point thirty-seven."

"Sir." Ellery stood to her fullest height. In order for them to take off, she'd have to sell this change in plans with no documentation. She hated how the room didn't seem to have enough air. How a man like Munroe could seem so necessary to some. Her heart sank at the thought, but she shoved it into a quiet, dark corner and kept on. This had to work. "I'm Dr. Ellery Stein, and this is my assistant, Reese. In my search of the destination location today, I discovered the mission's time period to be passive and the need for an equally intelligent assistant paramount to complete my research. There will be no room for the MI12. Please make adjustments accordingly."

As she spoke, the commander's long face took her words like a blow to his chin, cheeks reddening, chin dipping, chest puffing. "There is protocol—"

"We're aware. However, this mission is far too important. Protocol must not stand in its way." Ellery forced her expression neutral, bored almost.

The commander's dark eyes narrowed. "Mission Commissioner approved this change?"

"And the board." Ellery held his hard gaze.

"Documentation?"

"No time. This mission is urgent. We miss our window, and you know what could happen. Well, maybe you don't, but I assure you, as one of the Lead Researchers of the Historians, it would incur grave consequences."

The commander's lips thinned as he gave a single nod.

"Launch must occur at 1630."

The commander spluttered. "That can't be—there's no way—"

"I'm fully confident you'll find a way."

Shaking his head, he said, "I'll see what can be done, but my team won't be able to fully charge the battery, so we can't assure you all the energy you need for a round trip."

"The lighter weight should account for lost energy."

With a thoughtful twist of his head, the commander turned back to his team and began shouting orders, a new urgency pouring out of his tone.

Reese leaned in to Ellery and whispered, "I honestly didn't think it would work."

Ellery waved her off. They couldn't talk like that here and now. Maybe once they were in 2025.

"I hate that I'll be missing Family Time. I look forward to it every year." Reese's expression grew wistful.

"I never really noticed it." Ellery actually despised the stupid time. Without a family, what good was mandated, annual Family Time? It held absolutely zero purpose in her life.

"Step on the scale." The commander's eyes flashed as his gaze tripped from Ellery to another team member. "Mit, grab a new travel suit." Again, his attention shifted, this time to Reese. "Size, Miss?" The commander, whose label declared him Aaro, was in full mission mode and somehow was channeling Ellery's inner drive.

"S-s-small." Reese frowned, raising her arms as Mit wrapped a tape measure around her.

Mit smiled. "I'll take that into account."

Reese's cheeks blazed.

This was going to work. Ellery finally took a full breath, inhaling calm and exhaling excitement. Muscle Man's dark cloud wouldn't be ruining her research. Reese was dependable, noncompetitive—hence her still being an assistant—and her mind was as sharp as a HoverQuest's AI. Research missions required those with a mind for the task.

When Mit waved Ellery forward, she stepped into his workspace for her final measurements. The countdown proudly ticked away on the main mission screen. Twelve men and women swiped, ticked, and tapped in coordinates and code. Seeing the time travel mission command in action was like a work of art. A dance of brilliant minds coalescing into a finale that would send her into a history no longer available to their time period.

It was probably Ellery's turn to look wistful, but everyone was too busy to notice her. She double-checked her pack, only the bare minimum allowed. Time travelers needed to blend in, so they didn't carry clothing or other items. Nothing but essentials such as first aid and lifesaving amenities, including a day's worth of pocket meals, an unconsumable evil. She'd rather starve.

An arm around her shoulders and a tight squeeze startled Ellery.

"We did it! I honestly didn't think you'd be able to smuggle me onto a time capsule. But—" Reese spun, arms out, dancing to the beat of excitement that also pounded through Ellery.

"I couldn't have done any of this without you. This mission is counting on us to bring back the lost history. If 2025 still holds an account of the years prior, we could fill in thousands of blank pages in our history. Potentially discover the key to the families." Ellery shook her head.

It was hard to even imagine the present with a history. For so long, they'd simply focused on the now and what was to come with no rudder to steer themselves forward, with no anchor to hold them to a higher purpose.

History taught culture how to avoid danger, how to seek health and growth for the community, and how to value what was most important. Without it, men and women were aimless, selfish, easily manipulated.

"Hey, where'd you go just now?" Reese gripped Ellery's shoulders.

Ellery chuckled. "Just trying to imagine the present with a history."

Reese's eyes grew. "If we are successful, everyone will shout our names for all time's sake."

"But that's not why we do this."

"Maybe not you." Reese's eyebrows climbed to her blonde hairline. "But some of us wouldn't mind coming out of a shadow or two."

Hmm. Ellery did not know Reese felt that way. "Would you choose a different path for yourself?"

Reese grew still, her eyes solemn. "I'm beyond grateful to be your assistant." She scooped Ellery's hands into her own. "I'm not saying I regret working under you."

"But." Ellery winced inwardly. Whatever Reese said next might indicate a need for her to remain behind as well. No one was trustworthy. *No one.* Not even the smartest assistant. This was why Ellery did everything on her own. Right here. This.

"No *but*. However, a future that includes me working side by side as an equal to you is one that I could get behind."

Ellery let out the breath she'd been holding. "Any future that includes working side by side with you is a future filled with success and intelligence. I think—"

Dyce didn't care who witnessed an MI12 running down the corridor. If the mission's commander hadn't reached out to him ... He swiped a hand down his face and sped up. That researcher was a deviant!

This was why warriors couldn't ever let their guard down. People were like broken AI, spouting one thing and doing another. His eyes landed on Ellery first as he skidded to a stop.

Summoning his most formidable Team Leader tone, he filled the cavernous space with his bass. "How dare you?"

Ellery almost hid her wince, but the eyes always spoke the truth. Just as they had done earlier when he suspected she was up to something.

"Defying the Mission Commissioner is a heinous offense." Dyce fought to swallow the hurt trying to poke through in his tone. And to think he'd been praying their opportunity to spend time together would be one of hope and promise. He clenched his teeth.

Ellery straightened, as if her height did anything but enunciate her lack of strength and power.

"You thought you'd travel into the unknown without protection. And they say Lead Researchers are the smartest of us all," Dyce scoffed.

Cheeks flushing, Ellery balled her hands. "I'm not without means."

"Are you going to think an attacker to death?"

Ellery gasped. "It's a peaceful time."

"And you know that because we have a full account of all the happenings during that time period?" Dyce leaned back, feigning nonchalance. He had to get his temper under control or Ellery might report him for uncomely conduct.

A strange blonde stepped in front of Ellery, who'd frozen as if time itself stopped. The woman flicked a glance over her shoulder, squared off with Dyce, and lifted her chin. "It came to Ell—Dr. Stein's attention, she'd been paired with a brute who cared nothing for the research and might hinder the mission. Forced to make the only logical next step—to preserve the research mission—she made a call."

"Thank you, Reese. I'll take it from here." Ellery moved in front of the blonde, took a deep breath, and lifted those brown eyes to lock with Dyce's. "Thank you for your service. Unfortunately, it is no longer necessary, as this mission requires delicate finesse and a keen mind. As the Lead Researcher, it is well within my purview to dismiss your services. I have reset the protocols to accommodate Reese's smaller stature so we can include items necessary for travel to 2025."

Heat blazed through Dyce. Dismissed. She thought she could simply cancel protection. "Danger is everywhere."

"I am aware."

"And Reese is trained in protection protocols? She's able to ward off an enemy? Fight with whatever item is at her disposal? Assess your surroundings and protect you, even if it costs her life?"

Reese coughed. "I'm sorry. What?"

"I am assigned to protect Dr. Stein. Without me, it will fall on your shoulders to maintain her safety and the well-being of the research."

Reese's face paled. Good. The two women lived their whole lives in their heads. They had absolutely no idea the evil that existed beyond MI12's protection.

Ellery frowned, stiffened, then cleared her throat. "If I am lost, she can carry on the research without me. How would you suffice without the Lead Researcher, if perchance I am indisposed for some unknown reason?"

A below-the-belt hit. Did she somehow know he'd just failed a mission? Was she digging at his inability to keep his charge alive? He drove a hand through his already mussed up hair. "If you were indisposed, I'd find you and bring you back. But if you go on without me, you'll have no one to rescue you."

Ellery huffed. "It is not *if*."

Dyce leaned forward as if surrounding her with his strength might batter her into submission. Except she met him toe to toe. Thinking fast—for him—he shifted tactics. Smart people always wanted to be acknowledged for their minds, and they often dismissed the more physical needs of their bodies. Fine. He'd take their conversation into a realm she wasn't able to hold her ground in.

Silently, Dyce swept her feet out from under her. As if in slow motion, he finished the full circle and caught her head before it bounced off the tile floor.

Reese's scream echoed in the large warehouse.

The clatter of keyboards silenced.

Knowing a single move wouldn't be enough, Dyce turned and caught Reese's small neck between his biceps and forearm, closing it off in a triangle with his other arm.

"What are you doing? Release her at once," Ellery ordered from where she sprawled on the floor, clearly too shocked to move.

"Absolutely. As soon as you make me." Dyce widened his stance, ready for her attack.

Her eyes danced around the room, probably seeking a hero to come to her aid. Funny story, lady. He *was* the hero, and she'd sent him away.

She stormed to a nearby table and picked up a long, slender device. Spinning, she flung the item at Dyce's head. He easily ducked and held his expression calm, at attention.

Reese coughed. "Dr. Stein—"

"Let me think." Ellery jogged to the commander and searched his workstation while he stood several feet back, arms across his chest, his gaze switching between Dyce and the wily woman ransacking his organized environment. She turned back to Dyce, holding up a pen like it was a weapon.

Dyce chuckled.

"Don't," Reese whispered to him.

He raised an eyebrow she couldn't see but whispered back, "And why not?"

Her breath was hot on his arm. "She's easily provoked."

Holding the pen high, Ellery sprinted at him. Dyce shifted his grip, protecting Reese with his body, while capturing Ellery's tiny wrist in his hand.

She yanked back.

He refused to relent. If the woman needed a self-defense lesson, then he'd give her one. She was smart. She'd learn. "Finished?"

"Hardly."

He tilted his head, taking her in as she grew more and more frantic, trying to rip herself from his grip. "Now?"

"Never."

Dyce released Reese and spun Ellery to face him, gripping both her shoulders and bending down until they were eye to eye. "I've made my point. You are beyond intelligent, but you need me. I have your best interests at heart. My duty and calling is to follow orders, and that makes this mission my calling."

"No. It's *mine*."

"It's both of ours. And neither of us should dismiss the other." Dyce both willed and prayed for her to agree.

"Dr. Stein, listen to him. He's right. I couldn't have done all that."

Ellery scoffed. "I'll be the judge of that." She pulled from Dyce's grasp and paused, time ticking away.

With a deep breath, she finally shifted her gaze to where the commander seemed to fiddle with nothing. "Commander, I am sorry. It appears the plans have changed again."

Dyce cleared his throat. "Please return all protocols to their original settings. There's no need to mention any of this to anyone outside this room. Agreed?"

Shoulders relaxed, keyboards began clacking, and the room seemed to exhale.

Dyce moved to block her view of the team. "Listen."

He waited for her to lift her eyes to meet his.

"You are my team now. It's just you and me."

Ellery snorted, red creeping along her neck.

"I know I'm not the partner you are used to, but together with our unique strengths, we can accomplish the last leg of your research." Dyce's hand hovered, wanting to touch Ellery again but knowing he couldn't—shouldn't.

Ellery stepped back, as if aware of his desire.

Reese caught her as she stepped right into her space.

"Oh, sorry!" Ellery's cheeks flamed red.

Dyce shook his head. Poor thing couldn't get anything right. If left to her own devices, she'd tank her own mission.

Reese hugged her. "Going with Dyce is best."

"No. It's not." Ellery sliced her head to the right.

Reese stepped away, giving a longing glance to the capsule. "Make history, Dr. Stein. I'll see you when you return."

Reese turned and silently padded from the room.

It was obvious Ellery needed him. Something well beyond his understanding lurked just under the surface of the details Ellery gave him. He'd have to pay close attention to her, or she'd leave him behind again. Somehow, he had to gain her trust. It was imperative.

chapter
five

OF ALL THE confounding creatures Dyce had met in his lifetime, this whisper of a woman set him on fire in ways he'd never experienced before. Wild didn't even describe the hair trigger hidden inside of Ellery. Not even close.

"Lead the way." He waved Ellery down the long hall before him, away from the capsule, her attempted coup, and the team readying the ship that would propel them into the past. "We have a bit of time."

He shoved a hand through his hair as he followed, monitoring her, through the hall to the conference room. Somehow, he should have seen it coming—in fact, he did. He narrowed his eyes, a sharp pain wrapping around his chest, a result of his shift in duties. When forced to leave his well-oiled team to protect a lunatic researcher, the consequences would abound. In fact, she probably didn't know how close she came to death. Travel into the past without a protector. Insane. He snorted.

"Is there something you'd like to say?" She spun, her whole body coiled to pounce.

Heat sparked through Dyce. Grabbing her elbow, he pulled

her into the conference room. "You are Lead Researcher, but I'm charged with your protection. Yes, you can make research decisions, but no, you have no right to cut me out and set me aside. That must be absolutely clear in your mind. What you did here could have compromised your well-being."

"The research takes priority." Ellery placed her hands on her hips.

Oh, cute. "Right, and what happens to your research and knowledge if you die?"

Color drained from her porcelain cheeks, and she swayed on the spot.

Great. He'd done it now. First, he scared her off, and now he scared her witless. He held out both hands. "Sorry. That was harsh, but that's the world I live in." Gentler. He had to soften his voice, or she'd spook again.

Ellery glanced at the door.

"See. Together, as a team"—he tried to ignore the shadow that passed over her face just before she rubbed a palm over her heart—"I can battle the world back while you complete your research."

Shoulders rounding, Ellery took in a deep breath. "You're right." She held up a hand. "You are. It's a different team than I'd hoped for, but I can handle the research alone."

"Of course." Dyce searched her brown eyes as they seemed to warm up to him.

"I need you to understand. I'd risk almost anything to complete this research."

His heart hurt for her. That was no way to be ...

But then he realized they had that in common. "I understand that level of dedication."

She clutched her arms around herself. "I—"

Her gaze dashed to the door and then back to him. They were similar, but he'd never cut someone out of the team. In fact, he'd lay his life down for his team, for her. But his sacrifice would be so others could live. Hers seemed a bit of a waste, chasing ghosts three hundred years in the past. Memories weren't worth one's life. Especially those that had been lost for longer than either of them had been alive, since the war on data.

She swallowed and then lifted her chin. "I'm sorry. You probably think the Mission Commissioner saddled you with this lone wolf who makes rash decisions. A recipe for certain disaster."

"The thought had crossed my mind." The tension in his shoulders evaporated. "I'm glad we've found some common ground."

She searched his face, and he tried to radiate strength and protection.

"Okay." Some internal fortitude seemed to rise within her. "So, we do this together. Is there anything I need to know about your plans and expectations going forward?"

"I can't train you in thirty minutes before we take off, but stay as close as a shadow. Please communicate what you intend to do before you do it and remain open to my input, which is equally important. I understand you're willing to lay your life down for research, but let's let that remain our last option."

Ellery slowly nodded. "Understood. For me, I need you to allow the research to be our number one priority—aside from lives and such. I don't want us to take this risk only to fail. With my knowledge, if we come across anyone from the time period, and we probably will, please let me make first contact and only intervene if I'm in immediate danger."

"Of course. Do you have an estimated timeline for the return?"

"The initial quote in my research was six weeks with potential to remain longer depending on the needs of the research."

"What potential might affect the timelines?"

She closed her eyes, clasping her hands and taking a deep, cleansing breath. "Walking amid history." Her whole body trembled with excitement. "Conversing with the living ghosts of our forefathers." She squealed and jumped, sending a jolt through

Dyce. "Can you imagine meeting one of the twelve historically relevant family members? There's no telling what might arise, which is why I left room for whatever may be."

"I can't imagine it." Dyce tried to force his cocked eyebrow down, but it refused to settle over his eyes.

"I see your skepticism, but this is what I live for." She jutted her chin at him.

Great, so he could add offended to his list of crimes against Dr. Stein. "No. Not skepticism. I just might not share the same enthusiasm for dead people, but I love that you love them."

"Dead people will be very much alive in twenty minutes."

The thrill of the great Dr. Stein. "Right. We should make final preparations for the launch. So, we're good?"

She bit her lip and nodded. "We're good. No more taking off on you."

A sliver of tightness that had been coiled around his spine finally released at her promise. He didn't even realize he'd been concerned about a reenactment of her defiance, her betrayal. It certainly wasn't the best way to start off a new team dynamic, but she sure promised to be an exciting partner, and only two members on a team lent itself to some level of intimacy.

Heat blazed along his spine. No. Not that kind of intimacy. Just two made a small team. How hard could it be to ... He huffed. "Let's head out."

"Good." She led the way again.

What a spitfire.

How was Ellery going to make it through this mission with those blue eyes? Despite all her arguments, though, not once had she truly come to peace with leaving Dyce.

She needed Dyce so she could figure out the missing, possibly supernatural reason, for the Inn's longstanding history.

How he searched her face sent a flutter tickling her belly. She rested a hand over the spot to suffocate it. No butterflies allowed on this trip. No distractions. Her gaze wandered over her shoulder to find him watching her.

"Are you coming?" She held her breath for fear another pedantic or rude word might escape. Had she lost all access to her brain cells? This guy could conquer her single-handedly. That thought forced her breath out of her and drew her to a standstill.

He smirked.

She sincerely hoped he couldn't tell what she was thinking. In fact, *she* didn't even know what she was thinking. Tilting her chin, she dared him to attempt to pierce her mind with those blue eyes and their flashes of yellow gold that gave them the depth of the stars in the sky.

"Wasn't it you who was worried about making it to the launch bay?" He waved a hand as he passed her.

Heat spiked through her. Now, if she passed him, she'd look petty, but with him out in front, she was no longer the leader. For a beat, she let that thought sit with her until inspiration hit and she moved again, tailing him.

He spun. "What on earth are you doing?" He scraped a hand down his face.

"I'm shadowing you. At least, practicing it."

A softness entered his eyes, and she both hated and loved it. What was going on with her? Had she any mind left? Was the loss permanent? Without her cognitive acuity, she was nothing but a grunt, another useless mouth to feed in society. Did she even have any other redeemable qualities? *I must remain sharp and in full control of all my faculties for the endurance of this journey.*

"Practice is good. A few pointers." He balled his hand and released it, repeating this motion several times as he spoke. "Consider the sounds your feet make. Try to keep them as quiet as possible. Don't stare at my feet. That's a recipe for a trip and fall. People lead with their shoulders, so keep your eyes there, but also monitor the surroundings. If something happens to me out there, you might be left on your own, and you'll need to protect yourself with some basic self-defense and recon."

"Recon?"

"Just an awareness of your surroundings, noting the things and people who might be a danger." Munroe's expression grew scary somber.

Ellery nodded, feeling like he'd just shifted into a foreign language. "What do I call you?"

Surprise flickered in his gaze before he shuttered it away.

"The Commissioner called you Munroe, so I've been calling you that ..." She blinked, realizing she'd called him a bunch of names in her head, but only rarely Munroe. "In my head, but I wonder if that's what your team calls you."

His cheeks glowed. "Teammates call me Dyce."

An interesting name.

"Five-minute warning to countdown," chimed an AI voice radiating through the hall.

"We'd better hurry." Dyce turned to go.

To his shoulder, which she was now watching and refusing to enjoy, she said, "Call me Ellery."

Had he called her other names in his head too?

Within minutes, they were back in the cavernous warehouse and approaching different techs to dress and make final preparations. Ellery's priority became following Mit's orders as she strapped into her suit and avoided the commander's glare. An arm there and a cinched strap here, and she was ready within five minutes. She found Dyce waiting for her.

"How did you get finished so quickly?"

"It helps if you allow the person who knows what they're doing to lead you." He gave her a cockeyed grin.

She'd done that. Hadn't she? With a huff, she lifted her chin and led the way to the capsule, fighting back the shakiness in her limbs. This was it.

She lifted her foot over the footwell. History in the making. She sat down, and Mit buckled her in. He hooked Dyce in behind her and did a final dash check. A distant part of her mind blared a warning, but the cockpit filled with Dyce's warm musky scent, and her mind replayed the moment he told her she was a part of his team—his priority. Had she ever felt so special in her life?

Then the clock was counting down. The engine revved. Something crooned into a fevered pitch, and then her whole body seemed to suck through the mouth of a water bottle and explode out on the other side, but with all the wrong pieces in the most awful places.

A horrific explosion of pain rattled Ellery's head as it whipped forward, then back, slamming into her headrest. Her chest restraint gripped her firmly in the seat, but her guts seemed to twist and spin freely. Compelling herself to be strong, she willed her eyes open to catch the last of something brown and dark cracking as their capsule struck it. Then the ground came at her so fast she blinked her eyes closed again.

"What happened?" A whisper of her previous alarm, a sinking of the stomach, a deadening of the limbs, couldn't bring the story behind the sound to the forefront of her mind. But the rushing sound as the capsule scraped along the earth swallowed her voice. Their crash tore up some white powder, crushing slender brown things jutting from the ground that sent the capsule pinballing until it came to a sudden, silent rest, teetering as if on the side of a sharp decline.

Help us.

A sharp sound seemed to press against her skull, but it didn't make it through the ringing in her ears. The cabin flooded with a bright red light that only took slight breaks before flashing to full brightness again.

"Ellery."

A heavy hand landed on her shoulder, and she yanked against her restraints, lost in the horror of it all.

"Ellery, it's me, Dyce. We've crash-landed. We're on the backside of the location."

His words traveled down a long hall, barely making it within hearing distance. Her mind had filled with fuzz, and her ears sang a discordant melody. "What?"

The hand left her shoulder. A click rattled through her bones, and the capsule opened, thrusting their warmth into the world before sucking in a freezing wash of wind and white dust that swirled around her lap and settled on her clothing.

This was history.

chapter
six

An Enemy Watching

December 2025—Coordinates Ancient Elshaddai

"HELP HER, Lord. Just don't let me fail another one. Not again. I won't survive it." Dyce forced his muscles not to falter, shoved the blustery dust from his focus, turned from the night scene filled with horrors he didn't recognize, and triaged Ellery.

With practiced movements, Dyce did an inventory of her person, ascertaining her wound level. Ellery's skin was intact, pale but pinked from the ice in the air. The white dust drifted into his collar, on his eyelashes, and sprinkled with silent caresses along Ellery's still form. Why didn't she stir?

He'd sit with her for a moment. Wait for her to recover.

He leaned back, forcing himself to face his fear, and conducted a second search of her legs, arms, torso—the steady rise and fall of her breathing settled something jagged in him, letting the sharp, cutting pieces rest again. Dyce took his first full breath since the wild plummet from the sky. Only after he knew she was alive did he allow his eyes to skate along her flawless skin to the delicate spot where her lashes rested gently on her cheeks. *Flutter. Please!*

A subtle movement, small and discreet, would be enough to settle his racing heart and wrestle his fears back under control. A hair, loosened in the crash, lay across her nose. Removing his glove, he gently tucked it behind her ear.

"Come on, Ellery. Come on." He leaned forward, nearly closing his eyes as her unique lavender scent enveloped him.

Losing her was not an option. Not now. Not ever. The ferocity of his emotions surprised Dyce. Somehow, this spitfire researcher, who'd grown up in such a different world than he, had caught his eye—maybe more. But his approach needed to be cautious. She'd already willingly risked her life for this mission, so if he wasn't careful, if he gave too much of himself before he really knew where she stood, she'd run away with his heart, and he'd be left with nothing but heartache.

Something behind him in the darkness called out a slow "Who, who?" Hand on his weapon, Dyce spun to assess their surroundings. Something he should have done already, but with Ellery down, he'd prioritized her well-being.

A distant *whomp, whomp* filled the air. Dyce narrowed his eyes, forcing them to see in the blackness, but not even the moon shone on this night. He cleared his throat. The sound, more distant now, seemed to accelerate like blades on a very slow, soft propeller, and then the night grew eerily silent again.

Nearby, a protracted groan sent needles prickling along Dyce's spine. Without a historical record of this time period and their time's network to back their devices, Dyce couldn't predict the potential threats in the area, and without drones or hivizion satellites to read in his lens, they were vulnerable.

Dyce strained his ears, attempting to lock in on the origin of the sound. If it continued, he might need to assess the risk in person. His gaze flicked back to Ellery. The breeze kicked up and drew his focus to the white dust that swirled in the light of their capsule, landing in his collar again, and leaving in its place tiny wet puddles like dots.

Something in the black midnight groaned.

Leaving Ellery vulnerable to the elements and by herself wasn't an option, but still Dyce stepped toward the edge of the cockpit. If something was coming, he'd stop it before it got to her.

This time, a loud crack ricocheted through the area, and a crash stole Dyce's breath. Something was out there. Crashing like a bomb into the ground. His mind conjured all forms of dark figures and giant attack structures made of strangely formed ice and the brown objects spearing the sky. Nothing made sense in this new time period. What were the brown things they'd hit? The white specks that suddenly turned to wet drops when they touched his skin? Or the odd, disorganized sounds filling the empty area surrounding them?

Ellery let out a pained breath. He spun to see her head rolling from one side to the other. Dyce searched the cockpit. Grabbing a water bottle, he popped off the seal and pressed the nozzle to her lips. She drank without encouragement, and when she'd had her fill, she pushed the bottle away.

"Did we make it?" Her eyes searched his face and then danced across the night landscape before them.

"It's hard to make out anything beyond the capsule."

"Did you bring a light projector?"

"It would make us more visible." He fought the urge to say, *No go*, like he would with his team in Elshaddai.

She nodded, slowly. Confusion creased her brow. "But the cockpit is lit."

"That light doesn't travel far." Dyce swallowed back orders. He had to lead Ellery differently. She wasn't his trained team back home. No. Something in her called to him, drew him in like a tractor beam. He leaned closer. "Are you injured?"

"No. I don't think so." She unsnapped her buckles and rose unsteadily, reaching out and gripping his biceps to find her balance.

Dyce's stomach warmed.

"Are you smiling?" Her eyes danced across his face.

Dyce tried to stow whatever emotion he'd somehow

absentmindedly allowed to show. Better yet, distracting her would be his best strategy. "We made it to history."

A slow, glorious grin whispered along her lips, transforming her often strict expression into a brilliant smile that stole even to the corners of her eyes until, somehow, her whole being shone. "Do you smell that? This is the air our ancestors breathed!"

Ellery gripped her hands together in front of her, curiosity and excitement clearly overpowering all analytical thinking as she fixated on something outside the capsule. She was out of the cockpit and knee deep in the white fluff before he'd properly assessed their surroundings.

"Wait. I've not—"

As if the land itself swallowed Ellery in one gulp, she disappeared with a screech.

Planting both hands on the cockpit's edge, Dyce vaulted into the pitch-dark night. "Ellery. Call out. I'll come to you. Just remain still."

Of course, all her caution was gone. He shook his head.

"I'm fine. I think."

Spinning, he found he'd launched himself right over her. "Please, Ellery, danger is everywhere, in everything we don't know, hidden behind every dark corner. Every action you take without first thinking it through is reckless and puts us both in danger."

Her smile vanished. She chewed her lip. "I got carried away."

A calculated expression descended over her, as if being a researcher were a persona she wore. She bent at the waist, scooped the white powder into her hands, and lifted it for Dyce to inspect. "What do you think this is?"

"Not dangerous." He angled his body to monitor the darkness at his back.

"Clearly. But isn't it interesting? I mean, what purpose could it possibly have? And it seems to cover everything, like a cleansing material, or a replenishing of some sort. I'd take a sample, but look, as soon as I collect it, it transforms into droplets that trickle away. What do you think the liquid might be?"

"Possibly water? It reminds me of ice from the food center in our timeline."

Ellery drew her eyebrows together in an adorable face of concentration. "Could it simply be water? I'm going to circle the capsule, see what's on the other side. Is that okay?"

Her expression held acknowledgement and respect. Hope filled Dyce. "I'll escort you. Just be careful. The ground is not visible."

In her absent way, Ellery nodded and started around the nozzle of the capsule. Just as they found themselves on the other side, the voice called, "Who, who?"

At that moment, Ellery startled with a cry and slipped out of his sight.

In a nanosecond, Dyce's heart stopped.

"Dyce! Help!"

With a sudden intake of air, Dyce was in motion. "Ellery. Stay where you are." Her voice came from fifteen, maybe twenty feet away, loud and clear. But Ellery herself was completely invisible in the inky night. "Keep talking. I can't see you, but I can hear you."

Nothing in her life prepared Ellery for the sharp, shooting pain radiating from just above her ankle. It burned through her. Boiled her bones. Shattered her skin into a million pieces. As it climbed through her, it choked the very air from her lungs and stifled her voice as Dyce ordered her to call out again. But she couldn't. She couldn't even inhale.

Dyce seemed to slowly fall and slide toward her, but she still couldn't make her voice work.

What had she done? That was it. She'd spent less than ten minutes in history, and it broke her before she even got started studying all the thrilling details that surely hid in these lost days, months, and years. Her heart ached. Eyes burned. Her throat swelled until she couldn't even swallow.

Fire burrowed through her bones every time she even shifted her foot or leg. Movement was impossible. With the temperature as it was, she'd only last a short time before the end would come for her. Poor Dyce. All of this, the capsule, the research, the obvious concern radiating in waves from him, all for nothing.

Why suffer the trip to only fail so quickly?

In fact, the stars dancing behind her eyelids indicated she might pass out.

Why? Why me? Why not someone else?

"What happened?" Dyce's gloved hands cupped her face, his own so close she could feel his warm breath breathing life back into her icy cheeks.

"The ground just fell out from under me, and my foot caught on something underneath the white powder—" Ellery hated the sob that broke from her. It was all wrecked. Everything.

"It'll be okay. I've got you."

In the faint light of the capsule's cabin, Ellery could make out Dyce's feverish eyes. "I don't think I can—"

"I'll carry you." Dyce slipped his arms under her and moved to lift.

Ellery cried out. "Stop. No! You're making it worse. I can't move."

"I can't leave you here to die." Dyce clenched his jaw. He flexed as if to lift her again.

Ellery screamed.

Dyce's gloved hands shifted, one to cup her mouth and the other the back of her head.

How dare he!

"Quiet. Your cry sent whatever was watching us into the sky."

"We were being watched?" Ellery's stomach bottomed out. She fought back another wave of pain and nausea.

"Yes. Where are you hurt?"

"My leg."

He nodded. "Do not move. I'll get the med kit and light

projector to triage you." Dyce stared into her eyes as if he were willing her to obey.

"I can't move. That's already the problem." Ellery sighed.

"Good." Dyce stepped away, hesitated a beat, and then he was gone.

In the silence of the falling white powder and the foreignness of history, a dramatic shift in Ellery took her so by surprise, she gasped. Gratitude for Dyce's presence in this moment sent tears falling. What if Dyce had been left behind? What if her foolish, know-it-all attitude got Reese hurt, or worse, what if they were out here fending for themselves? There was absolutely no way two researchers could have handled this on their own.

It felt like only a minute had passed, but Dyce was back at her side, blinding her with a flood of light and dropping the med kit into the white powder beside them. "Describe the pain."

"It's everywhere."

He searched her expression. "Something seems different."

Could he read minds too? "I'm actually really glad you're here. I—my assistant and I couldn't have handled this on our own."

A deep, warm *hmm* radiated from his chest. "That's in the past. Let's focus on the here and now."

Ellery couldn't help but smile. And then they were both smiling, the light projector lying on its side in the fluffy white substance.

All too soon, Ellery was aware of the silence creeping in, making things awkward.

Dyce settled on his knees beside her. "It's too cold out here. I've got to get you up and moving. Before I can do that, I have to look. Okay?"

A creak awoke the night.

Ellery looked away into the darkness, wishing she wasn't broken, useless. What good was a mind if the body couldn't carry it to its work?

"I'll need to touch and examine the spot that's hurting you most."

"Please be gentle." Ellery leaned back against the slanted ground, grinding her teeth together in a preemptive move to keep herself from crying out if his probing hurt.

Unzipping the bag, Dyce placed a few items in his pockets before he ran a featherlight touch down from her knee. Three-quarters of the way, just a few inches above her ankle, his touch grew unbearable.

"Stop, stop! Please." Ellery breathed out through clenched teeth.

"Okay. Fine. I'm going to pull up your pant leg. I'll be as gentle as possible. But it might hurt."

"Please—"

"I have to do this."

"Just give me a second to—" Ellery took in the icy air, wishing she'd pass out already. She wasn't cut out for this kind of adventure. In her head, she'd only imagined interviewing an ancestor, diving into the databases that held the histories before they'd been lost, maybe walking along a path laid by one of the founding families. Nothing about getting hurt. Dying.

"Ready?" His eyes explored hers. In them, a deep well of strength seemed to firm up her own lacking stores of willpower.

"Never. But we've got to do it, right?" She took a deep breath and closed her eyes.

"Yes."

"Then do it." Knowing she wouldn't have the willpower to keep her eyes closed, Ellery looked away. "It'll hurt, but I can be strong." She hoped. *Be strong.*

"Okay."

It was a whisper that only dashed across her senses a second before pain licked up her leg. Turning away, Ellery bit down on her cheek. *Help. Help me. Help!*

"The skin is intact. Based on the bruising and your pain level, I suspect you've broken a bone, but we don't have the equipment to properly diagnose and treat it out here. I'm going to splint it so you can move. It will alleviate some of the pain."

"Does the kit have any pain medication?"

Dyce nodded, but his movements slowed. "Pain medication will slow your reflexes and dull your senses."

"Exactly." Then it hit Ellery. If they were in a life-and-death situation, again, she'd be worse than useless. She'd be a liability. At least, more of one than she already was. "Oh. I need to stay alert."

He nodded, watching her carefully.

"Would half a dose be a suitable compromise? I'm not sure I can move with this pain level." *Please, let me function with half a dose.*

"We can take that risk. I'll carry you if need be."

Ellery's stomach somersaulted at the idea of him lifting her into his arms. Physical touch wasn't a large aspect of research.

After a half dose and applying a zip-close splint that enclosed her entire leg and foot, sending warmth pulsing through her whole body, Dyce got to his feet and paused. "Are you ready? We have to climb this, collect what we need from the capsule, and seek shelter for the night."

Ellery groaned. "That sounds like a lot."

"Doesn't matter how it sounds, soldier. You've got research to complete, and it will not do it on its own. I've got you." Dyce reached down, scooped her up, and, without giving her a second to react, hoisted her in the air. Then, they were climbing toward the capsule.

"I thought you would only carry me if need be."

"It is need be. I'll set you to your own devices once the ground is flat and trustworthy. We can't afford injury elsewhere."

In what world was an MI12 more logical than a Lead Researcher? Only in history. Ellery huffed, creating a delightful cloud around her face that was there one second and vanished the next.

Just like time.

chapter
seven

The Secret

FIRST, Dyce would need to fashion a makeshift surface to carry both of their packs and Ellery, keeping her weight off her injured leg. Without equipment to mend the bone, the break, if it was a break, would take weeks if not months to heal. He shook his head, sickness swirling in his belly. Back home, it might take half a day to heal. Why Ellery believed this forsaken time period held all hope was beyond him.

"What?" Ellery's gaze searched his face, pain etched in the tightness around her eyes and the tension of her slender form.

"Nothing." He swung up and over the capsule edge and rested her gently back where she'd started, in her seat in the cockpit. He resisted the urge to strap her in and take her home.

Apparently, it was his turn to throw caution to the wind. He would no longer keep quiet, guard the amount of light pollution they released, or monitor their surroundings. He was on a mission to find shelter at all cost.

"It's bad." A tremble shivered just under her words. Barely. But it was there.

The boy's haunting face, at the moment his life ended, suddenly blazed to life in Dyce's mind. But this wasn't the same scenario. They could still find their way out of this. No one had a gun on Ellery. There weren't hostiles bearing down. At least, none that had stepped into Dyce's awareness, and he was hyperaware in a situation with a teammate down in a two-person team.

"No. It'll be fine," he finally answered, unable to look at her and lie, but they both were in danger because of her leg. He couldn't carry her for weeks, and if things went sideways, he'd need both hands to fend off an enemy.

And things always went sideways.

He quietly huffed as he turned away from Ellery's gaze that now seemed to bore a hole in his shoulder. Even without looking at her, he could tell she knew things were in awful shape.

"Your shoulders are so tense they're up around your ears, and you're throwing things like the ship has done you some heinous wrong. Level with me, Dyce. How bad is our situation?"

Dyce stilled. "I'm working on recalibrating the plan for both infiltration and extraction, incorporating the additional complication of your injury. I can't do that and commiserate with you regarding the status of our situation. Frankly"—he allowed his gaze to dance to hers, holding his expression under a firm lockdown—"how good or bad things are matters not. Our focus must remain on solutions and next steps."

A red light flashed just beyond the delicate curve of Ellery's face, reminding him how, after landing, the cabin flooded with a bright red light. Was it the same? The light seemed muted now, and he refused to even imagine what it might be about. Instead, the daunting task of carrying Ellery to safety took precedence— that and the hair falling loose against her cheek.

Sliding the hair behind her ear, Ellery gave a single curt nod. "True."

Her skin had taken on a sickly pallor. She must be in terrible pain. He grabbed a crate and rested it within a foot and a half of her seat. Wrapping his hand gently above her injury, he lifted her foot and placed it on the crate as he explained, "You need to keep the injury elevated."

When Ellery closed her eyes and leaned her head against the seat, Dyce turned to his work, paying close attention to any sound or movement she might make while also forcing his movements to be calmer, gentler, so as not to frighten her. She was so fragile and yet intensely fascinating. A force welled up within him, fierce and wild, readying him to tear the world apart to protect her.

He shook it off. But the weight of its sensation seemed only to dig in deeper, clawing into his heart and settling there as if it belonged. Oh, Ellery was more dangerous than any situation he'd ever faced before.

With a grunt, Dyce tossed first his pack, then hers, into the white fluff.

Ellery had opened her eyes and followed the trajectory of the pack. "I love this white substance. There's something peaceful and comforting about it."

"How do you know it's not designed as some sort of insidious weapon ready to kill us?" Dyce pulled out the long stiff tubing from the storage cubby. Somehow, he'd fashion it into a transport to pull Ellery and their packs behind him as he traversed the incline. He'd make it to the top and reevaluate once he scoped out more of the land. "Is it the same time here as it is back in our time period?"

"It should be. Time is constant. Ever changing, but in the same singular-minded march forward that every person experiences." Ellery's voice sounded pained.

Dyce frowned. Maybe she required more medication. If the impact broke her tibia, she might need enough to knock her out. A flat surface he could pull would be the only way to transport her if she were unconscious.

"What are you doing?" Her words held a hint of exasperation, as if he might have lost his mind and was literally tearing the ship apart.

Dyce almost chuckled. "I'm re-tasking some of our supplies. If I can find something like a tarp and some rope, we'll be all systems go."

"Oh, that's a relief. I was afraid the stress of time travel might ... have ..." Ellery's silence, at first, seemed to make sense.

But when the absence of her movement and her voice continued, Dyce's heartbeat sped up. "Ellery?"

Half of his torso was deep inside the cubby as he sorted through labels that meant little more than gibberish to him.

Without a reply, he grabbed something that might work and pulled out into a blast of cold air. He could barely make his voice whisper, "Ellery."

"It's so cold out here."

Alarm rattled through him like sharp heat and left him sucking wind like a fist to the gut. Shifting into the medic role, he set the items to the side, pulled off his glove, and pressed his fingers to her neck.

She took in a sharp breath as his icy fingers met the warmth along her throat. "I'm fine. Being still in this wind, it's making me feel strange."

Shock. He needed to find shelter and fast.

The mission to finish her research took priority over even injury. She stiffened her jaw and tried to step into the part of her brain that could compartmentalize, move the pain out of her thoughts, and focus on the things that mattered most. The mission stood paramount. Demanded her undivided attention.

And yet, the pulsing in her leg just above her ankle stole most of her focus. Her remaining thoughts danced between distractions.

First up on the list, the brute of a man warring with the innocent ship, and with him, her strange reaction every time he came near. And, oh, when he'd lifted her into the cockpit, her stomach had jumped in an incredibly enticing manner.

Second were the delightful experiences just beyond her reach because of her injury. A truth she maligned with her lack of physical prowess. Certainly she should have trained harder, but hours of research didn't accommodate a healthy workout regimen.

But probably third and most irritating was the flashing red light at the front of the cockpit. If she'd taken the time to read the manual instead of fashioning wild plans to leave with her assistant, then she'd already know what it meant. While Dyce dug in the cubby at the back, Ellery whispered her fingers along the side of the seat—really anything within reach—to solve the mystery.

Dyce rummaged in the loudest of manners. As she was about to say something, her fingers landed on a thin protrusion. Teasing the item out of the nearly invisible compartment, Ellery rejoiced at her discovery.

An intellipad clearly marked with the label: Emergency System.

Perfect!

Her gaze ravaged the device until her mind devoured every word and raged at the truth. With the short interval flash combined with the color red, it was absolutely certain—the crash damaged one of the fuel cells. She twisted to peer back at the broken lengths pointing up at the sky. They'd hit many of them as they landed. One of the brown stanchions could have easily battered and broken a fuel cell.

Worse. With only one working fuel cell left, they couldn't both return to their appropriate time period.

Ellery replaced the intellipad and grew deathly still. How could she abandon him here?

But she must. The research took priority.

Her breath grew shaky, shallow. This wasn't supposed to be how the mission went. In fact, Ellery hadn't predicted a single thing happening. With all of her intelligence, the vast ability of her mind, she still couldn't examine a path into the future.

She couldn't tell Dyce. Wouldn't. He was already losing it, thrashing about as if her injury were the worst of their mission.

If he only knew.

The research must live on. People back home needed to understand their roots. Where they came from would certainly help them determine their way forward. They were aimless in her timeline. Lacking real understanding of their place both in time and space. She couldn't abandon her life's work for one man.

She just couldn't.

Something warm and musk-like wrapped around Ellery as Dyce stepped near, dropping the items he'd collected. And when his fingers touched her neck, her pulse skyrocketed. "What are you doing?"

"Your vitals need to be monitored. You've suffered a debilitating injury." His fingers remained on her throat.

With his words, the pain flooded back in, almost wiping away the truth she had to keep secret.

"Are you feeling worse?"

Concern radiated from him, but all she could focus on were the questions swirling in her mind. What if he felt her erratic heartbeat? What if he could tell he made her *feel* things?

Think, Ellery. She wasn't some fool-headed child lost in a love story.

Then it hit her. What if he'd discovered the same thing she'd found out and now determined the best course of action was to kill her? He was MI12. They were mercenaries through and through.

"I'm fine. Did you find what you needed?" If he stepped away and refocused on the items he'd collected, then maybe she was wrong. Maybe he would protect her as he'd promised. In her line of work, the competition was cutthroat. Literally. But his team seemed to trust him.

Her gaze finally landed on his face, locking on his eyes and heating her skin.

He licked his lips and then, as if coming out of a deep reverie, said, "I'm going to finish making this, and then I'm going to have to lift you again. Do you think you'll need more pain medication to dull the injury?"

She shook her head. It would be this mission's trajectory to get all drugged up and then let out the one thing she could never tell him. That she would finish her research here and then abandon him to the past he never wanted to see, so she could save a future she never loved in the first place.

chapter
eight

A Whole New World of Problems

HOW DID anyone thrive in such a harsh environment? Dyce thanked God he was born in a century when atmospheric thermostats controlled climate, keeping territories at a constant seventy-two degrees. The ancients truly suffered.

"Everything okay?" Ellery's voice rang with a hint of pain.

"It would be better if we don't alert every shadow and creak of our presence." Hauling her wasn't hard. Her light frame and pack were nothing. But he must have slowed, otherwise she wouldn't have asked him if he was okay. Intentionally, he went through the motions of searching the area.

Ellery's whispered response whipped through the cold air in a tight hiss. "What is it?"

"Nothing ... yet." Dyce considered her as her gaze dashed to the solid spikes rising like still statues into the sky on either side of them. Fluffy ice and tiny green needles weighed their bowed arms down, hanging low, as if some terrible sadness consumed them.

"It seems perfectly peaceful out here with the fluff drifting quietly to the ground." Almost to herself, with a wistful note, Ellery said, "Fluff is a good name for it."

"It is." Dyce sighed. Shelter with warmth and food was

priority number one. If the right conditions presented themselves, Ellery might complete her research in a day. Then they'd trek with the sled back to the capsule. *Lord, let the conditions be right.*

"How long do you expect your research to take?"

"You're already eager to return?"

Dyce glanced over his shoulder to find her hand dipped in the white substance, drawing patterns with swirls and twists of her wrist. "I am accustomed to a plan, and as mission lead, I require intel to confirm our next steps."

"If there is tech in this time period, I should be able to acquire and store an in-depth outline of historical events in the portable database I brought in my pack." Ellery licked her lips. "Everything depends on the level of tech we face. Best-case scenario, I could have the data within a few hours. In a situation without tech, there's no telling."

Then let there be excellent tech.

The uneven ground suddenly dipped, and the sled fell to the side, threatening to tip Ellery and their belongings out. She let out a cry, and Dyce's stomach churned. Just imagining her injured leg hitting one of the thick spikes or crunching against the large rocks surrounding them chilled him to the bone. "Sorry about that."

"You can't account for every detail."

Something unique entered her tone, but Dyce couldn't help but focus on her distrust of his planning skills. "I can create a plan that will keep you safe."

But of course, she didn't trust him. She hardly knew him, and with her intelligence, she probably sensed his failure. The boy's ghost was haunting him. Dyce swiped a hand down his face.

"I know you can." Her whisper did nothing to quiet the raging inside.

Because what was the first thing that happened when they reached history? She took a few steps and fell, incapacitating herself. What had he done?

Wandered like an oaf behind her.

He shook his head with a grunt as his toe struck something

under the white fluff, now deep enough to cover the middle of his calf. The cold clamped onto him, writhed in his lungs with each breath, and itched against his bones. "It's my job to account for the unknown."

"There's only so much you can extrapolate from data. Sometimes it's only real experience that can provide a true understanding of a situation."

Were they even talking about the same thing? "I'm responsible for keeping you safe. With that failed, my next priority is to get you back home so you can receive treatment."

"I'm not leaving without my research completed."

"Exactly why I asked how long it might take. If you broke your leg above the ankle, you'll need medical care. Depending on the sit rep on location, your care might exceed their level of medical expertise."

"I'm certain in this time period they'd have developed a method for curing a broken bone."

"Back home, it would only take a few hours, maybe half a day."

"It's the price I pay for genuine experience. Other historians would *kill* to spend a minute in my shoes."

Her emphasis on the word kill sent a shiver down Dyce's spine. He knew the historians were cutthroat, but murderous seemed a bit much. They were brain-focused people. Weren't all smart people peaceable?

If the smart ones couldn't keep the peace, then there was no hope that he'd ever be out of a job. Keeping the peace would be a task only God could ever complete.

Suddenly, the weight in the transport shifted to center mass. Dyce glanced back to find Ellery staring at a giant hole in the thick cloud layer, revealing a black sky. He stopped and stared too. What was she seeing that he was missing?

"It's so beautiful." Her voice came out in a wisp.

Above them, the sky was awash in a thousand bright pin lights, and all around each was a glitter of sparkles that flickered with the movement of light. He spun slowly, soaking in the moment, and for that split second, there were no insurgents, no threats, no danger. There was only the enormous, brilliant moon peering back at him from the clearest, cleanest sky Dyce had ever seen.

"There's no yellow filter from the false atmosphere. The moon is pure, glowing, radiant white. Have you ever seen anything so beautiful?"

His answer required zero thought. "Yes."

He could feel her curious gaze searching his features, but he was so caught up in the moment's magic, he forgot himself completely. The breeze that first tickled along his face kicked up into a forceful punch that drew Dyce out of his daze.

A deep-throated groan reached out of the darkness from Dyce's left flank. His instincts instantly on alert, he fell into a crouch, laser pulled, waiting to spot the attacker.

"What is it?" Ellery whispered, fear palpable in her voice.

The wind picked the white substance up and blasted its icy shards into Dyce's face. He put up an arm for some protection but refused to relent and give up his surveillance.

"Is there something out there?" Ellery pushed up as if she would stand, but that wouldn't help anyone. Dyce held out a staying hand, wishing Ellery had learned the signals his team knew. One day, he'd have to teach them to her. For now, no one had his back. It was just the two of them, and Ellery could protect no one.

With the entire mission suddenly relying on his abilities, Dyce swallowed back his feelings, shoving them into a tiny box he intended to never deal with, and just as he finished his first three-sixty sweep, one of the tallest spikes, three over from the spot where he stood, squealed and in slow motion, folded.

Ellery screamed, curling in a ball, her leg awkwardly poking out at a strange angle.

Dyce let his arm fall and allowed an errant step toward the strange phenomenon as the spike seemed to dangle from its darker, almost-blackened skin. Its internal structure was flesh-colored, almost as white as the substance on the ground.

With a gust of wind, the spike released its top with a final scream. Split in two, the massive top half swung down at them.

Without another thought, Dyce flung himself over Ellery to protect her as tiny, sharp green projectiles, along with a blast of the thick white substance, flew from where the long arms of the spike had fallen.

When stillness returned and nothing but the ringing in his ears broke the silence, Dyce peeled himself off Ellery.

"Don't leave me."

His heart ached at her words. "Never."

A strand of her hair, dislodged from its peaceful placement earlier, trembled with the adrenaline thrumming through her body. He'd felt her body's reaction beneath him, and it burned him to leave her, even briefly, to examine the scene, but he bore the weight of every role in the team except one: the researcher.

"I'm going to inspect the incident." Dyce turned to the half of the spike that crashed just in front of them. "Any idea what these things are?"

"Pull me closer, and I'll look."

Even a hint of historical significance brought the researcher in Ellery to the forefront. Her fear tucked away and buried. *Good.*

She leaned over the edge of the sled where he'd moved her, and she ran her gloved fingers over the jagged tip of the spike's injury. "It's broken like a bone, but the material is softer, flexible, more like cartilage."

"Are you saying human bone is at the core of these spikes?" Nothing would make the night more horrifying than finding they were in some sort of boneyard.

"No." There was a chuckle underneath the syllable, and it made Dyce bristle. "I think this is plant life. Maybe something extinct in our timeline."

Dyce let his gaze inspect the remaining spikes standing tall. "I hope they don't all fall at the same time."

"See here."

He looked to where she pointed.

"There was a weakness in this one. Something had eaten away at its protective skin, and this"—she pointed to a black mark in the white internal flesh—"is some sort of decay."

"They won't all fall?"

"Doubtful."

Not impossible. The vision of their capsule tearing the tops off hundreds of these flashed in Dyce's mind. They certainly weren't impenetrable.

"We should continue on." No telling what amazing discovery they might make next. If only Ellery had her datapad. But all was fine. She had a perfect memory. This was the time to live and breathe history. One day, she'd fill a thousand datapads with the amazing stories of their mission. Then mothers could tell their children of history's great impact on their future. Her wayward people would find direction and peace, knowing where they came from and where they needed to go next.

"Agreed. I'll get us to the summit. This terrain matches the backside of our target location. The spikes are new and the white substance is different, but the incline is similar."

She hadn't even thought about the location. The world around her was awash with mysteries and hidden secrets.

Her stomach twisted. Secrets. She hated keeping secrets.

Over the bumps and bruises of the incline, Ellery allowed her thoughts to wander, noting the way the spike arms together wove above her, peeking through the shrinking hole in the substance above them at the stars beyond, seeking every little nuance of the fluff, how it fell, its varied shapes, how it sparkled under the moon's brilliant gaze. There was something magical about this place.

A silent whisper—no, more a nudge—seemed to bump

against her heart at that thought. But Ellery was a scientist. She didn't believe in magic.

Yet, the frightening questions that plagued her before they'd left, when she'd considered being lost in the quantum time-travel space loop with Dyce, now returned. She'd considered a wild discovery—supernatural, defying all scientific understanding—and somehow found room for it within herself.

In some ways, only something so outside of the scope of the known could explain what created Elshaddai.

The thought now warmed her.

But even in this white moonlit wonderland, Ellery barely had the courage to hope she'd secure the intel their timeline so desperately needed.

Suddenly, her transport tilted, and she no longer needed to hold on to its sides to remain on the makeshift device. Leaning up, Ellery took in the flat ground where the spikes seemed to grow fewer and farther between.

"I'm going to do some recon after I hide you under some of the spike debris. Do not move or make a sound."

Ellery nearly choked at the thought of being left vulnerable, broken.

Dyce drew near and grew still, his eyes dancing across her face. "What is it?"

Her emotion must have filled her expression. She pulled it back, forced her face plain again, and squared her shoulders the best she could. "How long does—I mean—is that necessary?"

Understanding lifted his eyebrows. "I need to check the surrounding area before entering. It's more open. With less cover, there's more potential to be seen. If there are hostiles, we'd be easy targets."

"Is there any indication someone here is going to kill us?" *Why on earth would anyone want to hurt complete strangers?*

"In my line of work, every person has the potential to inflict pain upon another.

367

"That's depressing."

"That's the truth."

"How long does it take?"

"I'll be as quick as possible, but I'll also need to be thorough. Do not interact with anyone or anything. Just remain still and quiet. Use this time to rest. We don't know what is going to happen next." Dyce systematically scanned their surroundings from where he crouched in front of her.

"Go. You're right. I'll be fine—silent and still."

His gaze locked on hers, and it was as if he was waiting for something.

"I promise."

He nodded, then stood, collected some of the debris, and rested it over her, forming a sort of shelter.

"This blind will protect you."

His words made no sense. Nevertheless, she nodded, giving the sky one last glance, only to find it fully awash with the thick covering substance again.

Then, with silent steps, he disappeared.

Ellery could never have predicted the overwhelming gulf of emptiness that swallowed her the instant he was out of sight. What would she do if he didn't return? She pulled her injured leg into a more comfortable position, and the mere shift sent shards of pain knifing through her. She couldn't fend for herself. If an insurgent took him out, she'd die of the elements, never able to share the mystery of history with her people.

Why had she fallen and hurt her leg? Why, the minute, the very instant, she lived an authentic experience, did it have to turn into such a disaster?

Time passed slow as death. Possibly her death.

There wasn't a timekeeper or device handy to tell the time that passed, but the sound of someone approaching brought Ellery such joy she almost threw off the blind and cried out.

"Hello, do you need help?" The female voice called to Ellery, and it forced Ellery's freezing hands to still and her breath to catch. "It's okay. I've come to help."

The woman worked to disassemble the blind, and Ellery's heart thrashed against her ribs. She both desperately wanted to meet this ancestor, regale her with stories of the future, and quiz her on the state of her present—and remain hidden for Dyce, following his instructions, keeping safe.

When a sweet face with bright red lips forming a perfect *O* made it through Dyce's efforts, Ellery sent her mind into overdrive with potential ways to protect herself.

"Oh, there you are. You must be frozen."

Ellery's heart nearly stopped.

Indeed, Ellery was freezing. The woman spoke Ellery's language. The likelihood was infinitesimal.

"Come, we must get you to the cabin." The strange woman stood and put both hands on her hips. "Where is your protector?"

How did this stranger from history know about Ellery's protector?

chapter nine

No Room at the Inn

"FREEZE!" Dyce's heart pounded out a warning against his ribs. If the strange-looking woman moved even a hair on Ellery's head, he'd end her time on Earth.

The woman tipped back, twisting to smile at him.

Smile? Maybe they didn't say *freeze* in this timeline. He'd better spell it out for her.

"Don't move." Dyce locked her in his sight. Did an ancient know his weapon could vaporize? Was she even aware of the risk he presented to her?

Completely ignoring him, the woman, short and stocky, placed both hands on her belly and shook with a hearty laughter that echoed into the midnight sky. "Why, I'm no threat, protector. Stand down."

Was she blind? He had his weapon locked on her. Clearly, she had no idea what it was capable of. "I'll not stand—"

"All is well. I've come to bring you good news. You've found what you're seeking—shelter." She tilted her chin down, giving him some sort of serious glare that seemed to indicate she thought she knew what they sought, but there was no way some ancient would have any intel on their intent.

The woman dropped her hands and stood straight.

He should have pulled the trigger the instant she moved, but something held his hand steady. In fact, an element beyond his own comprehension drew him to this woman.

Was it curiosity?

There was a peace about her. But even as he explored the idea further, he knew it wasn't that. Maybe it was her obvious comfort and joy in the face of his futuristic weapon. Surely, she'd never seen a weapon like his.

Did she have no fear at all?

His mind danced over their crash landing, Ellery's injury, the fallen spike, and his solo trek on recon. Fear that he'd mess up again tiptoed in Dyce's shadow through every moment of this journey. That Ellery, who couldn't fend for herself, would be left to do just that, or worse, an insurgent would kill her right in front of him, like—

The woman took a step closer. "You can holster your weapon."

"You're in no position to give me orders." Dyce wouldn't back down. Anyone could say they weren't a threat or give an order. No. Never. In fact, he leaned into his weapon and aim, ready for the certain danger coming for them.

"Fine. If you must interrogate me, could we do it in the warmth of my Inn? Temperatures are dropping out here." The woman's expression clearly showed she thought he was overreacting.

Didn't people during this time suffer skirmishes? Battles over territory? Where were *her* protectors? His gaze flicked over her shoulder to seek a hidden protector approaching. "The temperature is not my concern."

"Should be. The snow too."

Dyce didn't have a meaning for the odd word, *snow*, but as she spoke, his awareness of an uncomfortable chill nipping at his nose grew. He checked on Ellery to find it had painted her cheeks a lovely rouge. "I'll keep my weapon."

It was more of an order, a demand, than a request, but for some ridiculous reason, the strange woman said, "That's permissible. Soon, you'll realize you don't need it."

He scoffed. What kind of bargaining was this woman attempting to do?

Her breath circled her head in a cloud before vanishing. With a wink and an utter lack of concern, she spun on her heel, giving him her back, and was off before Dyce had moved a muscle. He trained his aim on her until her intent was clear. No threat.

Dyce would have to collect the transport and check in with Ellery. As he turned his attention fully on her, he found her face full of wonder as her gaze followed the woman who maneuvered the incline without the slightest indication of strain.

In a whisper, she said, "She might be one of our ancestors."

Dyce could only grunt as he shouldered the burden of the transport and, much less gracefully, made his way up the incline and to the foot of the tall Inn.

"It seems to be made of the same material as the spikes we just passed."

It wasn't the construction that caught Dyce's attention, but the sound of a thousand voices singing the most beautiful song he'd ever heard. "What do you think that is? Have you ever heard anything like it?"

"It sounds ethereal." Ellery seemed to say the last word with trouble. "Another wonder to make a note of for our historical restoration project."

Dyce swallowed. Of course, her focus remained on her work. At least this time, she called it *our* historical restoration project. It made his heart ache to think of her beautiful but trapped, always in an office, never out, experiencing life. Did her mind ever wander from her current project, or did her life's devotion only have room for one thing—work?

And worse, why was his mind wandering in this direction? He, too, should only think of one thing—protecting her. *Lord, what is going on with me?*

Ronte, one of the younger guys on his team, might have grown angry with her willful abandon of caution or the weakness in her fragile frame. Glancing back at his cargo, Dyce discovered Ellery contemplated him. "What?"

Her beautiful eyes flicked away, focusing on the light from the Inn, closer now, lacing the white substance with a warm yellow glow. *Strange.* "Is your pain worsening?"

Surprise registered on her face before she drew her brows together in a look of almost confusion or maybe conflict. "No. I'm fine. It's just ..."

She licked her lips, and Dyce couldn't look away, couldn't move another step. His heart and mind malfunctioned.

"History is so much more than I'd ever imagined." Something hid behind her eyes, but the moment the wind gusted again, her gaze widened and dashed just above Dyce's head.

Something cracked with an explosive sound.

He dropped the transport's makeshift handle, spun, drawing his weapon, and fell into a practiced crouch at the ready.

The white substance had accumulated on the roof and now slid, striking some decoration that hung off the roof's edge on its descent, emitting a clash and a clatter, as momentum carried it and the decoration to the ground in a deafening blast. In a few moments, it was all buried in a grave underneath several more chunks of the white substance.

"You can lower your weapon." The strange woman stood at the door, watching him as if he were the ancient. "Come on. You'll both freeze to death if you don't hurry."

Was the woman uneducated? Did she not know it would take much more time for such an experience to occur?

Ellery's mind whirled with the incredible secrets history displayed so lavishly before her and the one secret she must keep tamped down in her heart. *Ew.* When was the last time Ellery had considered her heart in any matter? But the results of her life's extensive research were sitting at her fingertips.

She couldn't help her eyes as they greedily sought the ancient decor, the colors and patterns, the warm browns and reds. So different from her time period's cold grays and solid chic.

And yet, there it was, nagging at the back of her mind, pinching her heart, weighing her stomach down, leaving her mind swirling even as she tried to ignore Dyce and his powerful muscles hauling her up the incline.

Why did it hurt so much to keep this one thing from Dyce? It shouldn't matter one iota if he returned with her. But even as she had the thought, she knew it was callous. Not like her. Not her truth.

Dyce abandoned the transport, lifted her in one smooth move, and carried her over the threshold—she almost snorted. There had been a time when Ellery believed that ancient marriage tradition would never happen for her. In fact, she gave it up completely for her work. And yet as Dyce hovered between the icy bluster of the outdoors and the warmth and spicy scents drawing them inward, something strange danced over her skin, leaving goosebumps in its wake, tickling her with a joy she'd not felt in ages. Her delight gripped her so firmly she almost missed the festive red and green bow just above her head with its spiraling ribbon dangling around odd green leaves.

"What could that be for?"

Dyce grunted. Either he didn't know, or she was too heavy. The latter thought made her stomach cringe. She needed to exercise more.

"Oh, it's mistletoe."

Ellery spared a brief glance at the woman, taking in the sparkle in her eyes, and finding herself smiling with her, even though she still didn't know the meaning of the word *mistletoe*.

"It's a tradition at Christmas—the best time of the year!" The strange woman danced as if to the music, but her hips and the beat warred with each other.

"Christmas?" Ellery let the word roll off her tongue. A curious tingle sparked through her again, this time starting at the roots in her hair.

The scientist in her refused to humor speculation about what was playing a part in the history she loved or the future she lived in, but something strange was happening in this woman's Inn.

"Ma'am." Dyce frowned.

What etched that level of grief into his expression? Things weren't that bad. She hurt her leg. She wasn't dying.

"Please call me Maggie." She waved a hand before hurrying outside and sweeping up both of their packs. She shouldered the burden through the door and deposited them on the mat at the foot of a long row of hooks. Disrobing her outer layer, she spun with a smile and hung the garment on one hook.

"Maggie, I'm Dyce, and this is Ellery, who potentially broke her leg in the elements. Do you have a medical kit on the premises?"

"Oh." Maggie shook her head and mumbled about knowing something.

Ellery couldn't quite make it out, and frankly, she didn't care. Her research surrounded her in bright, living color. She gripped Dyce's collar to twist and get a better look behind them.

Maggie took off. "I'll grab the kit."

Dyce pulled Ellery's attention back. "What is it? Are you in more pain? She'll be back in a minute, hopefully with something that will help you."

"No. I can hardly feel anything with the adrenaline thrumming through me."

"Adrenaline?"

"Please, just take me over to that shelving unit. I need to inspect those reference items. I'm not sure what they are, but they look like they might hold something important." She didn't want to explain her every thought to someone who wouldn't grasp her intent. She simply wanted to explore and consume everything she could while she still had the opportunity.

Dyce silently complied.

Ellery could hardly contain the excitement and gratitude welling up inside of her. Her eyes danced across the strange rectangular compartments, all different shapes and sizes, with words on the outside. "What do you think—?"

"Oh, that one's my favorite!" Maggie squealed as she silently peered over Dyce's shoulder. She set down a small red satchel. Perhaps her medical kit. A tall man hovered at the bottom of the stairs, watching Maggie.

Who was he, and when had she returned? She nearly scared Ellery straight out of the comfort of Dyce's arms. That thought reminded her she rested, cradled against his warm chest, and that in fact the Inn itself wasn't warm. It was his body that was warming her. A flush of heat raced to her cheeks. She squirmed.

Dyce grunted and adjusted his grip.

"What is your favorite?" Ellery didn't want to lose the chance to learn what these delightfully colored rectangles were.

Maggie pulled out a black rectangle with the word Bible on it. "This has kept me company through the ordeal of pulling this Inn from the wreck it was to the treasure you see before you. It was a miracle, getting it open in time for guests by December twentieth."

"It was," the man agreed.

"This is Alexander."

"Nice to meet you."

He nodded and muttered the same back, his gaze locked on Maggie.

In Maggie's hands, the rectangle was thick, surrounded by a sturdy black cover. When she ran her finger through it, it opened like magic, revealing slender leaves with a thousand words on each leaf.

Without thinking, the researcher in Ellery surfaced. "What is the specimen you hold?"

"Specimen? Oh! This is a book. Haven't you ever seen a book before?"

Dyce cleared his throat. "She's had a terrible injury. We should probably check how it's progressing. The elements are quite nasty out there, and she took a fall. I'm concerned she might have hit her head when she injured her leg."

Maggie's cheeks pinked. "Oh, no."

Even as he spoke, Ellery's leg throbbed. "I'm fine." Pain clogged her throat, making her words squeaky and awkward. Clearing her throat, Ellery said, "I'd love to know more about this book. Are all of these"—she indicated the shelving unit—"*books?*"

"Yes! I inherited quite a collection. It's probably my favorite part of the Inn, aside from the beautiful setting outside."

"Beautiful?" Ellery couldn't help how her brow drew together.

"Oh, the night keeps many secrets. But in the morning, when the sun's rays dance across the crystal ice on the trees and glitter off a thousand hills of snow, you'll see. It's more than beautiful— it's heavenly."

"Heavenly." Another word Ellery rolled around on her tongue. Her gaze landed curiously on the Bible.

"Here, you can borrow it." Maggie plopped the book on the nearby side table.

Dyce turned toward the couch. "I'm going to inspect your leg."

Ellery absently nodded as he rested her gently on the couch. He handed her the book, and her gaze never left the delicate pages as she carefully turned each one, greedily reading the words as if they might run away.

"You should try Luke. It'll tell you all about the real Christmas story," Maggie whispered, eyes on Dyce's work. "Oh, and Romans." She winked.

Ellery frowned.

"Am I hurting you?" Dyce's words came out choked.

"No. I just wondered." Ellery turned her gaze on Maggie, who observed Dyce's ministrations. "Do you have access to history?"

Maggie frowned, and with a chuckle that kind of made Ellery

feel crazy, said, "Of course. Online. There's everything going back as far as recorded history exists. Of course, the internet connection isn't the best out here. But it'll get the job done in a pinch."

"I believe I'm in what you call a pinch, then."

"Ellery, we can't focus on that right now. We have to assess your injury, come up with a plan to get you help, and then go from there. Your research, I'm afraid, must take a backseat."

"No." Ellery locked her gaze on Dyce. "Is it broken?"

Maggie swallowed. "I think it is."

Dyce huffed. "Yes, from what I can tell without a mediscanner."

"I've continued my research, and you've assessed my injury. No need for one to be exclusive of the other."

"Ellery, see reason."

"I'm quite certain I'm the only one seeing it right now."

Dyce's cheeks grew bright red.

Maggie cleared her throat. "I think I'll give you two a minute. Would either of you like a bite to eat or something warm to drink?"

Ellery said, "No—"

At the same time, Dyce said, "Yes."

With a flutter of hands, Maggie spun, muttering about hoping the other guests could sleep through the commotion and cocoa and cookies would have to do. Alexander followed her into the kitchen.

A moment later, Maggie bustled back in, flustered, with Alexander on her heels. Maggie carried a slim rectangle. What was it with this timeline and rectangles?

"Here's a laptop. You can research anything you want about history if it'll help keep your mind off the awful pain you must be experiencing." Maggie opened the lid and clicked a few square tabs with letters on them, and the screen brightened to a search bar.

Something giddy and wonderful washed through Ellery.

History, literally in its complete expanse and depth, lay at her fingertips.

Ellery searched for the most important events, breaking history into hundred-year components beginning with their current placement in the past and moving backward into the eighteen, seventeen, then sixteen hundreds. Her mind was on overload, with the Bible in her lap and the internet at her fingertips. The vast knowledge that all people in this timeline took for granted from their childhood history lessons to something as joyous and fascinating as the celebration they would have just the next day.

Christmas Day.

It was more than a researcher could ever hope for. More than she'd ever dreamed of. The origin of their winter holiday she had ignored every year was born out of this practice of Christmas that came from the birth of a very special baby.

It was while that thrilling thought absorbed her entire focus that Dyce's sharp fingers pressed a spot on her leg that stole her breath, and suddenly the world shivered and fell into darkness. Ellery fought and almost immediately lost her battle with consciousness after one last thought ...

Ooo, he better not have done that on purpose!

chapter
ten

When It Couldn't Get Any Worse

ICE SLITHERED through Dyce's veins. He'd made her faint. Had he pressed too hard? Or was the injury turning? They did that. Turned. The body's response to injury—shock—covered a multitude of wrongs, but eventually, the damage caught up with the injured.

"It looks broken to me." Maggie's voice wasn't more than a whisper, and it still grated on Dyce like a broken rotor. Alexander silently passed the red satchel to Maggie. She dug through it and handed Dyce some tape, two metal rods, and a small bottle.

"Thank you, but I'll handle this from here."

"Oh." She chuckled. "What's next then, tough guy?"

Dyce finally lifted his gaze to her and took in her elitist expression. "I'm trained in multiple forms of combat and triage medicine."

"If it's broken, she'll need to get to the hospital, but it might take them days to dig us out after this blizzard finishes passing through."

They didn't have days. In twenty-four hours, the shock would have completely worn off, and Ellery would feel all the injury except the very slight edge the medicine kicked away.

"You can use anything from my kit." Maggie waved her hand at the items he now held but was not applying.

Dyce got busy using the rudimentary items to care for Ellery. In their timeline, they had a slide-on sleeve that expanded and then hardened, form-fitting to the person's appendage, providing perfect support and protection for transport. Of course, they only transported the person to the next mediscanner in the city, and after an injection of nanites, the person walked out good as new.

Maggie, standing close by to Dyce with Alexander just behind her, placed a small, hand-sized rectangular device to her ear. After a strange rhythmic vibration that reminded him of a terrible type of rattling music, a voice, almost discernible as he listened in, spoke animatedly.

"Hi, this is Maggie Benson, owner of the Starlit Inn. I found a young woman at the edge of my woods. Her friend thinks she might have broken her leg."

More of the strange sounds rattled through, indecipherable.

"She slipped on the incline behind the Inn."

Dyce could barely make out the masculine voice's response.

"Yes. I'm not sure a fence would have helped in this situation. In fact, it might have hindered my helping them, but I'll take that into consideration as part of the remodel I've been working. Can you get an ambulance out here tonight?"

This time, Dyce leaned into Maggie's personal space, seeking the man's response.

"I'm sorry, Maggie. No can do. It's supposed to snow all night, with gusting wind and dropping temps. Maybe once they've cleared the main roads. I'll monitor that and send someone as soon as I can."

"Please let me know when you've sent someone." Maggie gave Dyce a pitiful, helpless sigh.

"Sure thing."

Dyce pulled away, not caring to hear any more of the man's words. Ellery's bag! Hope pulsed in his chest. Why hadn't he thought to check if a nanite injection was in their capsule's emergency kit? *Lord, please let there be something to remedy Ellery's condition.*

If something didn't work out, he'd have to haul her back to the capsule against her will. He dug through both bags, searching for a solution, but the only item his fingers grazed were the pills he already knew about. His gaze returned to Maggie's.

"Why are you glaring at *me*?" She held both hands up as if he were training a gun on her again.

People in this timeline were soft. Maggie'd probably faint at the sight of a protector in action. His gaze danced to Ellery, who was just as soft and would land right beside Maggie, curled in the fetal position. Man, his job was impossible.

He spoke slowly to not spook the fragile Maggie. "When I'm from—"

Alexander leaned forward. "When?"

Dyce swiped a hand down his face. "I meant where. It's been a long day and night."

Maggie narrowed her eyes.

"The city is so easy. The hospital is minutes away. I don't think I've ever been so far into nowhere that I couldn't get help." Dyce tightened the bandage, drawing the metal against Ellery's injury. She whimpered but didn't come around.

"I think she'll be out for the rest of the night." Maggie had folded her arms with her face propped on one hand, as if she, too, would like to crash.

"We should all rest. Morning is just around the corner. Let's reassess once we've rested." Dyce sat on the cushioned chair facing the couch.

"I'll put some more wood on the fire down here." Alexander moved to the firewood.

"And I'll grab the refreshments I meant to bring earlier. There are a few other guests in the Inn." Maggie darted to the kitchen.

Dyce studied Alexander's movements as he placed a few more pieces of varied, strange wedges of natural substance on the fire, noting how he handled the items he'd called wood and how the flames ate away at it. He could do that the next time the fire waned. Alexander brushed his hands together, removing debris just as Maggie reappeared carrying a tray filled with cups and strange plated items. Probably food. Then, after a lingering gaze on Ellery, Maggie nodded to Dyce, and the pair swept up the stairs.

Finally alone with his thoughts, Dyce relaxed. Now he could plan. But his mind and eyes kept returning to the soft curve of Ellery's cheek, the rise and fall of her breath, and the way she mumbled nonsense in her sleep. Was there anyone more beautiful?

He almost choked on his own saliva at that thought. *Lord, what is happening to me?*

Dyce imagined something lingered in history's air. Maybe a chemical expelled by the spikes outside or the snow they'd trudged through. That was what Maggie called the white substance—snow. He'd picked up on that much.

I can't take care of her here. I can do nothing.

Dyce ran a hand through his hair and leaned back, allowing his muscles to slacken and his spine to bow under the pressure he'd pretended wasn't overwhelming.

It's too much, Lord. I can't do this.

A warmth radiated from within Dyce. The scent of the wood burning, the crackle of the fire, the soft glow whispering along the walls seemed to speak to Dyce, draw him deeper into his feelings, really force his mind to release its death grip on the mission and take stock of more than just his work. A thing he'd already decided Ellery needed to do.

He was lonely.

Was this entire mission the Lord's way of reminding him to turn to his team?

A cool breeze skirted along the floor and whispered into Dyce's pant legs.

So, is that a no?

The breeze chilled his ankles and knees, and he rubbed his

hands to warm them again. There was something magical about Ellery. Her fire. Her indefatigable nature. It transformed her subtle beauty into something so much more stunning.

Unable to sit still anymore, Dyce stood and wandered over to the blaze. The orange flames licked along the back of the stones surrounding the fire. Transfixed, frozen in a past he never imagined, he was aware of Ellery on the couch. Her presence was indelibly marked on his heart, and he realized he could imagine a life with her by his side.

Now, who was being soft?

He scoffed and turned back to flop in the comfortable chair. Well, if he wanted a future with someone so vivacious and passionate, he was going to have to convince her to take more than a moment to scowl at him.

That was the real trick.

Imagining he'd rest his eyes and let his mind sort it all out, or even better, the Holy Spirit might whisper the answer into his heart, he leaned back, enveloped by the chair. The warmth of the fire soothed an ache he'd earned pulling the sled up the incline, and he allowed his mind and spirit to grow quiet.

Even as he listened for the Spirit's whisper ...

There was something he needed to figure out ...

He pried one eye open, and his gaze caught on the even rise and fall of Ellery's shoulder, and then he released his lid, seeking the comfort and warmth of darkness.

Pain arched along Ellery's leg, striking deep like a hammer, reaching into her hip, and radiating through her body like hot electricity. *It must be very early in the morning, with the fire almost out and the lights so low.*

She found Dyce slouched in the chair across from her. Some protector, sleeping on the job.

Ew. That was mean. Pain brought the worst out in her. Her level of intelligence should keep her from such thinking.

To ease the thudding in her hip, Ellery shifted, but it only made the pain worse.

Ellery gasped, the sound loud in the silence. Had she woken Dyce? Her gaze flicked to him, where she greedily took in how strong he seemed, even reposed as he was.

Focus, Ellery. You have a job to do. It's quiet. No one is around. This was her chance to really perform a deep dive into history using Maggie's device.

Opening it, the strange pictures displayed on the screen flummoxed Ellery. She tried to move through the picture, swiping the screen, but that didn't work. She didn't have time to figure out how to work the ancient device with its archaic manual manipulation. Forgetting herself, she shifted her weight again and nearly cried out, furtively glancing at Dyce, who hadn't stirred.

Her hand brushed a flat rectangle in front of the square letter keys, and an arrow appeared and shot across the screen. Ellery narrowed her eyes on the arrow, certain she was on to something important. Soon, she was clicking and swiping in a fury, beginning the historic search she'd been training for her entire life.

Nothing in her training could have prepared her for such an incredible discovery. The shock of the violence that seemed universal in all time periods, alongside the incredible compassion demonstrated after wild natural disasters. She was thankful her time period tamed the weather.

A warm breeze jingled a quiet bell nearby. Strange. Why was there a breeze inside? Ellery discovered a vent near the decorations of the inn, embedded within an elaborate green and red garland hanging on the fire's mantel were silver bells. After checking on Dyce, Ellery studied the silver as it shimmered with a hint of the deep red and orange of the embers. The silver bells reminded her of a word the innkeeper used. What was her name? Magly—strange name.

Right, the word was *Christmas*.

Pursuing the word Christmas, Ellery discovered the manger, Mary and Joseph, and the great sacrifice God made with His son. Tears traced her cheeks. But somehow, over the ages, they'd lost Jesus's precious gift. The device mentioned several things about the Bible, and so Ellery put the device to the side and picked up the leather-bound book Magly gave her. Soon, she'd lost sight of any period of time, letting the figures and wild happenings wash over her.

Over the next two hours, Ellery first absorbed Luke and the other Gospels, then Romans, and finally Acts, covering hundreds of years of history, but nothing hit her heart like the story of Jesus. Diving further, flipping all the way to the end, to a book titled Revelation, she discovered the Bible's twelve tribes. Narrowing her eyes, she immediately recognized those numbers and could finally connect their importance with the future.

This knowledge had to make it back. Her heart pinched, eyes sliding to where Dyce rested, and his locked with hers.

Jesus died for their sins—both of theirs—and now, she was going to sacrifice Dyce to share the good news with others. It was the right decision. But those bright blue eyes seemed to rip her heart to shreds.

"What's wrong?" Dyce sat up quickly. "You look upset."

A tear slipped down her cheek. She shouldn't tell him, but how could she pull this off without his help? She couldn't even walk. Couldn't do anything. Except, she could at least learn the history. She would ask Maggie to let her take the device to the future and seek help with more drive space to download additional intel.

Dyce moved from his chair and kneeled before her, taking her hand into his. "Look. It's going to be okay. I know your leg has got to be killing you, but we can go back today, get you in a mediscanner. I'm sure you've learned a few things, and you can share those. That'll be enough to get you approval for a second trip."

Ellery was already shaking her head.

"I'm not the Commissioner, but I'm certain—"

"No." Ellery sobbed. "The crash landing damaged the second fuel cell. There is only enough fuel to carry one of us back to the future."

Dyce rocked back on his heels. His eyes flicked to the cooling fire, then the lightening sky through the window. Then, strangely, he closed his eyes, and his lips were moving but making no sound.

"I can build a new fuel cell for the capsule." She probably couldn't, but she wanted to fix this.

"How? We can't even get out of the Inn and make it to a hospital." Dyce stood and paced the length of the room.

Tears streamed Ellery's cheeks. She furiously swiped them away.

"You go. You're injured. I'll be fine. Maggie will help me figure something out. Maybe I can work around her Inn. She's currently fixing it up." Dyce's brow formed a crease of concern.

"You'd let me do that?"

"Of course."

His words were so instantaneous, they would have toppled Ellery over if she were standing. "What if I can't make it back? What if the Commissioner doesn't approve my return? If he did, though, I could research so much more."

Dyce was at her side, gripping her hands in his, warm and strong. "Life will go on."

Ellery pulled her hands from his. "No." That wasn't good enough. "We're in the past. I could create a time capsule, seal and bury it. Knowing myself, I could make sure my team finds it."

Now Dyce was shaking his head. "We won't know if it worked until it's too late. Your mission is too important for us to just bury something and hope it's found."

"You have no idea how right you are."

"Did you already find something?"

"It's my life's work, and I'm sitting with the entirety of history at my fingertips. Of course, I've found something. I've found a thousand somethings. In fact, read this." Ellery pushed the Bible at Dyce, opened to Luke and what the internet said was called the Nativity story, the true reason for Christmas, her winter holiday.

He turned the pages slower than she would, but his eyes danced across the page, a myriad of expressions flickering across his sweet face. "The story of Jesus," he whispered without lifting his eyes. "I always believed there was more to what I was taught."

"Turn to John three, sixteen." Ellery could hardly contain the emotion welling up within her.

Dyce lifted awed eyes to hers. "God gave His Son. He loved us so much He was willing to give up His only Son to save everyone, including us."

"I know." Ellery still couldn't quite fathom that level of love. Something whispered through her, and her gaze found Dyce's. "It's an incredible love."

"Back home, everyone needs to hear this. This history, Jesus's life, is too important to remain lost."

"Will you carry me back to the capsule?" Ellery held her breath, wishing he'd say both yes and no. The heart was a strange organ. It suddenly flitted about like a loose paper on the breeze. Her skin prickled with warmth.

Dyce paused, swallowed, and then genuinely smiled. "Of course."

chapter
eleven

Becoming a Sacrifice

DYCE HATED it took him so long to recognize he was falling in love with Ellery. Why did he have to love her and lose her? Why would God give her a purpose separate from him? Couldn't God have prevented the fuel cell from getting damaged?

His thoughts battled like combat drones as Ellery told Maggie they'd be leaving and asked if she would lend the device to Ellery long-term.

"If the information is not on the device, but held somewhere in a super-cell of data, could we download it ..." Ellery paused, swallowed as if in pain, then continued. "And may I have it? I know it's a lot to ask—"

"I have another laptop. This is a spare I lend to guests. You can bring it back when you return." Maggie let her hand fall with a slap to her thigh as she seemed to take in the grim expressions around her. "Or not. Whatever you need."

"Can it hold all of history?" Ellery's voice held a note of childish wonder.

Maggie shook her head. "I'll help you download information to the device, and we can even load up a few thumb drives—"

"Hmm?" Ellery glanced at Dyce as if to ask if she'd heard correctly.

Their budding connection sizzled in his heart and spread outward to his limbs. As if, somehow, he lived his whole life disconnected from what mattered most, and now, in a thousand ways, it intertwined permanently, like gravity, with Ellery.

Except he had to let her go. This was her mission. The truth nearly knocked the wind out of him.

Maggie interpreted their silence correctly. "Storage devices. I don't know who came up with the name thumb drive, but it is about the size of a thumb."

Ellery let out a soft chuckle, but her face said she thought it was a terrible name.

"Thank you. If we could do that now, then Dyce will take me—"

"You're going back into that?" Maggie threw her arm out at the thigh-high drifts of snow. Two icicles hung on either side of the window as if to make her point.

"It's not ideal," Ellery whispered.

Maggie frowned. "There's something I'm not understanding."

Boy, was she right. Dyce stepped in to give some direction to the mess they were about to step into. "You said yourself, the emergency vehicle can't make it out here, and I'm accustomed to traveling through harsh conditions to complete a mission. I'll take Ellery to get help."

It was the truth.

Maggie sighed. "It's not ideal, but with the amount of snow that dropped last night, I'm thinking we'll be hunkering down for a long while. It's probably best for you to hike out to the main roads. I'll let the crew know. Then they can meet you there."

"Thank you." Dyce wouldn't meet them there. He didn't know how he'd explain things to Maggie, but he'd deliver Ellery to the capsule and return without her. Somewhere between now and then, and after praying his heart out, he'd come up with something to appease Maggie's reaction to his empty-handed return.

"I have something that will help." Maggie spun and raced back up the stairs. Dyce listened as her footsteps climbed another set of stairs and wondered how many steps were in the Inn. Everything went silent, and his thoughts whispered against the pain of letting Ellery go.

"This is hard," she said, as if reading his mind.

"Hm." What words mattered when one was about to let go of everything? It made God's sacrifice of His Son that much more poignant. Imagine. Even as Dyce thought it, his mind recoiled at the loss—the boy's dying face tripping across his thoughts. Ellery's sweet smile whispered on its heels. Letting go of one's own flesh and blood would be devastating. Dyce was strong. But he wasn't that strong.

"What are you thinking about?" Ellery glanced at the stairs as the pitter-patter of Maggie's return emphasized the passing time.

"Nothing."

Ellery scoffed. "That's not true."

Maggie rounded the end of the banister. "Let me give you one more thing. This one's for Dyce." She held up two large teardrop-shaped items. "Snowshoes."

"I'm sorry?" Ellery's cheeks pinked.

"They're specially designed to help you walk more easily in deep snow. It'll make Dyce's trip to the emergency vehicle on the main road a touch easier." Maggie glowed with triumph. "Now, let's grab some food and get you packing before your pain medicine wears off. Charlie at emergency services thinks the roads might be clear by nine this morning. It's probably an hour's hike in good weather, so you should leave in about an hour."

Dyce mustered his most disarming and grateful smile. "Thank you."

"Now, pass me that laptop, and show me what you want to download. While I was upstairs, I grabbed five thumb drives I had lying around. However, the hospital will have Wi-Fi, and you can access the internet then."

"Thank you. I'll feel better if I gather my research and have it all in one place."

Ellery was almost too smooth with her reasoning, but then again, she was brilliant. He smiled as the woman bent to download Ellery's research.

How many people would find a renewed love for their heavenly Father with this Christmas story? It was a miracle. And just in time to give the real reason for their winter family holiday. Dyce's mind traced over the names of his teammates, and a thrill tripped through him as he acknowledged how this news would impact each person he'd grown to love. His team. His family.

Though they might never see him again, they'd have the Bible, and there were many more stories beyond the story of Jesus's birth that could give his team the strength to heal and go on with the mission. "Maggie, would you allow Ellery to take the Bible with her as well?"

"That's a wonderful idea." She pressed the book back into Ellery's hands.

Ellery thanked her and said something else, and Maggie laughed, which made Ellery join her.

Lord, she's so beautiful. Thank You for giving her to me even for this short time. Help me let her go and trust You to take care of her while we live hundreds of years apart.

After placing their packs on the transport, Dyce plopped back in the padded chair and studied the women as they worked.

A warmth spread across Ellery's cheeks as Dyce's gaze never seemed to leave her while she worked. It sent curious sparkles tickling through her. She glanced up and their eyes met. Dyce didn't look away. It made Ellery feel seen. Known. It was comforting in a way she never imagined she'd feel in another's presence.

"Well, that's all of it." Maggie stood.

Ellery's gaze flicked to Maggie. "Thank you."

Maggie would never know the incredible impact she was having on the future of mankind.

"Yes. Thank you." Dyce stood. "I'll carry you out to the transport. I've already packed our items, and time is short. How is your leg?"

Ellery hated the spike of pain that struck her as he asked. Just focusing on it made it ten times worse. "Not getting better."

"Oh. That's awful." Maggie wrapped Ellery in a careful hug. "You take care and come visit me again sometime."

Ellery nodded and hugged the sweet woman back.

Dyce lifted her into his arms, which somehow seemed natural. How quickly her perspective had changed about him. Now, they'd lose whatever seemed to thrum between them. These moments spent living and breathing history taught her she'd been approaching life all wrong.

After another round of goodbyes, Ellery bounced along behind Dyce, who made excellent time with the miracle of snowshoes. Dyce navigated the woods at such an increased pace, they'd make it to the capsule in no time at all. Normally, the faster Ellery could travel from point *A* to point *B* the better, but this time, a mess of emotions swirled in her chest, threatening to spill out.

Maggie was so right. The world lay in a crisp stillness, encased in a thin layer of crystal. Boughs heavy with snow hung low to the ground, sweeping the fluffy white beneath. It seemed the world slumbered in a peaceful cleansing, glinting with the soft yellow light of the morning sunshine. Somehow, the scene delivered a tranquility Ellery had never noticed or experienced before.

She drew the quietness deep into her soul, hoping and praying it would remain there forever. That maybe one day, when she was whole and strong again, she might return and treasure it.

Dyce hesitated his steady decline to glance back at her. "You okay?"

"Fine." A lie. She didn't want to go. Her whole life she'd strained to touch even a glimmer of history, and now she was fully immersed and completely addicted. How could she leave it all behind?

Her leg throbbed with a steady, pulsing pain. It was their excuse to leave so suddenly, but she'd be leaving either way. She'd accomplished most of her mission. In her possession rested one of the greatest treasures her time would ever encounter. With time to study the twelve families' intersection further, she might be able to explain the conundrum plaguing her timeline.

All of Elshaddai would revere her name.

But her heart no longer beat for accomplishments or accolades.

Her gaze tiptoed toward Dyce's strong back. Over his shoulder, a brilliant red creature took flight, flapping its wings and crying at the sky.

I know, little one. I'm upset too.

Dyce's steps slowed as they met the devastation left behind by their capsule. Hundreds of spikes cut off at an ever increasingly sharp angle. The last ten were blackened by the heat of the fuel exhaust. A wide crater quietly sat covered in a blanket of snow as if the trauma never happened, and the only proof was a deep indent in the snow's structure.

Dyce stopped as Ellery slid up to the side of the capsule. With tenderness, he placed his arms under her and lifted her out of the transport. He stepped over the edge of the cockpit and settled her into her chair.

Their breath mingled together, and all Ellery could do was hold her arms to herself, forcing them not to clamp onto Dyce.

Dyce seemed to have no desire to remove his arms from her. Instead, he drew her closer, holding her in a hug so tight she finally gave in and let her arms wrap around him as well.

"I never thought history could be the gift it is," he whispered into her hair.

Ellery could hardly think around her desire to hang onto this man forever. He leaned back, leaving his arms securely around her, and took her mouth in a soft kiss that blew on the embers of Ellery's heart until everything inside of her blazed.

Dyce withdrew, searching her gaze as he finally released her and stepped back with what seemed no small amount of effort. "Be safe."

Ellery couldn't stop the tear that dripped down her cheek. "Be blessed."

Somehow, Dyce stepped out of the cockpit and was gone.

With trembling fingers, Ellery coded in her return, strapped in, and the capsule lifted into the air and whipped through the ages to return her to her timeline. She might carry the gift of history with her, and more than that, the story of Christmas and Jesus Christ's overwhelming love, but she had sacrificed her heart back in history.

chapter
twelve

The Beautiful Loop of Time

DYCE COULD BE HAPPY HERE. It would be certain if Ellery were still there, but he might just love history more than Ellery now. It had given him everything. A true story of his faith. An incredible love for Ellery. A chance to see the world as it was intended, not cement and steel, but a winter wonderland.

The snow seemed thicker, harder to manage as he trudged his way back. His legs felt dull, chilled to the bone, thick and heavy.

In some ways, he wanted to remain in the snow-covered land, free and wild, a new pain pulsing through him. God had brought him this far, and He would continue to carry him through this.

With the Inn just coming into view from the incline, Dyce recognized God's hand in history, the Inn, and the "magic" of this time period. Somehow, out of nowhere, when Dyce least expected it, God had given him not one but two unbelievable and overwhelming loves.

The true story of Christmas and Jesus's love for him, as well as Ellery who, after their kiss, stared up at him with so much love it took all his strength to let her go.

Maggie threw the door open. "What happened?"

"Ellery is on her way to help. I called in a favor with my team, and they—"

"Life-flighted her out of here." Maggie frowned.

Whatever that was seemed to make sense to Maggie and included flight, so it was probably close to the truth. She might even imagine Dyce was military or something like that. He'd let her. He didn't care.

Maggie's eyes grew wide. "You didn't go with her?"

"There was only enough fuel for one of us to travel the distance to home base." Dyce almost chuckled at how the truth was true while also allowing Maggie to understand it in her own way.

"Oh, I thought you two were—"

"We are. Now. Something about your Inn, the snow, the beautiful Christmas story. It awoke something in me. Something I didn't even imagine I'd ever need or want." Dyce allowed his gaze to return to the tree line. His mind danced down the incline to where he'd watched Ellery zip away in the capsule.

"The Inn is like that," Maggie whispered, staring at the tree line with Dyce.

How had his time period lost focus on the importance and necessity of love? And how had they lost the baby in the manger? Dyce would share the story far and wide. From now on, maybe he could somehow help make sure they never lost the story in the first place.

He crossed his arms and embraced the cold as the snow fell again.

"Come in when you're ready. It is really peaceful when the snow falls." Maggie turned, and the door clicked as she closed it behind her.

Alone.

The word sucked the wind from his lungs. After some time, Dyce turned to climb the stairs and enter the Inn, but there was a flash in the driveway leading to the house.

The capsule reappeared at the foot of the stairs. Fear struck him. What went wrong? Why would someone from the future come back so soon? Then he realized it could be anyone. Any change in the past had the potential to destroy the future. He swallowed. Had the insurgents overwhelmed his team? Taken the city? With a hand on his weapon, he approached the capsule, scanning and noting slight differences in the design from the one that carried him and Ellery to this timeline. Sleeker. Sharper. He cocked his head to the side, trying to make sense of it all.

Watching Dyce approach nearly stole Ellery's breath from her lungs. How would he react? For him, it would only have been minutes. For her, it had been months. Fifteen to be exact.

She'd planned this moment a thousand times and still, sweat slicked her hands. She hesitated to roll back the capsule's lid.

With a breath and a single command—"Just do it."

The top of the capsule receded into the base, and Ellery's gaze met Dyce's for the first time in what felt like ages.

A multitude of emotions passed over his face. Before he registered it was her, he stood with his hand on his weapon. But as his brain caught up with her presence, his hand fell to his side, and he leaned toward her as if she might be a figment of his imagination. In a whisper, he said, "Ellery?"

She chuckled. "I'm back."

"How?" His expression filled with astonishment and a hint of ... was it hope?

Ellery unbuckled and pushed her long hair aside as she stood and stepped over the edge of the cockpit. Even with such a detailed plan, it was frightening to take each step forward, but with a few touches to the control pad on her arm, the capsule disappeared.

"What are you doing?" Dyce stormed forward and stood forlorn in the center of the capsule's impression in the snow.

Ellery raised her hand to show off the bracelet on her wrist. "I can recall it at any time."

Dyce leaned back. "We can go home?"

Chuckling, Ellery nodded. "One day, sure."

Dyce's exhale formed a cloud that floated on a light breeze.

"But what kind of historian would I be if I didn't choose to live within the history I love and continue my research into the twelve families?" She pushed humor into her expression. It was okay he didn't sweep her into his arms. Maybe his feelings for her waned. Though it had only been a few minutes. Still, maybe they were never that strong. Though it should only have been a short while since she left.

"You look so—" He stepped a breath away. "My team?"

"All well. They send their love."

Dyce radiated relief as he gently cupped her shoulders. "Nice uniform, and the longer hair, I like it."

Ellery tried to keep the longing off her face. "For you, it's been but a few moments."

"For you, how long has it been?" His eyes seemed to register the answer before she spoke it.

"Fifteen months."

He leaned away from the words, dropped his hands. "You came back because—"

"It hurt to breathe air without you."

His eyes filled with a furious longing that mirrored her own. "You were right all along. We needed history, and something about the journey gave us this gift."

He wrapped her in his arms, and for the first time in her life, the sense of being settled and loved for all of her and not just her mind filled her to overflowing. "Merry Christmas, Ellery."

He kissed her again, and in her heart, she praised Jesus for His gift of love. When Dyce released her and captured her hand, she let her gaze wander to the beautiful Inn and the backdrop of the white-covered woods. "Merry Christmas, Dyce."

acknowledgments

I'm so thankful God pressed this beautiful, funny story into my heart in 2024. Over the time I wrote this story, my father grew sicker with cancer and eventually passed December 19, 2024. This story brought moments of laughter and helped me through a time when I easily could have lost my way. God's plans are always good!

A Quantum Christmas would not have been created without the wonderful brainstorming session at ScrivCon 2024 and the eight authors who inspired me at a time when my heart was heavy. So thank you to ScrivCon 2024 and those wonderful authors.

Thank you to my husband and children.

Thank you to Amber Mileusnich, who critiqued this story and cheered me on when I needed it most. Please know how much I deeply appreciate your help, especially during that difficult period of my life.

Thank you to readers for enjoying my out-of-this-world stories and for each and every review. Your words matter to me!

about the author

Jennifer Burrows has a message in her heart about God's love, and she's shared that when she was a musician in her father's church, as a missionary to underprivileged children in a third-world country, and as a wife who stood by her husband through terminal brain cancer that God miraculously healed.

Now, she's sharing God's powerful love through the art of fiction, raising awareness of supernatural influences, and helping others understand how to use faith in the face of adversity. Jennifer teaches in the greater Nashville area where she lives with her husband and their two children. Get to know Jennifer better at jlburrows.com, or connect with her online and on social media at:

www.facebook.com/jenniferlynnburrows or
www.instagram.com/jlburrowsauthor.

you may also like ...

A collection of novellas

On a day trip into the wilderness around Lake Tahoe, college students Ned, Tyler, and Everly stumble upon a monolith. No one knows its origin or purpose, but structures like this one have popped up all over the world, making national headlines. While not the local legend the group hoped to find, they decide to investigate, only to be engulfed by a blinding, powerful pulse of light. Instantly, the three friends find themselves in separate and drastically different worlds. They must quickly adapt to their new surroundings or perish.

If they can survive, the mystery of how to return to Earth becomes entangled in another question fundamental to our humanity. Where do I belong?

Get your copy here:

https://scrivenings.link/theneardistant

(an imprint of Scrivenings Press LLC)

Stay up-to-date on your favorite books and authors with our free e-newsletters.

http://scrivenings.link/join